# UNLEASHING
## FIRE

FALLEN LEGACIES BOOK 3

# UNLEASHING FIRE

## JULIE HALL

*USA Today* BESTSELLING AUTHOR

Unleashing Fire (Fallen Legacies Book 3)

Published by Julie Hall

Copyright © 2021 by Julie Hall

ISBN (paperback): 978-1-954510-05-0

ISBN (hardcover): 978-1-954510-04-3

ISBN (special edition hardcover): 978-1-954510-03-6

Julie Hall

www.JulieHallAuthor.com

Developmental and Line Editing by Rebecca Faith Editorial.

Proofreading by Janelle Leonard.

Cover design by Mirela Barbu.

Interior artwork by Salome Totladze and Kalynne Pratt.

# AWARDS

**Finalist, Speculative Fiction** / *Stealing Embers*
*2021 ACFW Carol Awards*

**Finalist, Paranormal & Supernatural** / *Stealing Embers*
*2021 Realm Awards*

**Finalist, Young Adult** / *Stealing Embers*
*2021 Realm Awards*

**Finalist, Readers' Choice** / *Stealing Embers*
*2021 Realm Awards*

**Gold Medal Winner** / *Stealing Embers*
*2021 Illumination Awards*

**Parable Award Finalist** / *Huntress*
*2021 Realm Awards*

**Young Adult Finalist** / *Stealing Embers*

*2020 The Wishing Shelf Book Awards*

**Finalist, Speculative Fiction** / *Huntress*
*2018 ACFW Carol Awards*

**Young Adult Book of the Year** / *Huntress*
*2018 Christian Indie Awards*

**Gold Medal Winner** / *Huntress*
*2018 Illumination Awards*

**First Place Winner, Religion** / *Huntress*
*2018 IndieReader Discovery Awards*

**Christian Fiction Finalist** / *Huntress*
*2018 Next Generation Indie Book Awards*

**Alliance Award (Reader's Choice)** / *Warfare*
*2018 Realm Makers Awards*

**Parable Award Finalist** / *Logan*
*2018 Realm Makers Awards*

**Gold Medal Winner** / *Huntress*
*2017 The Wishing Shelf Book Awards*

**Best Debut Author** / *Julie Hall*
*2017 Ozarks Indie Book Festival*

**Best Inspirational Novel** / *Huntress*
*2017 Ozarks Indie Book Festival*

**Second Place Winner /** *Huntress*
*2017 ReadFree.ly Indie Book of the Year*

**First Place Winner /** *Huntress*
*2012 Women of Faith Writing Contest*

*USA TODAY* **Bestselling Author**
*August 17, 2017 & June 21, 2018*

*Embers will enthrall fans of Cassandra Clare and Sarah J. Maas, or anyone who loves beautifully written urban fantasy with a sizzling-hot dose of romantic tension. Prepare to become addicted!*

**Audrey Grey**
*USA Today* bestselling author of the *Kingdom of Runes* series

*This delightful read was everything I wanted in a book and more. Author Julie Hall kept me turning pages far into the night, and I wanted the next book in the series the moment this one was over. Stealing Embers just may be one of the best books I've ever read. Well done!*

**Michele Israel Harper**
award-winning editor and author of the *Beast Hunter* series

*Crazy-talented Julie Hall has leapt onto my auto-buy-author list! Stealing Embers is an enthralling story, that easily ensnared me with its compelling characters and quintessential Nephilim concept! I need the next book—NOW!*

**Ronie Kendig**
award-winning author of the *Droseran Saga*

# Unleashing Fire

# 1

## EMBERLY

*A*fter seventeen years, my father finally stands before me in the flesh. His skin is as smooth as porcelain and glows like a low-watt incandescent light bulb. If he stood still, he could pass as a stone and metal statue rather than a living being.

"Wh-what are you doing here?"

After all this time, that's what comes out of my mouth first? Then again, no one else is saying anything. I'm not sure if the silence is from the shock of an eight-foot-tall seraph angel having just burst into the meeting room, or if they're all still reeling from the attacks on London.

Camiel's eyes spark—literally—and his mouth turns down.

"Come," he says.

Whoa. He might be my father, but he's not my dad. And I've never been one to answer to dog commands.

"No."

Steel shifts his body in front of me, but I side-step his protection, needing to stand up to this being on my own.

Camiel's face doesn't change, but he raises his wings a few inches before dropping them. The feathers rub against each other like knives. A warning?

"What do you want?" My voice is level and filled with false bravado.

Someone gasps. I don't blame them. Nephilim are raised to revere angels—and now I understand why. Camiel is a *force*, and he's barely said or done anything besides bust in the room and stomp around a bit. But he also abandoned me as an infant, leaving me defenseless against the darkness that lurks in this world and the spectrum one. As far as I'm concerned, this dude is just a supernatural sperm donor who hasn't earned my respect. No way I'm going to go all "sir, yes, sir" to his commands, even if it does look like he could smite me with a single glare.

Noise from the back of the room breaks the uneasy silence. It sounds like someone is moving through debris, but I refuse to break eye contact with the gilded warrior in front of me.

It's not five seconds later before Malachi strides into my peripheral view. "I think what Emberly means to say is, 'How can we be of service?'"

"That's not—" Steel jerks me to his chest, his hands squeezing my biceps in a silent plea to keep quiet. If Steel thinks it's unwise to speak up right now, it must be a *really* bad idea.

Seeing me manhandled, Camiel takes a half-step in Steel's direction. The ground vibrates under our feet, causing a chorus of muted shrieks from the Nephilim in the room.

Whoa.

Steel releases me, putting both arms in the air in a gesture of surrender, but stays pressed up against my back.

Camiel holds his gaze for a prolonged beat before turning his attention to Malachi. The cherub Elder flinches under his regard. Sweat dots his brow, and a bead drips down the side of his face.

He's terrified.

I scan the room. They all are. Even Laurent looks a bit peaked under his bronzed skin.

Maybe knowing the angel claimed me as his flesh and blood gives me a false sense of security? Or perhaps my lack of fear is because I wasn't indoctrinated with a lifetime of angel supremacy? Whatever the reason, I seem to be the only one in the room not about to pee my pants.

Camiel levels Malachi with a stern look. "You can hand over my daughter."

"Well, she's not really ours to . . . or rather to say—" Malachi gulps. "Yes, of course." He gestures for me to move forward.

*Now wait a minute.*

"I don't think so," Steel speaks up. He snakes his arm around my middle, anchoring me more firmly against his chest. Staking his claim.

Score one to the boyfriend for not wanting to hand me over to the absent parent I know nothing about. I knew I liked him for more than just his looks.

I can't say exactly what changes on Camiel's face when he turns his gaze on Steel, but it's scary. His irises swell, almost completely swallowing his pupils, and turn into swirling golden vortexes. With Steel at my back, I can't see his expression, but nothing about his solid presence says he's cowering in fear.

Camiel doesn't speak, just continues to stare.

And Steel just stares back . . . I think.

The room holds its collective breath and waits to see what will happen next. The tension ramps up my adrenaline production, and the twin slashes on either side of my spine tingle.

That's no good. If my wings break free, they'll punch a hole in Steel's chest. I try to lean away from him, but his arm tightens, staying my movement.

Sparks fly through the air and land on Camiel's armored shoulder. Tinkle pops back into existence as a flying squirrel. He grasps the shell of Camiel's ear with his paws and says something. When he's finished, Camiel turns his head to the tiny Celestial and lifts a single perfect brow.

"Really?"

Tinkle's head bobs. I almost can't believe what I'm seeing.

An angel, a Celestial, and a Nephilim walk into a bar . . .

A completely inappropriate snicker escapes me, and the attention of everyone in the room focuses on me.

Shoot.

I clear my throat. "Sorry."

At least the tingling along my spine has stopped.

"Your Celestial guardian says you are in danger. I'm here to take you somewhere safe." Camiel crosses his arms over his expansive, gold-plated chest, disgruntled from having to explain himself. I'll bet he doesn't have to do that often. As a seraph angel, he's the most powerful class in his species. Throw in the "Angel of War" title and, yeah, the guy definitely doesn't go around justifying every action or command. He probably just barks orders and expects to be obeyed.

That's not going to work with me. Until proven otherwise, he's a deadbeat dad first and seraph angel second.

"I don't need rescuing anymore. You're about seventeen years too late for that." Uh-oh. My bitter is showing. "Thanks, but hard pass. I'm good here." Why do guys continually think I need saving? I'm proficient in taking care of myself. I don't play "damsel" well.

"Your powers have awakened. You're ready. You will come with me."

"Ready? Ready for what?" I ask.

Camiel's irritated gaze flicks to Tinkle, who ducks his head. "All will be explained."

I cross my arms over my chest, which is admittedly awkward with Steel still wrapped around my waist, but it gets the point across that I'm not budging. The ground beneath our feet rumbles with Camiel's displeasure.

"New York has been hit as well," Sable shouts as she bolts into the room, holding her cell phone high. She skids to a halt when she spots Camiel's dominating figure and the Nephilim around the room bunched together like scared bunnies. Her eyes double in size and a gurgle of disbelief—or shock—bubbles up from her throat.

Camiel flares his wings, all six snapping up and out in a blink.

Gasps ripple through the room. The feathers align when extended, creating gilded shields behind him.

With a shake, he retracts them, and they return to their resting position at his back with a series of sharp clicks.

Was that an angel version of a mini temper tantrum?

"We're wasting time."

"There's the door." I point to the entrance he smashed to bits when he barreled into the meeting room.

A muscle under his left eye flutters, and I'm guessing he's considering whether I'm worth the effort. "Your mother would be disappointed."

I flinch. That was a low blow. My already bad mood goes from gloomy to tempestuous as I level the golden angel with my coldest stare. It's a hard look to misinterpret.

He widens his stance as if he's readying himself to absorb a blow. I'm tempted.

"I only meant she'd want you to meet her people."

Oh.

Some of the tension leaves my body, and I lean against Steel. "Who are her people?"

"If you come with me, you'll find out."

Tilting my head, I catch Steel's gaze. He frowns and gives his head a curt shake. I'm not ready to dismiss the idea as quickly, though. Tinkle was right about my father being a seraph angel, so he could have told the truth about my mother being from the angel-line. This isn't just an opportunity to learn more about my mother, but also a line of Nephilim that has been mis-classified as extinct for several millennia.

Camiel's gaze is fixed on Steel when I glance back at him. Tinkle goes up on his tiptoes to whisper in his ear once more. Still glaring at Steel, Camiel nods when Tinkle returns to all fours.

"You can bring your boy toy," Tinkle squeaks.

"Excuse me?" I ask.

"What? Is that not the right term? It's what Nova says you call him," he answers, gesturing to Steel.

Greyson, standing to my right, starts choking on nothing, and Steel's body goes rigid. I close my eyes and pray for the ground to swallow me whole.

"Sterling would die," Greyson mumbles.

I don't have time to do much more than scowl at him before Steel says, "We'll go," for the both of us.

"We will?"

"Now, wait a minute," Laurent speaks up.

"We should think this through," Sable adds.

"Emberly should go with him," Malachi chimes in. Oh my gosh, butt kisser much?

Now that the others have spoken, the room erupts in a chorus of voices. Everyone has an opinion on the matter and wants to be heard.

This is ridiculous.

"You really think this is a good idea?" I ask Steel, ignoring everyone else.

"A good idea?" He shakes his head. "Probably not. But I believe we can handle anything, as long as we stick together."

Steel skims his hand up my arm and then back down, and I go a little melty inside.

Clearing my throat, I erase the hearts from my eyes. I'm a big bad angel-born warrior. A fierce huntress. A few words and a light touch shouldn't make me go all mushy.

"But can we really? We're talking about a full-fledged angel. What if Camiel decides to barbeque you once we're out of sight of the compound?"

Steel arches an eyebrow.

"What? That's not out of the realm of possibility. We know nothing about him. What if he's a psychopath?"

"Enough!"

A wave of heated air gusts over the room, blowing back everyone's hair. The origin? A pissed-off seraph angel. Small flames dance over the knuckles of his clenched fists.

"Every minute that goes by, another Fallen slips through the barrier because I'm not commanding my army. You're disappointed by this reunion—I imagined it differently myself—but we don't have the luxury to waste time with this back and forth. I may not have had the opportunity to raise you, but I know no daughter of mine would be selfish enough to put her needs before the lives of innocents."

That was a proper guilt trip, and I'm firmly chastised. Heat rushes to my cheeks, no doubt reddening them to a deep rose color. I slide out of Steel's embrace, wrapping my hand around his to let Camiel know I'm not going anywhere without Steel.

"Okay. Let's go."

I move forward, tugging Steel with me. Something that might be relief flashes across Camiel's face.

"Wait!" Laurent jogs across the room to stand by his son. "Your mother will skin me alive if I let you run off again."

"I'd be more scared of Blaze and Aurora if you miss Christmas tomorrow," Greyson says.

"This isn't like last time, Dad. I promise. I'll keep in touch."

I shift my gaze to Camiel. Will that even be possible where we're going? The seraph angel doesn't give any indication he knows what I'm silently asking.

Laurent pulls Steel into a hug before letting him go. They give each other a tight-lipped man-nod before releasing each other. Greyson hugs his brother as well, whispering something in his ear.

I catch Sable's eye on the other side of the room, and she offers me a watery smile, understanding as well that I'm not running like before.

When he moves away from Steel, Greyson wraps me up in his arms.

"Tell Ash I'll contact her as soon as I can," I tell him.

"Will do." He plants a kiss on my cheek, then releases me.

Steel and I only take a half-step before Malachi calls out, "What should we do?"

Camiel glances over his shoulder at the angel-born Elder. "Assemble your people and do what you can on the ground in London and New York. Get humans to safety and eliminate any Fallen you come across. We'll handle shutting the leaks from the spirit realm."

Without waiting to make sure Malachi absorbed his commands, Camiel strides from the room with Steel and me in tow.

# 2

## EMBERLY

*I* watch Camiel's gilded wings sway as he marches in front of us, eating up the distance quickly as we traverse the desert, heading away from the Elders' compound.

Tinkle flits around my head. "How's Nova? Does she miss me?"

"Huh?" My mind is fully fixed on how surreal it is to be with my father, so it takes me a beat to catch on to Tinkle's questions.

"Is she okay? How did she react when Steel returned without me? Was she upset?"

I glance at Steel for help, but he only rubs a hand down his face and shakes his head.

"Yes, she was very upset when you were gone."

It's the truth, but also exactly what the Celestial was hoping to hear. The sparks trailing him as he zips along turn from silver to gold. I think that means he's pleased.

Camiel stops walking and does a half-turn, facing west.

Steel and I put on the brakes as Camiel's muscles lock and wings pull tight behind him. He tips his head to the side, listening for something. His eyes glaze over with a white sheen, muting their golden hue.

"What's happening?" I whisper to Steel.

"No idea."

"Tinkle?"

The tiny Celestial drops down on Steel's head. Steel peels his lips back in a half snarl as he swats at Tinkle, who deftly jumps out of the way and launches back into the air.

"Do you have to do that?"

"I don't have to, but I like to."

"Tinkle?" I prod again, hoping to halt a useless argument before it begins. "What's going on with Camiel?"

He stops buzzing in a circle around Steel's head and steers over toward me. He does a figure eight in the air before dropping to the ground. "He's communicating with his cohort."

"How? Telepathically?"

"How else?" he says.

Steel shakes his head at my questioning look, letting me know this is news to him as well. "Can all angels talk to each other that way?"

"Of course," Tinkle answers.

"That's handy," Steel replies.

"I'll say. Can they communicate with anyone like that?" I ask, thinking about my dreamscaping. Could telepathy have been passed down to me and manifest in my dreams?

Tinkle shakes his furry head. "No, angels can only talk to other angels that way."

Hmm.

An agitated growl rumbles from Camiel's chest. Turning right, he sets off again. Steel and I exchange a look before following. He doesn't seem any happier about chasing after Camiel than I am.

With a huff, I jog to catch up to the seraph. "What's going on?"

His steps are so long I have to step double-time to keep pace with him.

"I have to get back to my troops to stop more Fallen from breaking through to the mortal realm, but I can't do that until I drop you off." His face is hard, and the tone of his voice conveys annoyance. Ouch.

"Let's take care of that first. This thing with the Fallen—whatever it is—takes precedence."

Pressing his lips together, Camiel doesn't say anything. I wait a moment, still expecting him to answer me, but he doesn't.

"London is being destroyed right now. I've waited seventeen years to know where I came from. I can wait another day or two. Let's just go meet up with your troops. Steel and I won't get in the way. Promise."

"Can't."

"Why?"

Tinkle lands on my shoulder and pulls at my earlobe to get my attention. I swat at him to stop.

Camiel narrows his golden gaze on me and flares his nostrils. I feel the brunt of his stare like a physical weight, but I refuse to cower beneath it. I'm starting to get the impression Camiel is nothing more than an overgrown bully. How disappointing.

Tinkle yanks on my earlobe again. "Psst. Emberly. You're not supposed to question a seraph."

"I'm not questioning an almighty seraph angel. I'm questioning *my father.*" Yuck, that phrase tastes bitter on my tongue.

It doesn't look like Camiel is wild about the endearment, either. He frowns, and the color leeches away from his already pale skin. Still, his lips remain tightly sealed.

He doesn't want to answer any of my questions, fine. That's his decision. But I don't have to play this game.

Turning on a heel, I snag Steel by the arm and tug him back in the direction of the Elders' compound. He turns easily and nods, letting me know he's got my back. That feels . . . good.

"Stop," Camiel shouts from behind us. I ignore the command.

Steel peeks over his shoulder. When he faces forward again, his eyebrows are raised. "Get ready," he whispers.

I don't know what he means until a gust of air blows my hair forward, swirling the strands in front of my face and battering sand against my back. With a ground-shaking thud, Camiel lands in a crouch in front of us, halting our retreat. He fists his hands as he stands to his full eight-foot-plus height. White and blue fire runs across his knuckles and up his forearms. His wings, all six of them, flare out behind him. His golden gaze is molten, emotion churning in the depths.

He's intimidating, but I don't let it show.

"I said *stop.*" His voice is low and deceptively quiet.

Recognizing the threat, Steel tenses beside me. Tinkle zips in circles above our heads, raining down a fine mist of sparks.

The slashes on each side of my spine start to tingle. The longer we remain locked in this stand-off, the surer I am my wings are going to release here, in the mortal realm.

"Step back," I warn Steel as I shrug off my jacket to keep from shredding it. The tank top I'm wearing underneath scoops low in the back.

Steel moves to a safe distance, and I release my hold on the fire growing inside. My wings punch free. I flare them wide, mimicking Camiel's stance with my single pair of wings to his three.

Camiel's lips part as his gaze sweeps from the end of one of my gold wings to the other. The fire licking his skin extinguishes as he unclenches his fists. He folds his wings and they settle like a cape behind him.

Steel steps forward and grazes his fingers over my lower back, reminding me he's there.

"You look just like your mother . . . and me," Camiel's voice rumbles.

I don't know what to say to that, so I keep my mouth shut.

"I can't bring you with me because the angels don't know of your existence. If they discovered who and what you are, there are some who would sooner see you dead than take another breath. I need to get you somewhere safe so I can focus on the protection of others."

"Your own kind is a threat to Emberly?" Steel asks, his tone flat, but I know him well enough to hear the tremor of anger underneath.

"Some might be. The angels are torn in their views of Nephilim."

Since Nephilim were created from the union of Forsaken and humans, many angels consider us to be as much of an abomination as Fallen. I don't totally see the point of painting with such broad strokes, but the bigger issue now is that we could be in real danger from both sides of this conflict. If angels have killed Nephilim on sight, the angel-borns' reactions in the meeting room when Camiel busted in makes a lot more sense. I tuck my wings as the fight leaks out of me, and my emotions settle. There's a logical course of action.

"Steel and I will return to the Elders' compound for now. It's safe there."

Camiel shakes his head. "Not as safe as you think."

"Why do you say that?"

"Whatever caused the veil between the worlds to thin originated there."

Steel and I exchange a curious, questioning look.

"Once this situation is under control, you'll have the luxury of learning to trust me. For right now, I'm asking you to believe that I have your immediate best interests in mind and am bringing you somewhere safe."

"He's telling the truth," Tinkle says as he flies down and settles on Camiel's wide shoulder. "The angel-line village of Eden is very well hidden and protected by Celestials. You'll be safe there."

"The angel-line live in a hidden village called Eden?" I ask.

Camiel shoots Tinkle a glare. The little Celestial ducks, then blinks out of existence. Crossing his arms, Camiel awaits my response.

I glance at Steel, looking for some indication of what he thinks. His expression is blank, but he sweeps his thumb against the base of my spine and gives me a small nod.

It's probably wrong that a zing of anticipation shoots through my body at the thought of going to Eden when the world at large may be falling apart, but I can't help that I'm excited to know more about the mysterious angel-line.

Taking a deep breath, I lift my gaze to Camiel's. "All right then, let's go to Eden."

# 3

## ASH

The ringing in my ears won't go away, even though the alarms shut off five minutes ago. I absently rub my right ear as I help Blaze and Aurora get a board game set up in the bedroom. Eloise's mind is somewhere else as she stares out the window, and Nova and Sterling are glued to their phones in the other room. My phone keeps dinging, notifying me of messages I haven't checked.

"I like this game already," Blaze says with a smile as he inspects the cardboard box with the name "Trouble" scrolled in large bubble letter font. He shakes the top off and pulls out the board, immediately depressing the plastic dome housing the die over and over again.

The youngest twins were intuitive enough to know their mother was completely oblivious to their antics and wouldn't stop bouncing off the walls—literally. After Aurora knocked over a table lamp and Blaze embedded a fork into the drywall, I decided to try and focus their energy on something less physical while we all wait for news.

"What color do you want to be?" Aurora asks me.

I open my mouth to answer when Sterling snorts a laugh and my phone dings again. Reaching into my pocket, I switch the phone to silent. It will still vibrate, but that's slightly less annoying.

"Let me get you guys started, then I have to go check on the big kids, okay?" I tilt my head toward the adjacent room and heave an overly dramatic sigh as if checking on Sterling is the most arduous of tasks. Aurora giggles but nods. Luckily the board game is simple, and it only takes me a few minutes to get the pair started. Within that time, my phone goes off at least five more times.

Pulling the device from my back pocket, I stand and start scrolling through a group text message that includes all of us but is basically a conversation between Nova and Sterling.

Nova

**What's going on?**
**Why hasn't anyone messaged yet?**

**I'm never letting you guys leave me behind again.**

Sterling

**Chill, girl. Maybe Steel and Em are getting some alone time.** 😏

Nova

 😶 Greyson is with them.

Sterling

Nova

 Are you ever going to grow up?

Sterling

 Gosh. I hope not!

When I walk back into the room, neither of them looks up from their screens.

"Guys, I don't think spamming the group text with messages is helpful right now," I say. It's not a full second later before Sterling's phone dings and mine buzzes in my hand. I shake my head, but glance down at the new message.

Nova

> **Greyson, what's going on?**

> **I know you're checking your phone.**

Sterling

> **At least the alarm finally stopped. Is anyone else hungry for 🍗🍗 ?**

Despite his flippant comments, Sterling's leg bounces up and down and he keeps rubbing the same spot behind his ear. Nova is too focused on her screen to notice, but I do.

I say their names, but the pair ignore me and continue to poke at each other over text. Sighing, I type out a message.

> Stop texting!

> They'll get back to us when they can.

Both their heads finally lift in my direction.

"Ash, I didn't see you there," Sterling says.

"Clearly."

Nova opens her mouth to say something when the front door swings open and Greyson walks into the room. He looks a bit disheveled, and wariness clouds his eyes.

"Finally," Nova snaps as she pushes to her feet. "Next time you get to wait with the kids."

My jaw drops open. She didn't lift a finger to help with Blaze and Aurora. I'm about to call her out but shut my mouth instead. It's not worth it. Covering nervousness with sass is one of her coping mechanisms.

Eloise rushes in and heads for Greyson, her eyes bright with expectation. "Have they found Silver?"

Greyson blows out a breath. He shakes his head, and she deflates. With a wan smile, she pats Greyson's cheek and retreats to the far side of the room to stare out the window again.

"What's the update, Grey?" Sterling asks as he crosses the room to grab a bottle of juice from the fridge. He doesn't wait for his brother to answer before taking a swig straight from the bottle.

Greyson rubs his jaw, seemingly not in a rush to fill us in, which causes a ball of unease to wiggle in my gut.

"Where are Steel and Emberly?" I can't be the only one who's noticed their absence.

"You guys better sit down."

"Let me get this straight." Sterling holds up a hand, garnering all our attention. "Fallen have phased into the mortal world and are openly attacking London and New York. The Council's rallying all angel-born to fight, including novices from the nine academies. And Dad said we have to stay here?" The look on his face is half-disbelief, half-disgust.

Nova pulls out her phone and starts typing. "Speak for yourself. One call to my parents and they'll have me on the first flight to London."

Sterling crumples a napkin and chucks it against the

wall. "We're too old to be benched and relegated to babysitting duty."

Greyson drops into a chair. "We haven't gone through the metamorphosis yet. That leaves us at a disadvantage compared to mature angel-born." The look on his face tells me he's not drinking his own Kool-Aid. Greyson's status as "the level-headed son" won't let him outright disregard his father's wishes, but he's obviously conflicted. He's better at hiding his emotions than his twin, but I think underneath the façade, the news infuriates him as much as it does Sterling.

"That's a load of crap and you know it. Just because we haven't fully come into our powers doesn't mean we can't fight."

"Sterling. Language," Eloise warns, casting a quick look toward the bedroom where Blaze and Aurora are held-up with candy and their board game.

"Mom, I can assure you they've heard worse at the academy."

She shakes her head.

I sit back in my seat, pinching my lower lip between my fingers. I haven't quite decided which side of the fence I'm on. My instincts are the same as the others'; I want to jump into the fray and do what I was born to do, but there's no doubt this is dangerous. My parents may not be here like the Durands, but there's a good chance they'd want me to sit this one out as well.

"And that's where Steel and Emberly are?" I ask. "They left for London without us?" I ignore the tweak of pain in my chest at being left behind. I'm sure there's a reasonable explanation for why they went without us.

Greyson refocuses his attention on me. His gaze softens

as if he can see the small bruise their actions caused. Am I that transparent, or is he extra-attuned to my emotional tells? Both options make me a tad uncomfortable, and I squirm in my seat.

Clearing his throat, Greyson looks away. Is the news so bad that he can't even deliver it to my face?

"Right, about that. Dad wanted me to wait for him, but . . ."

Eloise straightens. "What is it, Greyson? Where are Steel and Emberly?"

"They left the compound, but they aren't headed to London or New York."

"Come again, Sparky?" Nova blinks at Greyson, suspicion darkening her gaze.

A crease of confusion forms between Sterling's eyebrows. "Where did they go?"

Greyson rubs his forehead, but quickly breaks under the weight of our stares. "Emberly's dad showed up and they went with him."

There's a beat of silence, then we all start talking over each other.

"What?"

"You're kidding."

"Was Tinkle there?"

"They found her dad? Who is he?"

The last comment is from Eloise, who still isn't in the loop about Emberly's lineage. She, like most everyone else, assumes that Emberly's parents are from one of the existing angel lines.

I'm on the edge of my seat for more news, but Greyson has to catch up his mother first.

"Yeah, so . . ." he starts, "Emberly's dad is Camiel. The seraph Angel of War."

Eloise's eyes widen and she brings a hand to her mouth. "A seraph . . . angel?"

Greyson nods.

"And her mother?" she asks.

Greyson slides his gaze to me. In Emberly's absence, and as her best friend, he's asking my permission to divulge her secrets. I give a small tip of my chin to let him know it's okay to continue.

"Her mother is from the angel-line."

Eloise takes a moment to process the information, then pulls herself together. Crossing her arms, she turns her attention back to Greyson. "So where did they go?"

Good. We're all caught up. Now we can get the information we need.

"They didn't say," Greyson answers. I have to smother a groan of disappointment. Turning to Nova, he adds, "They took their phones."

"A lot of good that's going to do them," she huffs.

The door opens and Laurent walks in. He takes one look at his wife's face and then sends Greyson a hard look. The skin around Greyson's eyes tightens in a wince, and his chin notches down as the weight of his father's disapproval settles on his shoulders.

"I asked you to wait," Laurent says to Greyson as he rushes to his wife's side.

Greyson lifts his hands in surrender. "I tried, but . . ." He lets the half-sentence hang in the air as Laurent slides his arm around Eloise's back and ushers her into the unoccupied bedroom, shutting the door behind them.

We can hear the rumble of Laurent's voice as he tries to

soothe his wife. Looking from the closed door back to Greyson, I frown, not liking what just happened. Doesn't Laurent understand how hard Greyson tries to toe the family line and how personally he takes his father's disappointment?

The room gets uncharacteristically quiet, each of us lost in our own thoughts.

I can't stop thinking about Emberly. After all this time, she's finally reunited with one of her parents. I can only imagine the emotional turmoil she's facing. I'm glad Steel is there for her, but wish I could be as well. The one big upside to this is that I don't have to worry about her physical wellbeing. I can breathe easier knowing a seraph angel has her back.

Sterling speaks up, his gaze intent on his brother. "We can't just sit around while everyone goes to war. This is what we're trained for, and the angel-borns are going to need every available warrior."

Greyson slides his tongue over his teeth. It's clear he's torn, and I'm with him there. I agree with Sterling to an extent, but what are we supposed to do? Hastily shooting out on our own has gotten us into trouble before, so maybe it would be best to just sit this one out.

Nova looks up from her phone. "Good news. I got us a ride out of here."

# 4

## EMBERLY

*I* slide off the back of the dragon, limbs shaky, hair wind-blown in all directions. When Camiel said we were traveling to the island of Cyprus, I'd assumed there'd be flying involved—I just didn't think we'd be shuttled over the Mediterranean Sea on top of Tinkle, transformed into a mythical creature. I would have preferred to fly myself, but Camiel said this would be faster.

"Well, that was an experience," Steel says when he lands next to me, his hair tousled in the way that makes me want to run my hands through it. Mine probably looks like I stuck my finger in a socket. His cheeks are pinked under his golden skin, and he looks nothing less than exhilarated.

"You enjoyed that," I accuse.

"What's not to enjoy?" He slaps the dragon's flank and Tinkle swings his horned head around and huffs. Swishing his tail, he aims for Steel's head, but Steel jumps deftly out of the way. "I think your Celestial is growing on me."

Off in the distant gold and pink spectrum sky, Camiel approaches, all six wings spread as he glides on currents of briny air. His gaze tracks back and forth over the horizon, ensuring we weren't followed.

"I beat you again," Tinkle says as soon as Camiel touches down on the shell-covered shore.

Camiel dips his head in acquiescence. Is that a half-smile on his face? "There's no one faster."

Tinkle's scaly chest puffs out and he wiggles his shoulders. In a blink, he explodes into a cloud of teal sparkles. When they dissipate, he's a flying squirrel once again. I may never understand why he chooses to spend most of his time as a squirrel when he can take the form of any being, real or imagined.

Steel raises an eyebrow and shoots Tinkle an annoyed glare. "You know a dragon would have been helpful when we were ambushed by Silver and the Forsaken in the mountains?"

"A real warrior could have bested a thousand enemies on his own," Tinkle retorts.

"This way." Camiel sets off inland, marching up a sandy hill in front of us. The ends of his wings drag along behind him, leaving divots. With the sun glinting off his gold armor and metal wings, he looks as fierce here in the spectrum world as he does in the mortal one.

Steel takes my hand as we ascend. I smile at him, then dip my gaze to where we're joined. My light skin stands out against his bronzed. His large, calloused fingers around my much smaller hand make me feel petite in comparison. Glancing up at Steel's profile, I feel a wave of gratitude that he's here with me. I don't know how I'm supposed to feel about everything being thrown at me right now, but Steel, my tether, keeps me from floating away in a sea of chaos.

We reach the crest of the hill, and Steel's eyes visibly

widen. He releases a low whistle. Swinging my gaze forward, I take in the village laid out around the small inlet below. Packed sand streets curve around white stucco houses with red-tiled roofs. I don't see any vehicles, but there are people down there. Some are winged.

Laughter reaches my ears, and I glance to the left to see a group of children playing in a grassy area among several wildly different animals. There's a monkey, a sloth, and a python in the mix.

What the heck is that seal doing shuffling around? Is it playing . . . tag?

The large-finned mammal flops after several of the children, who squeal and laugh in excitement.

In a burst of sparks, it transforms into a pig. Snorting loudly, it continues to chase the kids around.

Celestials.

"Friends of yours?" Steel asks Tinkle, who races between our feet and scurries off without answering.

"It's how these Nephilim stayed hidden for two thousand years," Camiel says as he nods toward the group of children and Celestials that Tinkle just joined up with. "Supernatural camouflage."

I watch Tinkle *poof* in a shower of sparks then zoom through the air over the playing children, sprinkling them with pink dust.

"If there are enough Celestials to hide all of Eden, why are the angel-line Neph still in hiding? Couldn't their Celestials have protected them?" I ask.

Camiel shakes his head. "Celestials' main powers include masking auras and shape-shifting. I picked your Celestial," he nods toward Tinkle, "because he has nominal healing abilities as well, which is a rarity among his kind. But they're a peaceful race of beings, childlike in a great many ways. If the angel-line Nephilim hadn't retreated to this sanctuary, they would have assuredly perished."

I turn to Steel. "*So* many things are suddenly clearer."

Steel snorts and then shakes his head. "All-powerful, indeed."

Zipping back to us, Tinkle transforms back into a flying squirrel before landing on my shoulder.

"What are we talking about?" he asks.

I open my mouth to answer him when Camiel cuts me off. "Nikias. There you are."

Camiel strides forward and clasps forearms with a slate-winged angel-born who walked up from the village.

"It's good to see you." Laugh lines crinkle at the corners of the angel-born's eyes as he smiles at Camiel, not a hint of fear on his face. When they finish their greeting, Nikias gazes past Camiel to me. "This must be her."

"Yes," Camiel affirms.

Oh, goodie. He already knows about me, but I don't know a thing about him or the angel-line Nephilim.

Nikias pauses to take me in, then takes quick steps toward me with his arms outstretched, reaching in for a hug. This time, when Steel positions half his body in front of me, I let him. You shouldn't come at a stranger like that.

Nikias stops short and drops his arms. Just a hint of a frown tugs his mouth downward.

"Nikias is safe," Camiel assures me. "I trust him with my life."

Interesting. A seraph angel trusting a Nephilim with his life. But just because Camiel trusts him, doesn't mean I do.

"It also doesn't hurt that he's technically my great-great-grandson-in-law," Nikias chuckles and then claps a hand on

Camiel's shoulder. There's a slight accent to the newcomer's words, as if he's pronouncing each syllable too exactly. It would make sense that English isn't his first language.

Camiel crosses his arms over his chest, his expression stern.

"You need to stop telling people that. I'm tens of thousands of years older than you."

"It doesn't make it any less true."

"Wait, if you're his great-great-grandfather-in-law, that would make you my . . ." I take a closer look at the angel-born. His deeply tanned skin is lined with age. He appears to be in his fifties by human standards, which is ancient for a Nephilim. He's as tall and muscular as any angel-born. His shoulder-length dark hair is tied at the nape of his neck, and thick brows sit over dark blue eyes. Blue eyes that look a whole lot like mine.

"Family," Nikias finishes with a smile when my sentence hangs in the air for too long.

I'm blown away. Yes, I met my father today, but his larger-than-life appearance makes it easy to mentally dismiss him as a relative—that and his stone-cold personality. In contrast—and despite my initial hesitancy—warmth radiates from Nikias.

I should have assumed I'd meet some distant family when Camiel said we were going to Eden. It's only logical, but I still wasn't prepared.

I step forward, grazing Steel's bicep with the tips of my fingers to anchor myself to something familiar. His arm muscles bunch as he watches me. Anxiety is written over his face—anxiety for me.

I offer him a small smile to let him know I'm all right. He nods and then slides an arm around me, bringing me to his side. I'm starting to like this vibe we have where we can communicate without words.

"And who's this?" Nikias asks with raised brows.

"Her boy-toy," Tinkle offers unhelpfully.

Oh, gosh. Not this again. I close my eyes and rub the bridge of my nose before opening them again. "Sorry," I whisper to Steel.

He chuckles, and the noise sends a shot of heat straight to my gut. "Oddly, I don't mind."

I shake my head. "Well, I do."

"Boy-toy?" Nikias' eyebrows hitch even higher, and he looks at Camiel. "And you're okay with this?"

The angel just grunts.

"Stavros is not going to take this well," Nikias says.

"It's an archaic tradition anyway," Camiel replies with a shrug.

"Says the thirty-thousand-year-old angel."

"I've already broken it once."

"What are you talking about?" I ask, putting an unintended end to their bizarre two-person exchange.

Nikias waves us forward. "You'll see soon enough. Come on. Let's get you two settled." Clasping arms with Camiel once again, they nod at each other before Nikias starts down the hill toward the village. I start to follow but pause when I realize Camiel hasn't moved.

"You're not coming with us?"

He shakes his head. "I'll return as soon as I can."

Right. Fallen in London and New York. Camiel is the Angel of War. Things to do, enemies to kill and all that.

I bite my lower lip. "What you said before about some of the angels' feelings toward Nephilim . . . London and New

York will be filled with angel-born right now trying to help where they can. Should I be concerned?"

What if my friends get caught up in that mess? I know they're not going to want to sit at the compound in Egypt, twiddling their thumbs while the rest of the angel-born army goes to war.

"My troops will be preoccupied with Fallen," Camiel says. My stomach drops. That's not overly reassuring. "I know you have questions." He lifts his arm as if he might pat my head or shoulder, but lets it drop to his side before touching me. It's an awkward moment for both of us. "When I get back, we'll talk."

I give him a tight-lipped nod. Considering the situation, it's probably the best I can hope for right now. Camiel turns toward the sea and launches into the sky. All six of his wings beat the air to gain altitude. I don't wait until he disappears before turning away. With a deep breath, I take Steel's hand and let Nikias lead us into Eden.

# 5

## EMBERLY

*A*lthough it isn't the literal interpretation of the Garden of Paradise, it doesn't take long to understand why the angel-line Nephilim named their sanctuary Eden. Homes are nestled between open gardens and small citrus groves that scent the air with lemon. Crushed turquoise seashells crunch under our feet as we walk along their streets. A few angel-born peek their heads out of windows and doorways to wave at Nikias as we pass. Their curious gazes only settle on Steel and me for a moment before they return to whatever tasks they were performing before our arrival. Tinkle flies high above our heads as a multicolored parrot. His colorful feathers stand out against the golden and pink spectrum sky.

"Most of the children are in school right now," Nikias explains as we continue down the mostly deserted streets. "We try to be as self-sufficient as possible, so most of the adults are either tending to our crops or training for battle."

"You train?" Steel asks as he scans the area. At first

glance he appears calm, but there's evidence of strain around his eyes that speaks volumes to me.

Nikias nods. "Yes, of course. Our warriors were long regarded as the best and strongest of all the angel-lines."

Steel's gaze fixes on Nikias, his expression unchanged except for the small lift of one eyebrow. "And yet you hide here on this island in your own self-contained paradise, rather than helping the rest of your brethren with the task of protecting humanity."

Part of me wants to scold Steel for his rudeness, but he does have a point.

Nikias is quiet as he assesses Steel. The only sounds are the crunching of the shells beneath our feet and the distant waves rolling into the surf.

"There's much you don't know about us and our history."

"I'm all ears."

A shadow flickers in my periphery and Steel shoves me out of the way—that's all the warning I get of the impending attack.

I hit the ground, shells biting into my hands when I land.

Flinging my hair out of my face, I jump to my feet in time to see Steel transform into a lion and swipe a paw at the gray-winged angel-born female that just dropped from the sky. Twisting out of the way, she lands a sidekick to his flank.

With a roar, Steel snaps at her, but she deftly dances out of the way before he can draw blood. She's up in the air and landing an elbow into Steel's spine before I have a chance to react. The force of the blow causes him to lose his footing.

Oh no she didn't.

I enter the brawl before she can get in another cheap

shot. My wings burst free, shredding my leather jacket.

Grabbing a fist full of her dark mahogany hair, I jab her in the kidneys twice and then kick her feet out from beneath her. She lands at an awkward angle. There's a snap of bone, but she doesn't stay down long. Arching her back, she leaps to her feet and spins to face me. One wing hangs limp and drags on the ground, but I hardly feel bad about the injury.

When she advances, I spin and extend my wings, not caring if I slice her across the neck or gut. Either will suit me just fine as long as blood flows, but I never connect. Instead, I absorb a blow from behind, right between my wings, and stumble forward.

Steel leaps over my head as I swing around, sending bits of shells spraying when he lands. A low and deadly growl vibrates the air as he takes slow, calculated steps toward her, backing her into a corner between two houses. With her wing broken, she can't fly away, but rather than fear, defiance shines in her eyes.

She palms a dagger sheathed at her side—the only weapon she carries. Lowering into a crouch, she swipes the blade at Steel at the same moment he pounces.

Someone shouts behind me, but I don't care because droplets of blood spray from Steel's shoulder as the Neph girl spins unnaturally fast out of the way.

I. See. Red.

"Mine." The word bubbles up from my chest. I rush forward, morphing completely the split second before I slam the girl into the side of the house, her body hitting hard enough that some of the wall behind her crumbles to the ground and a fissure snakes upward from the point of impact.

The whites of her eyes stand out, and I feel satisfaction that she's finally frightened.

My arm darts out, and I catch her by the throat, lifting her a foot off the ground.

"No! Emberly, stop!"

I dismiss Nikias' frantic shouts. This female is going to die. Slowly.

I start to squeeze my hand, cutting off her air supply. A smile stretches across my face as hers starts to redden. I'm enjoying watching the life slip from her. Only a faint whisper in the back of my mind says there's something very wrong with that.

She claws at my vice-grip on her neck and kicks out with her legs. Her feet smash harmlessly against my gold plates of armor. She's weakening and no match for my strength.

There's commotion behind me, but I'm singularly focused on my prey. I tilt my head, fascinated and enthralled as the fight starts to leak from her.

I'm sacked from the side and lose my grip on my victim. When I hit the ground, a heavy weight keeps me down. My vision is filled with brown fur, which is strange enough to snap me from my bloodlust.

Oh my gosh. I almost killed someone. A panic spiral starts when I realize what just happened. Yes, she attacked me and Steel, but she's still an angel-born, not a Fallen or Forsaken.

I begin to shake from adrenaline overload.

"Are you yourself again?" rumbles the furry blob.

Tinkle.

"Yes. I'm calm." Mostly. I shove at Tinkle and he rolls off me before lumbering to his feet. He's an oversized grizzly bear. I can't believe I wasn't squashed like a bug when he tackled me. He's as big as a mid-sized SUV.

"My work here is done." Tinkle explodes into a shower of sparks, transforming into a hummingbird. "Later," he says before flitting off. Where he's going or when he'll be back, I don't know.

Rolling on to my stomach, I push to my feet. My legs tremble like a newborn foal's. An arm reaches out to steady me and I look up into Steel's teal eyes.

"Are you okay?" he asks.

"Yeah, you?" There's a wound at his shoulder, but it's barely more than a scratch. It's not even bleeding anymore.

I went berserk over a minor injury.

"Hey." He catches me eyeing the tear in his clothes. "I would have done the same if I had the chance."

My frown deepens. Would he really? Maybe. But would he have enjoyed it as much as I just did?

The cold hand of fear latches onto my heart and squeezes. Where are these bloodthirsty instincts coming from?

"Is she all right?" I ask.

Steel side-steps, revealing Nikias kneeling on the ground next to the battered angel-born. He's saying something to her, and she nods in response. Lifting her gaze, she sends me a withering glare. Her light brown eyes stand out against her tawny skin. The look spears me, and I glance away, only now realizing we've attracted a small crowd. The stares the angel-line Neph send my way are no longer friendly. Instead, they are tinged with suspicion and accusation, and that makes my hackles rise. I took it too far, but that doesn't change the fact that we were attacked first.

"Nikias, what's going on?" Steel demands. "Camiel

promised Emberly would be safe here."

Nikias rises, helping the young angel-born to her feet as well. "You need to see Stavros and get that wing set before it heals improperly," he tells her. Glancing over her shoulder at the cock-eyed appendage, she winces.

"That's going to hurt," she says. Her voice has a smoky sound to it. Deep for a female. Unhurried and lit with the same touch of accent as Nikias.

"And whose foolishness is to blame for that?" he asks.

She glances in our direction, her hard gaze holding mine for a moment before she drops her head and admits, "Mine."

Nikias gives her shoulder a gentle squeeze. "I'll check on you later."

There's obvious affection in his eyes and I wonder at the relationship between these two. There's definitely a father-daughter vibe going on there.

The girl starts to walk away, one gray wing dragging along the ground behind her, when Nikias calls, "Shira."

She glances back at him, head cocked.

"We will be talking about this little stunt of yours then."

She scrunches her nose, but she nods before trudging away.

When she turns the corner, Nikias scrubs a hand down his face before turning to Steel and me. "My apologies. I assure you; you're safe. Nothing like that will happen again."

"How can you be so sure?" Steel's tone broadcasts his displeasure loud and clear.

"Shira is my great-grandniece." So that would make her my . . . aunt? Cousin? I'm not sure how I should feel knowing a blood relative attacked me. Up until a few hours ago, I'd never had any interaction with someone I'm related to. Now they're flying around everywhere—literally falling from the sky. "She's impetuous, suspicious of strangers, and thinks she can get away with anything. She can't." A dark look settles on Nikias' face, and although it's obvious he has deep love for the girl, I don't envy her. He's really going to lay into her later.

"Nik, do you need any help?" An angel-born male steps forward. The scowl on his face says he saw enough of the mini battle to be wary of me. He's technically weaponless, holding only a gardening hoe, but he white-knuckles the handle. In a pinch he could take a swipe at us with it.

I tug on Steel's arm, and he lets me pull him back a step. His gaze doesn't veer from the stranger.

Nikias waves the man off. "No, no. Everything is all right. It was Shira being impulsive . . . again."

An eternity passes before the man slowly nods and backs away. A smattering of about six or seven other angel-borns watch us from their houses or peek out from the nearest garden, but I ignore them.

Nikias releases a weary sigh. "Not exactly how I wanted to introduce you to Eden." The way he says it makes me wonder if he's worried whether I have a bad impression of his sanctuary, or his people have a bad impression of *me*. "Come. Once I get you settled in my house, the formal introductions can start."

I suck my bottom lip into my mouth and bite down, my anxiety flaring instantly. More new people. Yippee.

Reaching forward, Steel uses his thumb to tug my lip free. He rubs my bitten flesh, smoothing out the sting. My stomach bottoms out.

"None of that," he murmurs, offering me a tiny hint of a smile. "Remember, we got this."

The look in his eyes is so earnest, I almost believe him.

# 6

## ASH

*T*he tactical aircraft we board is nowhere near as luxurious as the private jet we took to the Elders' compound. Technically, we're hitching a ride with a contingent of angel-born warriors, but Nova's parents made sure there were seats for all of us. Though "seats" is a bit of an oversell. They're not much more than two rows of metal benches that fold out from the inside cabin walls.

Greyson sits on the bench across from me, staring at a spot on the ground. His brow is pinched in the same shell-shocked expression he's worn since we left his parents' apartment. Not wanting to disappear on them again, he'd insisted on talking to Laurent and Eloise before we left, but the blow-out between the twins and their father was epic.

Epically bad.

If Eloise hadn't been there to calm her husband down, it might have come to blows. Like most things in life, Sterling bounced back quickly. Greyson, not so much.

The twin brothers are startlingly similar at times, but as we've grown, the weight of responsibility settled on

Greyson's shoulders. In contrast, "responsibility" doesn't seem to be part of Sterling's vocabulary.

Sterling chats with Nova and an overly muscled Nephilim about how to work a flame thrower, while Greyson sits stoic and silent.

"Hey." Reaching forward, I tap Greyson's kneecap with my finger. He lifts his gaze from the imaginary smudge on the floor. "You okay?"

The pucker between his eyebrows smooths over. "Yeah, sure. Just getting my head in the game. Who knows what we're going to face when we land."

"That's true," I say, but don't for a second believe that's what occupies his thoughts.

"We're coming up on London City Airport. Landing time is roughly thirty minutes," the pilot announces over the speakers.

Someone shoves a black backpack into my hands.

"Here you go," says the burly warrior who was talking with Sterling and Nova. They both stand behind him with their packs already strapped to their torsos over their battle leathers. "Emergency parachute in case we can't land. Everyone without wings needs to have one."

The blood rushes from my head at the thought of free-falling, but luckily my deep skin tone hides the involuntary reaction. No need for anyone to know about my fear of heights. It's humiliating.

With a suddenly dry throat, I nod my thanks and shrug on the flat pack, wondering how a whole parachute fits inside. I fumble with the clasps, a fine tremor causing my hands to shake.

"Let me help," Greyson offers. He doesn't wait for my

reply as he fastens all the buckles and clasps. "You're all set," he says, then steps back.

"You sure it's tight enough?" I can still breathe, so I'm skeptical.

He shoots me a funny look. Uh-oh.

"Never mind." A weird gurgling sound that was supposed to come out as a carefree laugh rattles in my throat. "I'm sure it's fine."

It was surprisingly easy to get away with hiding a fear of heights at Seraph Academy. Our training was mostly on the ground. We learned to scale buildings and rocks, but we never got very high. A few feet off the ground isn't a problem for me, but a few thousand feet is.

Greyson's mouth turns down. "Are you all right?"

"Yep. Just wish I'd already grown my wings, then I wouldn't need this thing." That was a lie. As a dominion angel-born, I'm guaranteed to sprout a pair of wings when I come into my full powers, but I'm not looking forward to it. Given the choice, there's a long list of abilities I would have picked over flight.

"Okay." He isn't convinced. "Well, I wouldn't worry because—"

"Not worried."

"Uh-huh. I'm sure we'll be able to land safely, so it won't even matter one—"

There's an explosion somewhere outside and the plane banks. Hard. Anyone not seated and buckled gets flung across the cabin. Tossed clean off my feet, I body-check Greyson and we slam into an interior wall of the aircraft. His back absorbs the brunt of the blow.

When the pilot rights the plane, we slide to the ground.

There are groans throughout the cabin as people assess their injuries.

What was that?

Greyson lumbers to his feet, wincing. Even so, he reaches a hand down to help me up. We're only just on our feet when another explosion shakes the plane.

"All right. Everybody out," an angel-born I don't recognize yells. The end of her thick plait drapes over her shoulder, but whips back and nails Sterling in the face when she hauls open the cargo door. "Those with wings, phase to the spirit realm and we'll see you on the ground. Everyone else, if you see any dark shadows, do what you can to avoid them in the air." With that she phases and disappears from the mortal realm.

As people rush forward, I backpedal until I'm pressed against the cockpit door. I watch angel-born after angel-born fling themselves from the plane. Soon there are only a few of us left.

"Come on," Sterling shouts at me, waving his arm from his spot at the opening. All I can manage in return is a tiny head shake.

There's another explosion and the plane dips and banks. Sterling is thrown off balance and tumbles out of the aircraft. I think I hear him yell "Woo-hoo!" as he falls. With the plane still flying cock-eyed, Nova shakes her head and then jumps after him. After another two warriors exit the aircraft, it's only me and Greyson left. I'd probably be thankful he hasn't abandoned me if I wasn't so terrified.

We tip downward. The sound of the engine's whining fills my ears.

"We're going down," the pilot says over the speakers. "If

anyone is still here, time to bail out. I'm going to try to crash her into the river to avoid ground casualties."

Oh my gosh. This is really happening. I'm totally going to die.

"Ash, we gotta go!" Greyson's face is right next to mine, but I can only just hear him. The wind tosses my curls everywhere.

My muscles are locked. I cannot move.

"Ash!" He tries again to get through to me, but I can't even find my voice to tell him to leave me.

Not waiting for my permission anymore, he grabs me. Hefting me into the air, he forces my stiff legs around his hips and my arms around his neck.

"Hold on!"

I squeeze my eyes shut and do as he commands, knowing what's coming. In four swift steps, he flings us out of the plane.

We spin in a free fall. Greyson holds me with one hand and fumbles around my pack with the other. I think he shouts a curse, but it's torn away by the wind so fast I'm not sure. He works an arm between my back and the parachute pack, getting a better grip on me, then yanks his ripcord. His arm squeezes tight around my rib cage.

There's a tug right before we recoil upward, the parachute catching air.

"I've got you," Greyson assures me as we bounce and swing back and forth, but the truth of the matter is that I have him. It's a wonder he can still breathe with my boa constrictor hold.

Our descent slows and I almost start breathing easily, but when I crack an eye open, my blood pressure shoots right back up. We're falling into a world on fire.

"I can't steer. We're gonna land in the river." The words are barely out of his mouth when we're swallowed by a cloud of smoke. I hold my breath to keep from choking and press my face into Greyson's neck.

"It's going to be okay. I've got you," he assures me.

We smack into the river without warning and immediately sink in the frigid water. The impact stuns me for a moment, but then I detangle myself from Greyson. I lose him in the murky water as I kick toward the surface.

My head breaks free and I suck in a lungful of cinder-filled air. There's visibility along the surface of the water, but I don't see Greyson anywhere.

"Grey!" I shout, turning in a frantic circle. When a minute passes and I still can't find him, I dive below the surface, using my arms as well as my boot covered feet to search the river.

Thanks to my Nephilim abilities, I can hold my breath for almost ten minutes. Half of that time has already leaked away when my hand snags on something. I grab hold and yank, only to realize I have a chunk of the parachute fisted in my hand. I follow the material until I find Greyson, struggling against a knot of cords and fabric. Reaching for the sheath at my leg, I pull the dagger free and saw through the materials until he's detangled enough to ascend.

I'm relieved to see Greyson bobbing in the water when I swim to the surface. He jerks his head, flinging his short hair off his forehead.

"Thanks."

"No problem." But really, I'm the one who owes him thanks. I would have gone down with the plane if he hadn't hauled me out like he did.

"Greyson! Ash!" Someone yells our names, but I can't see much besides water and smoke.

"We're here," Greyson calls back.

"Bro, you in the river?"

Casting his gaze skyward, Greyson shakes his head, then sets off toward his brother.

We haul ourselves up and out of the river. Crawling over to a large patch of grass, we collapse. I need a moment to mentally recover from that ordeal. Pieces of ash float down from the sky like a light snowfall. It sticks to my wet clothing and then disappears. I'm shaking, and not from the cold—although London in December isn't warm.

Sterling calls our names.

"Over here," Greyson responds, and we push to our feet. The smoke has thinned, and I spot Nova and Sterling sprinting toward us. Grabbing a rubber band off my wrist, I twist my soggy hair up into a knot on the top of my head. I'm mostly in leathers, so the fish-scented water drips off me easily. Greyson runs a hand through his hair, pushing it away from his face, then checks the holsters and sheaths on his body, accounting for all his weapons.

"What were you guys doing in the river?" Sterling asks.

"The backstroke," Greyson deadpans.

"They obviously didn't land there on purpose." Nova has her phone out, her thumbs working as she talks.

I glance around. We're definitely in a park. There's a bridge stretching over the Thames not far away. "Where are we? And where's the rest of the group?"

"This is Bishop's Park, across from Putney. The others are battling Fallen on the other side of the river."

"We saw you guys bail from the plane late and followed

you over here," Sterling adds. "Did your parachute not work or something, Ash?"

"Or something," I mumble, my gaze flicking to Greyson, whose lips remain sealed.

Nova looks up from her screen. "My parents are near Buckingham. Something is going down there. They want us to join. It's less than five miles but won't take us long if we run. You two good?"

Running in squishy boots. Fun.

Greyson glances down at his own feet, probably thinking something similar, but gives the group a quick nod.

"Yeah, we got this. Let's go."

On a normal day, a five-mile run wouldn't have taken more than fifteen minutes. On the day London is attacked by Fallen, it takes forty-five. We stop once in Parsons Green to help a family of four—and their dog—out of a burning building. We stop again in South Kensington to pull a slab of concrete off a man's legs, which forces us to backtrack to leave him at a hospital.

It's only mid-afternoon, but the natural light of day is already fading. As we near Buckingham Palace Gardens, a shadowed creature drops from the sky, rattling the ground and freezing us in place as we assess the threat.

"Is that a Fallen?" I know what Fallen look like, but there aren't any distinguishable features on whatever is in front of us. It's just a dark mass of roiling mist, roughly the size of a Fallen.

"Yeah. Emberly said that's how she used to see them when she half-phased," Greyson says.

Poor Em. It's not that a shadowy blob would have been any more frightening than a Fallen in its original form, but this way you can't anticipate their attacks or plan your own. It sheds a whole new light on the fact that she faced these things all alone, with zero training.

I pull a handle from the sheath at my hip. With a flick of my wrist, a two-part blade snaps out, creating a short sword. Greyson's spear also elongates with the swish of his arm. Nova stands ready with nothing but a dagger, and Sterling pulls a double-sided axe from his belt.

"Where are we supposed to aim?" I ask.

"The middle?" Sterling answers right before the darkness rushes us.

It seems to be aiming for Nova. She bends her knees then vaults into the air. I think she's in the clear, but a wisp of darkness snags her ankle and flings her aside. She slams into a tree, shaking the bare branches.

It goes for Sterling next, who deflects the blows with the handle of his axe. Greyson and I flank it from behind. I swipe low the same time Greyson jabs the middle portion with his spear. I think we both make contact because the ends of our weapons come away dripping with a black substance. The shadow seems to stagger a few steps, then swipes at Sterling.

Sterling's black jacket is split open over his bicep, but that doesn't slow him. If anything, it feeds his adrenaline and determination. He swings his axe, which sticks in the air, the end buried in the swirling shadows.

Nova rejoins us and our unit surrounds the darkness.

Taking a few running steps, I jump in the air and slash my sword at the area where its head should be. Fresh Fallen blood coats the sharpened blade when I land, but I can't be sure where I wounded it or how badly. I'm about to take another jab when the shadows fall in on themselves, shrinking in size until they disappear completely.

"Did we kill it?" Sterling asks as he bends over to pick up his axe, which clattered to the ground when the darkness vanished.

I check my friends' faces. No one is sure of anything.

"Should we phase and check?" I ask.

Greyson puts his hand out to stop me. "No. We don't know how many more might be in the spirit realm. Best to leave it be."

I nod, happy to comply.

"Nova, are you okay?" I ask. Her hair is a little crazy, but I'm not one to talk. Somewhere along the way, my hair band snapped. My afro game is strong right now.

"Yeah, fine. Let's go. My parents are this way." She strides off toward Buckingham Palace with a slight limp. Nova could be missing an arm and still claim she's fine. Greyson scans my body with a concerned gaze as we both start after Nova.

"I didn't get hurt," I assure him.

"Just making sure."

"Hey, how about me?" Sterling asks. "I actually *did* get injured. I think it clawed my arm." He shrugs off his jacket and sure enough, there are four slashes on his bicep. They weep blood, but don't look too deep.

Greyson claps his brother on his uninjured arm. "Suck it up, dude. Chicks dig scars."

"Well, that means I'm outta luck because these marks will be as baby smooth as the rest of me in a few hours."

I shake my head. These two. We almost died in a plane crash, were attacked by a Fallen, and are in the middle of a mini-apocalypse—but they still make me smile. What would I do without them?

A blast rocks the ground, and a mushroom cloud rises from the other side of the palace. Shadows dart back and forth in the sky above the Royal Family's London residence. Shouts fill the ash-clouded air.

Nova takes off, ignoring whatever injuries she might have as she sprints around to the front gates—or at least to where the front gates used to be. The iconic black and gold entrance is a twisted mess of melted steel. Bodies are scattered here and there. Human guards. I don't even need a close look to know they're dead.

We come to a halt as three people in full tactical garb speed by us. They're swallowed by the black smoke from the explosion.

"Nova!" An angel-born male and female sprint toward us. I recognize them as Nephilim from the weapons strapped to their bodies. Humans don't tend to run around with serrated daggers and sais on their person. At least two sheaths are attached to each of their limbs.

Rather than embracing when they meet, each person lifts an arm and places a hand on the shoulder of the person to their right, creating a small circle. I recognize it as a common greeting between angel-born of the powers-line.

They break apart and Nova leads them over to us. Both angel-borns survey the area, staying alert and aware.

"These are my parents, Killian and Ciara," she says for my benefit alone, considering Nova's parents are already tight with the Durands.

Like most Nephilim, Nova's parents look young. Late twenties by human standards. Ciara's dark brunette hair is pulled back in a high ponytail that hangs in a thick wave down to mid-back. The only thing amiss on her is a smudge across her cheekbone. Killian's hair is closely cropped to his scalp, but I can still see the tint of red that Nova inherited in the low light of the almost-set sun. His exposed hands are smeared with blood, but there aren't any rips or tears in his clothing.

"Ash," Nova continues the hurried introductions, "and you know these two."

"Glad you made it here safely," Killian says, and Ciara nods her agreement.

"What's the situation?" Nova asks.

"Isolated attacks have been occurring all over the city since the early morning. The Fallen can't fully phase into the mortal world yet, but that hasn't seemed to slow the destruction they're causing." Ciara's bright green eyes narrow in frustration. "Angel-born are in both realms trying to protect the city. Human militias are trying to fight as well, but they don't know what they're up against."

We'd seen several of those groups as we traversed the city—humans carrying makeshift weapons like garden shears and tire-irons. One of our missions as Nephilim has always been to hide the existence of Fallen and the spirit realm from humans, but I don't see how that's going to happen after this. A supernatural invasion of this magnitude can't be covered up by a few slick spin doctors.

"Fallen aren't allowing aircraft to get close to central London and are holding off military around the borders of the city," Killian adds, then casts his gaze toward the palace. "It seems one of their leaders has taken a stand at Buckingham Palace."

"How do you know that?" Greyson asks.

Killian and Ciara exchange a look. I don't know them

well enough to be able to discern its meaning, but it amps up the sinking feeling in my gut.

"Just tell us," Nova says.

"He's angel-born," Ciara confesses, a crease forming between her eyebrows. "But light haired with silver-tipped wings. He can control angel-fire in the mortal world." She shakes her head. "We've never seen anything like it."

But we have.

"Thorne." The name slips through my lips, and Killian and Ciara zero in on me. "It has to be, right?" I ask my friends. They know as much about him from Emberly as I do.

"I suppose that's not unexpected," Greyson says.

"Where are the angels?" Sterling asks. "I get they're a reclusive bunch, but this is biblical-level destruction. Shouldn't they be here to lay the smack down?"

Greyson nods. "Camiel said they were going to try to close whatever holes in the veil are letting Fallen into the mortal world, whatever that means."

"Camiel, the Angel of War?" Ciara blinks at us.

I get it, we happen to know a lot of sensitive information novices wouldn't normally be privy to. But then again, my best friend is a magical, one-of-a-kind seraph angel-born, so it makes sense I'm in the know. "And who is this Thorne?"

"A seraph-Neph who leads an army of Fallen and Forsaken," Nova says. Another detonation shakes the earth and sends us all ducking as plumes of smoke rise from beyond the wrecked gates. "I'll have to explain later."

"Right." Killian and Ciara do a quick weapons check. "You all protect our flanks and back—we have to go in and help the rest of our cohort. There are eight angel-born in the courtyard."

"That few?" I ask. From what I know about Thorne, it will take more than that to take him down.

"We're spread thin right now," Ciara explains.

Killian and Ciara lead us through the mass of warped steel. We have to navigate through and over several charred bodies along the way. I try not to look too closely. Violence is a part of our culture, but these poor people never stood a chance. They didn't even understand the forces they were up against.

"Think a princess needs saving somewhere in that palace?" Sterling asks.

"Not the time, dude," Greyson whispers back.

"Prince Sterling has a nice ring to it," he says as he wipes a hand across his brow, smearing ash and Fallen blood over his forehead.

Nova shoots a glare over her shoulder at the brothers, and Sterling makes a zipping motion across his lips. I come level with her, moving forward with careful movements in the direction her parents lead. Shouts and barked orders come from the angel-born fighting on the other side of all this smoke.

I suck in a breath before we enter a particularly dense cloud. My eyes water, but after a handful of steps the air starts to clear, and I can see the white limestone of Buckingham Palace. There's a trench of fire blazing in front of the steps, cutting off our view of the battle beyond. A body is launched into the air from the other side and lands to our left.

Nova's parents rush to his aid. The man is already struggling to his feet by the time they reach him.

Nova releases a low-level whistle. I glance over and notice her gaze is fastened on the silver-winged Nephilim striding through the smoke and fire.

"Is he moving in slow motion, or is it just me?" she asks while tracking his movements. She palms a dagger in each hand.

"You can't be serious," I say.

"Dude may be evil, but it doesn't mean he can't also be smokin' hot."

I shake my head. "I can't even with that comment."

Thorne's gaze snaps in our direction. His pointed regard slides over me then snags on Nova and holds. With his face devoid of emotion, the experience is very Terminator-esque. The creepy factor of this whole ordeal just leveled up a thousand percent.

He raises his arm, and a golden ball of fire forms, sparking and spitting flames.

I think about the explosions and all the fire around us, knowing instantly he's the one who caused it. And now his attention is on us. Gulp.

"Time to cut the head off the snake," Nova says, then rushes Thorne. I shout for her to stop, but it's too late. Nova is talented, but with that angel-fire and the use of those razor-sharp wings, her talent won't be enough.

I start after her right as Thorne chucks the ball of fire. I hit the ground, but it doesn't faze Nova, who still barrels toward him. The fire zooms a foot over her head and explodes somewhere behind us. I don't know if he meant to do that, or if he just has bad aim, but I'm thankful for it either way.

When Nova reaches Thorne, she takes a swipe at him

with one of her daggers. The first bit of emotion shows on his face. I think it's annoyance.

Nova delivers a flurry of attacks that Thorne easily knocks aside.

I'm up on my feet and running toward the duo. In my periphery, I spot Grey and Sterling heading in the same direction. I pray we can reach the pair before Thorne decides to gut Nova with the tips of his wings.

"Watch his wings!" I yell, but I have no idea if she hears me.

Nova's movements don't slow as they circle each other in a dangerous sort of dance, but that doesn't bother Thorne, who continues to block everything she throws at him. I don't know why he hasn't gone on the offensive yet.

Greyson, Sterling, and I close in on Thorne and Nova at the same time, but they're moving so quickly, I'm not sure how to enter the fight without injuring my friend. I cast a worried gaze to Greyson, hoping he has a plan.

"Thorne!" Greyson yells. The silver-winged angel-born flinches at the use of his name, giving Nova an opening to nick his ribs. The hand he presses to his side comes away red, but he simply shakes the wetness off with a flick of his wrist. Rather than frustration at being injured, he tips his head at Nova as if to say, "well done."

What is happening?

With a downward flap of his wings, Thorne launches a few feet into the air. He lands in the middle of our group.

I backpedal at the invasion of space. Now at his back, Nova makes a move toward Thorne and he flares his wings, keeping her at a distance. He turns his head and gives her a side-eyed glance. "That was fun. But playtime's over. Come at me again and you'll watch your intestines spill."

I don't know if Nova believes him, but I do.

He turns back toward the three of us, placing particular attention on Greyson—though I can tell by the tilt of his head that he hasn't dismissed Nova outright.

"You know me?"

"Know of you," Greyson admits.

Thorne assesses Greyson and then Sterling and me. "Emberly's friends, I presume."

Sterling gives a half-nod. Thorne's mouth forms a cold smile that sends a chill down my spine. "I know of you too. Tell me, how's Silver?"

My eyes widen. He knows Silver went to us? Did he have her tracked to the compound, or was her surrender planned? Did she play a part in all of this? The timing of her disappearance this morning is certainly suspicious.

I don't dare take my eyes off Thorne to gauge Greyson and Sterling's reactions to hearing their sister's name. I'm guessing Thorne brought her up to distract us, but I'm not falling into that trap.

"She's just fine." Greyson's words are smooth, almost conversational. "Having a good time catching up with her family. You know about family, right? I hear you have a mother. Or rather . . . had."

Thorne's nostrils flare and his eyes deaden at the mention of Seraphim, his seraph mother. Emberly claims Seraphim was annihilated when she tried to take her body as a vessel. Thorne hadn't been there for that showdown, but he must have been informed by now.

Thorne lifts both hands. This time when the fireballs grow, they burn pure white. I can feel the heat of them pressing against my skin despite the flames already licking over the palace courtyard.

"I suggest you stay out of my way. I'll give you four a pass this once—for Emberly—but won't extend mercy another time."

That makes no sense. Emberly said they hadn't parted on good terms. I have no doubt this guy could barbeque us if he wanted, so I'm not complaining, but I also don't understand.

I take a half-step back, leery of those balls of angel-fire regardless of Thorne's assurance of safety.

Suddenly, Thorne's head snaps up as if in reaction to a call none of us can hear. Above our heads, the formless bodies of Fallen congregate in the darkening sky, undulating as if one giant being. Thorne presses his lips into a hard line as he gives his wings an agitated shake.

Something displeases him.

His focus returns to Greyson as he says, "When you see her, let her know that my offer still stands . . . for now. It won't for much longer."

With that, he chucks the angel-fire at me and the twins, and the three of us hit the deck. The heated balls sail over our heads. A gust of air sends sand and pebbles flying as Thorne flaps his wings. I cover my eyes against the grit.

"Nova, no!" Ciara yells.

I blink my eyes open in time to see Nova vault into the air and grab onto Thorne's leg. He glances down at her with a scowl on his face and tries to shake her loose, but she hangs on like a spider monkey.

He's already two body lengths in the air. Nova's added weight doesn't slow his ascent.

Ciara and Killian rush past as I hurry to my feet. They stop with their heads tilted up as their daughter soars away, attached to the appendage of a very dangerous Nephilim.

Killian pulls a throwing dagger from a sheath and cocks his arm. Ciara grabs her husband's bicep before he can let loose the projectile.

"Wait! You might hit Nova!"

It's hard to tell exactly what's going on, but it seems like Nova has managed to climb Thorne's leg and is trying to punch him mid-air.

Thorne's wings continue to pump as the two of them grow smaller, gaining distance and altitude.

Killian takes off. "Keep them in your sights," he orders as we sprint toward the gaping front entrance. Parts of it still smolder and the sharp smell burns my nostrils.

Just as we clear the smoke, I spot Nova and Thorne several stories in the air and at least half a football field away. Nova yanks on one of Thorne's wings and the pair spin. Ciara's hands cover her nose and mouth as she watches them spiral toward the ground and disappear behind a grove of trees. As a group, we immediately give chase, dodging tree trunks to track them down. Greyson and Sterling spread out on either side of me as we navigate the patch of trees.

Muffled shouts reach my ears, and relief floods my system. One of the voices is definitely Nova's.

I follow the ruckus, changing trajectory. Ciara and Killian are in the lead. They pull their weapons—Ciara a dagger from her thigh, Killian a crossbow from his back.

Nova and Thorne come into view straight ahead, trading verbal blows rather than physical ones.

"Down!" Killian shouts as he raises his weapon.

Nova spins. Her dark hair, free of its tie, whips Thorne in the face and he bats it away. Rather than hitting the ground like she should, she stands with her feet planted, arms straight at her sides and hands fisted. Killian lowers the tip of his weapon, releasing what sounds like a Celtic cuss word.

Thorne crouches and launches into the air—this time free of Nova's vice grip. Ciara and Killian take aim at the same time and their weapons—a bolt and dagger—slice the air. The bolt reaches Thorne first and nicks his thigh, making a small cut in his black leather pants. He spots the dagger and flicks it away with a snap of his wings, the metal edges creating sparks when they connect.

With a final scowl in our direction, Thorne flies off, getting quickly lost in the dark city sky.

"Nova. Are you all right?" Ciara pats down Nova's body, checking for injuries.

Nova remains uncharacteristically stoic, her gaze trained on the spot where Thorne disappeared.

"She's fine," Ciara tells her husband on an exhale when she finishes her inspection.

Furrowing her brow, Nova drops her gaze from the sky. "Well." She folds her arms over her chest. "That was vexing."

# 7

## THORNE

"What do you mean the gates are closed?" I modulate my voice to hide the torrid emotions souring my gut.

The Fallen replies in Enochian, repeating his previous statement word for word. The news hasn't changed: the angels sealed the rifts in the veil. More Fallen won't be able to enter the mortal world until the barrier is brought down for good.

Besides a small muscle tick under my eye that I can't control, I remain cold. Always cold. Emotion is a sign of weakness. And I'm not weak.

My mind brings up the unwelcome image of the auburn-haired Nephilim. I hadn't stayed cold then. If I had, I would have flown high and then watched as she fell, her body splattering on the solid pavement below. But that's not what I'd done. Instead, I'd cushioned the fall she caused. That momentary lapse in judgment is troubling. I quickly banish the frown pulling at my mouth.

The gray-skinned Fallen in front of me takes a half-step

back, misinterpreting my displeasure. I understand his unease. Bad things happen when I get angry.

"Dismissed." After a curt bow of acknowledgement, the Fallen strides to the edge of the roof, then launches into the air. His form blends into the bruised night sky, and he quickly fades from view. Suddenly weary, I keep my gaze fixed on the red stars above. "You played your part to perfection."

Heels click against the roof tiles as she draws near. The heat of her body warms my back when she cozies up to me. One of her arms snakes around my stomach and the other rests on my shoulder as she stretches to kiss the side of my neck.

I should probably feel something, but all there is inside right now is a block of ice.

"You're warmer than you used to be," I say.

"Am I?" She wiggles a bit, pressing her body more fully against mine, but I don't react.

Realizing she's not getting a response, Silver sighs. Her arms melt away and she slides around to face me—a silent demand to stop ignoring her.

I hold in my own sigh as I drop my gaze to her raven hair and then sweep it over her face. Her complexion has a bronzed blush that I'm not used to. Her lips are a full, red cupid's bow.

Silver has always been stunning, but there's no denying she's even more so now.

"Did you enjoy your family reunion? Were Mom and Dad excited to see you again?"

Irritation hardens her features. I'm purposefully baiting her—and she knows it.

"You know that's not why I went back."

I lift an eyebrow, staring her down. Challenging her. I'm not convinced her physical appearance is the only part of her that changed when Emberly transformed her from a Forsaken back into a Nephilim.

"That's not why *you* sent me back," she continues, her gaze narrowed. "I was content as I was. You know that."

"Content as a creature of the night?"

Folding her arms across her chest, she juts a hip to the side. Even though she's returned to me after fulfilling her part of the plan, I'm not sure where her loyalties lie. She's always been an effective manipulator. I'd be stupid not to consider she's working her skills on me as well.

"Yes. But now you and I are alike. You should be happy about that."

I clench my fist, blunt nails pressing into the fleshy part of my palm. My words grind out despite my resolve to remain stoic. "You overstep. There's only one other person like me, and you aren't her."

Silver flinches at my words and curves slightly into herself. I don't feel bad. I've never been anything but perfectly honest with her. She knows better.

After absorbing my venom, she straightens, wiping any traces of hurt from her face or body language. She tilts her chin up in defiance, molding herself into the Silver I know by leaning back against the ledge and adding just the right amount of arch to her back. From one breath to the next she goes from kicked puppy to sly vixen. Much better.

"She's attached to my brother. I've seen it myself. You don't have a chance of winning her heart."

I let one side of my mouth curve upward. Silly girl. "It's not her heart I'm after."

# 8

## EMBERLY

"*I*'d like to introduce you to your betrothed, Aero."

I blink at the male angel-born who steps forward. He drops to a knee, pressing a closed fist over his heart before standing again. Giving his head a quick twitch, he shakes dark curls off his forehead, but they stubbornly fall back into place.

Betrothed?

The group of people milling around Nikias' living room were invited to give me a soft introduction to the community, but this is anything but soft.

Scanning for help, I catch Steel's eye from across the room. Seeing the guy standing in front of me, Steel shoots me a look that says, *what's going on?* The one I try to scream back is, *get over here quick and save me from being married off.*

The crease between his brows deepens, letting me know he has no idea what I'm trying to say.

I start when a warm hand grasps my own. Completely thrown off, I don't think to snatch my hand back before the stranger bends forward and places a kiss on my open palm.

He quirks a half-smile at me, his dark green eyes peeking out from behind the fringe of walnut waves.

"I know we'll make a good match." The smooth timbre of his voice only ratchets up my discomfort.

"Ah. Um."

My hand is yanked out of the angel-born's and my body picked up and spun. I'm staring at the wall before I even register what happened.

"Don't. Touch. Her." There's a familiar growl in Steel's voice that says he's a hair's breadth from transforming into a lion. I guess he got my message after all.

I twist and peek at Aero from behind Steel's wide shoulders. The other male is as on-guard as Steel. His black wings are folded but arch up aggressively behind him. The scowl he sends Steel broadcasts his dislike loud and clear. I'm sure Steel's glare is no less menacing.

Aero's velvet voice drops an octave. "Step away from my betrothed."

Steel's muscles bunch. "Touch her again and I'll split you open from nose to navel." It sounds like he's juggling shards of glass in his throat as he speaks. I probably shouldn't find this show of dominance attractive . . . but I do.

"Don't threaten my son, cherub." The man who introduced me to Aero puffs out his chest and steps into Steel's space. I think his name is Stavros. He spat the word *cherub* at Steel as if it were an insult. Maybe to them it is?

An animalistic growl rattles Steel's chest and I know it will only take one small nudge to push him over the edge.

This is officially bad. Nikias invited a group of angel-line Neph over to his home to welcome me, but now we're one wrong move away from getting into another brawl.

And if these angel-borns fight as well as Shira, these odds aren't good.

I place a hand on Steel's shoulder, hoping to defuse the situation, but his body doesn't soften in the least. He's strung tight.

"I'm sure there's just been some misunderstanding." My gaze sweeps the room. Conversations cease as people wait to see how this plays out. I can't find Nikias in the bunch.

"There has been no misunderstanding," Stavros says. He tips his bearded chin up as he crosses beefy arms over his chest. "You were promised to us at birth. Your marriage to my son was written in the stars. Your union will produce strong angel-born."

Oh. Heck. No.

I will not be married off to some stranger to be used for breeding. No way, no how.

In a burst of light, Steel transforms into a lion. The low rumble of his growl vibrates in my chest. There are a few gasps throughout the room. I imagine they've never seen a cherub morph before.

"Father, perhaps this isn't the time." Aero looks back and forth between Steel and Stavros. "She's only just arrived and isn't yet used to our ways."

"Let's just get one thing clear," I say, finally finding my voice and backbone. I step out from behind Steel to move beside him, pinning Aero with a glare. "I don't know you. I don't know what promises were made or what magical stars were hanging in the sky when I was born, but we will not be getting married in the near *or* distant future."

A sound rumbles from Steel that sounds an awful lot like a snicker.

Aero scowls. Any traces of the flirtation he threw my way earlier disappear. "But—"

"Never gonna happen." I might have been shocked at first, but I am going to nip this thing in the bud right now.

"You don't understand the customs of our people," Stavros scoffs. "You are of the angel-line, so you will comply."

Steel releases another low growl and his hackles rise.

Nikias enters the room with a tray full of drinks. "Why is it so quiet in—" Catching sight of the stand-off between the four of us, he releases a curse. Setting down the tray, he moves toward us. Angel-born drift out of his way as he strides forward, his face set in a hard line.

"Stavros," he clips. "I told you this wasn't the time."

Stavros tsks. "What good is it not telling the girl the truth up front? She has much to catch up on. There are duties to be fulfilled."

I plant my hands on my hips. "*The girl* is standing right here and will make decisions for herself."

Steel moves one paw forward and Aero concedes a step, his hands fisting at his sides and twitching toward the blade sheathed at his waist. A spark of fury ignites in my gut and I command my wings to unfurl, purposefully scraping the sharpened ends against the stone floor in warning.

These Nephilim might also have wings, but mine are used for more than flight. They'd do well to remember that.

"Let's bring it down a notch before things get out of control."

We all ignore Nikias and instead remain on high alert. The elder angel-born pinches the bridge of his nose and mumbles, "This is not how I saw this going."

Turning his back on us, Nikias addresses the room,

telling everyone the festivities for the evening are over and thanking them for coming. No one speaks again until the partygoers clear out and only the five of us remain.

"Everyone stand down," Nikias orders, but is once again ignored. With a snap, his wings flare, and his voice booms, "I said. Stand. Down." Stavros and Aero are the first to back down. "Take a seat," he barks at the two.

With cautious looks in our direction, they lumber to the couch and sit on opposite sides. Nikias indicates Steel and I should take the chairs opposite them.

"I think it's safe to shift back," I whisper. In a burst of light, Steel's himself again. He places a hand on my lower back as we walk over to take our seats. Both of us eye the unfamiliar angel-borns with suspicion. When Steel lowers himself into his seat, his muscles are still taut and bunched. He's ready to spring into action at a moment's notice.

"Stavros, I know you have a lot of expectations where Emberly is concerned, but there are extenuating circumstances that nullify her contract. I told you this before the gathering began."

I exchange glances with Steel. He shakes his head and his lip peels back from his upper teeth, broadcasting his disgust.

I don't blame him. Arranged marriages without consent. Yuck. What century are we in? But I guess it makes sense that this angel-born community might not be up on modern concepts like free will. Their interaction with the outside world is severely limited.

"The contract is unbreakable." Stavros crosses his arms over his chest and leans back, challenge evident in the tilt of his chin. The light hits his hair just right to illuminate a thin streak of gray that shoots from his temple to behind his ear.

"That's not entirely true," Nikias says.

Stavros' eyes narrow. Aero's wide-eyed gaze bounces back and forth between his father and Nikias, that earlier confidence seemingly squeezed out of him as he begins to catch on to something I'm not picking up. Stavros and Nikias continue to consider each other. It's clear some sort of silent communication is happening between the pair.

"Emberly is not a full-blooded angel," Stavros finally says.

"Yes, true. But in this, she's more angel than human. There's nothing to be done if her angel nature is dominant in this area. It stands to reason that she's taken on more angel traits than just control over angel-fire and metal tipped wings."

"You're just trying to get out of our contract," Stavros argues.

And I'm just trying, and failing, to follow this conversation. Some of the stiffness has melted from Steel's frame. There's a contemplative gleam in his eye that tells me he's keeping up with this conversation more easily than I am.

Nikias rises and paces in the space behind Steel, his face a stone mask. "Either way, I won't force the girl into a match. It would make for an unhappy union for your son as well."

"Their happiness isn't necessary. The continuation of a strong angel-line is what's important."

Bracing his feet shoulder width apart, Nikias says, "It's too late. She's already made her choice."

Stavros flinches, then his eyes widen almost comically before landing on Steel beside me. "I don't believe it."

Aero's mouth dips downward, disappointment clearly written over his face.

"Father—"

"No," Stavros snaps. "Our family line will not be denied another time." He slams his fist down on the arm of the couch and the furniture groans.

There's obviously some history here I don't know about. I stay quiet and wait to see where this stand-off between Stavros and Nikias will go next.

As quick as a striking snake, Nikias has a blade to Steel's throat. Shoving out of my seat, a heated blast washes over me from head to toe and balls of angel-fire form in both palms. I don't need to look down at myself to know I've fully morphed.

"What are you doing?" With his chin tipped up and hands fisted, Steel's voice is deceptively calm.

Nikias' narrowed gaze stays on Stavros.

"Oh, shoot," Aero says from his seat next to his father. "It is true."

"I will give you to the count of three to lower the blade or else I'll barbeque you and burn this entire town to the ground. Feel me?"

The twin balls of fire in my hands itch to be released. My fingers twitch. The only thing holding me back is the concern that Steel will get caught in the crossfire, but with only a flick of his wrist, Nikias could slit Steel's throat from ear to ear. I have no good options.

As fast as he struck, the blade disappears from Steel's neck. Nikias steps away, sliding the dagger into its sheath at his hip and then lifting his hands to show he's weaponless.

Cracking his neck, Steel peers over his shoulder at Nikias. "Was that really necessary?"

"Steel, let's go. We're getting out of here." That was the last straw. We are blowing this popsicle stand. Literally, if I have to. Coming here was a colossal mistake. We just need to collect Tinkle on our way out and I am never going to lay eyes on this place—

"Is that proof enough for you?" Nikias' smug expression is directed toward Stavros.

Wait. What?

Stavros stares at Nikias, jaw working as he grinds his teeth. Aero lays a hand on the older man's shoulder. "Father. There's nothing to be done about it."

Stavros' nostrils flare. He shoves out of his seat and stalks from the room. Aero tips his head in Nikias' direction and shoots me a small smile of apology before following in his father's wake, leaving Steel and me alone with my however-many-greats grandfather.

Steel remains calmly seated, a brow arched as Nikias reclaims his seat in the chair next to him. I'm not nearly as relaxed. Angel-fire still dances over my fingers and licks up my wrists.

"Please, Emberly." Nikias indicates the place Aero just vacated.

"I'm a little too worked up right now to just sit and pretend the last thirty minutes never happened." I lift my fiery jazz-hands up as proof. I'll char that couch in an instant if I try to sit on it now, which is a tempting option. When I cross my arms over my chest, the angel-fire isn't more than a warm splash across my exposed skin. "Maybe you should start by explaining why you held a blade to Steel's throat."

Steel pushes out of his seat and walks toward me. I back up a step, not wanting to burn him, but he doesn't stop advancing. Reaching out, he cups my cheek.

"Steel, I don't think—"

"Hey," he interrupts. His thumb glides over my cheek-bone. "You've got this. You're in control."

My body begins to cool, and without a thought, the fire goes out. I lift a hand, my fingers brushing over the back of his own as my gaze connects with his. He bites down on his full lower lip, his teeth pressing into the soft flesh. The edges of his mouth lift in a lazy grin.

Hand to God, my toes curl in my boots and a swarm of hyped-up butterflies takes flight in my stomach.

"There you go," he whispers. Bending forward, he plants a chaste kiss on my forehead before stepping back.

I'm in a bit of a daze when Nikias clears his throat. Snapping out of it, I catch him rubbing at his mouth as Steel returns to his seat. It's obvious he's covering a smile.

So embarrassing. I really have to work on not coming undone at a mere touch.

Clearing my own throat, I settle on the couch, allowing my wings to hang over the low back.

"I'm not getting married. I'm seventeen." I realize he already knows my stance on this, but I'm setting the tone of this conversation.

Nikias nods. "I know."

Pressing my lips into a hard line, I lift my eyebrows, waiting for his explanation.

"Not all of our pairings here are arranged from birth," he starts. That's good to hear. "Only a handful of families from our line survived the attacks several millennia ago. In truth, the angel-line Nephilim probably would be extinct right now if it wasn't for Camiel. He found this refuge for us and helped make it look like we'd been erased from existence. Thriving wasn't even a thought in those early years. Survival was our one and only goal. So, the remaining angel-borns matched up the young with the most powerful abilities in the hopes of having strong descendants."

Listening to Nikias talk reminds me of a foster family I lived with who bred racehorses. They matched mares and stud horses based on favorable traits, able to get top dollar for a foal only if it had the right sire and dam. I shudder at the idea of thinking about people in those terms.

"Certainly you have the numbers now, so you don't have to do that anymore," I say. They've lived in peace for over two thousand years. They can't still be worried about extinction.

"We are very long lived, yet conception is difficult. It's uncommon for our kind to have more than one pregnancy throughout their lives." I shift my gaze to Steel, who is one of six children from his family.

"We're an anomaly," Steel confirms.

"Stavros was betrothed to your mother, and so the marriage contract between his family and ours was passed down to you and his son, Aero."

"What if Aero had been a girl? Would the contract be null and void?" I ask.

"No. It would have stood until there was a match to be made that might produce a child."

I scoff. "That's archaic."

"Old habits die hard."

"Are you saying that Emberly's daughter will be held to this contract?" Steel asks.

A flash of fresh panic gurgles in my gut.

"Whoa. Let's not get ahead of ourselves. Seventeen, remember?" I'm not looking to be a teen mom any more than a child bride.

Nikias dips his head apologetically and answers Steel. "Technically, yes."

I don't need another reason not to stay with these angelborns for any longer than I have to, but now I have one. I'm certainly not planning on popping any children out for a long, long, long time—if ever—but now I know to stay away from Cyprus and the hidden town of Eden if I ever do.

"But Stavros is going to back off . . . for now." Steel leans forward. Resting his forearms on his knees, his hands drape in between his legs. "Why would he do that?"

Good question.

"Yes, well . . ." Nikias clears his throat and for the first time looks uncomfortable. "There's a trait specific to angels that would exclude you from having to fulfill the contract. In a way, you'd be using the same technicality as your mother did to pass the agreement down to the next generation."

"What's the trait?" I ask.

Nikias takes a moment to consider his answer. I try to catch Steel's eye to get a read on his mood, but his focus is solely on Nikias.

"To explain properly, you need to know that time is not exactly linear for angels."

"Is that a complicated way of saying that angels can time travel?" This is getting interesting.

"Yes. And no. Humans were created to exist on a fixed timeline that only moves in one direction, forward. Whatever decisions they make in the present can only ever affect their future selves, not their past. In other words, no matter what happens today, it will never change what happened in the past. Does that make sense?"

Steel lifts his arms and steeples his hands under his chin.

I nod. "Yes, that's the general way time works."

"For the most part, that's the same with angels. Except sometimes their actions can send ripples back in time, leaving impressions in the past as well as affecting future events." He pauses and glances between me and Steel. He's building up to something big and the suspense is killing me. I lean forward, mirroring Steel's stance.

"In that way," Nikias continues, "when an angel finds their soulmate or partner or special someone, whatever you want to call it, it resonates with their past self."

How . . . odd.

"This isn't something that happens with angel-born. It's unique to angels. They call it soul-bonding. My working theory is that since you are technically more angel than human, you're similar to your father in that way. You've fallen in love already and picked your partner, or at least your future self has."

My wings arch up as I straighten my spine. "Love?" Technically speaking, Steel and I just got together. We haven't been a couple long enough to make proclamations of love for each other, yet Nikias just laid it out there. "That's a strong word. Aren't we getting ahead of ourselves?"

Nikias shakes his head. "If I'm right about this, which I'm pretty sure I am, you've chosen Steel at some point in the future, and that dictates how you've reacted toward him since the first moment you two met."

My cheeks are on fire. Having this conversation makes me feel incredibly exposed. I look to Steel, whose stony expression gives nothing away. "Have you ever heard about anything like this?"

He slowly shakes his head, but besides that remains

maddeningly mute. A relative stranger just proclaimed that I'm in love with him and he's just sitting there, calmly. How can he not be freaking out right now? Oh gosh, what if that *is* his freaked-out face?

"How do you even know about all this?" I ask Nikias, proud that my voice sounds relatively calm.

"I expect we know more about angels than the other Nephilim do, simply because we have more interaction with them. But in this particular case, I watched it unfold between Camiel and your mother, so I recognize the signs."

"What signs?"

"Your hyper-possessiveness is the most glaring one."

I scoff. "That doesn't mean anything. I would jump to defend anyone important to me. I'm a super-possessive person by nature, so that doesn't prove anything."

Nikias lifts his eyebrows as if to say, *you sure about that?*

Okay, that last part is a lie. I never showed a spark of possessiveness until I thought Steel's life was at risk, but Nikias doesn't know that.

I take a moment to think back on all the times I had that bizarre, growly "mine" reaction when Steel was in danger: the alley in Glenwood Springs, the time I found him half frozen in the mountains, when Silver ambushed us in Michigan, the arena at Whitehold, and even earlier today when Shira attacked us.

Biting my bottom lip, I fall back into the couch cushions with a huff. There's really no denying I go a bit out of my mind when he's in serious trouble. And then there's the fact that I morphed for the first time when I thought he was going to be sliced and diced by a group of Forsaken. Heck, when I'm really worked up, sometimes his touch is the only thing that can calm me down, like what happened a few minutes ago.

But those are all normal reactions to high-stress, life-threatening situations. Aren't they?

"I can see you're overwhelmed."

I release a half-laugh. "You could say that."

"I would have rather not have had this conversation with you. In truth, I'm sure Camiel can describe it better than I— after all, it's what bonded him to your mother. But considering how stubborn Stavros can be, it's best this is out in the open."

"What about Emberly's mother?" Steel finally speaks up. "Was she personally affected by Camiel's ability?"

Nikias' gaze comes to rest on Steel. "In a way, yes. Stasha dreamt of Camiel before the two ever met."

Oh, snap. This just got real.

I feel my eyes widen and hold my breath. That's too specific to be coincidental. I don't want to look, but my gaze drifts to Steel. He's staring at the floor, lost in his own thoughts. Finally, he nods and lifts his gaze.

"Okay."

"Okay?" That's it? That's all he's going to say?

Steel opens his mouth to speak just as the door behind him slams against the wall.

"That was a quick get-together. Did the dynamic duo lay the smack down on—oh shoot." Shira skids to a stop, taking in the three of us. Lifting her hands in front of her, she starts to take a slow step backward, as if she can slide right out of the room without us noticing.

"It's okay, Shira. You can come in." Nikias looks relieved for the interruption and pops to his feet. "It's been a long day. I think it's time to get these two settled. Could you show Emberly and Steel to their guest rooms?"

"Actually," Steel says, pushing out of his seat as well, "I have a few things I'd like to discuss with you, Nikias. Emberly can go on ahead of me."

I frown. That sounded an awful lot like a dismissal. Coming off that brain-exploding conversation, Steel's disregard doesn't feel good.

Shira looks between Steel and Nikias before tipping her face in my direction. The fading remains of a shiner rings her right eye, and one of her wings is bandaged. She puckers her mouth before nodding slowly. "Follow me, Princess."

# 9

## EMBERLY

"*Here* you go." Shira gestures me through the doorway with a wave of her arm.

The bedroom is unassuming. A small bed is pushed up against the far wall. There's a chest of drawers across from it and a rocking chair in front of the room's only window. A single daisy pokes out of a small bud vase resting on the sill. Neat, clean, functional, and oddly homey.

Going over to the bed, I run my fingers over what looks to be a handmade quilt.

"So yeah, this is it," Shira says from her place in the hall-way. "There's a bathroom down there." She points farther down the hall, then we both fall silent. Shira won't look me in the eyes, but it's clear from the way she holds herself that it's out of defiance, not deference. "I'm sure it's not as nice as what you're used to, but it's a place to stay."

I huff out a deep half-laugh. She obviously doesn't know much about me if she thinks I would look down my nose at this room. It's easily one of the nicest accommodations I've ever had.

Misinterpreting my meaning, Shira's eyes flare and then settle on me. There's not a drop of warmth in her gaze. This girl does not like me. But I suppose I haven't given her much reason to.

"I'm sorry about earlier." My gaze drifts to her bandaged wing. It's tucked in tight and high and looks uncomfortable.

Shira crosses her arms. "Are you though?"

I shrug. "You attacked us."

"You're the first outsiders to ever be allowed into Eden."

I lift my eyebrows. Is that supposed to excuse everything? "And that was reason enough to blindside us? Because we're new? Yeah, that makes sense."

Shira narrows her eyes and pulls her shoulders back. A wince flicks across her face when the movement jostles her wing, but she quickly covers it. "It's not safe for you two to be here."

"How do you figure?" I cross my arms, mirroring her pose.

"We're safe because no one knows Eden exists. Now that you're here, that's bound to change."

"I would never tell anyone where this place is." I scrunch my nose, offended she thinks we're untrustworthy.

"It's only a matter of time before more angel-born find out about us."

"Wow. So, your plan was to take us out so that your secret dies with us. Now I definitely don't feel bad about beating the crap out of you."

She curls her upper lip into a sneer. "I wasn't trying to kill you. I just wanted to test your fighting skills and abilities."

The words "so I can kill you later" are left unsaid.

After our scuffle earlier in the day, I was fairly confident

Nikias could get Shira under control, but now I'm not so sure. When she heals up, what's to stop her from coming at me again? Coming at Steel? She could hurt him, but I won't let that happen.

With that thought, a bubble of heat starts to percolate in my chest, warming my skin. I rub my fingertips together and they spark.

Shira's eyes widen and she takes a step back, her arms dropping to her sides. "Whoa, there."

"Where's Steel sleeping?"

With her gaze still fastened on my hands, she swallows and then jerks her chin to the side. "A few doors down."

"I want to share a room."

She shakes her head. "That's not happening. We're old school here. No canoodling before making it official."

Her words combined with the horrified expression on her face strike me as funny. My growing angel-fire fizzles as I realize how worked up I was over a non-threat. Even so, considering the issues we've had so far with Shira and then Stavros and Aero, I'd feel more comfortable keeping Steel close.

"Canoodling?" I smirk.

"I heard it in a movie once. We have television here," she snaps defensively.

"Seriously? You do?" I haven't seen very many modern amenities since we walked into Eden.

"Well, we have one. Sometimes we watch movies on VHS."

I don't even know if I've ever seen a VHS tape before. At least not in real life. I shake my head. It doesn't matter.

"I need a room big enough for Steel and myself." I straighten my back and put as much authority into my voice, faking like I order people around on the regular and hope it will work with her.

Shira releases a loud sigh, then cracks her neck. "Listen. You're both safe. I'm not going to come after either of you again."

"Excuse me if I don't believe you."

She pokes her tongue in her cheek, like she's the one who has the right to be annoyed. "I already told you I wasn't trying to kill you."

"No, you were just sizing us up to figure out how to take us out later."

She jerks back, her arms dropping to her sides. "Gosh, no. If you're staying here, I just want to know how capable you are of defending our people. Angel-line Nephs are the fiercest angel-born warriors. I wasn't sure if you measured up."

Oh. *Oh.*

I stomp toward Shira. She steps back until her wings bump against the hallway wall. Her mouth puckers and her eyes tighten from pain. I get in her face, raising an accusatory finger between us. "Let me get this straight: You attacked us just to make sure we met your imaginary warrior standards? You could have seriously injured us. You *were* injured."

"Seemed like a good idea at the time." The bravado in her voice and the rebellious tilt to her chin don't quite cover up the doubt shining in her gaze. Maybe there's hope for her after all.

"Nothing like that will happen again," Nikias says from down the hall.

Steel trails behind him, but his gaze hardens as he realizes something is going down between me and Shira.

I step back into the bedroom doorway, making space for Nikias and Steel. The hallway is wide, but three of us sport large sets of wings, making it difficult to gather closely.

"Everything all right?" Steel asks, looking only at me.

"Yeah. We were just getting the room assignments worked out."

Moving past Nikias, Steel leans in close and peeks over my shoulder. He's not touching me, but I can still feel the warmth coming off his body. I beat back the urge to sag into him. "Hmm. Bed's kinda small. Looks like I'm sleeping on the floor. Got any extra blankets?"

Nikias clears his throat. "We have another room for you down the hall."

Steel crosses his arms over his chest. "Nope," he says. He tips his head in my direction. "We're not splitting up."

I throw a smug look at Shira.

"That's not really how we do things here," Nikias argues.

"Don't care," Steel replies.

Taking a look at the hard set of Steel's jaw, Nikias must decide that it's not worth the argument. With a resigned shake of his head, he asks Shira to go collect some extra blankets and pillows and bring them to our room. She looks surprised that he caved but leaves to gather the bedding. Once we have everything we need, including borrowed sleepwear, Nikias leaves us with a request to leave the door open and a muttered, "Wait until your father hears about this." The look on Steel's face when the words drift back to us are half-amused, half-intrigued, but not one bit worried.

Steel and I don't say much as we slip under our respective blankets. I ask him what he talked to Nikias about, and he gives me a vague answer about wanting to understand the angel-line hierarchy. I thought for sure he wanted to quiz Nikias about this whole soul-bond thing—maybe see if there are any loopholes—but if he did, he doesn't fess up. I'm not brave enough to press the issue.

I try to get comfortable, but the bed is even smaller than I realized. My head grazes the headboard, and my feet hang over the end. I smack my knee against the wall when I try to turn over.

"I think this is a child's bed," I grumble. No wonder Nikias relented so easily. There is no way more than one grown person could fit in this space.

Steel chuckles on the ground below me. "Plenty of space down here."

I don't think he realizes how tempting that is, but I'm too on-edge to take him up on the offer. My mind is filled to the brim with revelations and whirling with concerns. Eden is a bubble set apart from the outside world, but in the quiet, my thoughts drift to the attacks we watched ravage London this morning. Burning buildings, razed monuments, shadow beasts swooping while confused humans ran for cover.

Has Camiel's angel army stopped the Fallen from coming into the mortal world? What's Thorne's end game, and can he be stopped? Have they found Silver yet?

I'm overwhelmed by a barrage of unknowns. My only measure of relief is knowing that my friends are safely cocooned in the Elders' compound.

Steel's breathing evens out quickly, but I toss and turn as much as I can in the small bed, convinced I'll never fall asleep. Despite my mind's unrest, I eventually succumb to the night's dark lullaby.

∾

"Emberly!"

Steel's concerned face fills my vision, his grip on my biceps just shy of painful.

"What—?" Icy water laps over my feet and salty sea air slaps me in the face. I'm confused and disoriented and a little bit freaked out.

The sky is just beginning to lighten. Warm, buttery rays of light streak across the sky and tint the Mediterranean waves. We're not only outside of Eden's boundaries, but also in the mortal world.

I backpedal and Steel jolts forward with me, refusing to relinquish his hold. A slice of pain registers on the bottom of my foot and my knee buckles. Steel steadies me before I crumple to the ground.

"Whoa. Just take it easy." He rubs a hand on my lower back, ducking down to my height and holding my gaze.

The last thing I remember was struggling to fall asleep in that baby-sized bed in Nikias' house. Now it looks like we're on the Cyprus coast. Could I have traveled through Eden and phased into the mortal world without a memory of doing either?

My freak-out jumps from mild to full-blown.

"Steel, what's going on?"

"You were sleep walking. At least, I think." With a pinched brow, he leans over and scoops me into his arms. He treks up a small dune and sits me down in the seagrass. Crouching in front of me, he picks up my foot. "You're bleeding. It looks like you cut it on a shell. Either from the beach or walking through Eden. It's already closing, but we should get it cleaned up when we get back."

The bottoms of my borrowed sleep pants are wet and

dusted with sand. There are dirt smudges on my knees and my left arm is covered in scratches.

"Steel." His attention shifts from the bottom of my foot to my face when I whisper his name. "I'm not a sleepwalker."

Something happened, but I have no idea what. Tremors race through my body as I stare at Steel like he has all the answers. He tries to wipe even the trace of concern from his face, but his eyes betray him.

"We'll figure this out," he says. I nod, not sure how else to respond.

I close my eyes and allow myself three more seconds to feel what I'm feeling and then force the fear and worry from my mind to make room for logic. I blink open my lids to find Steel waiting patiently for me to compose myself.

"Tell me what happened. At least everything you know."

He rocks back on his heels and rubs a hand through his disheveled hair, messing it up even more.

"I woke up and noticed you were gone about an hour ago. I thought you were in the bathroom at first, but when you didn't come back, I went to check. I couldn't find you in the house and the front door was open. When I couldn't find you from the air, I left Eden to check the beach. I didn't spot you until I phased."

"And when you found me, I just snapped out of it?"

"Not exactly." Steel frowns. "You took a swing at me first."

"I *hit you?*"

He rubs at his jaw. It does look a little red. "I wasn't expecting the attack."

I glance down at my hand. It looks all right, but it does feel a tad sore. I brush my fingers over Steel's cheek, moving them lightly over the area I connected with. He brings his hand up and covers my own.

"I'm so sorry." I hate the idea that I hurt him.

He lightly shakes his head. "You were out of it." He curves his lips into a small smile. The longer we talk, the less panicky he looks. "Don't they say you should never wake a sleepwalker?"

"I'm not—"

"I think they're over here!" I recognize Shira's husky voice coming from somewhere over Steel's shoulder.

"Don't say anything," Steel orders, then helps me to my feet.

I chew on my lower lip as Shira, Nikias, and a couple of vaguely familiar angel-born crest the hill.

"Beautiful morning for a walk, isn't it?" Steel says before anyone else can say a word.

"You were taking a walk?" Nikias asks, his voice filled with doubt.

Steel shoves his hands into the pockets of his sleep pants and notches his eyebrows up. "What else would we be doing?"

What indeed?

I keep my mouth closed and study Nikias, watching for his response. Finally, he glances at the angel-born with him and says, "Sorry. I guess it was a false alarm."

After a round of nods and waves, everyone takes off except for Shira and Nikias. Shira eyes me suspiciously, her gaze taking me in from head to toe. "Why are you so dirty?"

"Um." I glance at Steel, but he keeps his mouth firmly closed. My mind blanks. What would even make sense? "I wanted to build a sandcastle?"

That wasn't supposed to come out as a question.

Narrowing her eyes, Shira looks between Steel and me. Contemplating. Reading us. Seeing too much. She's sharp.

"You wanted to build a sandcastle before dawn?"

It's a flimsy excuse. All four of us know it, but I'm going with it. "I've never been to the ocean before. I've spent my whole life land-locked." At least that part is true. "I was . . . excited."

Shira glances at Steel, noting he's not covered with salt water and sand like I am. "And you didn't want to help?"

"Not a fan of sand," he says with a shrug, completely blasé about whether or not Shira and Nikias buy the lie.

"Honestly," Nikias starts, "I'm not sure I want to know what you two were doing out here. I'm just glad we found you and everyone is all right . . . albeit in need of a bath."

Steel chuckles, catching on to what Nikias insinuated much faster than I do. An amused smile brightens Shira's normally sullen features. When it hits me Nikias thinks we snuck off to fool around, I tell myself not to care, but even so, I can't stop the blush that warms my cheeks.

I clear my throat, ready to move on from this topic.

"Come on. Let's get back," Nikias says. He starts walking inland toward Eden, and Shira turns to follow him.

The lazy smile drops off Steel's face when they're a half-dozen paces away. His gaze sharpens when it focuses back on me. "We've got this."

He's said that before, but this time it sounds like a promise. I can only hope it's one we can both keep.

# 10
## EMBERLY

*S*hira keeps peeking over her shoulder and smiling at us as we trek back to Nikias' house. I'm glad someone is finding this amusing because my mind is too preoccupied by my little nighttime adventure to appreciate the humor. I didn't lie to Steel—I'm not a sleepwalker. I suppose it could just be a fluke, but the incident nags at me. My gut tells me something's not right.

Steel curses under his breath. I glance over at him as he knits his brow and scrolls through the messages on his phone, his gaze intent on the device in his hand.

"You're getting cell reception here?"

He shakes his head. "No. The messages updated when we were in the mortal world."

"Is everything all right?" I don't have my phone on me. My sleepwalking self didn't think to grab it.

He shoves the cell in his pocket, concern clearly written all over his face. "It was Grey. They're all in London."

"What?" The blood drains from my face. I'd hoped they'd

stay in Egypt. Last we heard; London was a war zone. "Are they okay?"

Steel runs his tongue over his bottom lip as he considers me, obviously hesitant to tell me something. "They had a run-in with Thorne."

"Oh my gosh." My heart starts to beat double-time. "We have to go right now."

Steel rubs at the day-old scruff on his jaw. "I'm not sure it's the best idea to be—"

"What's wrong?" Halting, Nikias turns to face us.

"Our friends are in London," I explain. "We're going to have to leave. Immediately."

Anxiety over what happened this morning gets swept aside, and I begin to mentally plan our next steps. Steel and I need to change clothes, but we didn't bring anything with us besides my wayward Celestial. If we can't get Tinkle to fly us up to England, we may have to double back to the Elders' compound to hitch a ride. It's doubtful we'd be able to get in or close to London using human transportation. There's probably a global lockdown on travel right now.

"Hold on. This isn't the time to run off ill-prepared." Nikias' gaze bounces back and forth between us. "We all decided this would be the safest place for you."

Um, no. Camiel decided that, and I didn't fight it. Those details aren't important now.

"Even so, we can't stay. Do you know how we can track down Tinkle?" I look up as if the Celestial may be flying somewhere above my head.

"Camiel may have a point," Steel says.

Refocusing on him, I lift my eyebrows. "You don't want to go help your brothers?"

That doesn't make sense. Steel will do anything to protect his family.

Shoving his hand in his hair, Steel begins to pace. Agitation rolls off him in waves.

"You know that's not it. We just need to take a moment to think this through. If we go to London, you'll have a bullseye on your chest." He stops in front of me. Placing his hands on my shoulders, he slides them down my arms until he grasps my biceps. "Thorne is going to want you back."

It's me. He doesn't want to put *me* in danger. He's choosing me over his family. That's . . . major. And although I'm warmed by his regard, I don't agree with him.

"Your brothers, Nova, Ash. They need us."

Steel takes a deep breath. "They're safe."

"You mean they're safe *for now*."

"You don't know why she can't leave, do you?" Shira cuts in. I'd almost forgotten Steel and I weren't alone.

"What are you talking about?" Steel asks. He drops his hold on me and angles toward Shira.

Shira looks to Nikias with a grimace of apology.

"It's the barrier between the realms." Nikias' gaze settles on Steel before sweeping back to me. I can tell he's not sure he wants to say more in front of Steel, but he's going to have to. "Our ancestors were messengers between the realms— the only angelic line that can travel back and forth at will. All other angels have to be granted permission to pass back and forth. After they fell from grace, the Fallen's rights to pass the barrier were permanently revoked. They've been clawing to find a way back into the mortal world ever since. They found a loophole when they sired our race, but Forsaken can't roam freely in the daylight, and many Fallen prefer their angelic bodies to Nephilim or human shells.

What the Fallen really want is to bring down the barrier between the realms."

Thorne's views about not having to bow down to humans whisper through my mind. "Bring down the barrier. What would that mean?"

"Hell on Earth," Steel answers for Nikias, who nods his agreement.

"At best, the Fallen would be able to phase into the mortal realm whenever they pleased. At worst, the two realms would merge."

"And somehow the angel-line Nephilim play into their plans?"

"We think so. It was the primary reason why we were hunted into near-extinction two millennia ago. The Fallen thought that eliminating our line would allow them to travel unfettered between the mortal world and spirit realm, but they got it wrong. Angel-line Nephilim are the key to unlocking the gates."

"What would happen if they get their hands on an angel-line Neph?" Steel asks.

"We're not sure how the Fallen were able to punch holes in the barrier, but we're concerned if they get their hands on someone from our line, they'll be able to bring it down for good. We're not completely cut off from the outside world, only mostly. There are a small handful of our kind not in Eden at the moment. When we heard Fallen were slipping into the mortal world, we called back any of our own stationed outside our community."

The pieces start to fall into place. "And Camiel knows all of this?"

"Yes," Nikias says. "He didn't bring you here only to keep you safe. He also wants to keep the world safe from you."

When we get back, Nikias shows Steel to a guest bedroom down the hall so we can both get changed and clean up in private. I hope to get a few minutes to talk to Steel, but by the time I'm presentable again, he isn't in his room.

I'm antsy and try to shake off my nerves. There's an oily feeling inside and I'm not sure if it's going to get any better until we talk privately. Voices drift up from the ground floor as I make my way down the stairs.

"There's no use arguing about this anymore. Nothing is going to get decided until Camiel returns. You're welcome to bring it up with him then," Nikias says.

"Camiel might be her father, but you are her angel-born guardian. As our culture dictates, you have as much control over this situation as he does."

Oh, goodie. Stavros is back and it sounds like they're debating my betrothal. I guess it was too much to hope that this discussion was put to rest last night.

Conversation doesn't stop when I enter the room. Nikias and Stavros are seated at a small table littered with coffee cups and a basket of muffins. Shira is nowhere to be seen.

Steel leans against the wall with a mug in his hand, a spectator rather than a participant in the negotiation. With a small smile and an amused glint in his eyes, he couldn't look more relaxed as he sips away. I prickle, a part of me preferring when he goes growly over this topic.

Spotting me, Steel tips his head, silently asking me to join him. I eye the basket of muffins as I drift past the arguing pair, not bold enough to snatch one.

"Want some?" Steel asks, holding his mug out. My nose twitches at the bitter smell of black coffee.

"Hard pass."

Keeping his gaze on me, he takes a long, slow drink. The voices on the other side of the room turn to static. Have I ever told Steel what a perfect upper lip he has? Hopefully not. His ego is already plenty inflated.

Clearing my throat, I tick my chin toward Nikias and Stavros. "Any updates there?"

"Naw. Same old. Stavros says you're contracted to his son and you need to marry quickly and produce a male heir." My jaw drops and Steel chuckles when he sees my reaction. "More or less," he adds.

I cock my head, a pleat forming between my eyebrows. "And that doesn't bother you at all?"

He shrugs. "Why should it?"

His flippant attitude bruises, and to cover the hurt, I take the coward's way out and snip at him. "Well, in that case, maybe I should consider his offer."

Steel laughs.

He. Laughs. At. Me.

My heart cracks. I thought we were on the same page about our relationship, but could it be that we aren't even reading the same book? Maybe this connection I think we have is only one way. According to what Nikias told us last night, I'm the one with the freaky angel-bonding mojo. Maybe my future self's feelings for Steel go unrequited.

Wobbling between confused and hurt, I start to spiral. Fast.

I know Steel wants me to be safe, but is it possible this is just a fling for him? A passing amusement to kill time? And if so, what happened to me being the flame that ignited the darkness inside him? Was that all a load of bull? Because if that were true, he wouldn't be laughing right now. He'd tear apart the room in a jealous rage and challenge Aero to a duel to the death.

I don't actually want that to happen—it's possible I've read a few too many romance novels in my life—but amusement isn't the emotion I expect from Steel over this betrothal mess.

I duck my head, sure that the hole he just ripped through my chest will reflect in my eyes. I turn to leave, but Steel catches my arm. "Whoa there, Princess."

I wiggle out of his hold. "Please don't call me that."

Steel's smile fades as the levity leaks out of him. "I see." He sets his mug down on a nearby end table. "Let me be very clear about something." Reaching forward, he grasps my arms and tugs me forward. I go reluctantly. Very reluctantly.

"You are mine, and I am yours. The only reason I find Stavros' posturing amusing right now is because I recognize it as a fruitless attempt to thwart what even fate can't undo. We're in this together until death, and even then, I won't let you go."

Oh. *Oh.*

Well, that's a little better.

"Besides, I have it on good authority that nothing short of a heavenly intervention could break the bond we have."

I glance at Steel from beneath my lashes. "And that doesn't . . . freak you out?"

Steel's normally hard features soften. His gaze brushes over my face and I swear I can feel it.

"Not at all," he says before dipping down to brush his lips against mine.

It's barely a taste. I want more.

"Can you please stop them from doing that?"

I break away from Steel to find Stavros glaring daggers at us. Nikias rubs at the smile on his face. Apparently, what we do in public doesn't bother him half as much as what we do in private. I get that.

"I'm afraid I can't."

Stavros' hard look swivels back to Nikias. "These are dangerous times. The cherub Nephilim has already failed to protect her once. We both know she'll be safest with her own kind."

Despite his earlier flippancy, Steel's arm wraps around my waist and he tugs me against his chest. I feel the rumble of his displeasure against my back. That was a low blow.

"If her safety was assured, Camiel never would have taken her from us to begin with. The only reason he brought her back now is because she's capable of defending herself."

Wait a second. An hour ago, Nikias was arguing this was the securest place on the planet, but now he's hinting at something else.

Stavros' face takes on a familiar shade of red and he curls his upper lip. "What happened back then was an accident, nothing more. To believe there's a threat in Eden is foolishness. If Stasha had never left with Camiel, Emberly would have been raised here like every other angel-born in our line. Her and my son would already be wed."

Nikias goes eerily still. An accident? A threat in Eden? I don't know the full history behind how my mother became a Forsaken, and I only have a vague knowledge of why I was hidden among the humans, but it's about time I heard it all.

There's a distinct chill in Nikias' voice when he speaks.

"We've been over this ad nauseum. You know the bond between an angel and their mate cannot be broken."

"But she is not an angel."

"In this way, she is. As the Elder of our line, I will hear no more of it."

Oh, snap. Nikias just pulled rank.

Stavros hangs his head, but his fists remain clenched. When he glances up, there's fire in his eyes. The streak of gray in his hair stands out against his dark features. "So be it," he mutters, then storms out, slamming the door behind him.

"Geez. He's tenacious. Is he going to be a problem?" I nod toward the door.

"No, not anymore," Nikias answers.

I'm not convinced. Neither is Steel. "Isn't that what you said last night?" he asks.

"Stavros waited a lifetime for Emberly's mother, only to have her snatched away from him by Camiel. He has some baggage where this marriage contract is concerned, but he's a good man."

Breathing deeply through my nose, I nod, content to let this go for now. Especially when there are more important matters to be discussed.

I'm about to ask what Stavros was talking about when something lands on my shoulder.

"Ahh!"

"Miss me?" Tinkle asks.

"Oh good, you're back," Steel says, and I blink at him in confusion. When has he ever been pleased to have Tinkle around? "Let's go. I need to check in with my brothers. I'm going to need you to get back into Eden." Yep, that makes more sense.

"What's the magic word?" Tinkle asks.

Steel stops in his tracks and does a slow turn, shooting Tinkle a flat look. I hope he realizes the little Celestial is not going to relent until he says please. Pulling his phone out of his pocket, Steel checks the battery life and then settles his gaze on me. "Let's finish the conversation about leaving after I get some more information, okay? If everyone's safe and out of harm's way, it may be best for us to stay put."

I nod. It's a reasonable course of action.

He turns to go but then stops. In two long strides he's in front of me. Slipping an arm around my waist and burying a hand in my hair, his lips seal over mine. The butterflies take flight in my lower belly immediately, but my eyelids only have a moment to flutter shut before he pulls away and heads toward the front door.

"Tinkle!" he yells over his shoulder.

"You didn't say—"

"Please!"

"Well, since you asked nicely." Tinkle jumps off my shoulder and coasts to Steel's as he opens the front door.

"I'll be back soon," he says right before he sweeps out of the house.

I stare at the closed door, my lips all tingly and my fingertips a bit numb.

"You okay?" Nikias asks.

"Oh, huh? What? Yeah. Good. I mean, I'm good." Gah. I'm not alone. Cue the epic blush.

Nikias chuckles. "Don't worry. It's nothing compared to Stasha and Camiel. There was a point I thought I was going to need to hose the two of them off."

I pull a face. Even though I never met my mother and

hardly know Camiel, Nikias is talking about my parents. There's still an *eww* factor.

"But there's no way I'm letting you two bunk up again tonight after what happened this morning. I may be sleeping in the hallway with a shotgun, too."

My face gets impossibly hotter. I'm enjoying the kissing perks of having a boyfriend, but I think I'm too shy for PDA. Steel certainly doesn't seem to mind it though.

I clear my throat, more than ready to move on from this awkward conversation.

"What was Stavros talking about? What accident?"

"Right. That." Nikias heaves a deep sigh, bolstering himself for the conversation he knows we need to have. "How about a walk?"

"Does this walk come with answers?"

He nods.

"Then I'm game."

Just like the day before, angel-born greet Nikias as we pass, usually with a wave or well wishes. There's an interesting blend of old and new world in Eden. There are no cars, yet sleek jet boats dot the crescent inlet the village huddles around. We pass people hand-tending vegetable gardens with hoes and spades, but as we near the outskirts where the homes give way to farmland, there are glass-domed greenhouses next to spacious fields with automated irrigation machines.

It's not until we reach an orange grove that Nikias chooses to speak. He picks a bulbous piece of fruit from the tree and passes it to me. "When you were a baby, only a few months old, you were poisoned."

I gasp, not expecting that. Was there ever a time when someone wasn't trying to kill me?

"You expect me to eat this after a statement like that?" I pass the orange back to Nikias. Peeling the waxy exterior, he splits it and brings a slice to his mouth. Sticky juice runs over his fingers as he bites into it and chews. He hands the rest of the fragrant citrus back to me.

"You survived, but Camiel believed it was an attack on you and convinced Stasha to leave Eden with him. It wasn't until he returned a year later that we even knew your mother was gone."

"You mean that she'd become a Forsaken?" Thorne told me my mother was a Forsaken—that she's the reason he and the rest of his army knew about me at all. But who knows which of Thorne's stories are truths or lies?

"Perhaps. You'll have to ask your father for the full story." There's sadness in Nikias' eyes that he can't hide. "Camiel won't talk about it with anyone. Whether to death or existence as a Forsaken, I only know that she's lost to us now."

The breeze kicks up and blows through the orange trees, shaking the leaves. I bite into a slice of the orange, the tangy pulp even more delicious than it smells.

"How can you be sure she's gone? Is Camiel's word that reliable?" I ask after I swallow.

"Yes, it is. There isn't a man, woman, or child here that wouldn't trust Camiel with their life. Who hasn't already. We would not have survived the last couple thousand years without him. But besides that, I know she's truly gone because if she were alive, she would never have parted with you. Camiel may have been the love of her life, but from the moment you were born, you became her sole reason to breathe."

There's a spike of pain in my chest and my eyes start to

prickle. I look down to keep Nikias from seeing my reaction, not because I'm ashamed of the emotion, but because I'm not ready to share it with anyone else.

I regain my composure, then ask, "Do you ever worry she might reveal Eden's location—assuming she was turned into a Forsaken? If she revealed my existence to them, what's to stop her from leading them straight here?"

Nikias shakes his head. "Eden is protected by Celestials. If you aren't an angel, the town won't be revealed to you unless you're guided by one. Even if a Forsaken knows the general area of our community, they won't be able to enter." He takes a deep breath. "I'm more worried about angels figuring us out. There are more than a few who wouldn't mind seeing us wiped from the Earth. The Fallen and Forsaken we can keep out—angels we cannot."

That's something to consider. The Nephilim outside of Eden are leery of angels, but the ones that live here have a deep-rooted fear of the ones they don't already know.

We walk down the rows of orange trees in silence for a few minutes. Nikias might not have the answer, but there's something else I have to ask anyway.

"Why did Camiel dump me with the humans? Was single parenting just not on his to-do list?"

Nikias regards me out of the corner of his eye before lifting his gaze skyward. The spectrum sun shines its rose-tinted rays down upon us, bathing his face in light.

"Camiel is the Angel of War. Thousands of angels are under his command, yet there are only a small handful of angels that know of Eden's existence, and even less—if any —that knew about Stasha and you. For angels, their rank isn't just a job, it's part of who they are. Being the Angel of War wasn't something Camiel could just stop doing, and so without Stasha, it was impossible for him to protect you. He couldn't raise you among the angels because there are too many prejudices toward Nephilim in their ranks. He didn't feel Eden was safe for you anymore and didn't trust other angel-borns. So, he hid you in the one place he didn't think you'd be found. I may not agree with his decision, but I know it wasn't made lightly."

And there was the truth of it, finally.

From a logical standpoint, perhaps Camiel had made the right choice. For better or worse, here I am, still alive and kicking. But does he have any idea what I went through to survive? The pain and suffering and abuse. Couldn't he have at least dropped in once to explain that I'm not fully human? Knowing would have made it easier to endure.

"I'd like to be alone, if you don't mind."

Nikias nods, a sad smile on his face as he lifts a hand to my shoulder and squeezes. "Of course. Take as much time as you need."

I wait until he's disappeared from view before I take off.

# 11

## EMBERLY

*I* only stop running when my body is about to give out. Bending over, I rest my hands on my knees and suck in long drags of air. Sweat drips down the sides of my face and plasters my shirt to my skin. The sprint through the fruit groves of Eden was by no means the farthest or longest I've ever run, but maybe the hardest. It's what I needed. My body feels pushed to its limits in the best way possible, and relieved of the tension that threatened to consume me after talking to Nikias.

I turn to start the trek toward the village when something drops from the sky, landing in a crouch in front of me. I stumble back a step as Stavros stretches to his full height, his usual thunderous expression firmly in place. He strides toward me, intent on eating up the space I just created between us.

Startled, I backpedal until I get tangled in the branches of a lemon tree. The spindly limbs catch on my hair and poke into my shoulders. I swat at the annoyance and rip out of its grasp.

"Stavros. What's going on?" No matter how intimidating he may be, I refuse to cower in front of this bully.

"You should have saved us all the trouble and died as an infant."

Shock seizes my muscles, so I don't react in time to dodge the blow. Stavros' fist connects with my cheek, and the impact throws me to my knees. I try to regain my footing, but he follows it up with a kick to the gut that sends me spinning into the trunk of a nearby tree. The branches shudder and a shower of lemons drop to the ground.

I wheeze for air, the breath stolen from my lungs. Stavros comes at me again. I duck and roll away from his next punch. His fist cracks against bark and the tree tips back, its roots spraying dirt everywhere as they peel from the ground.

What is going on? Is this another fake attack, like Shira's? Or is this the real deal?

Rolling his shoulders, Stavros stomps toward me. "You're an abomination."

My mind works double time to put together pieces that don't quite seem to fit. "You think I'm an abomination, yet you want me to marry your son? That's messed up."

He spits on the ground. "Marrying my son would have at least given you a purpose, but Aero is too good for you. I won't allow that to happen anymore."

Despite the situation, I almost laugh. Allow?

Stavros advances with deadly intent. "It's time I finished what I started. I'm not making the mistake of leaving you alive this time."

Finish what he started? This time?

I gasp. It was him. He's the one who poisoned me. He's the reason Camiel and Stasha fled Eden. The cascade of events that led to my being orphaned were all because of him.

Fury like I've never felt before builds in my gut and explodes. My transformation rolls over me in a heated wave, singeing the fruit trees around me. Stavros doesn't seem to have the sense to be afraid, but he should.

He's to blame, and he'll pay me back in blood.

Rage is like a living being thrashing inside my chest, overwhelming my conscience, my very sense of right and wrong. It screams at me to give over and give in, and the moment I do, I sink into oblivion.

I blink against the mid-day light. There's a keening moan and I look down to see blood. It's everywhere. It coats my hands and drips from my fingers. It's splattered over the front of my shirt and pants and puddled under my feet. I'm covered with it. Am I injured? Nothing hurts. In fact, discounting the horror and disorientation of the moment, I feel great. Better than great. Energized.

Another moan reaches my ears. I find its source lying on the ground a few feet away.

I was wrong. I'm not covered in blood—he is.

An angel-born is sprawled on his back in the middle of a row of citrus trees. There's a hole in his chest that bubbles and froths with blood. There isn't an inch of his face that isn't cut or swollen.

"Oh my gosh." Going to him, I drop to my knees. My hands shake as I try to figure out what to do for him while I work through what just happened. There's a blank in my memory, just like before.

"Stop the bleeding. I have to stop the bleeding," I whisper to myself. Answers aren't as important as saving this man's life. I go to put pressure on the gaping wound, but something isn't right. My hands sink into his chest a few inches before I snatch them back. There's no resistance.

It's not until that very moment that I realize there is a literal hole in the man's chest.

My whole body starts shaking. What happened here?

The man stares up at me with the one eye he can still open, fear churning in his gaze. He tries to speak, his mouth moving to reveal broken teeth and a dislocated jaw. My gaze catches on the streak of gray hair at his temple.

Oh my gosh, it's Stavros.

I stumble as I shove to my feet. A vague memory of Stavros' attack takes shape, but it cuts off the moment I decided to fight back.

"I'll get help," I promise, even though I already know it won't do any good. Angel-borns have amazing healing capabilities, but there's no coming back from something this awful. I don't even know how he's still alive.

I trip over a protruding root as I flee the orchard. I go to yell for help, but my throat tightens and only a squeak of a sound comes out.

The reality of the situation finally sinks in and fear slams into me like a tidal wave. I did that to him. There's no one else around. I'm covered in blood that's not my own. It had to be me.

Stavros attacked me, but does that make me any less of a murderer? Will anyone even believe that he attacked first? If I've learned anything since coming to Eden, it's that angel-line Nephilim protect their own. What will they do to me?

I make it out of the grove. Eden's town center and

Nikias' house are off in one direction, the ocean and freedom in the other.

Heaving from shock rather than exertion, I glance over my shoulder. Stavros is dead, or at least as good as. I shouldn't be looking for help; I should be running in the other direction. I need to leave this place before I'm punished for a crime I'm not even sure why I committed.

I could be in Turkey in a few hours. It's a big world out there. Lots of places a person could get lost.

My gaze locks on the distant waters. The sun's rays cause the peak of a crystalline wave to sparkle wildly. Freedom beckons me like a siren's song. The sweet melody dances on the breeze and for a moment, I soak it in. I consider what it would be like to hide from responsibility and consequences and these abilities I possess but don't fully understand. To strike out and leave this all behind. To carve out a life of peaceful solitude like I've always dreamed.

I let the idea wash over me and then pass.

Turning toward Eden, I take off, pumping my arms and legs as fast as I can with one thought in mind: Steel.

But I never make it.

# 12

## STEEL

"What do you mean she killed someone and fled?"

I couldn't have heard the angel-born correctly. I spent longer than planned on the phone with my family, first with my parents and then with Grey. After that, I had to track Tinkle down to get back into Eden, but there's no way things could have gone down the drain that badly in the last two hours.

Groups of angel-line Neph congregate in Eden's town center. I spot Nikias and Shira near the fountain. Ignoring the angel-born buzzing in my ear, I stride toward them. Nikias sees me coming and excuses himself from the group, Shira close on his heels.

"Steel."

"What's going on?"

"We're still trying to put together the pieces, but it looks like Emberly had a run in with Stavros and—"

Someone yells Nikias' name, cutting him off. There are

shouts from a group to our left and then people are shoved aside. Aero stomps toward us, his face ruddy with emotion. His wings are half-flexed, and he looks ready to take someone out.

"Where is she?" he demands as he steps into Nikias' space, only inches from bumping the older man's chest.

"Aero, you need to calm down," Nikias says. "We don't know anything for sure yet. It might not have gone down like it seems."

"My father is dead!" Aero roars, and an eerie hush falls over the square. "And she was seen fleeing Eden. We should have already put a group together to hunt her down."

There are a few murmurs of agreement from the crowd and my hackles raise.

"Watch yourself," I warn. The thought of Emberly hurt makes me want to break things. Preferably bones. I'm only just holding myself together. I need information, and I need it now. Refocusing on Nikias I ask, "Why would Stavros attack Emberly?"

"I should have listened to him," Aero says before Nikias can even open his mouth to answer. "He said producing strong heirs is important, but that she was no good. An abomination that never should have—"

My fist connects with Aero's jaw before he can finish his hate-filled speech. The crunch of bone shattering under my knuckles is satisfying. So is the sound of Aero flopping to the ground, knocked clean out from one hit. Shira drops to her knees to check on him, but I don't wait to make sure the scum is all right.

"That answers that question. Stavros must have temporarily overlooked his hatred of Emberly because of the possibility of suped-up grandbabies. He probably cracked when he realized that wasn't going to happen." I should have known something like this was coming. That guy had an unhinged vibe about him from the start. "Where were you when this went down?"

Nikias looks sick. His skin is pale under its natural tan and his mouth is pulled into a frown. "We'd just talked about why she'd been taken from Eden as an infant. She asked to be alone."

I scoff. "So much for this being the safest place on the planet for her."

I want to berate Nikias for failing to protect her from his own people, but it's not worth it. I have more important things on my mind, like tracking Emberly down and ringing her neck for running instead of coming to me. "Which way did she go?"

"Steel, if you'll just wait. We need to piece together what happened here and then gather our people for a search party."

I roll my neck, shoving down the urge to transform. "You do what you need to do, but I'm not one of your people. I'm going after her because she is *my* people. So, I repeat, which way did she go?" I let a little growl slip into my voice. "Don't make me ask again."

Aero groans at my feet, and Shira stands. "I'll take you."

"Shira," Nikias warns.

"If you could, I know you'd be out there looking for her right now. She's family—she deserves our support. You're the one who taught me that," she says with a pointed look at the angel-line Elder. "You need to stay and figure out what happened here. Let me do this. Let me help."

After a long moment, Nikias nods. Shira tests her wings,

extending them fully before tucking them against her back. The bandages from her tussle with us yesterday are gone, but they still look stiff. The set of her jaw says she's not going to let that get in her way.

"Come on." She tilts her head to the side. "She went north."

# 13

## EMBERLY

*J* jolt upright, jackknifing into a sitting position. The soft mattress beneath me absorbs the sudden movement. Looking down my body, I search for red. The last thing I remember was being covered in Stavros' blood, but the white tank top and jeans I'm wearing are spotless.

*Where the heck are my shoes?*

"Good. You're finally awake."

"Gah." I scurry away from the deep timbre of Thorne's voice. I roll off the edge of the bed, putting the large piece of furniture between us. Thorne lounges in a seat on the opposite side of the bed as if he sits on a throne instead of a basic wooden chair. With his legs wide and arms draped over the armrests, he silently considers me.

"You," I say, as if the word itself can hold the weight of my accusation.

Thorne lifts his eyebrows. The hair that usually flops over his forehead is pushed back, and the thin scar that runs through his brow up into his hairline makes his skin pucker.

"Yes. Me," he says calmly.

"What are you doing here? Wait, no. What am I doing here?" My gaze bounces around the spartan room. Is this another castle? The stones lining the walls aren't white, so I know we're not in the White Kingdom. Is there a secret Gray Kingdom? "Where is here?"

Thorne slants his head even more and his eyebrows hike impossibly higher. "You don't remember?"

I try to recall where I am, or how I got here, but there's another blank spot in my memory. I don't even have a hazy recollection of events. It's as if the last however-many hours —or days—of my life were erased. The missing time freaks me out even more than waking up to find Thorne holding vigil at my bedside.

Something else occurs to me, causing a wave of ice to flow through my veins.

"Where's Steel?"

Thorne lifts his upper lip and sneers. "How should I know?"

I release a relieved sigh. Steel's not here, which means he's probably still safe. My memory cuts out when I was searching for him.

Thorne sits back in his seat, looking more comfortable in my presence than he should. We're enemies, after all. The last time I saw him he was ready to sacrifice me to his mother. And then there's the small fact that I actually killed Seraphim. He can't be happy about that.

I scan for a weapon, but there's nothing in the room aside from the bed and the chair Thorne sits in. A down pillow isn't going to help me much.

"Where are we?" I ask again.

"Hmm. Interesting."

"Just answer the question."

"England."

My stomach drops out. "You mean to tell me I traveled all the way from Ed—" I clamp my mouth shut. I almost outed the angel-line sanctuary to Thorne. Clearing my throat, I go on. "How did you find me?"

A slow smile spreads over Thorne's face.

"I didn't find you. You found me."

"Right," I scoff. "Why in the world would I have wanted to do that?"

The sly expression on Thorne's face remains in place. I'm not at all comfortable with that look. "Well, it's obvious you've come to your senses and are here to join me."

"Yeah, no. I have not come to any senses." Shoot. That wasn't what I meant to say. "I mean, none of my senses have urged me to join you." Argh. That didn't come out right either. "I'm just saying, if anything, I came looking for you to kill you. I saw what you did to London and heard about New York. You disgust me. Innocent people were slaughtered."

That wipes the smug look off Thorne's face. "There are always causalities during a war."

"The humans aren't at war with you."

"Sacrifices have to be made to set things right."

I shake my head, saddened it's come to this. There was a time when I thought there might be a half-decent person buried inside Thorne. I was wrong.

"This isn't right. You're destroying lives. And all for what? So you can pound your chest and say you're king of the castle?"

Thorne spreads his hands. "Survival of the fittest. I didn't create the rules, I'm only playing by them."

"My mistake, I forgot I was talking to a sociopath incapable of feeling real emotions."

There's no mistaking the anger that flares briefly in his gaze. "Technically, I'm closer to a psychopath. I lack the impulsivity of a sociopath. As I'm sure you remember, I always have a plan."

Creepy.

"Well, this conversation has been a nice trip down memory lane, but I gotta go. Let's do this again never, m'kay?" I edge around the bed, heading toward the door to my right. I have no idea how I got to this place, but I needed to get away. I slide my hands over my back pockets, hoping I still have my phone, but I suppose that was too much to ask. If I can find a phone somewhere, I can call Steel. He's probably looking for me right now. I really need to stop disappearing on him. The stress is going to age him prematurely.

Thorne leans back in his seat. Throwing his legs out in front of him, he crosses them at his ankles. "I don't know that leaving would be a wise choice for you. But be my guest."

I freeze, eyeing him as he lounges in his seat, disturbingly relaxed.

"Okay, I'll bite. Why wouldn't I leave?"

He jerks his chin, indicating the window behind me. I retreat a step, unwilling to turn my back on him. Angling my face so I can still see Thorne in my peripheral view, I glance through the glass, rippled with age. Night has fallen, but the moonlight is bright enough that I can see the hordes of bodies outside. Thorne has a Forsaken army camped out below. I want to fist my hair in frustration. This can't be happening.

"I won't be your captive again, Thorne. Let me go."

"You're not my prisoner," he says with a wave toward the window and the Forsaken beyond. "I don't plan to stop you."

"But . . ."

"But I do think it would be prudent for you to wait until daylight, when the Forsaken take shelter from the sun."

I knew there was a catch. "Maybe I could take the lot of them. I didn't do too bad a job at Whitehold."

"Perhaps you can. From what I heard, that was a rather impressive show of strength. But I wonder if you could do it again? Of if you even know how you managed it the first time?" There's a whisper of a smile on Thorne's face that I want to smack off.

"Piss me off some more and you might just find out." I glance out the window again but stop counting when I reach fifty. Thorne's calling my bluff. He knows he has me, at least for now. "What do you want from me?"

"From you? Nothing."

I arch my eyebrows, not in the least convinced that's true.

Thorne splays his hands. "I didn't seek you out. You came to me. Since you seem to have no memory of why you did so, I can only guess at the reason myself."

Thorne pushes out of his seat and I scurry back a step. I don't want him any closer to me than he already is.

"I'd show you around, but I have more important things to do than babysit you this time."

Yet he had time to watch me sleep like a certified creeper. "How did you end up in this place? Did you have to murder a human family to make yourself feel more macho?"

"Disappointingly, no. There are a surprising number of

uninhabited castles dotting the European countryside. I had my eye on a bigger prize, but your friends showed up and ruined those plans."

My stomach dips at the mention of them, but I remember Steel said they'd come up against Thorne and were all okay. Even so, the thought of them facing off against Thorne scares me.

Crossing my arms over my chest, I press my lips together, showing Thorne I'm not going to rise to the bait.

Thorne chuckles darkly.

"I don't expect you to be here long, but you might as well settle in. Feel free to go wherever you want within these walls. The Forsaken aren't permitted in this dwelling."

"You have a messed-up sense of hospitality. You know that, right?"

He shrugs, then strides toward the only door in the room. When his fingers wrap around the handle, he pauses and looks over his shoulder at me.

"You know, it didn't have to be this way."

I know what he means, but he's wrong. Regardless of how much time I would have had with him at Whitehold, he never would've been able to convince me his way was right. I never would have fought at his side.

"It always had to be this way."

Something that might be sadness settles on his features, but I don't know if I'm seeing true emotion, or something put on to manipulate me. "Then in that case, I'm sorry for you."

What's disturbing is that he *does* look sorry.

He leaves the door cracked when he leaves, showing that I'm not locked in. I don't know what his game is, but I'm not letting go of this advantage. I'll search for a way to contact

Steel and be out of here the moment the Forsaken slither into their hidey holes in the morning. With free rein of the dwelling, it's highly unlikely Thorne's left something out that will be any use against him, but it won't hurt to look while I'm here.

I wait for Thorne's footsteps to fade, then slip out of the room.

# 14

## ASH

*S*terling shoves his hands in his pockets as he stares out the window. "This Christmas blows."

"Sterling," Nova warns from her reclined position on the couch.

"Well, it does," he whines. "I want a redo."

"I think there are more important things going on in the world right now than moaning over missing the Durands' annual Christmas feast." Nova rolls her eyes and continues to toss the lacrosse ball she's been playing with back up in the air.

"That's what I'm talking about. These poor people." He motions toward the glass, his eyes still fixed on the street below. "Some of them have lost everything they own. And they're the lucky ones."

Pushing up from my seat, I join him at the window. There's a family of five scurrying down the street. Heavy knapsacks hang off the backs of skinny-framed children. The father is carrying the youngest and the mother brings up the rear, keeping the children close. It's heartbreaking.

"What happened here isn't okay." I sigh. Shoving away from the sill, I walk toward the open plan kitchen to search for food I'm not really interested in eating. "Nova, any news from your parents about New York?"

We've been watching the human news stations from the comfort of one of Nova's parents' flats. Their building is one of the rare untouched ones in what turned into battle-field London. From what we've seen, New York didn't fare much better. The humans are confused over the attacks on two of their major cities, and rightly so. Their theories range from terrorists to aliens and almost everything in between—except the truth, which is a little bit of both and then some. Ciara and Killian are out with their squadron. They're supposed to get an update from Lyra, the power Elder. It feels like we've been waiting for news for hours.

There's a sharp knock on the door and our heads swivel toward the entrance. The lacrosse ball bonks Nova in the face.

"Ouch." She sits up, rubbing the bridge of her nose.

There's another knock, but this time it sounds like someone banging their fist on the door.

"Guys, open up," demands a muffled voice.

"Is that Steel?" Sterling asks right as Grey shoots out of the bedroom, making a beeline for the front door. He's been holed up in there for the last few hours, on and off his phone almost the whole time.

Reaching the door, Greyson yanks it open and sure enough, Steel stands just beyond the threshold. The brothers embrace quickly and then Grey ushers Steel—and a girl that is pointedly not Emberly—into the flat.

"Is she here?"

I open my mouth to ask who he means when Greyson

shakes his head and says, "No. Sorry, bro." Okay then. He knows something the rest of us don't.

Steel spits out a particularly colorful string of obscenities.

"Where's Emberly?" I ask as I join the small group in the foyer. I eye the girl standing behind Steel. She looks to be around our age. Her gaze doesn't settle any one place, but rather pops from one thing to another as if she's never been inside an apartment before. With a mane of dark hair, tawny skin, and standing almost six feet high, she fits the Nephilim mold, except for those light brown eyes. They're a shade of color I've never seen on an angel-born before.

"Gone," Steel says as he walks past me into the living room.

"Gone?" Nova asks, coming to her feet. "Gone where?"

Steel plows a hand through his already disheveled hair. "She took off. We don't know where."

I turn toward Greyson. "You knew about this?" I ask, thinking of all the time he spent on the phone this afternoon. I assumed he was talking to his parents, but it's clear that isn't the whole story.

Greyson grabs the back of his neck and grimaces. "Yeah. I didn't want to worry anyone just yet."

I throw a narrow-eyed glare at him. "We could have been looking for her."

Greyson lifts his hands in the air, palms up. "Where?"

He has a point. We need details.

"Yo. There's a super-hot chick standing over there." Sterling points at where the girl lingers in the entranceway. She's crouched and seems to be inspecting an outlet. How . . . odd.

"Right. That's Shira. She's Emberly's cousin, kinda. I'm a little confused on the exact family relation."

My eyes grow. "You found one of Emberly's relatives? How? Is she an angel-line Neph?"

"Yeah," Steel starts to answer. "There's actually a hidden—"

"Don't say another word." Shira pops to her feet and then stalks over to Steel, a thunderous look on her face. "You promised."

"Right." Steel sighs, looking exhausted. "It's complicated. I can only say she's here to help. Tinkle dropped us off. He's looking for Camiel. We're hoping he might have an idea about how to find Em."

Nova steps up to Shira, looking her up and down. "Are you the one who attacked Emberly and Steel?"

Right. Steel told us there'd been some kind of altercation with a fellow angel-born the first time he checked in with Greyson. He didn't give us many details and played it off like it was no big deal.

Shira sets her jaw and notches her chin up. "Yes."

"Respect. I'm Nova." She holds her fist out and waits for Shira to bump it. Shira glances at Nova's balled up hand and then her face, not having the faintest idea what Nova wants her to do.

"You just knock it," Nova says.

Bringing her hand up, Shira swats Nova's hand.

"Um. Close enough."

"Shira, this is Ash, and these are my brothers, Greyson and Sterling."

Greyson and I nod back, but Sterling looks gobsmacked. He manages to mumble something that might be a greeting but sounds more like toddler gibberish.

Baring her teeth at Sterling's weird behavior, Shira shuffles away from him.

I shake my head. Sterling, speechless. Never thought I'd see the day, but really not important right now.

"Emberly left on her own?" I ask, bringing Steel's attention back to the matter at hand.

Steel exchanges a look with Shira, his mouth pulling into a frown. "There was an incident and she took off. We think she ran because she got spooked."

That sounds like something she would have done in the past, but not anymore. Not after what we've all been through. "How sure are you she left of her own accord?"

A muscle in Steel's jaw jumps. "Pretty sure, but . . ." He has doubts too.

I sit on the couch, absently running the pad of my pointer finger across my lips as I try to piece together the situation from the limited information Steel shared with us.

Maybe whatever happened to Emberly scared her enough to flee, but what if there was another reason for her disappearance? Did she leave to try and protect someone? Maybe her presence was dangerous for other people.

She could be almost anywhere in the world. How do we find her if we don't even know why she disappeared?

A chime sounds and Steel reaches into his pocket, fishing out his phone. He swipes it open, and his face pales. His hand spasms, and he drops the phone. It lands on the carpet at his feet with a thud. The color returns to his face, and a vein throbs at his temple, then he phases.

"Shoot," Grey says and then follows Steel into the spirit realm. He's only gone a few seconds before he returns. "He's going to need a minute."

I snatch up Steel's phone. Flipping it over, I gasp when I

see the screen. There's a text from an unknown number. Under a picture of Emberly's sleeping face are the words, "Care to trade? – T"

"What is it?" Grey asks. When I glance up, I have the attention of the entire room.

Steel appears again. His hair even more disheveled than before, and his body as tightly strung as a bowstring.

"Thorne has her," I say as I hand the phone back to a heaving Steel.

"Who is Thorne?" Shira asks.

"A dead man," Steel answers.

# 15

## EMBERLY

*a*s castles go, this one is kinda lame. Most rooms are empty, without even the bare minimum of furniture. It's drafty, and as far as I can tell, only part of the structure is even wired for electricity. I can't find a phone, anything connected to the internet, or one shred of information that I can use against Thorne.

I stick my head into a room that looks like an old-fashioned kitchen. There's a giant hearth and rows of empty shelves. I hope there's a pantry somewhere because I'm hangry. I haven't eaten since yesterday.

"I told you, you'd run back to Thorne sooner or later."

"Sheesh." I lay a hand on my chest and feel the thump-thump of my heart through my shirt.

Silver sits in the far corner of the room, her heels kicked up on the worn wooden tabletop in front of her and her chair tipped back on two legs. There's a half-eaten red apple in her hand. She tips the fruit toward me as if in salute and then takes a big bite, the crunch extra loud in the cavernous space.

I peel my lip back from my upper teeth in a snarl, thoroughly disgusted I wasted the time and energy restoring her to a Nephilim. "I'd ask what you're doing here, but I already know."

Silver stops chewing and shoots me a toothy grin, not looking the least bit repentant. She ran back to Thorne the first chance she got, betraying the trust she was beginning to rebuild with her family. I guess it's no mystery anymore who caused the veil to weaken. If it was someone within the Elders' compound, it must have been Silver. I'm not overly surprised, but I am disappointed.

"Do you feel even a drop of remorse for what you did?" I ask.

Finishing her apple, Silver chucks the core onto the ground and rises to her feet. Her eyes go wide, and she presses a hand to her chest in mock surprise. "What I did? Whatever do you mean?"

"I know the disturbance that thinned the veil and allowed Fallen into the mortal world started in the Elders' compound. What I want to know is, how you could do it? People died. You betrayed your family. They trusted you, and you turned around and stabbed them in the back."

"Oh, honey. I'm not the one who thinned the veil between the realms." Silver's smile stretches as she saunters toward me. "You are."

"Silver!" Thorne barks her name from the doorway behind me. "That's enough."

"If you say so," she says with a shrug as she skirts me and leaves the room.

"My fault? What does this have to do with me?"

"Ignore her. She's disturbed."

At least we agree on something. But her accusation that I

not only played a part in the hell-storm that was unleashed on New York and London, but was the cause of it, grates on me. I'm distracted as Thorne crosses the room and pulls open a cupboard, showing his back to me as if I'm not a threat. His mistake.

Reaching into that deep part of myself, I start building my power. It's harder to do in the mortal world than the spectrum one, but not impossible. I wiggle my fingers as sparks ignite, stoking the heat inside as I prepare to release it on Thorne in a ball of angel-fire.

He rummages through the cabinet, pulling out ingredients for what looks to be tea or coffee as I grit my teeth, willing my power to come forth.

It's right there, ready for me to take, but when I reach for it, it sputters and dies, completely leaving my system.

What the . . . ? I stare at my hands as if I'll find some evidence of my power if I look hard enough. Nothing happens.

Finding a pot, Thorne fills it with water from a hand pump sink and sets it on a stove he has to light with a match. It's only after that task is done that he bothers to turn and face me.

"What?" he asks, his eyes narrowing.

"You're too relaxed. You're not concerned I'll get away. You're not scared of me."

He leans against the counter, a smile teasing the corners of his lips. "Maybe I'm just not threatened by you?"

I shake my head. "That's not it. Or if it is, there's a reason you don't see me as a threat. Something's not adding up. How did I really get here?"

"Your guess is as good as mine."

"Bull. There's more you're not telling me."

Crossing his arms, Thorne shrugs, looking as relaxed as ever. It sends a chill of trepidation down my spine.

"I never understood your attachment to that cherub, Steel. Maybe your subconscious is trying to tell you something?" Thorne suggests.

"You don't want to bring him into this." I have to swallow down a growl that tickles the back of my throat. Considering what happened to Steel at Whitehold, even the mention of his name on Thorne's tongue makes me ragey. I could have lost Steel forever that day, and the blame for that can be laid at Thorne's feet as much as his mother's.

"He's holding you back," Thorne continues, heedless of my warning. His gaze is sharp as he takes a step toward me. "Your cherub isn't strong enough to stand by your side, which is why he won't be there for much longer."

"Is that a threat?"

There's a beast inside me that starts to stretch, readying itself to defend Steel. Thorne either can't see the monster shining from my gaze or doesn't care about his own wellbeing.

"He muzzles your potential. Keeps you tame and domesticated. If you were free of him, you'd be unleashed. An unstoppable force. The world would be ours for the taking." Thorne's gaze is only a small step away from manic. "I should have disposed of him when I had the chance."

Wrong thing to say.

I fly at Thorne, my hands out in front of me, ready to claw his face off with my blunted nails. The flash of shock that skates over his features is particularly satisfying, but so is the crunch when I smash my fist into his nose.

I go after him like a feral animal, powered by not only my protective instincts, but my experiences at Whitehold. A thin line of trust had begun to build between us but was crushed by his betrayal—and I'm pissed about that, too. More so than I even realized. Despite the circumstances, I wanted to trust Thorne. I wanted him to be redeemable. All that frustration and disappointment and fury meshes together in a confusing ball of emotions that abruptly implodes.

Dropping down, I swipe a leg out and knock Thorne to the floor. I jump up to pounce, planning on pile-driving a few more punches into his face, but he catches me by the shoulders and tosses me across the room.

I slam into a table, my body snapping the top in two when it absorbs my weight. I shove pieces of it away as I get to my feet.

Thorne stomps toward me and I rush to meet him. We're a blur of fists and legs as we go after each other. For once we are evenly matched. I land a kick to his gut; he lands a punch to my ribs. I jab his chin; he elbows me in the temple.

I get a clean punch to his face and his chin snaps back, blood immediately welling from the cut on his lip.

"Stop," he growls at me, but I'm not finished venting my frustration.

Instinct and a whole lot of fury take over and I tap into my power. It's not as instantaneous or as strong as when I'm in the spectrum world, but the fire still builds in my body, and this time I'm not letting it slip from my grasp.

Bunching my muscles, I land an explosive front kick square in the middle of Thorne's chest, sending him crashing back into a row of shelves. I come at him, my fingers sparking and a ball of angel-fire growing. I'm ready and primed to let it fly when I sink into darkness.

# 16

## THORNE

*R*ed bleeds across Emberly's eyes and the fire on her palms sputters out. I cast a glance at the mess we made as I push to my feet, wiping the blood on my lip away with the back of my hand.

"Cutting it a little close there, aren't you Mother?"

Her face pinches in annoyance. It's odd to see Emberly's features twist into an expression I'm so familiar with on Seraphim's face.

"I didn't think she'd be able to get the best of you so easily."

Her words are a dig against me, but I'm so calloused to her displeasure, I hardly feel their sting.

I toe at a piece of splintered wood on the ground. Part of the table, perhaps? Maybe one of the shelves? We're not going to be here for much longer, so I'm not even going to bother getting someone to clean up this mess.

Silver comes flying through the doorway. Her black sheet of hair swishes forward, brushing her rosy cheeks as she slams to a halt. She's a beguiling creature. Undeniably beautiful, but I prefer seeing her as a Forsaken when her outward appearance more closely resembles her rotten core. That form, however less attractive, is more honest. I can hardly stand to look at her now.

"I was only gone for like, five minutes. What happened?" I roll my tongue in my cheek, annoyed.

"My son seems incapable of teaching his pet to heel."

My anger bubbles, but I smother the emotion before it can impair my judgment. It helps nothing if I lose my head over a few verbal jabs.

"Seraphim, you're back. Good," Silver says, her shoulders dropping in relief. "She's so annoying. Self-righteous isn't a good look. I was planning on hiding out in my room until she was gone."

Bending over, Seraphim picks up a large shard of broken plate. With a flick of the wrist, she launches it across the room. It smashes against the wall, showering porcelain everywhere. "You won't have to put up with her much longer. Once we bring the veil down completely, I'll stamp her out of existence."

I bite my tongue to keep my words in check. Seraphim taking over Emberly's body was never my preferred plan. Emberly could have been an asset. If only I'd found her before the angel-born indoctrinated her with their hypocritical sense of morality. But she made her choice, and now she's going to have to live with the consequences.

"Are you sure that will even be possible?" I ask with a tilt of my head. "Emberly is quite strong. You may find the task harder than anticipated."

Seraphim narrows her gaze. "Now that I'm unbound, it's

only a matter of time. Every hour I chip away at the girl's control without her even realizing it." She pauses and rubs her bare wrist. "Interesting how that trinket of yours gave me a bit of trouble."

I take extra care to keep my face blank. "Who was to know the spirit gem would suppress you to a corner of Emberly's psyche?"

"Who indeed?" She turns a saccharine smile toward Silver, who straightens under her regard. "I'm fortunate someone had the sense to recognize the issue and take action to rectify the situation. Your loyalty won't soon be forgotten."

Silver tips her head, pride shining from her eyes.

I cross my arms over my chest, ready to be done with this petty sniping and get down to business. "What are you doing here anyway? The angels closed the rips torn in the veil from your failed attempt to bring the barrier down. Your last message said you were making plans to recover the orbs, but you show up here empty-handed, with control over your host slipping in and out. Without those orbs we won't have the opportunity to try again."

Seraphim's nostrils flare and the skin tightens around her eyes. If she doesn't like the facts, too bad. We are where we are because of her. The Fallen who slipped through to the mortal world created a fair amount of havoc, but it was a far cry from the full-scale attack we planned. Her failure to fully bring down the barrier between realms on the first try crippled our strategy. Losing the element of surprise is a hard blow to absorb. I've no doubt we'll still succeed, but the victory will no longer be easily gained.

I brace for the brunt of my mother's anger. She doesn't take well to being called out, but her eyes don't even flash red. Her nostrils flare, but then all aggression leaks from her features. With a self-satisfied smile she says, "As a matter of fact, the orbs are being retrieved by the angel-born's friends as we speak."

I arch a brow. Interesting. "And how did you convince them to do that? By asking nicely?"

Her attempt at a coy expression comes out twisted, making her look unhinged. "Technically, I didn't do any convincing. That was all you."

I lift my chin, waiting for her to go on.

"I sent a message offering to trade the girl for the orbs and took the liberty of giving you the credit. That cherub of hers is quite smitten. I'd wager he'd do just about anything for her, including break into a secure Nephilim vault and steal the orbs."

I don't doubt Steel would trade anything for Emberly's life. If nothing else, he does have that going for him.

"So they believe we're holding her for ransom," I say.

Leaning back against the counter, I cross my arms and consider the strategy Seraphim put into play. It's a solid plan that puts all the risk on the angel-borns and none on us. Once we trade Emberly back to her friends for the orbs, Seraphim can return to the fold whenever is most advantageous. It solves one of our problems, at least, but the orbs aren't the only elements we need to bring the mortal world to its knees. "Any ideas about the other issue we encountered?"

"As a matter of fact, yes. I left a parting gift in Eden that is sure to send at least one of the reclusive half-breeds our way. All we need to do now is wait for the missing pieces to come to us."

I lift my eyebrows, grudgingly impressed. I run over the

new facets of this in my head. There are several places where things could go awry, but even then, the strategy is workable as long as the young angel-borns get those orbs out of the Elders' grasp, and at least one angel-line descendent follows Seraphim's breadcrumb trail out of their sanctuary. The key is to get the elements we need into play, and that's what Seraphim's been able to accomplish.

There's one issue. I told Emberly she could leave, and at the time, I meant it. I don't like being made a liar.

"I'll have to convince Emberly to stay longer. She's planning on leaving in the morning."

Seraphim peels her upper lip back from her teeth and scoffs. "I let her off her leash to replenish my strength, but it appears I'll have to stay in control since that's the safer option . . . for you."

"Are you sure that's wise?" I ask.

Seraphim tilts her head, narrowing her gaze on me. "If I didn't know better, I'd say you preferred the angel-born's company to my own."

"You're supposed to be keeping a low profile. If she has too many blackouts, she might figure out what's going on. You don't want to tip your hand."

Seraphim goes deathly still. A red glow sparks in her irises until it eclipses the dark blue of Emberly's eyes. It doesn't take a genius to understand I pissed her off, but she can get over it. She's being reckless. Her vanity is getting in the way of common sense.

"Know your place," she growls, her voice deepening beyond Emberly's natural tone. Doesn't she know by now that her scare tactics don't work on me? I stopped fearing pain years ago. It's a lesson she taught me firsthand.

I walk forward, passing her on my way to the door. Instinct urges me not to turn my back on her, but I won't give her the satisfaction of looking paranoid.

"I know my place," I say, then add just before I pass through the exit, "It's you who shouldn't forget it."

# 17

## STEEL

*A*sh paces back and forth in front of me. "I think we should tell Sable. She'll help us. I know she will."

I rub my bottom lip as I consider her suggestion. Sable took Emberly under her wing. I know the Seraph Academy headmistress cares deeply for Emberly, but enough to break every rule in the book? Is it a chance we can take?

"Who is this Sable?" Shira asks. "The less people who know, the better. This thing we're doing is very dangerous."

Ash frowns, clearly annoyed.

"Well then, what about getting help from your parents?" Ash's gaze bounces between me and my brothers.

"No, no, no." Greyson waves his hand in the air, stopping that idea before it starts. "They can't even know we're there. Between mom and dad, we'd never make it out of the compound again."

He has a point. From what I heard, they barely made it out the first time. Dad wanted everyone to stay at the compound, safe and sound. To get my parents' help, we'll have to let them know what we need, why we need them, and who we're planning on giving them to. There's no way they'd let us hand over the orbs to Thorne, even if it was to save Emberly's life.

Ash throws her hands up in the air. "Well, we're going to have to get help from somewhere."

"I have an idea," Sterling says. He's been uncharacteristically quiet, but I assumed it was because gawking at Shira took up all of his brain power. Maybe all this time, he's been deep in thought. He rolls a ball between his palms, looking nervous, which is also bizarre for my younger brother. "Blaze and Aurora."

No one says anything.

"I mean," Grey starts, "it could work. By now they probably know their way around the compound as well as Seraph Academy. If anyone knows how to get in and out of places quickly and unseen, it's those two."

Nova gives a husky chuckle and leans back into the couch. "It's not the worst idea we've had in the last hour."

I rub a hand across my mouth and do my best to silence the beast inside that roars at me to act. To rage. To destroy everything in my path to get to Emberly. That part of me is all instinct, but now isn't the time to rip the world in two. Now is the time for careful and meticulous planning.

"Blaze and Aurora are important people in your community?" Shira asks.

"Umm." Sterling grimaces. "Sure. Let's go with that." He starts to fidget under Shira's confused stare.

Looking at Grey, I nod once. He returns the gesture and pulls his phone out. "I got this," he says over his shoulder as he walks into an adjacent room.

"Wait up," Sterling says as he rushes to catch up to Grey. "I have a few ideas I want to discuss with the twins."

"Well . . ." Nova shoves to her feet. "I'm going to go raid my parents weapons stash."

"You think we're going to need weapons at the Elders' compound? Those are our own people." The look on Ash's face says how distasteful she finds the idea of fighting against other angel-born.

Nova shrugs. "I'm sure they have a few non-lethal options in their arsenal." She stops to consider that statement. "Maybe. Either way, I'd rather be over-prepared for a fight than under."

A smile breaks over Shira's face. She's a bloodthirsty one. She'll fit right in. "Can I come with you?"

"Sure, this way." Nova waves over Shira, who pops up and follows. I have a moment of hesitation letting the two of them bond, but then brush it off. They'll be fine.

Flopping back on the couch, I scrub my face with both hands. How did this happen? I can understand why Emberly fled Eden. She has a lifetime of flight instincts conditioned into her. When Stavros attacked and it ended in death, she was probably worried about the repercussions. I don't care a lick that she ended that scum's life—I have no doubt he's the one who started it. What bothers me about the situation is that she took off instead of coming to me. We'll be having a very in-depth conversation about that later.

"How are you doing?" Ash asks, her voice soft.

"Fine."

She arches an eyebrow. "Sure you are."

"I'll be better when this is over," I say with a huff as I stand. I start pacing the length of the living room. Even though I'm not looking at her, I know Ash's gaze follows me.

"How do you think she ended up back with Thorne?"

I stop pacing and run a hand through my hair. That's exactly what I'd like to know. Were we followed to Eden? Does he have a way to track her we don't know about? "It doesn't make sense." I'm missing something. I know I am.

"Do you think . . ." I glance at Ash when she doesn't go on. She absently rubs her thumb over her bottom lip, staring at nothing. With a blink, she slants her gaze toward me. "Do you think *she* went to *him?*"

An iceberg settles in my chest. It's the possibility I've been doing everything I can to avoid considering.

"No." I bark the word, startling Ash.

She frowns. "I don't mean it like that, Steel. I don't doubt that whatever you and Emberly have is powerful. I just wonder if there's a reason Emberly would go to Thorne. Maybe she has questions about her powers. Maybe they left something unfinished."

I clamp my mouth shut, refusing to admit it's a possibility. Until I hear otherwise from Emberly, I'm not going to believe it is.

"No. He took her. I know he did. Emberly would never go to him willingly." *Unless* . . . my mind whispers.

I stalk to the window, my gaze pointed outward, but I don't see a thing. Emberly was freaked the moment Nikias told us about our soul-bond connection. The news had the complete opposite effect on me. Learning there was something unbreakable between us had settled my soul. It felt right, but she could barely bring herself to look at me. At the time I didn't think it was the best time to hash out our relationship status. She was already overwhelmed from meeting her father and learning she had living relatives, but I was wrong. If we'd talked, maybe she wouldn't have bolted. My gut sours at the thought, but there's a very real chance she ran as much from me as she did from Eden.

"Yeah, I don't know what I was thinking. You're right. Emberly wouldn't do that." Ash stands and joins me in front of the window. She offers me a reassuring smile. It's a bit wobbly, but I know she's trying. "Don't worry, we'll get her back."

"I know." We will. There isn't another option.

# 18
## ASH

"*I* can't believe the success or failure of this mission rests in the hands of a child," Shira hisses as we follow Blaze through the dimly lit tunnel.

"Blaze is more than just a child," Sterling says over his shoulder. "He's a Durand." He flashes a toothy grin that doesn't impress Shira in the least. She bares her teeth at him in a snarl. Sterling's smile only kicks up a notch. At least he's not tongue tied anymore.

Blaze lobs a glare at Shira before waving us down the corridor that branches to the right. Sure enough, the little imps did know a way in and out of the Elders' compound. There are tunnels under the entire settlement as an emergency evacuation plan for the Council. The Elders are the only ones who know about its existence . . . until now. Blaze and Aurora sussed them out the day after they arrived and have been exploring them every day since.

Without realizing they were aiding in a heist, Nova's parents helped us arrange transfers back to the compound. The jet we chartered waits at a local airfield. Good to know that even in an apocalypse, most things can be bought for the right price.

We trek for another five minutes until we see a small figure hunched on the ground up ahead. Blaze darts forward, not waiting for the rest of us to catch up to his sister. When we reach Aurora, she has two long pins stuck into the lock of the door in front of her. The tip of her tongue pokes out of her lips as she concentrates on her task. It's less than a minute before we hear a soft *click*. With a triumphant smile, she slides her tools out of the lock and stands. Pulling a small case out of her back pocket, she waves it in the air.

"Thanks for the gift, Sterling." Unzipping it, she tucks the long metal pins back in their spot.

I cast my gaze to Sterling. "You got your eight-year-old sister a lock picking set?"

"Sure did."

"I don't know why I'm surprised."

"Neither do I."

"It's a practical gift," Shira says matter-of-factly. From the look on Sterling's face, you would have thought she professed her undying love to him.

Aurora's gaze narrows on the angel-line newcomer. "Who's that?" she asks with a nod of her chin in Shira's direction.

"My future wife," Sterling says.

Aurora and Shira both scrunch their noses.

"I would never consider a cherub as a life partner," Shira says.

Sterling's face falls. "What's wrong with cherubim?"

"They are weak."

Grey coughs into his hand to cover his laugh when Sterling's jaw drops open. Nova doesn't even try to cover her chuckle.

"Now wait a second," Sterling starts, but Steel slashes his hand through the air, ending what would probably be a lengthy debate between them.

"Enough, you two." Crouching down to his level, Steel addresses Blaze. "Stay here."

Blaze crosses his arms over his chest as he levels a glare at Steel.

"Don't give me that look. You're an important part of this plan. We need you here to act as a lookout and open the door for us when we get back."

With a sigh, Blaze nods. After quick fist bumps from his older brothers, we file through the door. I don't miss the glare Aurora throws Shira before she takes the lead. Looks like the angel-line Neph hasn't impressed the youngest Durand twin. I'm sure she doesn't care now, but if Shira sticks around, she's going to want those two as friends rather than enemies. Hopefully she won't learn that the hard way.

The six of us follow Aurora up the narrow stairway. Our feet pad soundlessly on the metal steps as we ascend.

It only took Blaze and Aurora two hours to locate a way into the vault once Grey put them to task. They are scary good at B&E planning. The little mischief makers are either going to take over the world one day or burn it all to the ground.

At the top of the stairway is another door. The landing is only big enough to hold three people, so I wait on the steps below along with Shira, Greyson, and Sterling as Aurora pulls out her tools and gets to work on the door.

The lock disengages with a groan and I hold my breath,

waiting for an alarm to sound. Not pausing, Aurora grabs the handle and heaves the door wide. I blink against the brightness.

"The orbs are in opposite directions," Aurora says. "All the artifacts are in glass rooms, so you won't be able to miss them."

"Good job, Aurora," Steel says with an affectionate rub across her cheek with his thumb. "Stay here, we'll be back as soon as possible." Lifting his gaze, Steel nods toward Grey, who stands behind me. "Five minutes and then we're out of here."

"Good luck," Grey says, then waves for me and Sterling to follow. Steel, Nova, and Shira take off in the opposite direction. Sterling casts a forlorn look at the other group before joining us.

"I'm sure you'll survive a few minutes away from our stunning new friend," Grey whispers.

"She is beautiful, isn't she?"

Grey nods, a half-smile tweaking his lips. "A knockout."

Frustration bubbles in my chest. If we get caught nicking these orbs, we're all going to be in serious trouble. Yet these two are discussing girls.

"Seriously?" I ask. "Do you really need to be talking about this right now?"

Sterling shrugs, not the least bit bothered by my ire. Grey's face darkens a shade. After quietly clearing his throat he mumbles, "sorry" and refocuses on the glass-walled rooms we pass.

"Up there," Grey says after we round a corner.

There's a blue glow coming from down the hall. Bingo.

We sprint down the corridor and find the orb nestled in

an open black box on a pedestal in the middle of the room, filling the space with soft blue light.

"That's weird," Sterling says. "I thought this one was gold."

"Emberly said it was blue before she touched it," I say.

"Then why is it blue now?" he asks.

I shrug. "Maybe after a certain amount of time, it changed back?"

"You know what's strange," Greyson says as he pulls open the door, holding it so Sterling and I can enter before him, "is that all these rooms are unlocked."

"The vault entrance is sealed pretty tight," I muse. "They probably figure no one is getting through it."

He lifts an eyebrow at me. "Yet we just waltzed in the back door."

"A door no one but the Elders are supposed to know exists."

Grey tips his head in concession.

There's a snap, and the room dims to its normal brightness. Sterling has shut the lid on the box and is carefully sliding it off the pedestal.

"It will really suck if this thing is weight-censored. Should have brought something of equal weight, Indiana Jones-style." He looks up from his task right before he lifts it from the pedestal. "We should get ready to book it, just in case."

Slamming his eyes shut, Sterling snatches the box.

I tense, but when nothing happens, I release a sigh of relief. This has all been remarkably easy.

Sterling opens one eye at a time, then frowns. "The Council's security is severely lacking."

Still holding the door open, Greyson urges us back through. "Let's just be thankful for that and get out of here."

"Agreed." I shoot Grey a smile as I pass, and he winks. Something about the gesture makes my cheeks heat and a spark races up my spine. I chalk it up to nerves.

We shuffle-run down the hall back the way we came. Excitement and relief bubble in my gut.

*I can't believe we did it.* Just as that thought breezes through my mind, a pair walks around the corner in front of us and we skid to a halt. All five of us freeze. Sable and Deacon blink back at us with matching looks of shock splashed across their faces.

We are in so. Much. Trouble.

"What is happening right now?" Sable finally asks. "When did you three get back?"

"Umm," Greyson fumbles.

"This isn't what it looks like," Sterling adds, which only makes Sable's gaze narrow in suspicion before dropping to the box in his hands.

Deacon presses his lips together as he folds his giant arms over his chest.

"Is that one of the orbs?" Sable asks.

Sterling shakes his head. "Nope. It's ah . . . a mini treasure chest."

I put my hands over my face. I can't watch.

"Ash?" Sable prompts.

I let my hands drop with a grimace. "That is an orb, and this is exactly what it looks like, but we have an excuse. Thorne has Emberly and is demanding the orbs for her release."

Sable brings her hand to her mouth to cover her gasp. Deacon lays a palm on her shoulder, his eyes conveying an uncharacteristic amount of concern for the headmistress. When he turns toward us, there's a hard glint in the depths of his eyes. "What happened? We want to hear it all."

I shuffle, shifting my weight from foot to foot, knowing that Steel and the others are probably waiting for us. There's a clock tick, tick, ticking in the back of my mind.

"We don't have time to—"

I cut myself off when a boisterous laugh echoes off the walls. I check over my shoulder, not seeing anyone, but knowing that someone might turn down this corridor at any moment.

"Shoot, we have to go." Grey's eyes broadcast his urgency.

"We're coming with you. This way," Sable says with a tick of her chin.

As a group we head back toward the secret entrance. It's less than a minute before we round the last corner; Sable and Deacon sail past the exit, but double back when they notice we're no longer following. We push through the door —all of us rushing to get through before we're caught—and slam it behind us.

I'm panting, but not from exertion.

Spotting Sable and Deacon, Aurora's eyes go round, and she tries to hide behind Steel.

In contrast to his little sister, Steel's face is a block of granite, cold and hard. He slowly hands the box with the other orb in it off to Nova, whose game face is also in place. Shira rounds out the trio with her chin tipped in the air and hands fisted at her sides.

Muffled voices sound on the other side of the door. No one says a word until they fade completely.

"Is the orb safe?" Steel asks Sterling, nodding his head toward the box clutched in his brother's hands.

"Snug as a bug," Sterling says, then shakes the box. Hearing the orb rattle around inside, I gasp and place my hand on the top, staying his movements. Sterling shoots me a grin but stops jostling the supernatural object.

"Are we going to have a problem?" Steel asks, eyeing first Sable then Deacon.

"Ash said you need the orbs to get Emberly."

Steel nods.

"Okay. Then you can explain the details to us on the flight out of here." Her gaze moves past Steel to Shira. "Including who she is."

Steel's motionless for three beats then nods. "Deal. Let's go."

He leads the way down the stairway back to the underground tunnels where Blaze waits. Aurora knocks on the door and Blaze swings it open, his gaze going as wide as his twin's when he sees Sable and Deacon. Wincing, he hunches his shoulders.

"Please don't tattle on us," Blaze pleads. "Mom and Dad will be so mad."

A tiny smile cracks on Deacon's face. Sable shakes her head.

"Come on," Steel prompts. After ruffling his little brother's hair, he nudges both of the young twins forward.

"Where are we?" Deacon asks, his blue gaze scanning the tunnel as Blaze and Aurora take the lead.

"Some sort of emergency evacuation route for the Elders," Greyson answers.

"Nice that they have a place to run to that no one else

can use if things go sideways, isn't it?" Steel asks, his words dripping with sarcasm.

Sable's eyebrows pull together, but I don't know if the look is frustration at Steel or the Council members. "I'm not even going to ask how Blaze and Aurora know about these tunnels." Hearing his name, Blaze turns his head in our direction with an impish grin. "Best not to ask if you already know you're not going to like the answer."

She closes her eyes and pinches the bridge of her nose. Within minutes we reach the mouth of the tunnel—a single-file opening that lets in the sun's natural light. Grey quickly explains to Sable and Deacon that we have an SUV waiting outside to take us back to the airfield. We're waiting on Thorne's directions for where to meet up.

The older Durand siblings say a quick goodbye to Blaze and Aurora. Aurora's eyes fill with moisture, but Blaze plays it off like it's no big deal.

"I'm staying here," Deacon announces. "Sable and I can't both disappear. I can cover for her absence."

Sable's brow furrows. "I didn't think about that. What are you going to tell people?"

"I'll tell everyone you're sick and that I'm keeping you quarantined in my room until you feel better."

"That'll raise a few eyebrows."

A deep chuckle rumbles in Deacon's chest. "Like I care."

Sable's cheeks darken and she casts a glance around to find all eyes on them. It's a miracle Sterling keeps his mouth shut. She clears her throat. "Yeah, okay. Thanks. I'll call you when we get settled. Let me know if there are any updates about London or New York."

"Will do."

Deacon catches her hand as she turns to leave. "Stay safe," he orders.

"I will."

Something crackles between the pair, but the tension defuses when Deacon spies Sterling quietly snickering behind Sable. Pulling a frown, Deacon drops Sable's hand and folds his arms over his chest as he steps back to join Blaze and Aurora.

We file out of the tunnels without further interruption.

"So, Sable . . ." Sterling starts as we jog to the black SUV hidden under a camouflage tarp in the distance.

"Mind your own business, Sterling," Sable snaps, casting a glare in his direction.

"Ma'am, yes, ma'am." Sterling probably would have mock saluted her if he weren't carrying the bulky orb box.

When we get to the car, Grey and Shira yank the tarp off. Steel is preoccupied with his phone, so much so that he's the last one to climb into the car. Rather than starting the engine, he twists in his seat.

"I have the location for the switch. We're headed back to the UK."

# 19
## STEEL

*T*horne stands in front of his Forsaken lackeys. I'd recognize the cocky, blond mama's boy anywhere. When our gazes lock, his eyes narrow, and he lifts his upper lip in a sneer.

*Feeling's mutual.*

The line behind Thorne is fifteen Forsaken across. It's a joke if he thinks that will be enough to subdue me. With how amped I am right now, it would take at least double that to put me down. Lucky for him I'm not planning on starting a brawl. It's true that I'm jonesing for a crack at the proud seraph angel-born, if for nothing else than to repay him for the cheap shot he took at me in the cell in White-hold, but I'm here for one thing tonight, and it's not to fight him.

I want my girl back.

Thorne's gaze breaks from mine and brushes over Grey to my right, then moves to Nova on my left and sticks. I catch the pulse of muscle in his jaw before he glances at the boxes in Nova and my brother's hands. His lips curl into a satisfied smirk. I clench my fists, my molars grinding with the unquenched urge to knock that look off his face.

I stop walking with a solid twenty feet between us. Grey and Nova follow suit. "We're here with the orbs. As you can see," I spread my arms, indicating the three of us. "It's just us. We're ready to fulfill our side of the trade. Where's Emberly?"

I expected to see her fighting like a hellion when we appeared, but she's nowhere in sight. The beast inside growls, but I tell myself not to get too worked up. This isn't the time to lose my head.

"I have to inspect the merchandise first." Thorne motions two Forsaken forward with a flick of his wrist. I nod to Grey and Nova, and they move forward as well, meeting the Forsaken at the mid-point.

Each of the Forsaken pulls out a large polished stone from their pockets. Spirit gemstones.

"Open it." Grey's shoulders tense at the order from the broad-shouldered Forsaken in front of him. We're not conditioned to play well with our mortal enemies. Greyson cracks his neck before setting the box on the ground and flipping the latch.

I hope the stone clenched in the Forsaken's meaty hand works. The orb in Greyson's box is the one from Whitehold. If the spirit gem doesn't work, we're all about to take a forced trip to the spirit realm. Although, that might not be a bad thing. I wouldn't mind being able to shift right now.

Grey slowly lifts the lid. Besides the brightness that spills over the area, nothing else happens.

"Satisfied?" he asks Thorne. Thorne tips his head in acknowledgement and Grey snaps the lid back down and latches it. The box remains between Grey and the Forsaken

—my brother is smart enough to know not to hand it over until we have Emberly.

The process is repeated with Nova and the other orb. The spirit gem does its job of nullifying the orb's powers.

"Your turn," I say, crossing my arms over my chest.

Thorne draws the moment out. The bastard. He finally gives a signal to one of his Forsaken, who jogs to the manor house behind them. I do my best to remain perfectly still while we wait. I won't give Thorne the satisfaction of seeing me squirm. The glint in his eye and the half-smile on his face says that he sees right through me.

It's an eternity before the front door creaks open once again. A female Forsaken struts out with a body thrown over her shoulder.

Not a Forsaken.

Silver.

My body jolts. I can't help it. The most likely scenario was that Silver ran straight to Thorne when she first went missing, but I hoped that wasn't the case. There's no denying which side she's on now.

Greyson takes a step in her direction before remembering himself and returning to stand sentry over the orb. His chest heaves with barely leashed anger.

If Thorne's intention was to throw us off, it worked. Only Nova manages to keep her cool. She inspects her nails as if she doesn't have a care in the world, but I know beneath that blasé attitude, she has a sharp eye on Silver. Nova's a warrior through and through.

Emberly's red-tipped blonde hair sways to the cadence of Silver's steps. When she reaches Thorne, Silver heaves Emberly off her shoulder and drops her to the ground.

Emberly lands on her back, her limbs splayed in all directions.

I take a step forward, a growl vibrating in my chest. I almost miss the scowl Thorne shoots Silver before wiping it from his face.

Crossing his arms over his chest, Thorne tilts his head in Emberly's direction. "Here's your prize."

"What did you do to her?" The words are hard to push out around the emotion building in my chest.

Thorne raises his eyebrows. "I didn't do anything. She's been napping a lot. You should get that checked out."

Silver chuckles and the sound makes me see red. She was given a second chance, and she not only threw it away but threw it in our faces. As furious as I am, I can't deal with her right now. Emberly is the priority.

"Let's be done with this," I growl, purposefully ignoring Silver, which I suspect makes her more annoyed than anything else.

Crouching down, Thorne slides his arms under Emberly and lifts her. I don't like the look on his face when he does so. There's a hint of tenderness there that he tries to hide, and the lion inside me starts to thrash. If we were in the spirit realm, I wouldn't be able to hold back my transformation. As it is, I have to pace to keep myself from charging.

So close. Just a bit closer, and this will be over.

We meet in the middle. Nova is five feet to my left and Grey five to my right. The orbs are tucked safely in the boxes at their feet, and Emberly is barely more than an arm's length away. Close enough that her sugary sweet smell tickles my nose. Thorne has her propped with her head resting against his shoulder. I want to rip his arms from their sockets to keep him from ever touching her again. He doesn't make the mistake of taking his gaze off me as he barks an Enochian command to the Forsaken who stand in front of Nova and Grey.

There's movement under Emberly's eyelids before they blink open. Her deep blue stare finds me immediately, as if she already knew I was there.

"Steel." She whispers my name like a prayer. Relief washes through my system. She's all right.

She blinks again and refocuses on Thorne. Realizing she's in his embrace, she bucks and lashes out. Stumbling back, Thorne tries to retain his hold on her, but she's not having it and delivers an uppercut to the soft spot under his chin. His head snaps back and he releases her.

That's my girl.

She lands in a crouch just as I reach her, wrapping my fingers around her biceps.

"Grab the boxes," Thorne shouts from his spot on the ground.

I'm about to yank Emberly and run for safe ground when she jerks out of my hold and rushes the Forsaken who snatched the box at Grey's feet, tackling him. The unexpected attack loosens the Forsaken's hold on his prize, and the box thumps to the ground, awkwardly rolling twice before coming to a stop.

"Greyson!" Emberly shouts even as she grabs the head of the Forsaken beneath her and twists. "Grab the orb!"

# 20

## EMBERLY

There's no way I'm letting Thorne get his hands on those orbs. I watch Greyson snatch the box at the same time I snap the neck of the Forsaken. Steel hefts me to my feet and we start running. I have no idea where we are. It's nighttime, but my enhanced vision allows me to see more than an average human. The rolling hills dotted with leafless trees and ancient stone walls indicate we may still be in England.

I spot Nova sprinting ahead of us with a black container identical to Greyson's. Orb number two. Greyson runs beside me. Thorne shouts furious commands behind me. I glance over my shoulder to see a small contingent of Forsaken hot on our tails.

They're close. Too close.

I put on the brakes so suddenly that the grass beneath my feet rips up, leaving a skid mark of brown dirt in the ground. The first two Forsaken I encounter aren't ready for the abrupt face-off. I clothesline them, putting a little extra *oomph* into the hit to collapse their windpipes. I kick at the next Forsaken to reach me, enjoying the crunch that sounds when his knee bends the wrong way. The only thing I regret is that none of my hits so far have been death blows.

Sensing movement behind me, I spin in time to see knuckles about to connect with my face. I don't even have time to wince before the fist flying at my face disappears in a Steel-shaped blur. He lands a knockout blow, then snaps his furious gaze to me.

The next group of Forsaken are almost upon us, but I have a split second to check on Greyson and Nova. Greyson stands frozen a dozen steps away and just stares at the Forsaken closing in on us. Nova jogs backward with the box lifted high and yells, "Kick their butts, girl!"

"Greyson, go!" I yell just as a Forsaken dives at me.

I fall to the ground and roll in a controlled maneuver that allows me to pop up behind my foe. I kick his face. Blood and teeth shoot out of his mouth. At the sight of the bloodshed, a savage desire to see more carnage blossoms in my chest. The craving is so strong, it heats my blood, making it feel like it's fizzling in my veins. With my common sense steamrolled by bloodlust, it's easy to believe that the only thing that will keep me from incinerating on the spot is to rain down retribution on this group of Forsaken.

I slam my fist into the downed Forsaken, only satisfied when his face isn't much more than a mess of pulp. Looking up, I search for my next victim and spot Thorne and Silver in the distance, charging toward us along with the remaining Forsaken. I zero-in on Silver, ready for a chance to finally tangle with the deceitful Durand sister.

I'm primed to take off when Steel shouts my name. His voice brings me a moment of clarity and by some miracle,

I'm able to rein myself in. Dispatching another Forsaken, Steel grabs my arm and forces me to sprint after Grey and Nova.

"Trust me," he shouts, understanding my desire to go back and finish off the remaining Forsaken. Releasing my arm, he grasps my hand instead and squeezes.

Nodding, I pick up speed, a little shaken by the strength of my bloodthirsty instincts.

Nova and Greyson disappear over a small hill in the distance. I can hear Thorne and the Forsaken yelling in Enochian behind us, but their voices are soon drowned out by a loud thump, thump, thump noise high in the sky. Above us, a helicopter starts raining fire down on Thorne and the remaining Forsaken. I want to stop and watch the show, but Steel tugs me forward.

Before we reach the crest of the hill, an SUV bumps over the top and swerves to a stop in front of us.

"Get in," yells Sable from behind the wheel. I almost can't hear her over the noise from the helicopter blades and gunshots.

The back door is thrown open. Ash waves us forward. When we reach the car, Steel practically tosses me inside. Sable hits the gas before Steel even shuts the door behind us, fishtailing the vehicle on the soft grass.

I swivel in my seat as we career away from the action. Forsaken either lay motionless on the ground or have phased into the spectrum world. I see Thorne in the distance, his legs braced wide as he watches our escape. A line of bullets from the chopper above heads straight for him. My pulse picks up speed as I watch.

Why isn't he phasing?

The SUV's windows are tinted and we're so far away I

know there's no way Thorne can clearly see me, but it feels like he's staring right at me.

It's not until the very last moment that Thorne disappears, phasing out of the mortal world and into the spectrum one. The bullets intended for him find purchase in the grass and soil instead of his tissue and bone, and the emotion I feel over that isn't rage or disappointment, it's relief.

"It was too easy," Greyson says.

"Too easy?" Sterling's eyes round as he stares at his brother. "Are you kidding me? Did you see the mad skills we used to pull that off? We have Emberly. We have the orbs. That's a win, man."

"I'm not debating the outcome. I'm just saying that if Thorne really wanted those orbs, he would have fought harder for them. A dozen or so Forsaken is nothing. Especially compared to Emberly's power."

"She was passed out. Maybe he thought she'd stay that way?" Ash adds.

"I agree with that one." Shira points at Greyson. "It wasn't a very hard-fought battle."

I'm still having a hard time believing the angel Nephilim is here. I know she doesn't like me. I don't have an abundance of warm fuzzies for her either. If things hadn't gone south with Stavros back in Eden, I'd like to believe we would have eventually worked toward tolerance and perhaps mutual respect. To think she left Eden for the first time in her life to help Steel find me is a surprise. Maybe I misjudged her?

"Hi. I'm Greyson. We've actually just spent the last two days together." Greyson gives Shira a wave.

Shira shrugs. "You all look alike to me."

"Hey." Sterling looks crushed at her comment. Nova chuckles from her perch on the sofa arm next to him.

Sable, who I've been told joined the group when they stole the orbs, crosses her arms over her chest. "The important thing now is to figure out how to get the orbs back to the vault. Deacon says they haven't been reported missing yet. It's only a matter of time before someone notices they're gone. They won't be safe until we return them."

"That's a good point." Greyson rubs his mouth. "Maybe Thorne wasn't as concerned about leaving with the orbs because he plans on coming back for them. Could he have put a tracker on Emberly?"

Eight sets of eyes turn to me, including Steel's. He hasn't spoken much since we bunkered down in the safehouse, but hasn't let me leave his side, either.

Hunching my shoulders, I curl into the couch cushion behind me.

"Stand up, Em," Sterling says. "Let's take a look."

I glare at Sterling. "Pass."

"It's not like it would be in plain view," Greyson says to his twin. "If anything, it would be embedded in her skin or he would have made her ingest it. Unless you've developed X-ray vision in the last few hours, you're not going to be able to see it by looking at her."

"Should she strip to check for incisions or weird bumps under her skin?" Sterling suggests.

"Hmm. Maybe." Greyson looks thoughtful. "She'll need someone to help her. There are places on her body even she can't see."

Sterling grins, and I'm convinced he's about to volunteer for the task. "I'm sure Steel could lend a hand."

My cheeks instantly heat. "Oh my gosh, you two. Stop. Thorne didn't sneak a tracker on me." I don't think.

"How can you be sure?" I feel Steel's question rumble against my side because of how tightly he's pressed against me. "You said you weren't conscious for most of the last two days."

I chew on my bottom lip but pop it free when Steel's gaze moves pointedly to my mouth. "Well, yeah. There's that."

"He must have dosed you with something to keep you out. Embedding a tracker on you isn't out of the realm of possibility. Heck, maybe he put one on you back at White-hold. We still don't know how you ended up with him to begin with, since you can't remember anything past when you laid Stavros out."

Anger radiates off Steel like rays of sunlight. I know it's directed at Thorne—at least for the most part—but that doesn't make it any easier to ignore. His emotions have been simmering since I woke up while Thorne was trying to swap me for the orbs. Steel's body vibrates with them, and my guess is that it's only a matter of time before they boil over. I can't decide if I want to be there when it happens or not.

"Getting Emberly checked out is a priority," Sable says. "Killian and Ciara probably have something that can scan her. Nova, can you contact your parents?"

Nova nods. "I'll give them a call. How many of us are going?"

"Yes." Sterling fist pumps the air. "Ask them if they can

pick us up in that sweet Apache chopper. Shira and I had a blast shooting Forsaken."

Shira rolls her eyes. "They didn't let us operate the weapons. We fed Killian ammo and Ciara piloted the bird."

Sterling's smile fades. "It was still awesome."

"Let's split up." Sable stands, palming her phone as well. "Which half of you want to volunteer to help me sneak these orbs back into the compound's vault?"

The idea of being separated from the orbs gives me a rush of anxiety so strong, words burst out of me without a thought. "Wait. No."

Sable and the rest of my friends blink back at me. "What's wrong?" she asks.

My body sends signals to my brain that I don't know how to interpret. A thin layer of sweat breaks out along my hairline. Jitters run up and down my legs, and I have to clasp my hands in front of me to keep from fisting them. All I know is that I don't want to be separated from those orbs, but I don't have any idea why.

"It's just," I start, not quite knowing what I'm going to say. And then an idea hits me. "You said Tinkle was looking for Camiel, right?" My gaze darts between Steel and Shira, the last two to see the tiny Celestial.

They both nod back at me. Shira's eyes narrow suspiciously, but that's nothing new. She's been wary of me since before we even met.

"We should wait and give the orbs to Camiel."

Sable starts to shake her head. "Emberly, I'm not sure—"

"We already know the orbs aren't safe at the compound. If you could get them out, someone else could."

"That's highly unlikely."

"But possible," I press.

Sable sighs. "It's the safest option we have."

"But it's not," I argue. "They would be safer with Camiel and the angels than with the Nephilim." Sable's eyebrows rise, but I forge on. "If Tinkle went to find him, it's only a matter of time before they both show up. We can hand the orbs off to Camiel then. We just have to stay hidden from Thorne and his army of Forsaken minions until then."

Sable doesn't look sure. My friends seem to mull over the idea as well. No one speaks for several moments. I hold my breath. My heartbeat thumps so loud, I'm sure everyone can hear.

"The Council wasn't able to find out anything about the orbs. Perhaps Camiel would be a better guardian," Sable finally relents.

The weird sensations running through my body start to ebb. Sweet relief floods me.

"Okay." Sable nods to herself. "We'll keep the orbs, but only for now. If Camiel doesn't find you in the next couple of days, they're going back into the vault. Until then, our top priority is getting you checked out. Besides the possibility that you're carrying a tracking device, we have to get to the bottom of this missing time."

I open my mouth to argue and then clamp it shut. My blackouts are concerning. I'd like to brush them off as no big deal, but they're anything but. Instead of making a fuss, I nod in agreement.

I feel Steel's gaze on me, heating the side of my face. As the group starts to break apart, everyone going in different directions, he tips his head toward a closed door, indicating he wants to talk. I'm suddenly nervous to be alone with him. He probably has questions I won't know how to answer, and it doesn't help that he still looks furious. And in truth,

I'm always a little nervous to be alone with Steel. His regard leaves me slightly breathless and lightheaded, but in the best way possible. I stand to follow him into the empty bedroom in the cottage we're holed up in but find the delicious part of being alone with Steel is absent—leaving only a heavy pit in the bottom of my gut.

# 21

## EMBERLY

"*A*re you . . . angry at me?" The words are out of my mouth as soon as the door clicks softly closed.

Steel plows a hand into his hair, raking his fingers through the raven strands. "Yes. No."

Turning his back to me, he paces to the other side of the room. He hunches, placing his hands on the windowsill. His muscles bunch under the thin cotton of his shirt.

Gnawing on my lower lip, I slowly mirror his steps, crossing the distance between us until I stand directly behind him. Indecision churns in my belly. I tentatively raise a hand and flatten my palm on his back. I can't not touch him right now. He's hurting, and the urge to offer what comfort I can is overwhelming.

He heaves in a breath, his body shuddering on the exhale. A single point of contact isn't enough right now.

Moving in closer, I slide my arms around him, pressing my upper body against his back. I rest my cheek on his shoulder. Warmth grows in my chest and blooms outward. I need the physical contact just as much as he does.

"Why did you run?" His softly spoken words vibrate against my chest and stomach.

"I told you, Stavros attacked me."

"I know that. But why did you run from *me*?"

I inhale, holding the breath a moment before letting it out. "I didn't. I was on my way to find you when I blacked out."

It doesn't make sense, but it's the truth. I'm not sure that's enough for him. This isn't about me disappearing. I mean, it is, but it's more than that. So much of Steel's identity is founded on keeping his loved ones safe because of the one time he didn't. Couldn't. I can only imagine what it felt like for him to find out I was gone.

"Steel." I loosen my hold and with gentle hands, urge him to turn and face me. He leans back against the window. Sealing his hands on my hips, he pulls me into the space between his thighs. I press a palm to his cheek, feeling the roughness of several days' stubble as he slips his thumbs under the hem of my shirt and draws small circles on the skin above my hip bones. It's thoroughly distracting, and it takes me several heartbeats to remember what I was going to say.

"I can't promise that nothing bad is ever going to happen to me. In fact, I can probably guarantee that it will. Thorne and Silver are still out there planning who knows what, Stavros might have spread his prejudice against me to other angel-line Nephilim, and Fallen might pour into the mortal world at any minute."

"Is this supposed to make me feel better? If so, I need you to know that your pep talks need some work." He's serious, but also not. There's a spark of humor in his gaze.

"But what I can promise you," I say, ignoring his comment, "is that I won't run from you, only toward you."

Steel wraps an arm around my waist and hauls me into his chest. Dipping his head, he runs the tip of his nose over the column of my throat. Catching my breath, I tip my head back to give him better access.

"That will be a welcome change," he murmurs against my neck with a chuckle.

"Hey, come on now. You've done your fair share of running, too. You peeled out of Seraph Academy so quickly that I had to dodge flying gravel."

Steel makes a sound low in his throat that's an awful lot like a growl. It might sound menacing, but I can feel his smile as he places a soft kiss behind my ear. A delicious shiver works its way down my spine.

*Yes, please. More of that.*

"If you say so," Steel chuckles.

Shoot. I said that out loud? How embarrassing.

I start to pull away, but Steel swipes his lips across the same sensitive spot and I'm not thinking of much else other than his warm mouth. Wrapping my arms around his neck, I slide a hand into his hair, pulling a bit at the strands when he tugs on my earlobe with his teeth.

I want to taste him. I need to taste him.

I maneuver my lips to align with his, but he dodges my advance. Bending low, he swipes my feet out from under me. The world tilts. My mind is already muddled, and the unexpected movement makes me yip in surprise. Before I can clear my head, he sets me down on the bed and stretches out beside me. His hand dives into my hair, and he tilts my head before lowering his mouth to mine.

At the touch of his lips, a fire ignites.

These aren't sweet kisses. They're possessive and claiming and intense, and I can't get enough. Each new slant of Steel's mouth causes a zing of pleasure to shoot through my body. After all we've been through in the last few days, I need the reminder that he's here and mine and not going away, and apparently Steel does too.

I grasp his biceps as he holds himself over me, but he's not close enough. Trailing my hands to his mid-back, I pull him down on top of me, loving the way it feels to have his body pressing mine into the mattress.

I trail a foot over his calf as we continue to kiss. When I scrape my nails over his ribs, he wrenches himself back up onto his forearms. Gulping in deep lungfuls of air, his chest expands and contracts, brushing against mine with each inhale.

His lips are swollen and his hair in complete disarray. He's never looked hotter.

"You have to stop looking at me like that." His voice has dropped an octave and the sound alone makes my toes curl.

I shake my head.

"I'm trying to be good right now, Em. This is moving a bit fast. You're really . . . inexperienced."

I could take that as an insult, but I choose to use it to my advantage instead.

"Exactly why I need the practice." Pushing up on my elbows, I place a soft kiss to the corner of his mouth. "Is this all right?" I ask, fake innocence dripping from each word.

Steel doesn't move a muscle, but his gaze tracks over my face. I lean forward again and slowly rub my top lip over his bottom one before ever so slightly pulling it into my mouth for another kiss.

"How about that?" I ask, letting my lips brush over his when I speak.

I'm about to deliver an open-mouthed kiss when he cracks. His weight drops back onto me. A deep groan rumbles in his chest and against my own as he cups my face and claims my mouth once again.

That's better.

He nips at my bottom lip, and my mouth opens on a gasp. Taking advantage of the movement, his tongue sweeps into my mouth. If my eyes were open, they would have rolled back into my head. As it is, a galaxy of sensation overwhelms my mind and sparks burst behind my closed lids.

I can't seem to take in enough air, but I don't care. Breathing is overrated.

Just when I think things can't get any hotter, Steel's fingertips brush my naked ribs, and I short circuit. I freeze, my muscles locking as my mind whirls in indecision.

Sensing my change in mood, Steel stops kissing me. He stares down at me as he catches his breath, just as much a beautiful mess as he was a few minutes ago.

"Are you all right?" he asks.

I bite my bottom lip.

It's just too much . . . or maybe not enough? I'm not sure which, and that uncertainty is what finally makes up my mind.

"Maybe you were right. This may be more than I'm ready for right now."

As my body cools, I'm confident putting on the brakes was the right move, but that doesn't make me any less embarrassed. I try to duck my head, but with Steel hovering over me, there's nowhere to go.

"Hey, look at me." He uses his fingers to guide my face back in his direction. "There will never be a situation where saying, 'no,' 'not now,' or 'we should wait' will be a bad thing. You and I, we aren't on a timer. We won't expire. Whatever pace we decide to set will be the perfect one for us."

That's it. He's done it this time. I'm dead. Good and truly dead.

He kisses my nose and says, "How about we head back out there and help figure out how to save the world?"

"You guys in—Yikes!"

A door slams, and our heads swivel toward the room's entrance.

Through the closed door I hear Ash's muffled, "Sorry. So sorry, you guys. I didn't see anything . . . much." Followed by Sterling, "Why is your face red? Are you holding in a fart?"

"No!" Ash's voice is indignant. "I walked in on . . . um, or rather, I just found Steel and Emberly."

Sterling laughs. "Is that all? Did I ever tell you about the time I caught them sucking face in an alley?"

"Who cares," Shira yells from somewhere else. "They're soul-bonded. You're going to have to peel them off each other for the next couple of decades at least."

"What's soul-bonded?" Sterling asks.

Closing my eyes, I groan.

The door pops open again, but this time it isn't Ash standing there, it's Sable.

So. Much. Worse.

"You two," Sable points at us. "Up and out."

She leaves the door open and stomps away, giving the rest of the house a great view of Steel and me plastered together on the bed.

Ash winces and turns away, giving us what little privacy she can. Greyson and Sterling don't afford us the same courtesy as they openly cheer, throwing catcalls and kissy noises our way.

I drop my head to the mattress and cover my face with both hands as Steel moves off me, his movements stiff.

"Is this what it's like getting caught by your parents?" I ask.

Taking my hand, he pries it away from my face and helps me stand. "I don't know."

I lift a brow at that, unconvinced he's never been in a compromising position before.

"Never got caught," he says with a grin.

I narrow my eyes, even as I struggle to tame my breathing. "I hate you."

He chuckles. "We both know that's the opposite of the truth." He rubs at a spot on his neck. "I might have a hickey to prove it."

My eyes go wide. Wow. He really went there.

"Too soon?"

"Way too soon," I confirm.

"Steel. Emberly. Get out here," Sable calls. I grimace when her command elicits another round of laughter from the peanut gallery.

Seemingly unconcerned by Sable's surly demeanor, Steel loops an arm around my shoulders. Leaning down, he plants a soft kiss to the crown of my head, and I go a little melty. I almost don't care about my disheveled appearance as he leads me out of the bedroom and into the living room where the group is resettling.

"Glad to see you're in a better mood, bro," Sterling says with a toothy grin.

"Sterling, don't tease," Sable chastises. "It's beneath you."

Sterling shakes his head. "It's really not."

"Where's Shira?" I ask, mostly to steer the conversation in another direction. Nova is in the kitchen, speaking on her phone.

"Upstairs," Ash answers. "Something about checking in with her grandfather."

"But they don't get cell service in Eden."

"Where?" Ash's eyebrows pull together in confusion.

I glance at Steel and he gives a slight shake of his head. Bending down he whispers in my ear. "They don't know about Eden. Shira has a way to communicate with Nikias though."

Oh.

"Never mind."

Nova saunters into the room, sliding her cell into her back pocket. "Okay boys and girls, pack your bags. Our ride is on its way."

# 22

## EMBERLY

"*S*he's clear." Killian nods at me to drop my arms as he steps away with the scanner. "There's nothing on her broadcasting her location."

Well, that's a relief.

"Sorcha just arrived," Ciara says. "She's ready to meet with Emberly."

"Oh shoot. You called in one of the Elders?" I ask.

Ciara nods. "Sorcha is probably our most skilled healer. As the virtue Elder, if anyone knows what's going on with these blackouts, it will be her."

My gaze tracks to Sable, who leans against a janky metal table in one of the power's underground bunkers. This one happens to be in a sewer. The smell is less than pleasant. "Doesn't that blow your cover?"

"Sorcha knows how to be discreet. Once the orbs are secure, I'll head back to the compound."

Killian and Ciara exchange a less-than-pleased look. Apparently, they helped with the exchange only because they were repeatedly assured the orbs wouldn't actually be handed off to Thorne and were to be returned to the vault straightaway. They were less than thrilled to find out we still had them, with no plans to immediately return them to the Elders. Sable argued with them behind closed doors for almost an hour before Nova's parents reluctantly agreed to go along with our plan.

"I'll go topside and grab her," Sable offers, then jogs to the ladder that leads to the street level.

She only just disappears from view when the metal door on the opposite side of the room groans and pops open. Nova and Steel walk through, both with an impressive number of new weapons strapped to various parts of their bodies. Steel immediately makes his way to me, throwing an arm around my shoulders and tucking me securely under his arm. A cylinder bulge pokes me in the hip.

"Is that a tear gas grenade, or are you just happy to see me?" I ask.

Steel glances down at the canister, then looks at me with a cocky half-grin. "Powers have all the best toys."

I'd say, "typical boy," but Nova looks equally excited about her haul. She shows off a retractable baton to her parents, demonstrating how she can use it to knock her opponent to the ground before stabbing them with a tactical knife.

We're a weird bunch.

"Did they find anything?" Steel asks, his voice losing any hint of lightness.

I plaster on a smile, hoping to put him at ease. "Got the 'all clear' from Killian."

Some of the tightness leaves his muscles. "Good. The others will be happy to hear it too."

Sterling, Ash, Greyson, and Shira all stayed behind at the

safehouse this time. Hopefully they're getting some much-needed rest.

I hear Sorcha's lyrical voice and only have a few seconds to explain to Steel what she's doing here. He lifts his eyebrows, but the moment Sorcha's foot touches down in the dank room, he clears his face of all emotion, giving her only a blank slate to analyze.

That's skills right there. I need him to give me a lesson.

Leaning over, Sorcha brushes the grime off her pants before looking up. Gone are the flowy dresses she favored in Egypt. Instead, she's swathed from head to toe in fitted black battle leathers. Her red-tinted hair, with its vein of white, is pulled high in a tight ponytail.

She scans the room as Sable leads her over. The soles of her steel-toed, knee-high boots thump on the damp concrete floor with every step. Those babies are made for combat rather than stealth.

"Emberly. Steel." Sorcha nods at both of us. Her freckles stand out even more against her dark clothing and the severe hairstyle. It's such an American thing, but I'm convinced my name sounds better when she says it in her Irish accent. "It's good to see both of you doing well." Sorcha's gaze fixes on me. "At least, relatively so. That was quite the exit you two made."

"Right." I don't remember her being in the meeting room when Camiel busted in the door, but it would make sense if she was. She's an Elder, after all. "I'm not sure angels know the meaning of *subtle*."

Her forehead pleats as she raises her eyes. "Met many angels besides your father?"

Ah. "Well. No."

A soft smile lightens her face and makes the laugh lines

that branch from her eyes more defined. She leans in as if sharing a secret but doesn't do much to lower her voice. "Me either."

"Thanks for coming on such short notice," Killian says as he steps forward and shakes Sorcha's hand.

"This is our daughter, Nova," Ciara says after she, too, shakes the Elder's hand. Nova bows her head in an uncharacteristic show of deference to the virtue leader.

"I've heard positive reports about this one," Sorcha says with a smile and diverts her attention to Nova. "We're expecting great things from you."

Nova is tongue-tied for a moment before catching herself. She quickly clears the shell-shocked look from her face before answering, "Of, course."

"Now, Emberly. It's time I take a look at you."

Before Sorcha can take even a step in my direction, a shower of sparks rains down on us. A small furry creature appears and sails over our heads.

"I win again!" Tinkle yells.

"Tinkle!" Nova rushes forward as Tinkle drops to the ground and turns into a golden retriever, his tail thumping to a rapid beat. He plasters slobbery dog kisses all over her face when she kneels down to pet him. Killian, Ciara, and Sorcha watch with slack-jawed gazes as Nova starts to baby talk to the Celestial while rubbing his belly. I get it. Celestials are the fabled guardians of the angel-born. Seeing one in the flesh would leave any Neph in awe, but I'm willing to bet Tinkle's antics are what pushed them over the edge.

I glance at the ladder that leads up to the surface. Just like when Tinkle appeared in the meeting room in the Elders' compound, he won't be alone. I have no idea how Camiel is going to fit through the narrow opening. His eight-foot height and six metal wings give him a pretty hefty girth.

Steel slides closer, also waiting for the inevitable. Grabbing my hand, he gives it a squeeze to let me know he's here for me. I'm looking at him when a wave of hot air blasts through the room, tossing my hair in every direction.

The adults in the room drop to a knee, their heads bent in reverence to the mighty seraph angel that just appeared. Nova stops petting Tinkle, her eyes round like saucers, but Steel and I remain standing.

Even these few days apart dulled my memory of the power of Camiel's presence, but I refuse to bow before him —or worse, cower. I may understand him a bit more after spending a short time in Eden and talking to Nikias, but he's going to have to earn my respect. As of now, he doesn't have it.

Camiel's molten gold gaze doesn't stray from me, and despite my bravado, I start to sweat under his regard.

"You're well?" he asks, and the question takes me by surprise.

"All things considered?" I shrug. "I guess."

He tips his chin up. "Good. Come. I'll escort you back to Eden."

Now, wait a minute.

I hear Nova whisper "What's Eden" from somewhere behind me. Shira is going to be furious when she finds out Camiel spilled the beans.

I shake my head and lean into Steel. "Naw. I'm good here."

The gold in his eyes swirls with displeasure. He crosses his arms over his chest, and I wonder vaguely if that is his "I mean business" stance.

"You need to go back. I can't keep leaving my troops every other day to pull you out of trouble."

He can't possibly be serious. My internal temperature spikes. The low rumble in Steel's chest says that he's not happy either.

"I'm not even going to get into the fact that your appearing act right now is the definition of too little, too late—let's not forget it was my friends that got me back from Thorne—but let's talk about Eden, shall we? You want me to willingly return to a group of Nephilim that you took me from as an infant because one of them tried to murder me?"

Sable gasps. Still kneeling on the ground, she lifts her head to watch the exchange. Killian, Ciara, and Sorcha's gazes are on us as well, even as their heads remain bowed.

"Nikias told you." I can't tell if he's relieved or frustrated, but I don't spare much time to dwell on it because I'm far from done.

"Oh, yeah. He told me. And I only feel a little guilty about putting Stavros down, considering he tried to poison me as a baby, but there could be more—"

"What?" Another rush of fiery heat blasts throughout the room, blistering my skin. Steel pulls me behind him as Camiel marches forward. A layer of white fire outlines the angel's body. "Stavros did what?"

Oh, shoot. I forgot he didn't know about that part.

I nudge Steel out of the way. I'm tough enough to fight my own battles.

"Yes. He admitted it when he attacked me. And considering—"

"You were attacked?" Camiel shoots a hard look in Tinkle's direction. The flames encasing his body swell, making it clear the Celestial jumbled some of the facts. Tinkle tucks his tail and lowers his dog body toward the floor in submission.

Closing his eyes, Camiel extinguishes the white fire licking over his body. Running a hand through his blond locks, anger and anguish linger on his face. It's the most human I've seen him look, and I'm oddly comforted to know that underneath his perfect shell, he's capable of those emotions. The fact that he seems genuinely distraught over my well-being doesn't hurt either.

"The point," I continue, "is that the angel-line community is probably not the safest, or most hospitable, place for me right now. There could be others like Stavros who consider my existence blasphemous, and I did kill one of their own. My guess is that there are more than a few angel-borns in Eden out for my blood." I can't help but add, "And as far as I'm concerned, you gave up your right to tell me what to do or where to go when you left me to fend for myself with the humans seventeen years ago." The room falls silent when I finish.

"Leave us." The ground rumbles with Camiel's deep command, but the only ones who listen are Killian, Ciara, and Sorcha, who quickly beat feet for the nearest exit. Sable stands but doesn't move. Transforming into a flying squirrel, Tinkle climbs up to Nova's shoulder and hides himself in her hair.

Steel shifts even closer, and Camiel tracks Steel's minor movement. He knows we're not backing down. The angel's lips press together in annoyance.

"Nova." Ciara's voice snaps in the silence, but Nova waits until I nod to saunter toward the door her parents hold open for her. Nothing about her slow steps says she's in a rush. I already know that Steel would give anyone, even the mighty Camiel, the finger for trying to separate us, but I'm not sure whether to be impressed with Nova's ability to keep her cool in the presence of a seraph angel, or a bit worried for her sanity. Sable holds her ground but has the sense to appear frightened.

The door slams shut, leaving the four of us together. "I'll repeat anything you have to say back to them anyway," I tell Camiel before he can put up a fuss about Sable and Steel. "They're not leaving."

The mighty seraph rolls his shoulders, and three sets of sharp wings bob behind him. Leveling me with a glare, his eyes glaze white. I've seen this happen once before when he—

"Ahh."

A stabbing pain pierces my brain, forcing me to slap a hand on the metal table next to me to keep from tipping over. Squeezing my eyes closed, I press a hand to the side of my head and concentrate on breathing through the pain. Steel seals his arms around my waist, anchoring me. The others are talking, probably trying to get my attention, but I can't make out their words past the throbbing agony.

Voices elevate and then fingertips softly touch either side of my face. Finally, the pain starts to ease.

When I open my eyes, my vision is blurred and filled with gold. After a few blinks, it starts to refocus. Camiel stoops in front of me. He's so large that even down on one knee, his head reaches my chest. Sable stands behind him, a hand raised to her mouth as she stares between Camiel and me with wide, round eyes.

Steel's elevated heartbeat thumps against my back. He bears the burden of my weight with his arms wrapped tight around my middle and his chest pressed up against me. As the pain continues to fade, I steady my legs, but don't pull away. I can't yet stand without his help.

"I've caused you pain," Camiel says. His eyebrows pinch as he frowns.

Raising a hand, I touch my temple and try to use my fingertips to soothe away the pain.

"You caused the monster headache?" I ask, my mind struggling to keep up after its hard reboot.

"Not intentionally. I was trying to communicate with you as my kind does. I thought, given your predominate angel attributes . . ." His gaze shifts to Steel and then back to me, clueing me in that he knows about the soul-bond. "That we would be able to link telepathically. I've tried to reach you that way many times over the years. I never knew I was hurting you." I catch the hint of regret in Camiel's voice.

"Were you able to speak with Stasha that way?"

Camiel shakes his head. Soft wisps of his white-blond hair brush his shoulders with the movement. "No. But your mother was full Nephilim. You are not."

"I'm not a Nephilim? Then what am I?"

In a fluid motion, Camiel rises, giving his wings a soft shake when he reaches his full height. "Something else."

That's not ominous or anything, but I don't have the bandwidth to dwell on my specific species classification right now. In the grand scheme of things, it's just not important.

"I've had acute headaches for years. I just assumed . . ." Could all those times I had sudden, piercing pain have been because Camiel was trying to reach out to me? Does that mean he didn't fully abandon me?

Closing my eyes, I inhale deeply through my nose,

waiting for the lingering discomfort to fade. "That was worse than it's ever been before."

I feel the rumble of a growl in Steel's chest, but he doesn't speak. Instead, his near-bruising hold on me tightens even more, but I don't mind. His solid presence is soothing.

"Probably because of my proximity. The geographically closer angels are to each other, the stronger the signal is that we send back and forth. Nothing happens if an angel tries to communicate to a human or Nephilim in this way, but your brain must be receiving the signal, but struggling to interpret the message." He crosses his arms. The pose is intimidating, but there's a new softness on his face. "Perhaps it's something we can work on in the future, but for now, I won't try to reach you that way. I . . ." Camiel clears his throat. "I apologize for the discomfort I've caused you over the years."

Did that just happen? Did a seraph just apologize to me?

I twist to check with Steel. His gaze moves from the golden angel to meet with mine. He gives me a tiny shrug and a quick nod.

"Well, um . . . you didn't know." I duck my head, suddenly embarrassed. "So, there's really nothing to apologize for."

Camiel heaves a sigh and when he exhales, his shoulders slump. He rubs a weary hand over his face, his head just shy of hanging, and his wings droop limply behind him. From one breath to the next he goes from the image of a proud warrior angel to a beaten-down mortal with wings.

"This wasn't how any of this was meant to be," he murmurs.

"Any of what?" I ask.

He lifts his gaze. His eyes look tired. "Stasha, your mother, loved you with all her heart. And her heart would have broken if she knew the hardships you were forced to endure."

My chest constricts when he talks about the mother I never knew. The one I never let myself dwell on, because it was easier to believe she never existed than to think she threw me away.

"We were overjoyed when you were born, but things turned dark so quickly. This was never the upbringing we planned for you. But at the time . . ." He shakes his head. "It was the only way I could think to keep you safe. I'm sorry we weren't there for you all these years. Sorry I wasn't able to keep her safe." Camiel lifts his hand and cups my cheek. The sheen over his eyes most likely mirrors my own. "But I know she would have been very proud of the woman you are becoming."

A tear drips down my cheek, and Camiel wipes it away with a sad smile before stepping back. In this moment, I don't see him as a mighty seraph, the Angel of War, Commander of legions of warrior angels, but instead, I see him as a man who lost the woman he loved and was left broken because of it. A man that felt he had no other choice but to hide his daughter—the only connection he still possessed to his wife—in a realm full of strangers.

But maybe there's still hope.

At some point during Camiel's confession, Steel loosened his grip on me and now rubs a comforting hand up and down my arm. When his fingers wisp over the back of my hand, I turn my own and twine ours together.

If I could restore Steel and Silver, there must be hope for my mother as well.

"What happened to Stasha? Where is she now?"

Camiel's face shutters. Any gentleness in his features burns away, leaving a hardened shell behind. "I will not talk of it."

"It's just that, I may be able to help her. I was told she became a Forsaken." Dropping Steel's hand, I lift both of mine and stoke some of my power. Not a lot, but enough that twin balls of fire spark to life in my palms. Sable gasps, having never seen me bring forth my power in the mortal world before. I close my hands, extinguishing the flames. "I can do things. I may be able to bring her back."

Hope blooms in my chest, filling me with warmth. Maybe there's a chance to reclaim all I was denied. Camiel placed me with the humans to hide and protect me when he lost Stasha, but if I could bring her back, perhaps we could be a family.

Camiel shakes his head once. "No." The word echoes off the wall, a clear warning not to proceed that I refuse to heed.

"But I've done it before."

I catch a glimpse of Sable. Her face has gone bone-white and she shoots me a look of concern. I guess I should just be grateful that her head hasn't exploded. Arguing with a seraph is probably high on the angel-born list of no-nos.

"I'm well aware of what you can do." Camiel's voice has gone steely cold.

I blink back at him, thoroughly confused. Did I misinterpret his pain? Does he not feel strongly enough about my mother to even try and fight for her? Or is his hatred of Forsaken so deep that he doesn't want Stasha back now? A kernel of anger settles in my gut and takes root.

"If she's a Forsaken, there's still a chance for her. If you refuse to fight for her, that's fine. But you can't stop me." I lift my chin in a silent challenge. Camiel's nostrils flare, and a gush of phantom heat buffers against me, but I won't be intimidated.

"I said no because Stasha is gone." I open my mouth to argue, convinced he still doesn't understand the situation correctly, but words freeze in my throat when he continues. "And I know that she is, because I am the one who killed her."

# 23

## EMBERLY

*A* strangled gasp chokes its way out my throat. "How could you?"

Maybe it's not true? Thorne said she was still alive. But Tinkle said she was dead. It was easy to believe that by "dead," Tinkle meant she was a Forsaken. That's what I wanted to be true. Would Thorne lie about something like this? Gosh, yes. Yes, he would.

"Emberly," Steel whispers in my ear, rubbing a hand along my back to calm me, but I don't want to be pacified. I yank out of his hold, stomping forward until I crowd Camiel, ready to force answers.

Questions crowd my mind, one spilling over another in a jumbled mess, but face to face with Camiel I'm only able to push one word out. "Why?"

"Because she would have been the death of you."

I stop breathing. I'm pretty sure my heart skips at least two beats.

"She would have led the Fallen straight to you, so when I found her, I did exactly what she would have wanted me to had she been in her right mind, and blasted her with enough angel-fire that only char remained."

I stumble back as if hit by a physical blow.

Camiel not only killed her, but he killed her to protect me.

"It was a decision that forced me to rip my own heart out and burn it to ash." His gaze travels from me to Steel and back again. "Pray you are never faced with such a decision, for it may not be something you will ever fully recover from. I know I won't. If I had to do it again, I would, but I will speak of it no more."

The room falls silent. As if Camiel pulls the heat from the air, a chill sets in, driving through my flesh to settle in my bones.

There's a hollow knock on the metal door across the room, then Sorcha pokes her freckled face through the opening.

"It was quiet, so we were wondering if we could come back." Her wide-eyed stare trails from me to Camiel, then back again.

"Yes. We're done here," Camiel says without looking at Sorcha. He crosses his arms over his chest and steps to the side, allowing the others to re-enter.

Nova's parents and Sorcha give Camiel a wide berth as they re-join us, but Nova strides right by the golden warrior, close enough that her arm almost bumps his as she passes.

Tinkle's eyes peek out from behind the cascade of her locks, but the black glassy shine is the only part of the creature I spot.

"Nova," Steel warns quietly as she slides up next to me in a blatant show of support.

She tips her shoulder in a lazy shrug, and something a lot like "deadbeat dad" hisses from between her lips. My eyes widen, and the air in the room heats once again.

Oh, snap. I'm not the only one who heard that.

I glance at Nova, not sure if I'm more surprised by the show of fearless loyalty, or just her general fearlessness.

When the room stays silent but heats up a notch, she clears her throat, hinting at her true level of discomfort.

Despite everything, I smile. The girl might be a bit of a head case, but she's my head case.

"We have a matter to discuss with you," Sable says, pulling Camiel's attention away from the auburn-haired beauty.

Right. The orbs. We need to get them somewhere safe and very far away from Thorne. Now that Camiel is here, we can hand them off to him and be done with them.

A wave of anxiety floods my system. I slap a hand on the metal table to keep my balance, drawing the attention of everyone in the room. As quickly as it happened, the sensation dissipates.

What was that?

Steel's hand on my lower back slides to my rib cage as he leans forward into me. "Emberly?"

"Umm . . . sorry," I say, not meeting anyone's gaze. "Head rush."

Maybe some air would be a good idea?

I open my mouth to announce that I'm going to the surface. Let the adults deal with the orbs. They've never brought me anything but grief, and I'll be glad to get rid of them. But I can't quite seem to make my mouth form the words or my feet take the steps. Sable goes on, explaining to Camiel about the orbs and how she wants to give them to him for safekeeping. Worse yet, I have to tamp down the urge to shout that he can't have them. I clench my muscles, sealing my mouth to keep words from escaping.

Everyone is heedless of my inner turmoil, except Steel, who is close enough to feel me stiffen.

"Hey," he whispers in my ear, and when I don't respond, he pulls me to the side. My feet move with his firm urgings, but my attention is still on the conversation about the orbs.

"What's wrong?" he asks, but I only shake my head.

How do I explain something to him that I don't understand myself? My visceral reaction to giving up the orbs makes zero sense.

"You're correct. The orbs are indeed very dangerous," Camiel says, and I realize I must have missed a bit of the exchange. "But I can't take them. Angels are forbidden to touch the orbs. We are not even allowed to get near them. Our power interacts with theirs in unpredictable ways."

Relief is fast and sweet, and in that moment, I am completely myself again. Shooting Steel a smile, I ignore his frown and re-join the group.

I raise my hand unnecessarily. "Would now be a good time to mention that one of the orbs changed colors and short circuited a bit when I touched it?"

Camiel's gaze darkens. "Don't touch it again."

I salute him. You don't have to tell me twice. At least Steel's instincts were correct when he kept me from the orb we took from Whitehold.

"So, we'll return them to the compound vault then," Sorcha says. Killian and Ciara nod their agreement and a fresh tendril of anxiety trickles through me. "I've been keeping people from discovering they're missing. Sneaking them back in shouldn't be too difficult."

Camiel shakes his head. "No. They need to be returned to their origin. Only then will they be safe. If we only knew they'd been unearthed, all this," Camiel gestures toward the ceiling, which I take to mean the destruction wrought against London, "might have been avoided."

"If the angels communicated more with us, you would have been aware."

"Nova!" Ciara snaps at her daughter, who only looks a smidge remorseful.

"I'm just saying," she says.

Camiel's gaze fixes on Nova. Is that a hint of a smile I see?

"Maybe that should change?" I widen my eyes when Sable speaks up. She's not one to go against the establishment. Although she did help steal the orbs, so maybe I haven't given her enough credit. "If we opened a line of communication between angels and Nephilim, I think it would serve both our peoples."

Camiel heaves a sigh. "I don't disagree. But angels are . . ."

Stubborn. Elitist. Prejudice.

". . . set in their ways. There would be opposition."

"Perhaps their ways should be challenged?" Sable suggests. "If an influential angel, one that your kind looked up to, were to take steps toward change, I have no doubt it would make an impact." It's obvious Sable's talking about Camiel.

"If by 'impact' you mean stick a target on my daughter's back, then yes, you'd be correct."

Nope. I don't like the sound of that.

Sable frowns. She glances at me and then back at

Camiel. "I don't see how brokering an exchange of information between our kinds would put Emberly at risk."

"The more interaction between angels and Nephilim, the higher possibility that Emberly will be discovered. The safest thing for her will be to remain hidden."

"I've spent my whole life hiding," I speak up. "I understand you want to protect me, and I appreciate that, I truly do, but I think that's something I'm about ready to put behind me. I have a life." I glance over my shoulder to see Steel standing behind me and then turn my attention back to Camiel. "I'd like to start living it."

The room falls silent. I don't expect this is an argument anyone is going to win right now, but hopefully it gives Camiel something to think about.

"Have the leaks been plugged? Will more Fallen pop into the mortal world?" Steel's voice rumbles behind me. His words aren't particularly hostile, but agitation hovers under the surface.

Camiel's ageless gaze rakes over Steel. I look back and forth between the pair as they have a silent standoff. Finally, Camiel lifts his head in a quick nod. A glimmer of respect shines in his eyes. Or maybe I'm just reading what I want into it.

"Yes. As far as we can tell, the veil is intact. And it should remain that way as long as—"

A violent *boom* cuts Camiel off. The ground shakes and the sky falls. I drop to my knees. Something heavy strikes me on the back, shoving me to my stomach. A plume of dust fills the air, and I can't see my hand in front of my face, let alone anyone else. I gasp and the particles coat my lungs, sending me into a coughing fit.

There are muted shouts, but it's hard to make out the

words over the ringing in my ears and my own violent hacks.

The pressure on my back disappears. Someone cups their hands under my arms and hauls me to my feet. There's a sharp pain in my lower back, but it's bearable.

"Where are you hurt?" Steel says. I can only just make out the top of his gray-powdered head as he pats me down.

"I'm fine," I choke out, my coughing finally subsiding. "What just happened?"

The air is still filled with too much dust and debris to see very far, but from what I can tell, the ceiling just caved in.

Done with his body check, Steel rises to his feet. He's covered in so much dust, it looks like he rolled around in flour. He waves a hand in front of his face to try to clear the air, but it doesn't help.

A trickle of blood leaks down his face from a cut above his eyebrow. He's hurt, but it's just a cut. Even so, instant rage boils my blood and that voice deep inside whispers, "*mine.*" I force myself to chill.

A sudden gust of wind blows grit in my face and sends my hair flying in every direction, but it clears the air a bit.

Camiel stands in a pile of rubble. His face, hair, and golden armor are covered in a thick layer of gray dust, but he appears otherwise unaffected. He flaps his wings another time and I close my eyes, turning away to keep from getting a face full of concrete dust. When I look back, I can see even more of our surroundings. Beams of sunlight illuminate the area.

What the heck? We're two stories underground. Was there a bomb?

Besides Steel and Camiel, I can't see any of the others, but then a mound of rubble starts to shake. Steel and I exchange a quick glance. We start forward at the same time only to be stopped short when the mound explodes, chunks of concrete flying.

Camiel twists and flares his metal wings, shielding Steel and me from the fallout. When he lowers them, Tinkle is there as a teal-scaled dragon. He shakes his body and then folds his outstretched wings. Like little chicks next to a mother hen, Sable, Sorcha, Killian, Ciara, and Nova lie or crouch on the ground on either side of him. Tinkle sheltered all of them from the initial cave-in.

I breathe a sigh of relief as they jump to their feet, pulling whatever weapons they have. Their eyes are wide as they scan for the next threat.

"Thanks, bud." Nova runs a hand over Tinkle's scales, giving him an affectionate pat. Maybe I should be annoyed that my Celestial didn't instinctually try to defend me. But I'm not. I'm just thankful that he protected the others. Keeping people I care about safe has become just as important as my own well-being. Maybe even more so.

"This shouldn't have happened." Ciara's face tips up as she inspects the hole above us. The faint trill of sirens wails in the distance. Maybe for us, but maybe for something else going on in the city. It's possible Fallen are attacking London again. "The shelter is fortified against bombs. It should have held."

"I'll go to the spirit realm to scout," Camiel says as he cracks his neck. Dust and small debris trickles off him like falling snow.

Sorcha gasps and yells, "Look!" pointing toward the opening above, where a form made of shadow and mist stalks back and forth around the periphery.

A shadow beast.

Another monster appears, and now there are two. Are they part of Thorne's army that came through before, or is there a tear between worlds that Camiel missed? The second option chills my blood.

The angel-born immediately start looking for a way to get to the surface. With a growl, Camiel disappears, only to reappear less than fifteen seconds later, his eyes filled with rage. "I can't fight them in the spirit realm. They're only corporeal in the mortal world."

"So, fight them here."

"I can't."

"Why not?"

"I can count on one hand the number of times an angel has been revealed in all his glory to a human," Camiel growls.

"You're worried about humans seeing you?" How can that be a concern right now? "London was torn apart by shadow beasts. I think seeing an angel would actually be a welcome sign for the humans."

Camiel bares his teeth and starts to pace. "It is forbidden."

I shake my head, more than disappointed. My expectations for my father were already low, but this is next level.

"Emberly, let's go," Steel calls, holding his hand out to help me start the climb up and out.

Everyone else is halfway to the surface. Tinkle is a tabby housecat and easily scales the rubble next to Nova. They're going to need Camiel's help when they reach those Fallen. Angel-born are fierce, but they are strongest in the spectrum world. I might not be an expert at battle strategy, but the shadow beasts have the high ground. They're going to pick us off at the rim of the opening.

I stoke my power. I've manifested my wings in the mortal world before, so I know I can do it again. I concentrate on moving the energy inside to where my wings will emerge along my spine. I build my energy, yet hold it back, not really sure if what I'm doing is correct.

Sweat beads and then trickles down the side of my face. I reach a point that seems almost unbearable and then with a scream, I let go.

With a rush, my wings unfurl. My gold battle armor covers my body. I was only shooting for wings so I could fly out of here and distract the shadow beasts, giving everyone a chance to get on level fighting ground, but I'm not sorry I have battle armor and weapons as well.

I shoot Camiel a withering look. He might have reservations about revealing himself to humans, but I don't.

I crouch, and with a mighty flap, fly into the air.

# 24

## EMBERLY

*I* shoot into the air like a bullet, soaring over the shadow beasts by at least twenty feet before dropping to the ground between them in a crouch. My plan works: I have their full attention. The mist and shadows that conceal their true form roll and undulate as they draw near.

My pulse skyrockets, which is saying something, because it's been thumping wildly since the initial explosion. I know the shadow beasts are Fallen, shrouded in a blanket of darkness, but as the creatures of my nightmares stalk closer, I find it hard to breathe.

This is the first time I've seen a shadow beast since Steel and Sable whisked me off to Seraph Academy. I've witnessed a number of horrors since then, but something about this particular incarnation of evil makes my muscles lock in fear.

Memories of the terror inflicted on me since early childhood flip through my mind on a slideshow, and so I miss the first attack. A thick tendril of smoke and shadow snaps toward me, catching me in the gut. I'm thrown back. I flare my wings, but it barely slows my body down. I slam into the marble side of a building with a bone-jarring thud.

Stars wink in my vision as I slide to the ground with a groan. I shake my head to clear it just in time, as the shadow beasts are almost on me again.

Shoving away from the building, I head straight for them, dropping low into a baseball slide at the last second. Flaring my wings, I try to find purchase on their bodies with the sharpened metal tips of my feathers, but my wings ghost through the shadows as if there's nothing there.

I grunt in frustration and pop to my feet, spinning in their direction. I know how to fight Fallen—Thorne made sure of that—but this is totally different. In this form, my enemy moves within the shadows, making it difficult to anticipate an attack or land hits. The familiar panic from years of attacks threatens to overwhelm me again.

"Emberly!" Steel yells my name as he pulls himself up and out of the crater in the middle of the street. His chest expands and falls as he pants for air. Most of the concrete dust from the blast has shaken off him, but I notice a blood stain and rip in his jeans on one knee. Dried blood from the cut on his brow is smeared across half his face, and fresh blood drips from the tips of his fingers.

My heart squeezes, lancing a spear of pain through my chest. He was the last one to start the climb, but the first one to appear. He must have clawed his way through the rubble without regard to injuries.

He spots me, and his eyes widen.

"Down!" he shouts, and for once I listen.

I hit the ground, my gold breast plate clanging and grinding against the pavement as one of the shadow beasts shoots over my head. I think I'm in the clear until a claw rakes across my back, splitting skin and muscle.

I scream in pain, more than half convinced I was just reverse-gutted. Did the monster tear one of my wings off?

I work up the courage to check, straining my neck and twisting to assess the damage. I still have both feathered appendages, but there's a deep laceration that starts on my shoulder and runs across my spine. It stops mid-back, right under where my wing is anchored and my armor starts. There's a gash on the metal that goes almost all the way to my hip. If I hadn't fully morphed into my battle armor, this injury would have been much worse. As painful as it is, I can't let it stop me.

I gather my power as I push to my feet. Blood slides down my back and drips to the ground. I go a little queasy. It's warm and sticky, like someone dumped chocolate sauce on me. I'm sickened, knowing what the sensation actually is, but when the shadow beasts headed for Steel suddenly divert their course to rush me instead, I'm glad for the injury.

The now-familiar bloodlust that keeps overtaking me starts to wake, but I stamp it down before it grows out of control. Operating on instinct alone won't bring down these monsters. I can't afford to lose my head right now.

I grow a ball of angel-fire between my palms and smile. "That's right, you creepy blood-sniffing monsters. Come to mama."

The angel-fire heats and turns white. I chuck it at one of the shadowed blobs, and the blaze engulfs it.

Bingo.

The darkness shrinks until there's nothing left and then

the fire puts itself out. I'm not exactly sure what just happened, but I'm going to take that as a good sign.

I don't have time to create another fireball, so I feint to the left when the other shadow beast nears, then coil and launch over its head at the last moment. Steel catches up with me when my feet hit the ground.

"This is how the Fallen used to appear to you? This is what you faced on your own?" he asks.

"Yep. Good times, right?"

His eyes soften. "I'm so sorry."

He opens his mouth to say something else, but I shove him to the side when the remaining shadow beast takes a swipe at him. A column of shadow and mist would have landed right on his head if I hadn't pushed him out of the way.

I appreciate Steel's empathy, but this isn't the time for a heart-to-heart.

Palming the daggers attached to the metal bracers on my thighs, I slash at the shadows, satisfied when one comes away with a layer of black ichor dripping from the blade.

Finally.

I press my advantage and step into the shadow's space, my arms arcing and jutting in a flurry of motions that are purely instinct at this point. I'm not sure how many of my attacks have found purchase, but I gain feet as the beast retreats to avoid each slash.

Suddenly, a spearhead punches through the shadows, the tip narrowly avoiding my head.

I reel back and the spear is yanked out the way it came in. The shadow dips, as if the creature concealed inside the mists has dropped to its knees. Sorcha stands on the other side of the pulsating darkness.

"I'll finish this one," she shouts. "Go help with the others."

The others?

I turn to see my friends battling no less than four more shadow beasts. Even Tinkle has joined the fray; he fights by Nova's side as a cheetah, darting around the dark entity and slashing out with his claws when he gets the chance.

Camiel is nowhere to be seen.

Disappointment is a rock in my chest, pressing painfully against my heart. I'm frustrated at myself for feeling anything at all, but when I made the decision to open myself up to people, that meant exposing myself to all sorts of heartache. I lock down that part of myself as best I can and sprint toward the nearest enemy.

Steel's battling a shadow beast on his own and with his bare hands, only really able to punch and kick to keep the Fallen at bay. There's a tear in his shirt across his chest where he's been clawed, and that makes me livid.

With daggers still in hand, I leap into the air, aiming the blades at the middle of the dark entity. They sink into something solid and hold, jolting me to a stop when I don't release my grip. The creature whips around and my body flops with it. Tired of feeling like a rag doll, I lift my feet and push against the mass of shadows. When I connect with something solid, I rear back, yanking the blades out and flipping to the ground.

Both daggers are covered in black Fallen blood, but I'm not done with this beast yet.

Dropping to the ground, I swing in a circle, flaring my wings and slashing my blades. I'm a whirling dervish of death.

The shadow beast topples to the ground, but the dark

smoke and mist doesn't dissipate. It's difficult to kill these creatures when their vital organs and head are hidden within a swirling vortex of shadows.

I'm about to summon another ball of angel-fire when Steel appears. Lifting a block of concrete above his head, he smashes it down. His hands disappear into the dark mists for a moment before he hoists the chunk up again and repeats the motion several more times until the gray piece of concrete is splattered with black blood and his chest heaves from exertion.

It's super violent . . . but I'm kinda into it.

Steel doesn't take his eyes from the shadow beast at our feet until the last bit of darkness vanishes. When it does, his gaze snaps to me and the intensity makes me flush. A battle still rages around us. This is not the time to stop and ogle him, but I can't seem to help myself. Even all dirtied up, he's just so hot.

"Are you hurt?" he demands, his head obviously not in the same gutter as mine.

"Oh, yeah. I'm fi—"

"You're bleeding." His tone is just short of accusing.

In the commotion, and my mental mini break to admire him, I'd forgotten about the wound on my back. I start to say that it's nothing when he turns me around so he can inspect it himself. I close my mouth. In truth, it's a pretty deep cut. I'm lucky I've been able to still fight.

Steel peels the hair off my back and throws it over my shoulder. Some of the saturated strands slap me in the face.

Ew.

I cringe as his fingers drift over my sticky and crusted back, bracing for when he finds the wound, but the pain never comes.

"It looks like it's already closed, but this is a lot of blood."

"What?" I strain my neck to peer over my shoulder, not convinced a gash that deep could have sealed so quickly, but all I see is blood-caked skin. "It has to still be there." I turn in a circle, trying to get a better look.

Cursing, Steel pushes me out of the way. I hit the ground hard and look up just in time to see Steel take the impact from another shadow beast.

This one moves like a freight train and slams into the side of the nearby building hard enough that chunks of brick and glass rain down from above.

Steel was in the middle of that collision.

I shove to my feet, growing a ball of angel-fire between my palms even as I rush the creature before me. I lift my arm to chuck the piping-hot orb when I'm tackled from the side. The wind knocks out of me as I'm pounded into the street.

The new shadow beast is on top of me, and I expect a claw to rip into me at any moment. I can't see anything in the vortex of darkness, but with my hands trapped between my chest and the oppressive weight on top of me, I prepare to blast this monster anyway. My fingers just start to tingle when the creature is ripped off of me and flung into a parked car, the metal and glass crumpling with the impact.

Camiel stands between me and my attacker. His six wings are splayed wide as he marches forward. He reaches into the darkened mist. Grabbing hold of the beast hiding inside, he lifts it over his head. With a roar, Camiel jerks his arms apart and tears the shadow beast in two. He lets go of the pieces and the shadows dissolve. I blink at where the creature disappeared and back at him.

Whoa.

"Did you just rip a Fallen apart with your bare hands?"

"Yes," Camiel answers distractedly, as he scans the area for more enemies. Or maybe he's checking for humans. I haven't seen any—hopefully if there are any in the area, they'll stay hidden—but it doesn't mean there aren't some watching from the buildings around us.

"That's badass."

Camiel refocuses on me. "What?"

"Just that, I'm impressed. And also, a little freaked out."

Camiel clearly doesn't know what to make of that.

Steel.

My heartbeat kicks up as I jump to my feet. I turn a quick circle to get my bearings and see him running toward me covered in an obscene amount of red and black blood. A little too much to find sexy this time, but the pressure in my chest melts away. He's okay.

I do a quick check and locate the rest of our group. Banged up, bloody, but all standing. And not a shadow beast in sight.

Movement out of the corner of my eye has me turning my head up and to the right. I get the briefest glimpse of a blond head of hair before it vanishes—Thorne. He must have phased into the spectrum world to fly away. I'm not surprised in the least that he's behind this seemingly random attack.

Without wasting time to explain, I phase into the spectrum world. Even in the middle of a downtown war scene, the area is washed in colors more vibrant then even the lushest landscape in the mortal world. I spot a few colored auras, telling me there are some humans close by, but pay them no mind. They can't see me in the spectrum world and

I'm looking for something specific—the shine of Thorne's silver wings.

I spot something to the west, in the direction of the setting sun. I flap my wings in a powerful downstroke to give chase, but my right wing isn't working correctly. I end up only getting a couple of feet of altitude before I drop.

Steel phases into the spectrum world in front of me just in time to see my spectacular flying fail.

"Whoa." He wraps his fingers around my biceps and steadies me. "What's going on?"

"Thorne. I saw him in the mortal world and followed him here." I jerk my chin toward the horizon behind him. "I thought I spotted him flying off that way. I was going to go after him, but something's wrong with my wing." I give them a test flap, and sure enough, the right one's range of motion is limited.

Steel's nostrils flare and he bares his teeth. "Where is he?" His speech is more growl than actual words, but I get what he's asking.

I scan the sky, but then shake my head. "I don't see him anymore."

In a flash, Steel is a lion. He releases an angry roar, his hackles raised along his spine. When the noise tapers, he transforms into a giant eagle and immediately takes flight. A sound of frustration bubbles up in my throat. He's going after Thorne and I can't follow.

"Where's he going?" Nova asks.

I spin to find everyone, including Camiel, behind me. I suppose at this point the spectrum world is just as safe for them as the mortal one.

"I thought I saw Thorne," I explain.

Camiel's gaze snaps in Steel's direction, then he shoots into the air after him.

A knot of unease settles into my gut, but I don't exactly know why. Is it because I'm worried they won't find Thorne, or that they will?

# 25

## EMBERLY

"Well, if that was Thorne, I wouldn't want to be him right now." Nova's lips twist into a frown. "Camiel and Steel will give him the worst beating of his life if they find him."

I'm not sure she's right about that. I think of the faded scars peppered over Thorne's face and hands, the only exposed skin he ever allowed me to see.

"Maybe I should go too," squeaks Tinkle, who is back in his flying squirrel form and perched on Nova's shoulder.

Reaching up to pat Tinkle on the head with two fingers, Nova shakes her head. "Naw."

"But I'm the fastest," Tinkle says with his fuzzy chest pushed forward.

Nova smiles. "If you left, who would be here to watch my back if another Fallen attacks? I can't lose my wingman."

Tinkle's tiny face scrunches in concentration and then he says, "Good point. I should hang back. Just in case."

I shake my head. Little dude is an awful protector, at least to me. I think Nova might be his soulmate, though.

Sable steps forward and sweeps her gaze over me from head to toe before she relaxes her shoulders. My heart warms when I realize what just happened—she checked me for injuries. I'm suddenly really glad the group brought her in.

"We should find somewhere safer to go," she says. "There may be other Fallen or Forsaken in the area. My guess is that Thorne is trying to recapture Emberly."

It guts me to think I just put so many people's lives in danger. I turn to Killian. "Are you sure I'm not being tracked?"

Killian nods once. "Positive. If you were broadcasting a signal, I would have picked up on it. I checked you over twice. You're clean."

"Then how in the world did those shadow beasts find us?"

Something drops from the sky and hits the pavement with a thud, causing a small tremor.

"It's probably because you didn't have a Celestial shading your location," Camiel says as he straightens from the crouch he landed in.

"I thought angels never revealed themselves to humans?" I say with a raised eyebrow. We're in the spectrum world now, but we weren't when he tore the shadow beast in two.

"And now I can count on one hand and one finger how many times that's happened." His face hardens. He's not the least bit happy about that.

"Where's Steel?" I ask.

One side of Camiel's mouth kicks up. "Your chosen is slow."

There's a loud caw and I look up to see Steel soaring toward us. He lands gracefully, transforming the instant his talons touch ground. His eyes narrow on Camiel as he strides to my side. "You have three times as many wings."

Camiel shrugs, all six of his golden wings bobbing with the motion. "So?"

Steel pops his jaw but doesn't rise to the challenge.

"What happened with Thorne?" I ask.

Steel releases a heavy breath and tries to run a hand through his hair, but it gets stuck and he has to yank it free. "We lost him."

"Lost him," I echo. "How?" I skate my gaze to Camiel, who appears equally frustrated by the news, before looking back at Steel.

"This is a big city," Steel says. "There are a lot of places to hide."

"But you did see him, right?"

"We saw something, but we were too far away to be sure."

It's my turn to huff. If we'd caught him, there was the potential for this all to end quickly. Instead, Thorne's free, issuing orders to his Fallen and Forsaken army, and planning who knows what.

I turn my mind toward something else before my blood starts to really boil. "You think the Fallen found me because Tinkle wasn't shielding my aura?" I ask Camiel.

"Most likely. Your power shines like a beacon without him." Camiel's gaze shifts to where Tinkle is perched on Nova's shoulder. "He'll stay with you from now on." The way he says it makes it sound like a promise and a command.

Tinkle casts a glance at Nova and then launches into the air, gliding over to me. Properly chastised, he burrows into my hair, yanking the fine strands as he hides himself. I reach back to pat him, and he snaps at my finger.

"So, if we need to get in touch with you, should Tinkle leave me or take me with him to find you?"

It's not like Camiel has a cell phone we can call him on. Oh, shoot. For that matter, neither do I anymore. Thorne probably still has it.

Camiel rolls his tongue over his bottom teeth as he considers the issue. Communicating with non-angels probably isn't something he does often. Rather than giving me a straight answer, he simply repeats himself. "Without a Celestial shading you, the Fallen will find you right away. He isn't to leave your side."

I shrug. "I guess we just hope it doesn't come to that then."

He opens his mouth to say more, then closes it. A moment later, a white film slides over his golden gaze.

"What's happening right now?" Nova asks.

"He's talking to an angel."

"Seriously?" Her eyes widen. "That is wicked cool. I want that ability."

I nod back at her. "Samesies. Apparently, it's just an angel thing though."

"Tragic," she says with a head shake.

"We need to talk about these orbs," Sable cuts in, reclaiming the conversation while Camiel is distracted with this one-on-one. Ciara and Killian nod their agreement. "We need to get them secured before they can be used again. I don't even want to think of the ways the world will be reshaped if the barrier between realms is ever dropped completely."

Hell on Earth. That's what it would be like. Even the thought of it makes me shudder.

"The less people that know about the orbs' true power, and their new location, the better," Sorcha adds. "You should be the ones to return them." She looks at all of us in turn. "Perhaps gather the others who already know and split into two teams. I'll handle explaining their disappearance to the Council."

I grimace. That does not sound like a fun time.

"Come," Camiel says, his sudden reentry into the conversation jarring. "We need to find a secure location to plan."

"So, no one will know the location of both orbs. Only the teams who hide them will know where they're placed?" Killian asks.

All twelve of us—not counting Sorcha, who already left to return to the Elders' compound—are congregated in a studio apartment in the West End, another safe house. We're packed in like sardines. Thank goodness for high ceilings or we would never fit—Camiel especially with his enormous body.

Camiel nods. "The less people who know the orbs' location, the better. On their own, the orbs are relatively benign. It's when they're together that the issues arise."

I snort, and heads all around the room snap in my direction. Whoops. I lean back into Steel, not liking the attention. I hold my hands up in front of me. "Sorry, it's just that a good amount of trouble was caused by them separately. I wouldn't exactly refer to them as benign."

"Relative to the amount of trouble they can cause together, they are."

I tip my head toward Camiel in agreement. He has a point.

"We need to split into groups," Sable says. "My suggestion is to designate a team lead to know the precise spot where the orb should be placed. They can tell the rest of the team the general location. Let's mitigate the possibility of being in this situation again."

Sable's proposal of only having two people know the exact location of the orbs makes sense, but I don't like it. I don't know why. I start to get that itchy feeling I had in the bunker and can't stop myself from speaking up.

"Is that really the best idea? What if something happens to the team lead? The others in the group won't know where to take the orb." There was a bit of reason to that argument, so it didn't raise too many eyebrows.

"Yo, Em, you're savage," Sterling says from his spot against the wall to my left. "Haven't you ever heard of, 'no man left behind'?"

I duck my head and seal my lips. Words want to pop out of my mouth, but I'm determined to keep them in this time.

There's an awkward pause that settles over the group, but I refuse to break it.

Finally, Sable claps her hands together. "Let's get everyone split up. Greyson, Sterling, and Nova, you're with Killian and Ciara. Steel, Ash, Shira, and Emberly, you're with me."

Sterling raises his hand. "I think I should switch with Ash."

Sable shoots him a "what are you up to" look.

"The guy and girl ratio will be more even then."

More than one person rolls their eyes.

"Do I get a vote?" Tinkle asks, speaking up for the first time since Camiel ordered him to stay with me. "Because if so, I think Steel and Nova should swap."

Sable shakes her head and turns to speak with Camiel and the other adults.

Dropping my head into my hands, I scrub my face as the conversation digresses from there.

Steel stops me from rubbing off my eyebrows, tugging me as far away from the group as the room will allow.

"What was that before?" he asks. His tone skews toward concerned rather than accusatory, but I still prickle at the question.

"It just seemed like a better idea for more people to be informed." I can't meet his gaze.

"Hey, look at me."

I don't want to, but I do, and our gazes lock. Reaching forward, Steel places both hands on either side of my neck and gently massages the tense muscles.

Oh. That feels nice.

I can't help but go a little gooey at his touch. My tongue darts out to swipe along my bottom lip and Steel tracks the movement. His pupils dilate and then return to normal. Leaning forward, he crowds me, and I don't mind one bit. The air between us warms, and I wish we weren't sharing the same space with so many others, including my angelic father.

"Not again," someone groans.

Steel and I turn our heads at the same time to see Shira and Sterling standing a few feet away. With their heads cocked, they study Steel and me as if we're a museum display.

"I already told you they're going to be awful because they're soul-bonded," Shira says.

Oh. No.

Sterling cocks his head at Shira. "You mentioned that phrase before. Soul-bonded. What does it mean?"

Shira's gaze swings to Steel and me. I shake my head, hoping she'll catch on that I don't want this to become a thing.

She grins. "They don't know?"

I narrow my eyes at my angel-born relative. "It's personal."

With a chuckle, she turns and walks away.

"Is this what it's like having a sibling?" I ask Steel.

"Only the tip of the iceberg," he answers with a smile.

Sterling glances at Shira's retreating form, then back at Steel and me. "What am I missing here?"

Steel looks to me with raised eyebrows and then shrugs as if to say, "it's up to you."

Even if I wanted to get into it, now isn't the time. Maybe after we've defeated Thorne and his army. Or maybe never. Yeah, never is good too.

I give my head a minute shake, and Steel takes it from there.

"Looks like Shira and Greyson are getting along well." Steel tips his chin toward the pair on the other side of the room who are no doubt engaged in a very innocent conversation. "Do you think she's into him?"

It takes effort to keep from laughing when Sterling's mouth puckers and his gaze jumps to them. It's evident to anyone with eyes that Sterling is crushing on my distant relative. He stalks off, marching a straight line toward his brother and the brown-eyed Neph. I wonder if Shira's informed him of her sub-par opinion of cherub angel-born yet? If anything, that may pique his interest even more.

"Don't you think you're a little old to still be messing with your brothers like that?" I ask Steel.

He chuckles. "Never."

Even as I smile back at Steel, my mind begins to wander. So much has happened in the last few days, I don't even know how to start processing everything. Eden, finding out I have a hidden branch of relatives—one of whom is an actual angel—the revelations about Steel and me, killing Stavros without the memory of doing so, my blackout and sleepwalking episodes, Thorne's plans for world domination and destruction...

I rub my forehead. The list is even longer, but those are the highlights.

"Hey, you all right?" Steel asks. The longer we're together, the more in-tune he is with my moods. I can't say that I mind. It's comforting to know he's looking out for me.

"Yeah, I'll deal," I tell him truthfully. "It's just ... a lot has happened in a short amount of time. I wish I could hit 'pause' and take a moment to breathe and get my bearings."

His brows drop low. His mouth twists to the side as he searches my face. "I get that. I'd really like to get to the bottom of these blackouts of yours. Sorcha didn't get a chance to look you over, even though that's why she came. There's got to be something going on there."

I nod. "I agree. There are some moments that I just don't feel like myself. Like something's tweaking with my emotions and responses. I know that doesn't make sense, but..."

I let my words peter out, unsure of what I'm really

saying. Part of me wants to wave these incidents off as stress or a side effect of using my powers more fully, but to not take this seriously would be foolish. On the other hand, London was razed and there's a threat that the world as we know it could change forever—and not for the better—if Thorne succeeds in bringing down the veil. So how valid is it to ask everyone to stop what they're doing and pay attention to my mood swings?

"Hey." Steel resumes his gentle kneading at the sides of my neck. He waits until I meet his gaze before going on. "I don't know what's going on, but we'll get to the bottom of it, together. I promise."

I nod, forcing a weak smile, but I can't help but wonder if Steel is making a promise there's no way he'll be able to keep.

# 26

## EMBERLY

*W*hen Camiel finishes his conversation with Killian and Ciara, he turns and heads my way. His gilded wings shift with every step, and Greyson and Ash have to jump out of the way so they don't get clipped. The powerful seraph angel doesn't even seem to notice—or maybe it's just that he doesn't care.

"I have to leave," he says when he reaches me. He delivers the news coldly, and I wonder if he's annoyed that he feels like he has to update me. "I have to return to my army. The attack today makes me wary there's another tear in the veil we missed."

"Okay," I answer with a nod, expecting Camiel to leave immediately. Instead, he remains planted in front of me, frustration hardening the lines of his face. "I mean, I get it. You have an army to command or whatever it is you actually do." I don't mean to say more, but the silence is getting awkward. "So . . . I will see you later . . . sometime . . . or whatever?"

Oh gosh. Someone please slap a piece of duct tape over my mouth.

"If I had a choice, or rather, if there wasn't—" Camiel releases a grunt. He can't get a complete thought out without cutting himself off. Is the mighty angel . . . tongue-tied?

I press my lips tightly together to keep words from slipping out, determined to wait him out.

A lungful of air leaves his chest with a rush right before he speaks. "There will be time for us. Stasha—" Camiel clears his throat. The powerful cords and tendons in his neck restrict with the mere mention of my mother's name. "She would have wanted things to be right between us. I'm determined to make it so."

He places one of his hands on my shoulder. His angel-paw is so big it reaches from the base of my neck to my bicep. He squeezes lightly, and I take that as his gesture of comfort. I'm not generally a hugger—in fact, up until I entered Seraph Academy, I hadn't ever truly been embraced, but the urge is strong enough that I decide to go with it.

Stepping into Camiel's space, I wrap my arms around his stomach, overlapping my hands behind him, and rest my head on his metal-plated chest.

I tell myself it's all right that he isn't hugging me back—it's probably not an angel thing anyway. But it's something small that I can give him to let him know I'm open to seeing what the future holds for us.

I twitch when his arms drop on my back, and he squeezes me to him. He's a bit rusty at this for sure, and there's a second or two when I can't breathe because his grip is too tight, but then he seems to get the hang of it.

It turns awkward again when it's obvious that neither of

us know how to end a hug. I pat his lower back with both hands and clear my throat. He gets the hint and drops his arms.

I step back with my eyes cast on his gold-encased feet.

"Thank you, for that," Camiel says. There's a gentle cadence to his voice I've not heard before. I lift my gaze and he gives me the briefest of smiles. "That was . . . nice." He furrows his brow. "Although, I don't think I did it correctly."

The fact that we are both horrendously bad at such a small gesture makes me smile. "I'm no expert myself. Maybe we can work on it together?"

I brace for rejection. I can't help it. It's just in my nature. It isn't until Camiel says "I'd like that" that my muscles relax and the tension leaks from my shoulders. The knowledge that he cares warms my heart. I'm basically one big toasty marshmallow of feelings at this point.

"I'll see you soon," he says. This time when I nod, Camiel disappears into the spectrum world immediately. With his large body no longer blocking the rest of the room, I notice how quiet it's become. Everyone is staring at me, which makes me want to fold into myself.

Sable claps her hands together and starts to issue orders. The room comes alive again as plans take shape for the next day. Killian and Ciara pull their group together and I see Greyson making a list of supplies. Sable calls Shira over. Sterling is so busy frowning in their direction that he doesn't hear Killian calling his name.

"You good?" Steel asks, stepping close.

I tip my face up, a smile lifting the corners of my mouth. "Yeah. I am."

Somehow, Sterling convinces Ash to switch groups with him, and I can't say I'm all that surprised. I shake my head as he grins at Shira, who is either too naive to notice his interest, or doing an excellent job ignoring his advances. I don't know her well enough to figure out which one it is.

The groups will part ways in the next few minutes, and I saved my goodbye with Ash for last.

"You take care of her," Ash says to Steel.

I'd like to think I take care of myself, but my heart warms at her concern. Especially when Ash pulls back from her hug with Steel to shoot me a wink, telling me she knows I can handle myself.

Steel meanders over to Greyson and Nova to say goodbye and give Ash and me some privacy. I join hands with my bestie, and we stare at each other for an elongated moment. There's a soft smile on Ash's face, but the wetness in her eyes betrays her emotions. When my vision blurs from my own gathering tears, I know my poker face isn't in place either.

I hate saying goodbye to her again. There's a piece of my heart that will always belong to Ash. My soul feels stretched when we're apart.

"Are you sure you want to switch spots with Sterling?" I think his crush is cute, but I'd rather have my best friend with me on this journey than pander to his whims.

She chuckles lightly. "You say that as if saying no to Sterling is ever an option."

"He is rather persuasive."

"And to think Aurora and Blaze have learned all his tricks." Ash widens her eyes comically. "Those two are going to be an unstoppable force someday."

"Let's just hope they use their powers for good."

Our laughter brings levity to the situation. We hug and when we pull away, Ash's gaze strays to the corner, where Steel talks with Greyson. I'd classify the look on her face as wistful.

The plot thickens.

"Interesting." I struggle to hold back a smile.

Ash looks back to me. "What?"

I lift my brows and shoot Greyson an exaggerated stare. Maybe I should have seen this coming, but I totally didn't.

Ash's eyes bug out and she shakes her head. Her dark curls bounce back and forth. "Oh no. No, no, no. You do *not* have the right idea about that."

My grin only grows. "I approve. He's definitely the most levelheaded of all the Durands."

Ash busts out laughing, and I catch Greyson and Steel turn their heads to look at us. Oh shoot. Nephilim have super-sensitive hearing.

Leaning into Ash I whisper, "Do you think they heard us?"

Her face reddens. "Let's hope not because as embarrassing as that would be for me, I think you'll actually get more flak from Steel if he heard you say that."

She has a point, but despite all the craziness around us, a conversation about cute boys is just so normal, I can't stop grinning like an idiot.

"It's really not what you're thinking, though. I just worry about him sometimes because it doesn't seem like anyone else ever does." The sincerity of her words shines in her eyes as well. And gosh, she has a point.

Greyson may be a fun-loving trickster like his twin half the time, but he's also always the one who seems to have to bail his siblings out of trouble. He never complains about it, but Ash is right—Greyson probably does get overlooked next to the issues whirling around the rest of his family members. He needs someone looking out for him, too.

"What are we talking about?" Greyson asks as he slides in next to Ash.

"Nothing. Nothing at all," she answers quickly.

"Smooth," I cough into my hand as Greyson frowns.

"It really is nothing," Ash assures him.

"It's time to head out," Killian says loud enough for his voice to carry over the chatter. "Blue team with me. Red team with Sable."

With one final, wobbly smile, Ash nods at me and then heads over to join Nova and her parents.

"I've got her back," Greyson assures me.

"You promise?" I ask, looking up into Greyson's blue-green eyes.

His gaze shifts toward Ash and hardens with determination before it swivels back to me. "On my life."

That's the best I can ask for.

With a quick hug and a brotherly kiss on the forehead, Greyson turns and follows in Ash's wake. As I watch Ciara grab one of the orb boxes as the group heads toward the door, sludge starts to roll in my gut. In a few minutes, the only link I'll have with the other orb is a single phone connection.

We were all forced to ditch our cells. Some of us—Sterling and Nova—took it harder than others. The only people who still have a way to communicate are Sable and Killian. They both have an untraceable phone that's only to be used to contact the other group in case of an emergency. And not even a "someone is dead or dying" emergency. Nothing short of "the barrier between the worlds has evaporated" or "the planet is about to explode" warrants use of the devices.

An itchy sensation burns behind my sternum as I force myself to remain planted in place while the other group files out, taking the orb with them.

What is wrong with me? I hate the orbs. I should be happy to see it go. Good riddance magic-orb-of-death that can cause the destruction of the world as we know it. Hope to see you never. But instead of relief, I find myself breathing through the impulse to grab it and run. I'm a half-step away from going full Gollum on the orbs and rocking in a corner with them while chanting "My precious." This is ridiculous.

"What's wrong?" Steel asks.

"You've been asking that a lot lately," I say, forcing false flippancy into my tone.

"I'm well aware," Steel says without cracking a smile. I let the brittle expression drop off my face. It feels fake, and that's not something I want to do with Steel.

"Truth is, I have a bad feeling about separating the orbs, but I don't know why. I've been getting panicky with just the thought of letting one out of my sight." I lift a hand in between us to reveal the fine tremor that's preventing me from holding it steady. "I hate the orbs, both of them. But I feel . . ." I stop to really search my emotions. "I feel *desperate* to keep them in my sight."

Steel reaches up and sandwiches my hand between his palms. His touch grounds me and the jitters I'm feeling start to subside. He runs his tongue over his bottom lip while he thinks.

"Okay," he finally says. "I trust your instincts. I think I have an idea that will help."

With my hand still captured between his, he tugs me over to Sable.

"You two ready?" she asks when we stand in front of her.

"Almost," Steel says. "But I'm going to need that phone."

Sable cocks her head. "For what reason?"

Steel glances at me before returning his gaze to Sable. "Emberly has a bad feeling about the orbs being separated. I think she should have control over the phone."

Sable's gaze tracks over to me. "Is that so?"

I nod.

"Hmm." Sable's mouth twists to the side. I shift my weight from foot to foot. I won't blame her if she says no. It's an odd request and the reasoning doesn't quite add up.

"Here you go," Sable finally says, and slaps the rectangle device in my hand. "Guard it with your life and let me know immediately if the other group calls."

I blink down at the phone. That was so easy, I'm almost confused at what just went down, but I can't deny that my anxiety is already starting to wane.

"Better?" Steel asks, and I nod.

"Thank you," I tell Sable.

"I trust you," she says with a smile. "Now let's grab what we need and get going. I want to get out of the city and bunked up for the night. We have a busy few days ahead of us."

I clear my throat, having to push past the ball of emotion suddenly clogging my airway. "I'm good to go."

*I trust you,* she said. It's such a simple phrase but means so much. It should make me happy to have Sable, and the rest of my friends' trust, but for some reason, it fills me with dread instead.

# 27

## EMBERLY

*W*e only make it twelve blocks before we come across the first gang of Forsaken. Spotting them, Sable holds a fist in the air. We duck behind whatever cover we can find while she investigates.

So far, we've relied on the shadows to conceal us as we travel on foot through downtown London. Public transportation is completely non-existent at this point, and vehicles are loud and draw unwanted attention. We're working under the assumption that Thorne knows we still have both orbs and will try to reclaim them. Our objective is to stay away from any Fallen or Forsaken, and get this orb hidden so it can't be used.

Tinkle has gone invisible and scouts the streets ahead of us. He releases a small burst of sparks at every corner to let us know the coast is clear.

Steel and I crouch behind an abandoned taxicab. The large, round-roofed vehicle covers us completely. Shira and Sterling hide behind a dumpster to our left. I peek through the windows, but I don't see Sable anywhere. I drop back down and shake my head to let Steel know I didn't see her.

"We wait," he whispers.

It's a full ten minutes before I hear the faintest brush of feet against pavement. Sable rounds the front of the car then squats next to Steel and me.

"There are six," she whispers. "We could easily take this alley and circumvent them, but . . ." She presses her lips into a line and releases a breath through her nose before going on, "They're harassing two humans."

Shoot. The plan was to avoid contact with the enemy, but if we turn around and leave those humans, they're as good as dead.

"I can handle six alone," I say. It's getting easier to bring forth angel-fire in the mortal world.

The planes of Steel's face harden and his nostrils flare, but he doesn't contradict me, even though I know he wants to.

It's Sable who shakes her head. "If even one of the Forsaken flees before you can eliminate them, they'll run right to Thorne and tell him where we are. We're close enough to the city's perimeter that Thorne will know we're headed out of London. The more we can keep Thorne in the dark, the better. You're the last one we want them to see. The likelihood that they'll recognize any of the rest of us is pretty low."

I rub a hand against my forehead. She has a point. The other angel-born are skilled at fighting and I have no doubt they could take the Forsaken, but against six, the possibility of injury is high.

"We can't not help them," I say.

Sable huffs out a breath, then peers over the hood of the

car. The group of Forsaken aren't visible from our vantage point, but the frightened humans' shouts chafe my eardrums.

"Steel, give the backpack to Emberly. I don't want that orb anywhere near those Forsaken."

Steel shrugs the black bag off his back and hands it to me. After I slip it on, he helps me tighten the straps while Sable goes to update Shira and Sterling.

"Be careful," I tell him.

"Aren't I always?"

"I seem to remember having to save you from being skinned by Forsaken the first time I ever ran into one."

"That was after I saved you from them, right?"

"Yes, and then got knocked clean out."

"Is that what happened?" he asks, rubbing a hand over his chin. The beginning of a grin teases his mouth. "I don't exactly remember the details anymore, but I'm sure I was much more heroic than you're making me sound."

When the others creep out into the open, Sable gestures for Steel to follow. Planting a quick kiss on the crown of my head, he takes off after them.

I do my best to settle my heart and let my friends take care of this group of Forsaken on their own, but it's hard.

Metal crunches and glass shatters. A scream echoes off the buildings around me, and I'm on my feet and running before I realize what I'm doing.

Sterling shouts up ahead. The sound is followed by a Forsaken shriek that reminds me why I'm not in the fight to begin with. I put on the brakes and duck behind another car.

I thump my head against the door as I clench my fists, beyond frustrated I can't jump in and help. One frustration leads to another, and I'm suddenly furious at the angels for staying hidden in the spectrum world. Nothing about that makes sense. This system is messed up and broken. I can almost understand the rationale to keep the spectrum world and all its creatures hidden from humanity so that people can live normal lives, but the cat is so totally out of the bag now. Shadow blobs attacked London a few days ago for the entire world to see. What is the point of angels still remaining hidden?

If it were up to me, there'd be an angel standing guard on every street in London right now.

There's a crash, and I hold my breath. My insides go itchy when silence blankets the night.

Turning, I slowly rise to peek over the hood of the car just as Sterling and Shira walk around the corner. Sterling brushes his hands off, his hair wet with Forsaken blood. There's a huge smile on his face. Shira looks equally invigorated.

I breathe a sigh of relief and then jog over to them.

"Did you see the look on the mohawk guy's face right before I dropped the dumpster on his head?" Sterling slaps his hands together to simulate the smashing sound it must have made.

"No, because I was busy pummeling a Forsaken into the brick wall. You know, my grandfather always talks about how vicious Forsaken are, but all and all, I'm not overly impressed."

I open my mouth to ask about Steel and Sable when they appear as well. Sable helps support a light-haired human male who favors his left leg. One side of his torn shirt and neck are covered with blood. He holds a piece of cloth to his throat.

"Please tell me I'm not going to turn into a vampire."

I'd laugh, but the look on his face says that he's one hundred percent serious. And in a way, I don't blame him. If one of the Forsaken just nom-nommed on his neck, and considering the recent events, vampires don't seem like that far of a stretch. I remember thinking something similar the first time I laid eyes on the Forsaken who broke into Seraph Academy.

"No, you're going to be just fine," Sable assures him.

Steel cradles an unconscious girl in his arms. He tries to keep her head propped up on his shoulder as he walks, but it keeps lulling over his arm. A trail of sparks follows in his wake.

"Thanks for the help," Steel says as he strides by Sterling and Shira.

"What?" Sterling asks. "We did help. I killed at least one and a half Forsaken."

Ignoring everyone else, I rush over to Steel. "Is she hurt?"

A light weight lands on my shoulder and I glance over to see Tinkle in his flying squirrel form. "I think she might be dead," he says.

Steel shoots Tinkle a look and then shakes his head. "She's fine. At least physically. She passed out when Sterling squished one of the Forsaken's heads under a dumpster."

I wince. "I can understand how that would be the last straw."

Steel hefts the girl back up and her head knocks against his shoulder before slipping back over his arm. Getting closer, I brush a clump of red hair off her face. She looks young. Older than me, but still in her twenties for sure. I'm sad for what has happened to her tonight, but she's lucky to be leaving with her life.

"There's a hospital a couple blocks back," Sable says, still supporting the majority of the guy's weight. Dude looks super out of it. "We're going to have to go drop them off. Sterling," she shouts, "get over here and take over for me."

Something explodes in the distance. We can only see a flash in the sky, but the ground beneath our feet shakes and it seriously spooks the guy Sable is trying to hand off to Sterling. Falling to the ground, he curls into a ball and starts sobbing.

This is going to be a long night.

It takes us the rest of the night and a good part of the morning to get to the safe house outside of London. Even though we are miles and miles from the city center, smoke still taints the air. By the time we arrive at the suburban row house, I've been up for almost fifty-six hours. I'm dead on my feet. As I ascend the stairs to the front door, Steel lays an anchoring hand on my lower back to keep me from swaying too wildly.

Technically, the rest of the group should be more tired than I am. They traveled from London to Egypt to steal the orbs from the Elders' compound, then back again while I was passed out in Thorne's stolen manor house in the countryside. I wouldn't be surprised if Steel hadn't had more than a handful of hours of sleep here and there since I fled Eden. But even so, no one seems to have sunk to my level of exhaustion.

"I want everyone resting," Sable says once we've all shuffled through the front door. "One of us will stay up and we'll rotate every hour. If you're not up guarding, I want you asleep. This is the last guaranteed sleep we're going to get for a while."

The plan is to rest up for part of the day and then set off again mid-afternoon. Considering the Forsakens' limitations in the sunlight, it would be best if we could travel during daylight hours, but we've all been go-go-go for days.

"Where are we headed next?" Shira asks.

"South," is all Sable will say. "I have first shift. Everyone else, find a place to bunk down."

"I call the master bedroom for Shira and me," Sterling says.

Shira blinks at Sterling, then makes a big show of walking into the living room and laying out on the only couch large enough for sleeping.

"That's cold," Sterling says with a frown.

Shira snorts and then turns her back on us, wiggling into the cushions to find a comfortable position.

I spy a door down the hall and make a beeline for it, praying it's a first-floor bedroom and not a half bath or closet. I don't care if there's only a toddler bed in there, if there's enough room to lie down, even if I have to do it on the ground, that's where I'll be for the next few hours. I'm not climbing any more stairs. When I push through the door, I breathe a sigh of relief to see a sparsely furnished guest bedroom with a full bed up against the far wall.

My mind chants, *bed, bed, bed* with every step I take until I'm faceplanted into a slightly funky-smelling pillow. Don't care about the odor, I'm already half asleep.

The bed dips and sways and I don't bother checking to

see who just climbed in here with me. It could be Sterling and I'd be cool with that right now.

"I don't think it's a good idea for you two—" Sable's words drift off.

A dark chuckle comes from beside me and, despite my exhaustion, a delicious chill skates down my spine. That's definitely Steel.

"You don't have anything to worry about. She's dead to the world."

He's not wrong. I garble out something completely incoherent without cracking an eyelid.

"Just make sure you both get some sleep. No . . . distractions."

To that, Steel just chuckles again, and the door clicks shut. I wonder if Sable realizes he never agreed to her terms. But considering I can't even summon the energy to flip over or take my shoes off, there's not much for her to be concerned about.

Nails click against the hardwood floors and Steel says, "Don't even think about jumping up on this bed. There's a perfectly good sofa chair against the wall."

Tinkle says, "Rude," after releasing an animalistic huff. There's rustling on the other side of the room that I assume he's settling into the spare chair. I'm glad he didn't try to squeeze on the bed, but not even Tinkle's dog breath could keep me from sleep at this point.

The mattress shifts again, and I think Steel must be settling in, but the next thing I know, he's tugging one of my shoes off. I try to tell him I can do that, but my face is still buried in the pillow and I can't seem to summon the energy to turn my head.

After he's removed both my shoes, his arms slide under

my body and he gently turns and lifts me into the air. Using some sort of magic, he manages to pull back the comforter before placing me back down.

I peel my eyelids open to slits and mumble my thanks. I drift away with the feel of Steel's mouth against my skin as he places kisses on each cheek and my forehead before finally brushing his lips against my own.

# 28

## EMBERLY

*I*'m jarred to the surface, suddenly fully aware. The lingering scent of mildew from the pillow beneath my head tickles my nose. I lay on my side with my hands folded in front of me. My slow, rhythmic breaths tickle the back of one of my hands. Steel's body warms my back and causes my body to sway ever so slightly with each of his deep exhales. Muffled voices sound from down the hall and then quiet again.

I'm awake, but also not. No matter how hard I try, I can't so much as crack an eyelid or wiggle a finger.

Am I experiencing some sort of sleep paralysis?

A husky chuckle vibrates in my head and a bolt of adrenaline shoots from my chest out toward my fingers and toes. My internal alarms blare but I can't even get a muscle to twitch. Even my breathing remains modulated and even.

*I was wondering when you would finally regain awareness. It will be so much more satisfying for me this way*, a female voice purrs inside my head.

What the what?

*I could have left an hour ago, but I was hoping this would happen. After hiding in your psyche for all this time, it would be anti-climactic if you just faded away.*

That voice. Seraphim.

*You're . . . you're dead. Gone. You can't be here.*

**Oh child,** her voice is laced with amusement. *What you know could only fill a teaspoon in an ocean of knowledge.* It feels like each word burrows through bone, scratching against my skull before fading. *I didn't die. I've simply been lying in wait. And what a fruitful endeavor that turned out to be.*

I don't know what she means. I don't *want* to know what she means. What I want, is to wake up from this horrible nightmare.

**Let me show you what I can do.**

My body stirs and starts to slide out of the bed. My sock-covered feet touch the ground. My weight shifts to the balls of my feet as my body rises—but I am not doing any of it.

My muscles contract and release as I glide to the end of the bed and look upon Steel's sleeping form. He has an arm thrown over his face to block the early afternoon sunlight that shines through the window. I'm so intent on watching him that I don't notice Seraphim has commanded my hand to grab the dagger sheathed at my thigh until the weapon is heavy in my palm.

A slow smile stretches over my face and dread punches a hole through my chest.

*If you hurt him, so help me—*

**You'll what?** Seraphim taunts. **Kill me? Good luck with that.**

The only way I can think to kill her, would be to kill myself.

*You think I won't sacrifice myself to protect him?* I will. Without a moment's hesitation.

**What I think is that you'd try to find a more creative solution before it came to that. You're nothing if not a survivor. But apparently, I still haven't made my point. Even if you wanted to harm yourself, you couldn't. You no longer have control of this body.**

With that, I walk forward, creeping up on Steel. My arm raises and the blade in my hand comes to rest a hair's breadth from Steel's jugular.

*No! Stop. Please, don't do this.* I'm begging, but I don't care. Inside my mind I'm kicking and screaming and fighting like a hellcat, but it doesn't make a difference. I can't control a single movement. Seraphim could end Steel with a flick of my wrist and there is literally nothing I can do but watch.

The blade is removed from Steel's throat, and a rush of relief floods me. Mumbling something incoherent, he shifts in his sleep. My heart weeps. He's right there, and I can't reach him.

**Lucky for him, killing him would be noisy and messy.** My head tilts as Seraphim looks her fill. **He's also very pretty. He'll make an exquisite vessel, but he's not the prize I have my eye on today.**

Utterly in control of my motions, Seraphim turns my body and heads straight toward the black backpack in the corner of the room. As a Great Dane, Tinkle snores softly from his perch on a muted orange armchair.

*Wake up!* I silently beg, but Tinkle is known as a deep sleeper and not likely to be roused.

Bending over, my hands reach for the bag and soundlessly swing it over my shoulder. It thumps lightly against my back.

With motions far more fluid than I've ever possessed, Seraphim pulls on my shoes and heads toward the exit. I want so desperately to take one final glance at Steel, but I can't force my head to turn.

The door clicks shut behind me, and I want to sob but can't so much as make a peep. I'm halfway down the hall when Shira calls to me. Seraphim glances back, hiding a smirk against my shoulder. My hand lifts and for a moment I fear Seraphim is going for the dagger again.

*Seraphim! You leave her alone!* I scream.

I try to gather my power. Maybe a rogue flame or spark will tip Shira off that something isn't right? I can feel the energy running on currents throughout my torso and limbs, but it won't obey my commands.

Rather than reaching for a weapon, Seraphim waves my hand and gestures for Shira to follow. Shira's eyebrows bunch together, but she starts forward.

Once out the back door of the house, my legs start pumping as Seraphim forces me to run down the alley.

*Where are you taking me?*

"Emberly, wait. Where are you going?" Shira calls, but Seraphim just picks up the speed. Shira's feet slap against the asphalt behind us as she gives chase.

"That's right, little bunny. Hop right into my trap."

There's nothing stranger than feeling words bubble up my throat and fall from my lips when I'm not the one who put them there.

A wave of satisfaction overtakes me, momentarily eclipsing my own frantic emotions. When the surge passes, I'm left alone with a magnified sense of panic and fear from knowing that even my innermost sentiments can be over-shadowed by Seraphim's will.

I go wild. Unleashing a bevy of insults and shouting in my own mind as if I were a banshee releasing a cursed scream. I imagine myself bouncing around the confines of my own head. I hold out hope that I might be able to scramble Seraphim for even a moment and then snatch back control. A few seconds is all I need. That would be enough time to warn Shira.

*That's enough noise.* Seraphim mentally swats at me like I'm an annoying mosquito. *The novelty of your presence has worn off. Time for you to go away.*

I can't even enjoy the twinge of annoyance in Seraphim's voice because the moment she issues her command, I am helpless to do anything other than fade away.

# 29

## EMBERLY

*M*y eyelids feel like sandpaper as I slowly blink. Keeping them open for more than half a second is impossible. No matter how forcefully I order them to remain open, they keep shuttering closed. It takes a dozen tries to keep them opened to only half-mast. Even then my vision is blurred, and I have to reach out to my other senses to figure out what's going on.

I'm sitting in a chair. Wait, no, I'm *tied* to a chair. My hands are immobile on the armrests. The restraints bite into my wrists when I try to lift them. A rope is wrapped tightly around my stomach and another is secured over my chest and around my shoulders. The coarse fibers of the binding poke through my shirt, making my skin itch.

My head is filled with lead and weighs a million pounds. It takes me three tries to lift it, and when I do the fuzzy outline of Thorne's white-blond head hovers above me. Giving my head a shake, I blink rapidly, and my vision begins to sharpen.

Thorne's midnight-blue gaze searches my own. "Ah. There you are."

I groan.

"Did you drug me?" My words and body are slow. Drugs seem like the obvious culprit.

"No. It's just taking your body a little extra time to reorient itself to your commands."

Say what?

"You haven't been yourself," he says by way of explanation.

I think he means that figuratively, until I remember the strange dream I had of the voice inside my head. My breath catches when reality comes crashing down on me. "Seraphim." A knot lodges in my throat, and I have to swallow around it. "That was . . . real?"

Thorne's face is almost emotionless. Almost. There's a shimmer of something that looks a lot like anger buried in his gaze that betrays the apathy he's clearly trying to portray. "You didn't destroy her in the merge. You've carried her with you since you left The White Kingdom."

I don't want to believe him, but I know it's true. It explains too much. The blackouts. The mood swings. My propensity for violence. She's the foreign entity slithering deep inside. I did my best to write it off, but I can't anymore.

The implications of what Seraphim's possession really means crash down on me like a thousand-pound weight. Tremors wrack my body, and I go into a state of semi-shock.

I'm the one who walked Seraphim into the Elders' compound and handed her the means to further her plans. I'm the reason the shadow beasts were unleashed into the mortal realm. I'm the wolf in sheep's clothing. It's what Silver tried to tell me at the manor house that I didn't want to hear. Knowingly or not, my hand was the one that struck the match, and unless I figure this out, it will be my hand that sets the world on fire.

"It was her. She's the one who combined the orbs and caused the holes to appear between worlds. And she used me to do it."

Thorne tips his chin in acknowledgement. "The perfect sleeper-spy."

My body stops shaking as fiery conviction erupts. I'm not going to let her win.

"I'll fight her."

I'll erect mental barriers so high she'll never be able to reappear. Never mind that I don't really know how to do that. I'll figure it out.

"You won't be able to," Thorne says. He leans back against an intricate wood desk and crosses his arms. "She's too strong and has too large of a foothold for you to beat her back."

I shake my head, refusing to believe him. "That can't be true. I'm sitting in front of you now, fully in control. I just have to keep her out."

Indefinitely.

"You can't. Not without that." Thorne nods toward my hand. I look down and see an unfamiliar bracelet bracketing my wrist, an inch-wide strip of gold bent into a "C" shape. Its design is chunky and crude, as if it was hastily put together and without thought, but the white gem embedded in the top is familiar. It's the same shade and texture as the gemstone that adorned the bracelet Thorne gave me to lessen the effect of my aura on the Fallen. He said it would protect me from them. I took that piece of jewelry off the night before the attacks on London and New York.

I look at Thorne, whose hooded gaze gives nothing away. "You sent Silver to the Elders' compound to convince me to take off the bracelet."

It's not a question. I know he did. Silver's surprise change of heart now makes sense. She didn't come to us only to be restored to a Nephilim. If she had, she wouldn't have run straight back to Thorne.

"Did I?" he asks with a tilt of his head. "If you'll remember, I was very specific about you not removing that bracelet, ever. It was your choice to take it off."

"So, you didn't want your psycho mother to take control of my body and destroy the veil between worlds?" My tone is mocking. He's never going to convince me that wasn't his plan all along.

"I'm simply reminding you of the facts. I imagine things would be different now if you'd only trusted me enough to heed my warning."

"You're kidding, right? You were ready to let your mother take my body and consume my soul—or whatever crazy unnatural thing happens during the merge—and you expected me to trust you after that? Are you delusional?"

"I didn't say that I expected you to trust me, only that things would be different now if you had."

I don't understand him. I probably never will. But one thing I do know is that this conversation is going nowhere.

"You had both orbs. Why wait to use them?" I ask.

He rubs his bottom lip, seemingly considering how much to tell me. "There was one very specific ingredient we never had. One we've been tracking for years."

He gives me a pointed look, and the blood drains from my face. Me. They needed *me* to bring down the veil.

"Without the blood of an angel-line Nephilim, the orbs' full power can't be activated. Once we had you, we were missing an orb. It was quite the conundrum. Fortunately, Seraphim has been planning her revenge for thousands of years and her contingency plans have contingency plans. When it was obvious you weren't going to help us of your own volition, we found a loophole."

It's hard not to feel stupid for playing right into their plans. Especially because I knew something was off after what I assumed was a failed merge. The bloodlust that overtook me several times was beyond anything I'd ever felt before, but I ignored it, hoping it was all in my head and would go away rather than facing it.

"If Seraphim had access to both orbs and me before, why didn't she bring the veil down completely? Why rip a hole in it at all?"

His shrug is deceptively nonchalant. "More angel-line blood is required than we realized."

"Are you planning on bleeding me dry to rip the barrier between worlds?" I release a brittle laugh that sounds a touch manic. "That's going to be pretty inconvenient for mother dearest, because if I'm not mistaken, she's stuck with this body. I die. She dies."

Thorne tilts his head. "You're not the only angel-line Nephilim we have access to anymore."

My heart skips a beat. I swear it does.

"From the moment you slipped off that bracelet, Seraphim heard every word and saw everything that you have. You've provided us with plenty of useful information. Frankly, more than we bargained for."

I want to sob. He knows. He knows about the angel-line Nephilim. He knows about Eden. And it's all my fault. Is there a single person I haven't betrayed?

I search for hope to latch onto and find it. "You can't bring the veil down without the orbs. You'll never find them again. You had your one chance, and you won't get another."

"You've already brought me one." Thorne gestures to the corner of the room and sure enough, the black backpack sits there.

I try to shrug, but my bindings prohibit the movement. "So what? One is hardly useful on its own."

Thank goodness we split them up. Now it makes sense why I felt so desperate to keep them together. That was Seraphim flipping out. I feel dirty knowing she's been manipulating my emotions like that for days, but I don't have the bandwidth to be creeped out by the situation right now. My freak-out will have to wait.

"You're right. But Seraphim will retrieve the other one quickly."

I huff out a humorless half-laugh. "You say that like it will be easy."

"Not as Seraphim it wouldn't, but as you." Reaching behind him, he grabs something and holds it up.

Oh no. The phone. The one Sable gave me that can contact the other group. If Seraphim calls the other group, of course they'll think it's me and lead her right to the second orb. We put contingencies in place so that the two groups wouldn't know where the orbs were, but that phone is the link between the two. Sable and Steel won't even be able to contact the other group to warn them not to give up their location.

The look Thorne gives me is almost pitying. "We're so

far ahead of you and your friends, we're not even playing the same game anymore."

I push past fear, and fury explodes in my chest. My power starts to rumble, and I stoke the flames. I'm going to burn my way out of these restraints and then Thorne and I are going to rumble. It's a battle that's far overdue. His skills as a fighter might surpass my own, but my power has grown exponentially, and he has no clue what lengths protecting my loved ones will drive me to.

I release my power, but rather than lighting me up like a bonfire, the energy rebounds back into me and fizzles.

No.

I snap my gaze to my other wrist, and the red gemstone Seraphim used to subdue me in Whitehold sparkles back at me.

I rage in frustration and thrash as far as my bindings will let me. Thorne stands by and watches my tantrum without saying a word. When I tire myself out, I stop my fruitless attempts. Panting, I glare at Thorne. He stands before me, cool and collected as a block of ice. The perfect winter prince, devoid of emotion or empathy.

"The truth of the matter is that I would have preferred you at my side as yourself. But again and again, you keep making the wrong choice. So, here we are." He splays his hands wide.

"If that's the case, why are we even talking right now? What do you need from me that you don't already have?"

Thorne seems taken aback by that question, but I can't imagine why. What's the point of this little tête-à-tête? He went to at least a bit of trouble to bring my consciousness to the surface and block Seraphim from making a sudden appearance. But to what end? Does he just want an audience to hear his villainous monologue?

Turning away, Thorne skirts the desk and walks to the window. With his back to me, he jams his hands into his jeans. The white t-shirt he wears stretches across his shoulders as they hunch. In a weird twist, this is the most human I've ever seen Thorne. He seems almost . . . vulnerable.

Perhaps I've been going about this all wrong. Could he be talked out of this scheme? Maybe he brought me back because there's a tiny part of him that actually wants that. I used to think there was a conflict in Thorne; maybe I was right all along?

"Thorne." I make sure that my voice is soft and non-threatening. "This isn't right. None of it. Somewhere deep down you know that and don't want to go through with this. You haven't had the opportunity to know any other way, but this isn't the only path. You can choose another."

His muscles bunch before relaxing again. He half turns his head so that all I can see is his profile. "You don't know what you are talking about."

"Maybe not. But we could try, together." I wet my lips and dig deep for something that might get through to Thorne. "You were right, we are the same."

He turns to me. The look on his face tells me he's not buying what I'm selling.

"We are the only two beings of our kind, but it's not the only connection that binds us. We didn't have a soft upbringing. We didn't have the love in our lives that we should have."

I press on, desperately hoping that something I say will sink in and take root.

"No one else will ever understand the ties that bind the two of us together. I believe that now."

To my surprise, my words ring true. Whether I like it or not, some of our damage matches. Without Steel, Sable, and all my friends to ground me, who's to say I wouldn't have been manipulated toward evil and destruction as much as he has? The thought alone makes me shiver, and I send up a silent prayer of thanks for all my found family, including the father I may never get a chance to truly know.

"But you don't have to go through with any of this. We can find a better way."

The room falls silent, and we just stare at each other. I beg him with my eyes to pick a better way, but there's an emptiness in his gaze that makes my blood run cold. Did he hear anything I just said?

With a sigh, Thorne walks toward me. When he reaches for my wrist, my blood pressure spikes. He's going to take off the bracelet, my only defense against Seraphim.

"Don't do this, Thorne." My voice is half-command, half-plea.

With his fingers on the warm metal band, he stops his movements and looks me in the eyes. "It's already been done." No matter what he says, I still read regret in his gaze. "Our fates have already been decided, so there's no use fighting against them. You want to know the reason I brought you back?"

I nod, and not only because I'm frantically trying to buy myself some time. I truly want to know.

He brings his other hand up to my cheek, moving his thumb back and forth over my skin. "It was so that I could say goodbye."

Leaning down, he presses the softest, chaste kiss to my

lips. It's over before I even have the chance to react. He steps away as I struggle for words. In his hand is the bracelet with the milky gemstone, my only protection from his vicious mother.

"Goodbye, Emberly."

# 30
## THORNE

When the door clicks shut, Emberly's desperate screams for me to return are barely muffled. My hand tightens on the doorknob even as I command it to let go. Her pleas pinch at a part of me I didn't know existed. My only comfort is that with the spirit gem missing from Emberly's wrist, Seraphim will reclaim her dominance soon enough. The next time I lay eyes on her, I have no doubt the self-assured gaze of my mother will stare back at me . . . but is that really a comfort?

Ripping my hand from the door, I force myself to leave.

Weak. That's what I am. I'm going to pay for that stunt. Seraphim is going to be livid I suppressed her, and I can't say that I blame her. And all for what? So I could say good-bye? What kind of garbage is that? I don't even understand my own actions. Emberly may be the only other being that rivals me in power, who is worthy to lead beside me, but that doesn't mean I owe her anything. I am on the precipice of seeing all my plans come to fruition, and I'll be damned if any sort of sentimental attachment is going to ruin it all.

I need to get my head on straight, and there is only one surefire way I know how to do that.

I clench my jaw as I turn the corner. I can no longer hear Emberly's cries unless I strain my senses. I consider turning back and listening until I become numb to her pleas, but there's a much more effective way to achieve my goal.

Arriving at the room I've commandeered for myself, I shove the door open. It bangs against the wall with the force. I kick it shut, and the frame rattles when it latches.

The sight of myself in the floor-length mirror—hands clenched, chest heaving, a flush high on my cheeks—gives me pause. It's been years since I let myself get this unhinged. Emotions—even the anger Seraphim gives into so frequently—make you vulnerable, and that's something I refuse to be anymore. The patchwork of scars over my body are the proof that I paid a steep price for that education. Some marks have been there for so long, I don't remember not having them.

The thin scar that runs through my left eyebrow stands out as I gain control of my breathing. I'd earned that one at age six. I made the mistake of crying over a broken arm during training. Seraphim, disgusted by my reaction, backhanded me into a wall. One of her sharp claws cut a path through my brow straight up to my hairline. That was the last time I ever cried.

With a sneer at my reflection, I reach back and yank my shirt up and over my head, tossing it onto the ground. I stride toward the chest at the foot of the bed, flip open the lid and grab the worn handle of the scourge. Faint white lines spiderweb over my hands, and I'm missing the tips of my left index and middle finger.

When I was younger, wielding a sword with my left

hand was difficult for me. For a month I was forced to face off against Fallen, only allowed to defend myself with that one arm. Every time I touched a weapon with my dominate hand, Seraphim took an end of a finger. It only took two times to learn my lesson, and, because of it, I'm evenly skilled with both arms.

It was well worth the payment.

Standing in the middle of the room, I breathe deeply to center myself. Even after years of discipline, sweat still beads my brow. Just another sign of the weakness that needs to be beaten out of me.

My knuckles ache as I grip the handle even tighter, my frustration past the boiling point. Emotions churn in an internal vortex that must be stopped.

I jerk my arm up, snapping my wrist over my shoulder. The metal barbs of the whip's tails catch on old scars from my youth and tear bloody paths over my skin when I force my hand to wrench the flagrum away.

The first rivers of blood cause something inside to break. As I repeat the motions, allowing the barbs to shred my skin, I know it won't be long until I'm numb once again.

# 31

## EMBERLY

*E*ven with my super-fast healing abilities, my throat is so raw I can't yell anymore. I want to be mad at Thorne—and part of me is—but there's something going on with him that I don't understand. Beyond his ability to free me, Thorne can't be my concern right now.

Like a snake uncoiling, I can feel Seraphim slithering inside, spreading an oily patch of darkness.

I look down at the red gemstone keeping me from using my powers. I melted my bindings once before while under the suppression of this particular stone, but that had been in the spectrum world, where my power is strongest. Right now, I can't so much as bring my body temperature up a degree. I'd scream in frustration if my throat wasn't already so damaged.

Sucking in a deep breath of air, I close my eyes and mentally remind myself that I'm a fighter.

*Get it together, Emberly. You've been in tight spots before. Six months ago, you didn't have any powers to fall back on, and you still managed to pull through. You can get yourself out of here, just think.*

I give myself another three seconds to freak out, then snap out of it. I tug at each of my bindings, looking for loosened knots or extra give. If I have to break a bone to free myself, I won't hesitate to do so. There's barely any wiggle room and all my thrashing only manages to strengthen the knots.

Moving on, I check the integrity of the chair. It's solid wood, with a layer of padding under my butt and behind my back. It doesn't even creek as I shift my weight, but wood has to be easier to break than rope.

The chair is oversized, so my feet don't lay flat on the ground. My legs aren't tied, which is currently the only advantage I can find. I try to rock forward, thinking that if I can tip onto my feet, maybe I can break apart the chair, but it's too heavy, and I can't get the leverage I need to stand.

Frustration threatens to thwart me, but I don't let it.

Kicking my legs forward, my toes brush against the wood desk in front of me. Vigorously swinging my legs back and forth, I scoot the chair forward a few inches. It's just enough to allow me to kick off the front flat panel of the desk, which sends me tipping backward. I hit the ground hard enough to knock the wind out of my lungs.

I didn't hear so much as a crack of wood with the impact. Now I'm stuck on the ground, still immobile and staring up at the flat white ceiling.

Stupid antique chair built to last several lifetimes. Why couldn't he have tied me to a cheap IKEA one? I would have snapped it in half by now.

I take a beat to catch my breath. Closing my eyes, I allow

myself two deep breaths to get centered, and that's it. When I open my eyes again, it's game on.

I turn my attention to the bindings circling my wrists, so tight they're just shy of cutting off circulation, but they're my best shot. I have zero leverage now that I'm on the ground. I'm worse off than I was a minute ago, and that's infuriating.

Eventually, I work in a little wiggle room, but it comes at the sacrifice of my skin. I rub my wrists past the point of raw and they drip blood onto the ropes encircling them. It's painful, but the lubrication that the blood provides makes it possible to move my hand back and forth about an inch.

I realize the bracelet with the red spirit gem is going to be harder to free, so I laser my focus on the other hand. I tug and pull and yank as I try to free myself. The darkness inside that I now know is Seraphim grows stronger every minute. I don't have even a second to lose. I have to free myself and find someone to lock me up until we figure out how to yank her out of me. I won't let myself dwell on the possibility that we can't be separated, or that her full possession is a definitive eventuality, like Thorne suggested. I simply won't let myself go there. This is my body, and I'm not giving it up to that monster.

The pain in my hand is excruciating. The coarse rope rubs against my skin, making it crack and split. I've broken some of the delicate small bones, but it doesn't matter. Skin and bones heal.

I bite my lip to keep from shouting as the rope scours over the thickest part of my hand, cutting deep into the first set of knuckles. With the help of the blood and skin loss, my hand finally slips free.

I don't waste a moment loosening the binding on my

other hand and then I have two working arms. I try to take off the bracelet with the red gemstone, but just like the last time, it won't budge. With a grunt, I refocus on freeing myself. The ropes around my stomach and chest are more difficult because the knots are in the back, but now that my arms are free, I manage to wiggle out of them.

Dashing to the door, I put my ear up to the wood to listen for movement. I have to be smart about this escape if I'm going to pull it off.

I stretch my hearing to the limit, but don't pick up even the lightest footstep. I'm out of the room in an instant and rushing down the oversized hall.

Shoot, where are we? A real palace this time? Thorne really does like extravagant living. The ceiling hangs at least twelve feet above my head and drips with multiple chandeliers. Old timey portraits line the walls and the ornate carpet runner screams opulence.

I pad along, not making a sound, but pause when I hear a muffled moan from behind the closed door I just passed. I freeze, feeling like I've been in this position before. But just like my failed escape attempt in Whitehold, I can't stop myself from investigating.

Creeping closer to the door, I press my ear against the wood. The room beyond is silent, except for the labored breaths I pick up with my angel-born hearing. Slowly turning the knob, I crack the door enough to see through a sliver of space. A girl is tied to a chair in the middle of the room. Her head is tipped forward, and her dark hair falls in unruly waves, curtaining her face from me.

Pushing open the door, I rush to her side. Falling to my knees, I work at the knots of the ropes securing her in place.

"Come to finish the job?" she croaks.

Startled, I glance up into one light brown eye. The other is swollen shut. Half her face is caked with dried blood and the other half is puffy.

"Shira?" My fingers move frantically on her bindings. "What are you doing here?"

Her mirthless chuckle turns into a wet cough.

"Like you don't know," she gets out. "We should have never trusted you. That's the only reason you overpowered me." Her voice breaks more than once and hatred—pure abhorrence—shines from her one good eye.

The memory of Seraphim leading Shira from the house comes back to me.

I shake my head. "That wasn't me."

"I was there when all this happened." Shira dips her head toward her shoulder to indicate the damage to her face. "This was most certainly your handiwork. Tell me, did you come across Stavros on accident, or seek him out?"

Her accusation that Stavros' murder was premeditated hits its mark. I have to remind myself she doesn't know what she's talking about.

"I didn't hurt you. It was Seraphim, not me. It's complicated."

She makes a noise that may be a scoff, but it's hard to say with her wheezing every breath.

My words tumble over each other as I work on loosening the knots. "Apparently, she didn't die during the ceremony like I thought. We merged; I just didn't realize it."

"You're a Forsaken?" Even though it obviously hurts, Shira jerks away as far as her binding will let her. "We let a Forsaken into Eden?" Disgust drips from each word.

"No, it's not as simple as that." I stop for a moment, because maybe this does make me a Forsaken. But it can't, because I'm still me. At least, I am some of the time. The sunlight doesn't bother me, and I don't have fangs. The thought of drinking blood makes my stomach roil. Technically, I'm something else altogether, but now isn't the time to figure it out. "Listen, I'm going to get you out of here, but when you're free, I need you to run." I catch Shira's one-eyed gaze and hold it. "I need you to run, even from me."

A scream of rage makes me flinch. It echoes in my head where I know only I can hear. Seraphim is now fully aware and mad as a viper. For all my boasting to Thorne about mental shields and keeping Seraphim out, it feels like my control is slipping like sand through an hourglass. I'm not going down without a fight, but how do I fight something like this?

I get one of Shira's hands free and move on to the other. Before I can loosen the knot, she grabs a handful of my hair. I scream for her to stop, but she slams my head into the corner of the wooden arm and my vision winks out.

My body slides to the ground, and I can't make any of my limbs move.

Seraphim's husky chuckle echoes inside as I slip away.

# 32

## THORNE

*I* barely have time to throw a shirt over my shredded back. It hasn't been long enough for the wounds to scab over. Blood starts saturating the material, but there's nothing to be done about it. The silent alarm on the room Emberly's in was tripped, meaning someone entered the room, or she's on the move. Either way, I have to act fast.

I take off so quickly my body would be a blur to the human eye. There's yelling to my right. I slam through the doors where the brown-eyed angel Nephilim is being held, to find Emberly on the ground laughing. The other angel-born captive is half-freed. The dark-haired one hurls insults even as Emberly continues to chuckle and push to her feet. A trickle of blood runs down the middle of Emberly's face. The drops dribble off the tip of her nose.

"You stupid half-breed," she says as she stares down at the bound girl. "If you hadn't just done me a favor, I'd rip off each one of your fingers and feed them to you. I only need you alive right now, not whole."

Not Emberly any longer. I straighten my spine and slip on a mask of complete and utter disinterest in preparation for my reckoning. Emotion will only fuel Seraphim's retribution.

The angel-born stops her rants, and her good eye widens as she regards the person in front of her, only now realizing who she's dealing with. Emberly must have freed herself and tried to free this one as well when Seraphim regained control.

Seraphim lifts a mangled hand and twists it back and forth to inspect it. Her upper lip curls in a snarl.

"Stupid angel-born, always damaging the package," she mutters.

I clear my throat and she twists toward me. Red glints in her eyes, then fades as her temper flares.

"You're really not her?" the Nephilim girl asks.

Seraphim sucker punches her in the temple. The Neph girl's head snaps to the side and then she's out cold. Her body slumps against the ropes still fastened around her chest. Seraphim shoots the girl a look of disgust before turning on a heel and heading straight for me.

"You owe me an explanation," she says, then shoves through the doors and out into the hallway.

I follow in her wake.

"There's a vast difference between what you think I owe you and what I actually do." I probably shouldn't poke her, but my mother's control has begun to chafe.

"You were born to be a thorn in the side of my angel brethren, not my own," she snaps.

I spread my arms out wide, recklessly inviting Seraphim to take a good look. "I am what you made me, Mother. Any grievances you have against me fall at your own feet."

She comes at me, striking my chest with so much force, I slam into the wall. I don't so much as flinch as my battered back takes the brunt of the impact. I learned how to conceal my weaknesses at a very young age.

"What was that all about?" Seraphim snarls in my face. Her hands are fisted in the front of my shirt. "And be careful how you answer. You may be my son, but some acts are beyond forgiveness. I might decide I have no use for you after all."

"Watch yourself," I growl. My chest expands from the lungful of air I suck in through my nostrils. "I'm not a fledgling to be manipulated by your every whim. The Fallen and Forsaken are as much my subjects as they are yours." I push into her space, forcing her back a step. "Maybe even more. One day you may find that you've pushed me too far."

Dropping her arms, Seraphim puts space between us and goes deathly silent. There are several beats when the only sound is my ragged breathing.

"Good." Seraphim tips up her chin. A satisfied smirk appears on her face. "You should never let anyone take what is yours. Not even me."

I narrow my eyes, wondering if this is a trick.

"I trust you won't be slapping that bracelet on me in the future, and whatever sort of closure you felt you needed was finally satisfied?"

I roll my tongue against the inside of my cheek, glad she's not attacking me anymore, but suspicious of where this conversation is going. Rather than answer, I cross my arms across my chest. The movement rounds my back and a few of the cuts that weren't split open when Seraphim smashed me against the wall start to weep.

I was prepared to feed her a lie about questioning

Emberly for information, but I decide then and there I'm not going to explain myself.

Seraphim chooses to pretend my silence on the matter is capitulation. "Good," she nods. "Now, I will forgive your lapse in judgment under one condition. Retrieve the second orb."

# 33

## STEEL

The porcelain lamp shatters against the wall. I know from experience that it won't help Sterling feel any better.

A plate is the next victim, and it explodes into a million white shards that sprinkle to the ground.

"Bro, you need to calm down," I say to my brother right after he launches a mug with a roar.

He disregards my command and pulls a mirror off the wall, smashing it at his feet. This is ridiculous.

Jolting forward, I wrap my arms under Sterling's armpits and secure my hands behind his head. He thrashes and tries to flip me over his shoulder, but my little brother hasn't gone through metamorphosis yet and doesn't have his full strength. He may be a formidable fighter, but he's no match for me. At least not yet.

"I said—Calm. Down!" I shout in his ear.

Sterling huffs and puffs, but finally stops squirming. "How are you not raging right now? Your girl is missing too."

I grind my molars together. I'm well aware of the situation. What Sterling doesn't know is that I'm right on that edge. Heck, his breakdown is probably the only thing that has kept me from my own. With two Durands out of control, we would have brought the whole house down, and a fat lot of good that would do for us. What we really need right now are level heads.

I release Sterling and give him a not-so-gentle shove. He stumbles on the rubble he created before finding his footing.

The front door opens and shuts, then Sable walks in the room. Her gaze sweeps the mess and then bounces between Sterling and me. I hitch a thumb in Sterling's direction, my lips pressed into a hard line.

She crosses her arms over her chest and levels Sterling with a hard stare. "So, smashing everything in sight when you're angry is the Durand male way to cope?"

"Apparently, only when we lose our women," Sterling mumbles as he kicks at a broken picture frame.

"Shira isn't your woman," Sable says.

"Yet," Sterling retorts.

Taking a deep breath, she shakes her head, but doesn't engage my brother further. "No one has heard from Emberly, Shira, or the other group."

I poke my tongue into my cheek. My blood boils with a toxic mix of frustration, anger, and fear.

Sterling stalks over to the window that overlooks the barren backyard and alleyway. "We'll have to track them. They couldn't have gotten far."

"We don't know that," Sable says. "If Emberly and Shira phased, they could have flown in any direction. They could be *very* far from here by now."

Sterling jerks his gaze from the window to stare at Sable. "They only would have flown if they left of their own will, and that makes zero sense."

"I agree it doesn't make sense, but it's a possibility."

Sterling's eyebrows pinch. "No. No, it's not a possibility. They wouldn't have left us voluntarily. Someone came and took them." His gaze snaps to me. "Tell her, Steel. Emberly wouldn't do that to us. She wouldn't do that to *you*."

My mind has been almost solely fixated on that very thought since the moment I woke to find Emberly missing from bed. She was gone—again. But she'd promised never to leave like that. She promised she'd come to me. And I believed her. So, what happened?

The resolution I came to is almost too frightening to think of, but the more I dwell on the possibility, the more I wonder how I didn't see it before.

"I don't think Emberly left us. I don't think Emberly was in control at all." That was as painful to say as I thought it would be.

"What do you mean?" Sable asks.

"Something has been off with Emberly since we brought her back from Whitehold. The day of the first attacks, I had to douse her in cold water to wake her. When we were in Eden, she sleepwalked out of the village and threw a punch at me before she woke up. Then there's all the missing time. She traveled all the way from Eden to England without a single memory of how she did it or even why. We've been so preoccupied with the orbs and stopping Thorne that we didn't take Emberly's condition seriously. Rather than investigating what was going on with her, we pushed it off."

Shame balloons in my chest. I, more than anybody else, should have put her first. I should have made her not only a priority, but the top priority. If I had, I have no doubt we wouldn't be in this position. If—when—I get her back, I won't ever make this mistake again.

Sable cocks her head, a thoughtful expression puckering the skin between her eyebrows. "And you think you know what happened?"

I nod. "I do." Crossing my arms over my chest, I plant my feet, physically preparing myself for what I believe to be true. "I don't think Emberly grabbed the orb and the phone and took off. I think Seraphim did."

# 34

## EMBERLY

*E*very moment is like drowning in an abyss. I can't see anything, and the more I fight, the deeper I sink.

*Seraphim!* I scream, or at least I think I do. I can't even hear my own voice. The only thing I can truly feel is the sharp tang of panic as it churns and grows and swallows me whole.

What am I going to do?

For all my boasting to Thorne about keeping Seraphim at bay, I folded faster than a house of cards. Swooping in and taking control of my body with ease, Seraphim shoved me so deep inside my own psyche that I may never find my way out.

*Seraphim!* I try again, but still nothing.

What if I'm already gone? I can't feel my body. Can't hear, see, or smell a single thing. Who's to say that Seraphim hasn't already pushed my soul into the void, or whatever it is that actually happens during possession? Am I going to be stuck in some strange type of purgatory for the rest of eternity?

If I could breathe, this is the point where I would start to hyperventilate, which, in turn, would make me want to throat punch myself for falling apart.

*Pull it together, Emberly. You've been in tough spots before. Admittedly, not this tough, but panicking isn't going to help anything.*

I need something to ground me. An anchor in this world of nothingness.

Steel.

I may not be able to feel anything tangible, but my emotions still swirl inside me. When I think of Steel, a vortex of longing and love wraps me in a comforting embrace. I grab on to my memories of him like a tether.

A blurred image starts to appear. I focus on the first time I saw Steel, and the picture crystalizes. He appeared in the spectrum world, standing between me and a group of shadow beasts. Taunting them. Daring them to attack. He was so arrogant and bossy, yet even then there'd been a spark between us.

I think about those first weeks at Seraph Academy. The bitter taste of Steel's contempt rushes to the surface, followed by the confusion I felt over his hot and cold treatment.

Our relationship hasn't always been puppies and roses, but apathy was never one of our issues. Even the toxicity from those early days gives me life right now.

There's a crack in my heart as I remember Steel leaving the academy to search for Silver. Those days, I did my best to push him from my thoughts, only to have concern leak through the instant my guard dropped.

I see Steel standing next to his bike, his hair too long and his clothes hanging loose. Relief and anxiety twist in my gut. Our attraction started to bloom into something beautiful after that, but we weren't given the time to wipe the slate clean and start again before I was stolen away to Whitehold.

I know what round of emotions come next, and I fight to stay open to the sensations. Even though they are branded into the very fabric of my soul, my own protective instincts scream at me not to go back. I push through and let the fear and hopeless agony wash over me. In the moments after the merging ceremony, Steel is there, but also not. His eyes stare at me, but all I see is Legion.

The heartache was like nothing I'd ever felt, but I welcome the burn, the fiery furnace of emotion that is my lifeline to reality. Some part of me comes awake with every layer I peel back.

I move past the pain of losing Steel to embrace the sweet relief of his return. The beautiful moment he confessed the depth of his feelings for me. The euphoric state of rightness in his arms. Like finding the home I didn't know I was looking for.

Something powerful grows inside me. The sweet and the harsh mix in a crazy kaleidoscope of emotions, fueling me. I can see it now, shining like a beacon in the darkness. A spark of my power appears as I strain for Steel. It swells as I rip my soul bare and dive into every emotion I have for him.

Something beyond instinct drives me forward. All I need to do is reach out and grab hold of the energy. It's mine after all. Mine to mold and manipulate.

With Steel still in the forefront of my mind, I press into

my power. The light eclipses the image of Steel, but that's okay because I can still feel him.

Steel is mine, today and forever, and nothing can change that. The depth and breadth of my love for him only makes my power burn brighter. He's seared upon my soul.

There was no one before him, and there will never be another.

I let my love for Steel and my power consume me. It leaks into every crevice of my being and forges a bond through time and space that irrevocably links the two of us. And as the bond solidifies and strengthens, I feel him. I feel Steel on the other end.

With a powerful tug, I pull him to me.

# 35

## STEEL

"Seraphim?" Sterling pushes away from the wall. "You said Seraphim was dead."

"Yeah, that's what we thought."

Sable brushes her tongue over her top teeth. "I see where you're going with this." She studies the ground as the pieces slide together for her as well. Bringing a hand up, she rubs her fingers against her bottom lip before lifting her gaze. "I don't want to believe it's true, but it does make a sick sort of sense. If the merge was successful, then Seraphim's been there the whole time."

"Wait, wait, wait!" Sterling waves his hands in the air. "Are you saying that Seraphim possessed Emberly and has been controlling her since Whitehold? There's no way. That would make Emberly a Forsaken and we've all seen her out and about in the daylight." He scoffs, then levels me with a hard look. "And don't you think you would have known if you made out with Seraphim instead of Emberly?"

I suppress a shudder. "Yeah, I definitely would have known.

But I don't think Seraphim was always in control, just at certain times. And Emberly is more angel than most of us, and Seraphim is a seraph Fallen. Maybe possession isn't typical between them? The one thing we know for sure is that we don't know everything about Forsaken and possessions. Silver's proof of that. And when Legion merged with me, I can't say that I was in control, but I had moments of lucidity during that event. Maybe Seraphim has been biding her time, waiting for her moment. We don't actually know what her endgame is."

Sterling doesn't want to believe it, but even he starts to see how it makes sense. "But what about Shira? That doesn't explain why she's gone too." He shakes his head. "The only thing that makes sense is that someone came and took them."

"What are the chances that someone broke into the house and got away with both Emberly and Shira without one of us hearing anything?" I ask my brother. "It makes more sense that Seraphim, acting as Emberly, convinced Shira to leave the house."

"Why would Seraphim bother with Shira?"

"I don't know. Maybe Shira got in her way when she was leaving? Maybe Seraphim needs her for something? For all we know, Seraphim may just want information about the angel-line."

Sterling opens his mouth again, but I stop him by cutting my hand through the air. "Whatever question you have, I can assure you, I've already asked it myself and come up empty. The most important thing right now is to find the girls and bring them back."

"No." I glance sharply at Sable when she contradicts me. "Bringing the girls back is not the most important thing.

Our top priority is to get that orb somewhere beyond reach. The orb is our focus."

Sterling frowns at Sable, not liking that comment one bit. I squeeze my fists tight enough that the bones in my fingers start to ache.

Taking a deep breath, I stop myself from punching a hole in the drywall. As I already know, and Sterling just demonstrated, smashing things won't accomplish anything.

"Let me be very clear about my intentions." My voice drops so low it's almost a growl. "If the choice comes down to saving the world or saving Emberly, I'll choose Emberly every single time. If you want to keep your eye on the orb, that's fine, as long as you don't get in my way. Because from here on out, whatever stands between me and my girl will be destroyed."

Sable's gaze widens. "Steel, you can't possibly mean that?"

"I've never meant anything more."

I get that Sable's gotta do what she's gotta do, but the same goes for me. I already let Emberly down—more than once—and I don't intend to do it again. When I find her, I might just spirit her away to a remote island and wait out this apocalypse. Thorne be damned. The orbs be damned. The world be damned.

A spray of sparks rains down on us, breaking my stare-off with Sable. Tinkle pops back into the mortal realm, gliding until he lands on a broken side chair. He takes in the domestic carnage before coming to rest on me. "Do you feel better now?"

"Wasn't me this time." I tilt my head in Sterling's direction, and his cheeks turn ruddy.

"Actually, I do feel a little better," he says, lifting his chin a notch.

"You Nephilim males are weird," Tinkle says. "Hey, are there any cookies around here?"

"Tinkle," Sable stops the little Celestial before he can start scrounging for food. "What did you find?"

"Oh right. Yea, sorry." He rubs his tummy with a tiny fur paw. "I haven't fed her second lunch, so she's angry with me."

"You refer to your stomach as 'she' and you think we're weird?" Sterling asks.

"Yes. So?" Tinkle blinks back at my brother.

"Tinkle," Sable prompts a second time.

"Right, right. I found their trail. My sense of smell is surely the most sensitive of all the Celestials. If Camiel had appointed any other of my kind as Emberly's champion, I'm positive she would have been killed by now. But since it was me—"

"Where does the trail lead?" I growl.

"Well, you see—" Tinkle's mouth continues to move, but I don't hear anything. I shake my head, blinking my eyes against the sudden fuzziness clouding my vision. My limbs go numb, and I lurch forward, catching myself on the back of a couch. As the energy drains from my body, I slump to the floor. Sable and Sterling are both there in an instant, probably shouting my name, but I can't hear them. My eyelids droop, and the next moment, I'm dead to the world.

# 36

## EMBERLY

*S*teel materializes in front of me. Not a memory. Not an image of him in my mind's eye. The actual living, breathing Steel.

Throwing his head back, he fists his hair and shouts, "Not this dream again."

Dream?

I gasp. This is it. This is the origin of Steel's dreams about me. Nikias said that when an angel chooses their person, the event is so significant that it bounces back in time, creating ripples. This is why Steel knew me before we ever met. Like a distorted reflection in the water, the dreams were glimpses, or echoes, of this very moment. But this—this is what starts it all.

Soul-bonded . . . it's true.

The high of the realization is snuffed by the harsh light of reality. How unfair to have finally forged this connection when I most likely won't be around much longer to bask in it.

"I gotta wake up," Steel mumbles to himself. He rolls his

tongue over his top teeth as he takes me in, longing shining in his eyes. "You're so beautiful." He releases a sigh, and the word "torture" escapes on his breath.

I glance down at myself. I'm clothed in my full battle armor. Gold covers most of my body and the weight at my back is a sure sign that my wings are out as well. Steel is dressed in the same clothes he was when I—or rather Seraphim—snuck out of the bedroom.

Stepping into Steel's space, I take his face between my hands. Two days' worth of stubble is rough against my palms.

It's the best thing I've ever felt.

Part of me wants to lean in and soak up as much of him as I can. These could very well be our last moments together, but there's no time for that. He needs to know about Seraphim, and Shira, and how to save the world from a Fallen invasion.

"Steel, no. This isn't one of your dreams." A crease forms between his eyebrows. "This time it's happening for real. Do you understand what I'm saying?"

I drop my hands to his shoulders and wait for his response. He searches my face. Reaching forward, he rubs strands of my hair beneath his fingers. "You feel real, but you always do." Leaning forward, he skims his nose over my cheekbone and inhales. "Strawberries and spice," he says when he pulls back. "But that's not new either."

"Steel, we don't have time for this." He needs to snap out of it and get with the program.

"Ah, and there's the difference. I can understand every-thing you're saying. That's a first. Your sentences are usually broken up and disjointed."

"Yes, exactly. I'm here." I wave a hand at the misty nothingness around us, not exactly sure where "here" is, but that detail is inconsequential right now. "You're here. We're here together, but I have no idea how much time we have. I don't know how much time *I* have left."

"What do you mean?"

Right, time to drop the bomb. "The merge with Seraphim worked. She didn't die like we assumed. She's been with me ever since we left Whitehold. She's the one who caused the breaches in the veil between worlds. She killed Stavros and brought me to Thorne. She's the one who snuck out of the house earlier today. The mood swings, the missing time, the sleepwalking—all of it. It's been her, working through me, all along. And now she has complete control over my body."

I suck in a deep breath of air, then hold it, waiting for Steel's reaction.

He nods once. "Right. What else?"

I cock my head. "No questions about that bit?"

I thought for sure he'd argue with me. Or maybe pepper me with questions about how all of it was possible. Immediate acceptance was the last thing I expected.

"I already worked through most of that. I figured you were possessed by Seraphim."

My mouth drops open. It takes a second for me to find words. When I do, they are clumsy and inarticulate. "But, but, how? When?"

"You said you'd never leave me again. I believed you." He runs his thumb over my bottom lip and tugs it out from between my teeth. I didn't realize I was chewing it. "When I woke and you were gone, I knew there were only two possibilities. Someone took you, or you walked yourself out the door. You said you wouldn't leave me like that again, and there's no way someone would have abducted you right underneath my nose. When it finally occurred to me that Seraphim might not be gone, everything fell into place. It was so obvious." He swallows and his Adam's apple bobs. "Emberly, I'm so sorry I didn't see it sooner."

I capture one of Steel's hands and hold it between mine. I know Steel well enough to understand this is something he will beat himself up about, and that's not fair.

"No, don't do that. Don't go down that path." I shake my head. "This isn't your fault. I didn't even realize she was still here, and she was taking up residence in my own body."

"I still should have known." Pain-filled remorse slashes across his features. "Where are you now?"

I don't want Steel to steer our conversation in a different direction, but there is still of bucket of information he needs to know. "I'm not exactly sure. Somewhere fancy. Long hallways, high ceilings, lots of room. I don't think that's going to narrow it down much for you. And I'm with Thorne again."

Steel's gaze darkens even though I'm sure he already considered that a possibility.

"Shira is here, too. Seraphim lured her out of the house and then knocked her out. Thorne told me they think the barrier didn't drop completely before because Seraphim didn't use enough of my blood, or because they need a full angel-line Nephilim to complete the ritual. When they get their hands on both orbs, they're going to try again, but use Shira's blood this time. They're determined to obliterate the barrier between the mortal world and spirit realm, even if they have to bleed Shira dry to do it."

Steel rubs the bridge of his nose. "I may not let Sterling in on that little factoid. He'd likely start raging again."

"Raging?"

"He didn't take Shira's disappearance very well. He tore half the house apart."

"That doesn't sound like Sterling."

Steel shrugs. "The males in my family don't take well to people taking what they consider to be theirs."

I grimace. "Just don't put it that way to Shira. She won't find that flattering."

"Noted."

"You need to find this place and get Shira out of here. Without her, I don't think Thorne and Seraphim will be able to bring down the veil completely. They may be able to punch some more holes in it, which would be devastating, but the world can recover."

"They won't be able to do anything just yet. They still need the other orb."

"With the sat phone connection to the other group, and Seraphim masquerading as me, I don't think that will be an issue much longer. I think we need to work under the assumption that they're going to collect the other orb very soon . . . if they haven't already."

Steel curses under his breath. "All right, just hang tight. We're coming for you. Right before you yanked me into this dream, or whatever it is, Tinkle said he'd found your trail. I'll find you."

"Steel, I need you to listen to me." I take a deep breath, fortifying myself for what I have to say next. "When you find me—when you find Seraphim—you have to kill me."

He's shaking his head before I utter the last word. "No. I won't do it. There will be another way to end this."

"There might be, but there's no time. Seraphim has complete control of my body. She will hurt and kill people. Innocent people. You kill me, you kill Seraphim, too."

"You can't ask me to do this. I won't."

"I am and you will. There was a time when you asked the same thing of me."

His eyes narrow. A muscle ticks in his jaw. "That's a low blow."

"It's just the truth. There are more important things in this world than us. Than me. I expect you to do the right thing."

He huffs out a humorless laugh. "Then you expect too much."

Steel steps forward. He bumps into me, throwing me off balance. Before I'm able to move back a step, he slips an arm around my lower back and anchors me against his chest. His voice goes low and growly. "Let me make one thing abundantly clear: I will watch the world burn before I let you go."

The breath catches in my throat, and it's a moment before I can speak again. "The world is more important than I am."

He shakes his head. "Nothing is more important than you."

"Your job is to shelter and protect those who aren't strong enough to defend themselves. That's who you are. The Nephilim exist to protect people from evil."

"That may be true, but *I* exist to love you. To protect you. To be with you. I won't give that up. If that makes me a selfish bastard, then I. Don't. Care."

I'm dead. His words have carved a path straight through my heart.

A tear leaks out of my eye and drips down my face. Steel

catches it with his fingers before it drops off my chin. His features soften as his gaze tracks over my face. He twines his other arm around my back so I'm captured in a full embrace.

"Emberly, you are the other half of my soul. I will choose you above everything else for the rest of my existence. So no, I won't let you go, and I certainly won't kill you."

"But Steel, don't you understand? I'm already gone. I was lucky to get through to you this time. Seraphim has me completely shut out. The state I exist in isn't really an existence at all." Another tear joins the first, and now I can't stop more from falling. "You won't really be killing me; you'll only be helping me move on."

It hurts to say, but it's the truth. This moment between us is a gift, but that's all it is. It won't change anything. Seraphim has such a strong hold on me that I won't be able to surface again, and Steel needs to understand that so he can do what needs to be done.

"You're wrong. You're not gone. You're here with me."

"But I'm not. Not really. I think," I choke on the words, but they need to be said. "No, I *know* you need to let me go."

"Never."

"Then the world will fall and burn, and it will be all our fault."

"So be it."

# 37

## STEEL

*E*mberly yanks out of my grasp. I make a move to capture her again, but she puts her hands up to stop me. In the nightmares she always asks me to kill her, so I don't know why I didn't see this coming.

"You don't mean that," she says.

"Oh, but I do." I cross my arms over my chest to keep from reaching for her as we have a silent stare-off. I'd think it was cute if the stakes weren't so high. "Do you have any idea why Seraphim waited this long to take over your body?" I ask, switching into problem-solving mode. "Did it take her a while to gain enough strength to overcome you? Was she biding her time to gather intel against us?" Maybe I'm grasping at straws, but I believe there has to be something we can use against her.

Emberly glances down at her bare wrist. "The bracelet Thorne gave me—the one with the white spirit gem—kept Seraphim suppressed without us knowing. I took it off at the Elders' compound and that night, she created the holes in the barrier between worlds. After that, she voluntarily suppressed herself to gather information and get the orbs back."

"Emberly, that's it—the bracelet." I can't stop myself from reaching for her again. When my hands wrap around her biceps, she doesn't push me away. "We'll get it back on you to put Seraphim down until we can figure out how to destroy her for good. It's back at the compound? Where exactly did you leave it?"

She absently chews on her bottom lip as she thinks. Her gaze tracks up and to the left as she pulls up the memory.

"I took it off in the bathroom in the room I shared with Ash. I set it on the counter, but I have no idea if Seraphim did something with it after that. I don't remember seeing it the next day, but that morning is hazy."

I can work with that. I'll call Deacon and have him scour the room until he finds it.

"But there's another one here. Thorne used it to wake me up."

"Wake you up?" Just the mention of Thorne ignites my wrath, but I keep it under wraps.

"He put it on me and it blocked Seraphim. I think he just wanted to say goodbye. When he took it off, Seraphim didn't regain control until I got knocked out."

I swallow a growl. That prick. I'm well aware Emberly has a soft spot for Thorne, but as if he hasn't already hurt her enough, he has to mess with her head as well? It's like he's twisting the knife he already stabbed in her back.

I shove the thoughts of dismembering Thorne to the back of my mind. "That means there are two opportunities to get that bracelet on you. That's good."

She continues to gnaw on her lip, a concerned crease between her brows.

"This is going to work," I assure her. And I believe that because it has to. There isn't a universe where I exist without her. "You just have to hold on a little while longer."

She nods but still looks uncertain. I duck my head and press a kiss to her lower lip, because watching her chew it is making me crazy. I can't not have a taste. She gasps at the sudden movement, and I take advantage of that as well, deepening the kiss, reminding her what she has to hold on for.

Emberly is like fire in my hands, and she consumes me completely.

I'm not prepared when she's ripped from my grasp. Thorne holds her with one arm locked around her middle and the other pressing a blade against the column of her throat. I go to grab a dagger, but in this place the only weapons I have are words.

"How are you here?" I demand.

"Funny thing about dreamscaping," Thorne says, a sardonic grin kicking up one side of his mouth. "It's a seraph power."

"Thorne, let me go," Emberly demands. She keeps her head tipped back to keep from cutting herself on Thorne's blade, but fury that almost matches my own burns in her gaze.

"Afraid I can't do that. There's no way to bring you back while you're still connected to him. Something tells me the moment I lower this weapon, the two of you will suction back together like octopuses."

I don't know if Thorne can actually injure Emberly in this strange, dream-like state, but I'm not willing to risk it. With the dagger threatening Emberly, I can do nothing but snarl at Thorne.

"How did you even know to come here?" Emberly asks. She's capable of more rational thought than I am right now. The visions of Thorne's demise cycling in my head take up a lot of space.

"Seraphim's comatose stare tipped me off something was up. Time to say goodbye, Emberly. We have places to be."

"No!" I reach for Emberly, but Thorne yanks her back and they disappear into the shadowy mist.

I shout her name, but it just echoes in the void. I'm too late. She's already gone.

# 38

## ASH

Snowflakes drift down from the sky and settle on the damp ground. Most of them melt quickly, the temperatures not low enough to make them stick, but I'm still chilled to the bone. Scotland is undeniably beautiful—even in the middle of winter—but this wet cold is not for me.

"You hangin' in there?" Greyson asks. His blue-green stare checks me over from head to toe as he chews on the inside of his cheek.

I nod, and it dislodges a drop of water from the tip of a curl on my forehead. The icy bead drips on my nose, making me flinch. I swat it away, then shove my hands back under my armpits for warmth.

"You didn't ask if I'm okay," Nova says, peeking around Greyson from the other side.

"That's because you're not shivering like a newborn puppy."

"Hey, come on now," I say. "That's not really an accurate —ah . . . ah . . . ah-choo." I lift my gloved hand up in front of my face just in time to keep boogers from rocketing from my nose to the ground. Pulling my hand away, I grimace at the wad of snot in my palm.

"Ew, Ash," Nova pulls a face, "that's nasty."

Nova, ever so helpful.

"Here." Greyson digs into his coat pocket and hands me a napkin. I do my best to clean up the mess. Thank goodness my cheeks are already reddened by the chilled air so he can't see the heat that just shot to them. That was embarrassing.

"Where do you think the others are right now?" Greyson asks.

I tried my best not to think of the other group over the last day. I hate that we had to split up. Not knowing how they're doing is a special sort of torture, but right now, I welcome the change in conversation. Anything to keep my mind off the cold and divert Greyson and Nova's attention from the giant loogie I just shot from my nose.

"I'll bet they're somewhere warm," I say as I stomp my feet to get some of the feeling back into them. "Watch us be on our way to the North Pole to bury this orb in a glacier, and they get to throw theirs into a volcano in Hawaii. If that happens, Sterling's really going to owe me."

"But just think, if we go to the North Pole, maybe we'll meet Santa Claus," Greyson says with a chuckle.

"I'd be down for that as long as the big guy has some peppermint tea waiting for us when we get there." Mmmm. That sounds amazing right now.

Greyson rubs his hands together to create friction and then blows into them for warmth. "What if he has a house made of real gingerbread and we can eat whatever we want in it."

"That was a random thought, but I'm fully behind it. It sounds delicious." My stomach rumbles at the thought of peppermint tea and gingerbread. "The elves have to be a completely different species, right? Do you think they really have pointy ears?"

"It would be creepy if they didn't. Without the ears they would look like regular people, and that would just be weird."

I nod, fully agreeing. I'm about to make a comment about reindeer when I catch Nova just staring at us.

"What?" I ask.

She shakes her head. "You don't actually believe in Santa . . . right?"

I'm about to reassure her that Greyson and I are just messing around when he says, "Come on, Nova. You know there's a kernel of truth in all the myths."

He bounces his eyebrows up and down and then throws her a wink.

Nova opens her mouth to reply when we hear the distinct trill of a motorcycle engine. We turn to the road to find Ciara riding toward us. She stops and cuts her engine, pulling her helmet off but not dismounting.

"We're all set," she announces. "We have beds for the night and a flight out of here at first light. Come on, let's get inside and get you guys warmed up."

Yes. I am all about that. The only rest we got last night was between Oxford and Birmingham in the back of a bumpy box truck. We all crammed into a hatchback from there and drove north. When we hit Scotland, we traded the car in for motorcycles and have been riding country roads up through the highlands all day. We arrived in Inverness less than an hour ago and have been waiting on Killian and Ciara on the outskirts of town.

I flex my fingers as I throw my leg over the seat of my motorcycle. They're stiff, but I'll be okay. I survived the ten-hour drive to get here, so I can manage another ten minutes. With everyone mounted and the orb safely tucked in Greyson's saddlebag, we follow Ciara through the charming town. The modern is mixed in with the ancient, but parts of the small highland town make it feel like we've traveled back through time; stone cathedrals, small pubs, bookshops, and even a castle.

We pass through the town without stopping and head east, hugging the inlet. Eventually, Ciara veers away from the water and leads us along several winding dirt roads until we arrive at a farmhouse. Cutting off our engines and dismounting, Ciara tells us to stow our bikes off to the side.

I see a chimney with gray smoke puffing out the top and can almost feel the heat of the fire thawing my frozen skin. I start toward the front door when Ciara calls to me.

"Not there, Ash. Over here."

Scrunching my eyebrows, I skirt the house with the rest of the group and have to stifle a groan when Killian steps out from a barn behind the house.

"What? No room in the inn?" Nova asks her dad with a grimace. At least I'm not the only one disappointed by the accommodations.

"This is low-profile," he answers.

Nova picks up a piece of her damp hair and lets it drop again, her mouth askew in an exaggerated frown. I have to turn my face to hide my smile, knowing she's upset she won't be able to blow out her hair tonight. I catch Greyson's eye as we enter the barn and he smirks back at me. He's as familiar with Nova's grooming habits as I am.

I'm pleasantly surprised to find that it isn't a functioning barn after all, but rather a bunkhouse. Three sets of bunkbeds flank the walls to the right and left. A narrow farmhouse table is set up down the middle. There's a door off to the right that I really hope is a fully functioning bathroom. A hot shower sounds like heaven right now.

"What smells good?" Greyson asks, making a beeline directly to the table in the center of the space. A basket sits on top, along with plates and silverware. Opening the basket, he pulls out a bowl of mashed potatoes, a loaf of brown bread, and several rounded objects that look a bit like baked potatoes.

"Our hosts were kind enough to provide us some dinner," Killian says as he slides onto the bench seat and starts to pass out plates.

Nova groans as we all take a seat. "Not haggis."

"Haggis is delicious," Greyson says as he piles his plate full of potatoes, a piece of bread, and one of the potato-shaped objects.

Nova scrunches her nose. "Only if you enjoy eating liver, heart, lungs, and other animal bi-products all cooked in sheep stomach."

Greyson shrugs. "Tastes like sausage to me."

My enthusiasm for dinner drops significantly as I watch Ciara cut into a chunk of haggis. It does look a bit like ground meat and gives off a hearty smell that boarders on pungent. I'm about to grab a plate and load up on potatoes and bread when Greyson sets his in front of me.

"Eat up," he says, then starts piling food on another plate for himself.

"Oh." I'm caught off-guard that he served me before he took food for himself. I blink down at the plate before remembering myself. "Thank you."

"No prob." Greyson already has another dish in front of him and forks a mound of potatoes into his mouth.

I cut into the haggis and the aroma hits me. It's not bad, per se, but it is strong. I poke at the soft yet crumbly mixture.

Greyson nudges me. "Just pretend it's sausage. I mean, are intestines really that much better than stomach?"

"I don't know if that helps," I confess.

"Should I remind you what's in hotdogs?"

"Please don't."

Greyson chuckles and dives back into his meal. I bring a smelly bite to my mouth and take the plunge. I chew slowly. Greyson wasn't wrong. It does taste a bit like a peppery, earthy sausage. If given a choice, I wouldn't order it off a menu, but it's not awful. My next bite is larger as I really dig into the meal. It helps if I squash it all together and wash it down with water.

Conversation throughout dinner is light-hearted, but grinds to a sudden halt when a ringing sounds from Killian's backpack.

"Is that the sat phone?" Nova asks, her fork paused halfway to her mouth.

The ring sounds again, and Killian is out of his seat and rummaging through his bag in a flash. He picks up the call before the third ring.

"Sable, what's happened?" he asks in place of a traditional greeting.

I hear a female voice through the mic but can't make out the words. Killian's eyes widen and he shoots a glance at his wife, holding her gaze. "Emberly, slow down. Where's Sable?"

Shock squeezes the breath from my lungs, and I drop my fork. It clatters loudly on the plate and then thuds to the tabletop.

"Where is the orb now?" Killian pauses as Emberly says something. He runs a hand through his dark hair. "You know I can't tell you where we are. If you're separated from the group, you should make your way back to the Elders' compound and wait there."

This one-way conversation causes my anxiety to skyrocket.

"Dad, what's going on?" Nova asks.

Killian shakes his head, then strides toward the door at the back of the barn. Ciara jumps from her seat, following him with a warning for the three of us to stay put.

"That can't be good," Nova says when the door bangs shut after her mom.

"We probably shouldn't jump to any conclusions," I say, but my mind whirls with possibilities.

What if Thorne found them and attacked the group? What if he has the orb? What if Emberly is hurt? Why isn't she with the rest of her group? What could have happened to separate her and Steel?

My gaze drifts to Greyson, whose eyes are glued to the back door where Killian and Ciara disappeared. Two of his brothers are with that group. He's silent, but I know him well enough to see the concern written across his face.

"Well, something's wrong," Nova goes on. "That phone was only supposed to be used in extreme emergencies." Nova pushes her plate away from her. "And how did Emberly get it, anyway? It's supposed to be with Sable."

Killian and Ciara re-enter the bunkhouse, silencing our speculations. Walking over to his bag, Killian crouches as he re-stows the phone. I hold my breath as I wait for someone to tell us what just happened. It's at least thirty seconds before Nova breaks.

"Mom. Dad. What happened?"

Ciara breathes deeply and casts a glance at her husband. Standing, Killian crosses his arms over his chest.

"The other group was attacked. We're not sure about the current status of the other orb." Killian pauses and then glances at Greyson. "Or the rest of the group."

Greyson's eyebrows twitch toward each other. He leans forward, placing his elbows on the table in front of him.

"Is Emberly hurt?" I ask, unable to muzzle the concern for my best friend.

"Emberly got separated from the others. She isn't sure where they are now."

He didn't answer my question.

"This doesn't change our mission," Ciara chimes in. "We're still flying out at first light. If Thorne does have the other orb, it's more important than ever we get this one hidden."

She's right—I know she is—but worry for my friends overwhelms me. I couldn't hear Emberly's words, but her voice was frantic. That's not like her. She may still be working to control and hone her abilities, but she's the most powerful angel-born I know. Perhaps the most powerful one in existence.

Shy of death, is there a plausible reason why Steel would allow himself to be separated from her? If it was between the fate of the world and Emberly, I think Steel would choose Emberly. I saw it in his eyes when Thorne tried to ransom her for the orbs. Steel would have happily handed the supernatural objects over if it meant Emberly would be returned unharmed.

"Greyson?" Killian's voice breaks the momentary silence that has settled over the group. "Are you going to be able to stay on mission?"

He rubs his mouth and nods. Dropping his hand to the table, he says, "I understand what has to be done."

"Good. Let's finish this meal and get ready for bed. The more sleep we can get, the better shape we'll all be in tomorrow."

I look down at my half-eaten haggis. What's in my stomach has already soured. The likelihood of me getting the rest of my meal down is probably about as good as the possibility of getting sleep tonight, which is to say, slim to none.

Picking up my fork, I push food around the plate while my mind churns. I know I won't be able to settle it until I do one thing: I need to talk to Emberly.

# 39

## ASH

"*A*sh, what are you doing?" I spin with the phone clutched in my hand.

"Greyson," I say on a half-gasp.

Greyson's gaze lands on the phone right away, then snaps to my face. I was so careful making sure everyone was asleep before I nabbed the sat phone and snuck out of the bunkhouse. Did I not check Greyson well enough, or had I made a noise to wake him?

"Ash," Greyson says again, taking a tentative step forward. "Why do you have the phone?"

He knows exactly why, but I can't help stating my case. "We can't just leave her out there alone. You know that. Emberly is new to our world. She probably doesn't know who else to call for help."

With his mouth set in a hard line, I watch a war take place on Greyson's face. Indecision rides him hard. Duty is just as important to him as loyalty to friends and family. I just need to tip the scales.

"Don't you want to know about your brothers? One of

them could be hurt, dying. Do you really want to look back on this moment and know that we did nothing to help?"

Greyson flinches and my heart tweaks. I don't want to wound him, but it's the same track that keeps running through my head. What if there's something we can do to help them, and we don't? I can't live with that, and I don't think Greyson could either. I know that Killian and Ciara are being extra careful right now, but what could be the real harm in checking in with Emberly?

"It will just be a quick conversation, I promise."

With a sigh, Greyson ushers me farther away from the barn. "It's best if Killian and Ciara don't find out about this call."

Once we're a good distance from our sleeping teammates, I quickly dial and listen to the phone ring. And ring.

I glance at Greyson after the fifth ring. Maybe we're already too late?

He lays a hand on my arm and squeezes, offering what comfort he can.

Finally, the line picks up.

"Have you decided not to leave me for dead after all?" Emberly's words bite, which isn't like her.

"Emberly, what's happened? Are you all right? What do you need?"

I'm met with silence.

"Emberly?"

"Ash. Is that you?"

"Yes, it's me." I breathe a sigh of relief. She seems annoyed, but okay.

"Oh, Ash." Emberly starts crying. Big sobs loud enough that Greyson can hear.

"Put her on speaker," he says.

I punch the button and Emberly's cries echo in the night. I'm extra glad we moved away from the barn.

Emberly's usually levelheaded. She hasn't had an easy life, so to hear her so rattled has me extra anxious. Even Greyson looks antsy from all this crying.

"Em, this is Greyson. Can you tell us what happened?"

"It was awful. There were Fallen and Forsaken everywhere, so many that I had to run. We got separated and when it was safe for me to return to where we were ambushed, no one was there. I found Sable's backpack with the phone, but besides that, there was only . . . blood."

Greyson rubs a hand over his mouth, his eyes haunted.

"Where are you now?" I ask.

"I'm in a half blown-out house outside of London. You guys, I'm so scared. I don't know what happened to any of them, but I'm terrified that—" She breaks down and starts crying again.

"Is the house safe?" Greyson asks.

"No. I know it's not." There are sniffles on the other line as she tries to compose herself. "I want to join your group, but Killian wouldn't tell me where you guys were. I can't be alone. I've been alone for my whole life, and I just can't do it again."

Greyson and I exchange a glance.

"We're leaving in the morning, Em," Greyson says. "You wouldn't be able to join us even if you did know where we were."

"Wherever you are, I'm sure I could fly to you. You couldn't have gotten that far in the last day."

My eyes plead with Greyson. After everything that's happened with Emberly this past half-year, I've never heard her this undone.

"Please, you guys. You're all I have," she begs. I can't help the tear that slips from my eye and tracks down my cheek. Greyson's gaze is fastened to it as it drops to the ground.

"All right, Emberly, listen carefully to everything I tell you." I meet Greyson's eyes, and he nods once, letting me know he's okay telling her. "We leave at daybreak, so you have to make it here before then."

A crash wakes me from my fitful sleep. I roll out of the bunk and on to my feet, reaching under the pillow for the dagger I stashed there last night even as I rise to my full height.

A fist heads straight for my face, and I block it with my arm and then strike out with my free hand. My blow lands harmlessly against my attacker's shoulder but throws them off enough for me to regain my footing. In a split second, I categorize the male's features and size him up.

Tall, dark-haired, gorgeous, pale white skin. Forsaken.

I slash out at the monster with my blade. The tip slices a shallow cut across his chest, which angers him more than it does any real damage, and he comes at me again.

As we exchange blows, others battle around me, but I'm too busy fighting this Forsaken to assess the situation. I only know they've found us and it's bad.

I'm about to drop low and take the Forsaken down when an explosion blows the back of the barn wide open and sends me flying forward. I smash into the wall and slide to the ground. Ringing in my ears covers all other noise.

Shaking my head, I push to all fours. I glance up to see Greyson running at me. His mouth is moving, but I can't hear anything over the ringing. He waves his arms, but I don't know what he's trying to tell me.

I start to push to my feet when I'm tackled by a Forsaken. The large male slams me to the ground. My head snaps back and connects with the concrete floor. A wave of nausea rolls up from my gut that I'm only just barely able to hold down.

The Forsaken above me bares his teeth. His sharp fangs lengthen as he tips his head back, preparing to strike.

I rear up. Twisting my torso, I nail the Forsaken in the face with an elbow strike. Using my momentum, I flip the male on to his back. With my knees planted on either side of his hips, I throw a jab to his face and then his trachea. His larynx collapses under my knuckles, and he starts to choke. He wheezes and gasps as my hearing returns.

I'm looking for a weapon to finish him off when Greyson reaches me. He wrenches me off the Forsaken and to my feet. He has a cut that runs through his left eyebrow and trickles blood down his face. He wipes at the blood, smearing it over the side of his face. He's covered in dust and small debris from the explosion but looks relatively okay. He yanks me toward the door.

"Wait, I haven't finished him off."

I scan the ground for my dagger as Greyson hauls me backward. The Forsaken is still writhing on the ground, but he'll be good as new in a few minutes. A solid stab through the eye-socket and into the brain will end him, though.

"No time," Greyson shouts.

I look up to see Nova and her parents fighting off a group of Forsaken in front of the hole that was blasted in the back of the bunkhouse. They're doing a good job of holding the Forsaken at bay. With their backs to each other, Nova, Killian, and Ciara fight like a well-oiled machine. Ciara shouts commands that cause them to dip and dive and attack as a group. It almost looks like a choreographed dance.

"I've got the orb. We have to get it out of here."

Right. We have to protect the orb.

Shoving through the front door, Greyson and I take off for our bikes. I feel wetness on my feet and realize I don't even have shoes on. My socks soak up the morning dew, but I don't have any time to do anything about it now.

We reach the bikes, and my feet skid over loose gravel as I scramble to mount the ride. The motorcycles will be loud, but we have a better chance of escaping with transportation than on foot.

Both our engines rev to life at almost the same time. I shoot a glance at the farmhouse. Instinct screams at me to protect the humans inside, but I know it's more important to keep this orb from the Forsaken.

Greyson and I peel out with absolutely no finesse. Both our bikes kick up dirt and gravel, and mine fishtails before I'm able to right it again. We really punch it and take off down the dirt country roads at speeds dangerous even to someone with angel-born reflexes.

The sky to the right is starting to lighten. It's almost dawn. The Forsaken will be trapped once the sun rises. Their attack strategy doesn't make sense.

My gaze zeros in on the black pack on Greyson's back as he zips down the road in front of me. The orb we have is the one taken from Whitehold. Emberly said that it not only forced everyone into the spirit realm, but also allowed Forsaken to walk in the daylight. Their plan must be centered around getting the orb to allow them to move during the day.

My muscles are tight as we careen around a bend in the road. I don't know where Greyson is headed, but there's no time to flag him down to ask. We need to put as much space in between us and those Forsaken as possible.

How in the world did they find us?

Someone drops from the sky, landing in the road in front of us, and we have to swerve to keep from crashing into him.

Greyson and I bank in opposite directions, but we're going too fast to maneuver safely and both end up putting down our bikes. The gravel road eats at my clothes and exposed skin as I skid across it, the weight of the bike pressing me down. I grit my teeth to keep from yelling in pain.

I finally slide to a stop. Ignoring my injuries, I shove the motorcycle off of me, then stagger to my feet.

"You have something that belongs to me."

I spin to find Thorne only a half-step away. His hand shoots out and clamps around my throat. He lifts his arm and brings me into the air. My toes brush back and forth against the ground as I try to find purchase.

I strike out at Thorne, hoping to get him to drop me. He tilts his head away from my sloppy punches and squeezes his hand around my throat. I stop my attack and claw at his hand, trying to loosen his grip to get a full swallow of air.

His hand tightens even more, and his eyes narrow. "Where. Is. My. Orb?"

Hanging onto his wrist for leverage, I kick my feet forward and into his chest. The attack takes him by surprise, and he drops me. I fall heavily to the ground, landing on my skinned shoulder and hip, coughing as I suck in sweet oxygen.

Thorne reaches for me again, but Greyson plows into his side, sending them both to the ground. Greyson only has the upper hand for about a half second before Thorne is back on his feet. He yanks Greyson up by the straps of the backpack and delivers an uppercut that has Greyson airborne before crashing back to the earth.

Greyson rolls to the side and spits out a wad of blood and saliva, then shoves to his feet. Thorne advances on him.

"That pack strapped to your back looks promising. I'm not in a particularly bloodthirsty mood this morning. How about you give me a look, and if the orb is there, I'll let you two leave without any more injuries?"

Greyson snarls in response.

Thorne shrugs. "Don't say I didn't warn you."

Thorne moves so fast I have a hard time tracking him. One moment he's ten feet from Greyson, and the next he's standing behind him. Greyson only has enough time to half-turn before Thorne kicks his knee. I hear the crunch of bone and Greyson crumples to the ground.

I take off toward the pair. I have nothing to fight with except my fists, and that's not going to be enough to take down Thorne, but I have to try.

Thorne yanks the backpack off Greyson. While he's distracted digging through the contents, Greyson swings his arm in an arc and embeds a knife in Thorne's thigh.

Thorne staggers back, eyeing first the knife in his leg, then Greyson. With his gaze latched onto Greyson, he pulls the box with the orb out of the bag.

He's about to flip the latch, opening the box and exposing us all to the orb's power, when Greyson brings his other arm up and aims a handgun at Thorne. Without hesitation, Greyson squeezes the trigger.

The shot rings out. All three of us freeze.

My eyes widen as a red splotch blooms in the middle of Thorne's chest. Thorne doesn't even look down as he flicks his wrist. The top of the box opens, and we are forced into the spirit realm.

Thorne's silver wings punch out. With the orb in his grasp, he jumps into the air. The downward thrust of his wings sending him high into the sky. A single drop of blood lands on my shoulder as he shoots over my head and disappears into the early morning sunrise.

# 40
## STEEL

*S*able slams her phone down on the counter. After a night of fruitless searching, we broke into a mobile phone store in Chelsea. Sterling was able to get cell phones working for all of us. Sable just got off the phone with Deacon.

"Thorne has the second orb," she says. "He attacked the other group in northern Scotland and took it an hour ago."

I scrub a hand down my face. The good news just keeps coming.

"Are the others all right?" Sterling asks.

Sable nods. "Some injuries, but nothing life-threatening. They're on their way back to London."

I shake my head in disgust. "None of us even made it out of the UK. Deacon needs to find that bracelet."

"He can't search for it himself because he's here, in London. There's a temporary base within jogging distance. But he's going to send someone to look for it."

Keeping my mouth shut, I nod. Finding the bracelet

Thorne has somewhere in this city is probably going to be my best bet, but I want the other one just in case.

Sable takes a deep breath. "Deacon is going to update Sorcha and the rest of the Elders about the orbs. This is too big to keep under wraps."

Sterling lets out a low whistle. "We're in so much trouble."

Sable looks weary, but considering the night we've had, I'm sure we all do. The number of Forsaken in London has grown exponentially in the last twenty-four hours. Either Thorne's orders or the open hunting grounds brought them in droves. We weren't looking for fights, but it was impossible to avoid them. As soon as the sun went down, we spent as much time helping humans stupid enough to walk the streets at night escape attacks as we did searching for Emberly and Shira. And the few Forsaken we captured and questioned either didn't know anything about Thorne's plans or were willing to die to protect them.

We're banged up and bruised. Each of our clothes is splattered with blood, our own and Forsaken, and we have nothing to show for it. My hands itch to grab something and throw it out of frustration, but I fist them instead.

"Once the Council learns about everything going on, we're going to be the least of their worries. Let's just keep our focus where it should be," Sable says right before Tinkle pops back into the mortal realm directly in front of her face. She lets out a yip, and he drops to the counter.

"Why'd you yell?" he asks.

"Was materializing right in front of my face really necessary?"

"Of course not," he says, and blinks back at her, clearly not understanding her angst.

"Did you find anything?" I ask.

Tinkle takes in a breath. His furry shoulders lift up and then sink as he hangs his head. "No. I couldn't find any trace of Emberly or Shira on either side of the river. It's like they disappeared."

I have to walk to the other side of the room to compose myself. I hung a lot of hope on Tinkle being able to lead us to Emberly. Impotence causes frustration to boil in my gut. I can't do anything for her if I can't find her.

Sable sighs. "I know you've done everything you can. It's time for you to find Camiel and let him know what's happened."

Tinkle scurries behind a cardboard advertisement sitting on the display counter and peeks his head out at Sable.

"I can't do that," he says.

"Why not?"

Tinkle's voice quiets, and I have to re-join Sable and Sterling to hear him. "I lost her again. Camiel will be angry. Very angry."

Sable exchanges a raised-eyebrow look with me and Sterling, and I'm reminded of when Camiel described Celestials as "childlike."

"Are you worried that Camiel will hurt you?" Sable asks.

Tinkle shakes his triangular head and clutches his paws together in front of him. "No." His eyes widen. "He's going to yell at me."

Sterling snorts out a laugh, and Tinkle swivels his head in my brother's direction. "It's not funny. He's really loud."

If Emberly's life wasn't at stake, I'm sure I'd find this little convo amusing as well, but as it is, we don't have time for this.

It takes Herculean effort not to bark at Tinkle. What I

really want to do is ring his neck, but that won't get us anywhere with him. If only Nova was with us. She'd be able to get Tinkle to walk through fire with only a flip of her hair.

I bend over so my face is closer to the creature, doing my best to keep my voice at a reasonable level. Emberly is a saint for putting up with his antics. "Camiel may know a way to bring Emberly back. We're going to need all the help we can get to stop Thorne and Seraphim. We need you. *Emberly* needs you."

His whiskers twitch. As a flying squirrel, Tinkle doesn't have eyebrows, but if he did, they'd be furrowed in determination.

"All right, yeah. I'll do it."

I let out a burst of air. If that last attempt didn't work, my next move was to threaten his life. I'm glad it didn't come to that.

"But for the record, I'm not doing it for you, Lover Boy. I'm doing it for Emberly."

"Yeah, yeah, sure. That's fine." I don't care if he does it for an imaginary friend as long as he gets Camiel, and fast.

"We're going to need you to find Camiel quickly and then let him know what's happened. That Seraphim has possessed Emberly and they have both orbs," Sable says. "Now that they have everything they need, they could bring the barrier down at any moment."

"I got it. And don't worry, I'm superfast. I'll get to Camiel in a flash." As if to prove his point, he shoots into the air. A line of silver sparks trail after him as he zips around above our heads.

I bite my tongue to keep from snapping that it took several days for Tinkle and Camiel to show up the last time

Emberly went missing. I just have to hope that this time will be different.

Tinkle lands on a cell phone display across the room. "The next time you see me, I'll have an oversized seraph with me."

"Wait," Sterling calls with a hand in the air to stop Tinkle from disappearing. "Can you get a message to Shira's family?"

Tinkle cocks his head. "The angel-line Nephilim never leave Eden. They won't be any help if that's what you're thinking."

"That may be true," Sterling admits, "but they deserve to know what's happened to Shira. If what Emberly said about Thorne and Seraphim's plans are true, Shira's in a lot of trouble right now."

Reaching out, I clasp my brother's shoulder. "We know she's still alive."

He glances over at me. "For now."

He's not wrong. Shira's safety isn't guaranteed. I didn't tell him that Seraphim roughed Shira up pretty badly, only that Emberly saw her. I was worried knowing her physical condition would send Sterling over the edge.

"I'll make sure Nikias finds out," Tinkle says with a nod, then blinks into the spirit realm.

Sable grabs the mobile phone and shoves it into a pocket. She checks her holsters then grabs her pack off the ground. "Let's go meet up with the others. We can regroup and figure out our next plan of action."

Sterling follows suit and starts gearing up. I never relaxed, so I don't have to.

The makeshift base is in a park southeast of us on the other side of the Thames. We make our way over Chelsea

Bridge, walking straight down the middle lane because there are no moving vehicles on the streets. Most of London either fled the city or is hunkered down in hiding. Forsaken, angel-born, and random military convoys are the only ones still traveling the streets. I haven't paid too much attention to what the human military has done since Thorne unleashed Fallen into the mortal world, but I'm sure they still have no idea what they're truly fighting. The time for keeping humans in the dark about the real world has come to an end, but that barely concerns me. Let the Elders work out that mess.

We're halfway across the bridge when a prickle of awareness lifts the hairs on the back of my neck. I slow down and then stop to scan the riverbanks. It's quiet. Eerily quiet. But I don't see anything suspicious.

"Bro, you coming?" Sterling calls from where he and Sable wait for me. They've made it to the other side of the river while I loiter in the middle of the bridge.

I make another visual sweep of my surroundings. There's nothing but abandoned vehicles littered on the bridge. Maybe I'm being paranoid?

I nod, then yell, "Yeah, I'm coming."

I'm three paces into my jog when a car in front of me explodes. The blast punches me head-on and sends me flying backward. I slam into one of the bridge's main support pillars and then flop to the ground. I hear two more detonations. When I struggle to my feet, a black cloud has swallowed the end of the bridge.

"Steel! Steel!" Sterling yells my name loud enough for half of London to hear.

Pulling out my newly acquired phone, I arch my back

and twist, working out the kinks from that impact. That sucked.

Sable picks up on the second ring. "Are you okay?" she asks.

"Yeah. Tell Sterling to stop shouting."

Sable relays to Sterling that I'm all right and he stops calling my name.

"Three car bombs took out the bridge," Sable says.

As the smoke from the blasts start to clear, I can see there's no way to the other side unless I phase and fly over. Reports have confirmed that the spirit realm is flooded with Fallen, so we've been cautioned to stay in the mortal world. I run my tongue over my teeth as I consider my options.

"I know where Brockwell is," I say. "I'll head up to the next bridge and meet you guys there."

I'm already jogging back the way I came. I don't know what triggered those explosions, so I don't feel comfortable being exposed. I give each vehicle I pass a wide berth, just in case.

"We can meet you at the next bridge," Sable offers.

"Naw. Don't waste the time. Go on without me. I'll be less than twenty minutes behind you."

Sable is quiet for a moment. She doesn't like the idea of separating, but it doesn't make sense for her and Sterling to back track. Finally she relents but doesn't let me go until she gives me advice about avoiding Forsaken. I nod like I'm listening, but really, my mind is already on what route I'm going to take.

I head north toward the next crossing, keeping the river on my right and a keen eye on each building I pass. It doesn't take more than ten minutes to reach the Vauxhall Bridge. I pause before crossing, not because I'm worried about another bomb, although I should be, but because something about Emberly's description of where she's being held starts to nag me.

I turn over everything she told me, which isn't a lot. Fancy. Old-fashioned. High ceilings. Ornate hallways. Lots of rooms. She said it reminded her of a palace. Buckingham Palace would be the obvious choice if I didn't already know that thanks to Thorne, half of it burned down the first day of the attacks.

The answer comes to me and I don't know how I didn't realize it before.

A hotel. She's in a nice hotel. A nice hotel with lots of rooms and historical fixtures. That's got to be it.

There are a ton of historical hotels in London, but some of the nicest ones aren't far from here. I'm looking for old English opulence, and I know exactly where to start.

Sable and Sterling will be expecting me, but now that I have a location in my head, I can't pass up the opportunity to check. At worst it will be a detour; at best I'll find my girl.

Forgetting the bridge and heading north along the Thames, I take off at a sprint. The world around me blurs as I head straight toward The Savoy.

# 41
## STEEL

*S*omething is definitely going on in that hotel. In the last thirty minutes, five Forsaken slinked from The Savoy to the adjacent theater using their awnings as cover from the sun.

I dig in my pocket for my phone. It's time to alert Sable to what I've found. There's a tightness in my body that says Emberly's close. Even if I have to search each and every room in this giant hotel, I'll find her.

The phone is at my ear and ringing when Silver steps out of the hotel. Everything in me freezes, turning me into a living statue.

Rather than scurrying to the theater adjacent the hotel, like every Forsaken that I watched emerge from The Savoy has done, she strolls forward. Silver tips her face skyward when she clears the awning and soaks in the sun, something she wasn't able to do for ten years as a Forsaken. There's a smile on her face as she enjoys the small luxury.

The phone clicks as someone picks up the call. I think I

hear my name, but I'm so caught off-guard by Silver that I barely hear anything.

The last time I saw Silver she was with Thorne. I'm now positive this is the right place.

"The Savoy. Silver's here. I'm going in," I say, then hang up. I don't need to elaborate. I know they'll come.

My first obstacle is Silver. As I war with myself about what to do, I miss my opportunity to strike. Someone calls her name and she glances over her shoulder, baring her teeth at the person who spoiled her moment. Turning, she strides back inside.

Silver won't hesitate to take me out the first opportunity she has, so I can't afford to give her concessions she won't offer in return. I harden my heart, reminding myself I already lost her ten years ago. She made her decision; she picked a side of her own free will, and she's going down with the rest of them.

After crawling out from my surveillance spot under a car, I do a quick check to make sure all my weapons are secure. I have knives strapped to my right ankle and hip, a crossbow slung over my shoulder, three tear gas grenades strapped to my lower back, and two machine pistols fully loaded and holstered against my ribs. I'm the most effective in my lion form, but I can't rely solely on my shifting abilities. It's a trade off, but if I stick to the mortal world, I won't have to deal with any Fallen.

I skirt the building, looking for a point of entry. It's safe to assume that Thorne has guards positioned at each of the traditional entries, so I want to avoid those.

There's a prospect three floors up: a window cracked open. After checking my surroundings, I start to scale the side of the building. The ornate ledges and carvings in the stone aid my ascent.

I hoist myself over the last ledge and strain my hearing, not wanting to drop into an occupied room. Not picking up anything, I nudge the window open farther and slip into the room. My feet land on the carpeted floor without a sound.

Crown molding, tray ceilings, a four-poster bed, and dark mahogany furniture garnish the bedroom. There's a sitting room to my right that I don't bother exploring, but instead pad straight to the door, cracking it an inch to scout the hallway. When I don't hear or see any Forsaken, I move into the corridor.

It's not exactly how Emberly described, but I'm not concerned. Seeing Silver confirmed that I have the right location, but I've also stayed here before and know that not every floor is identical. I need to make my way down to the floors with the banquet halls. The ceilings are the highest there and the hallways the most ornate, fitting Emberly's description the closest. It's as good a starting point as any.

As I move down the hall toward the stairway, I slip my twelve-inch knife from the sheath and hold it at the ready. Just as I adjust my grip on the weapon, the door on the left swings open. I pivot and land a front kick to the gut of a male, catching him completely off guard.

Hunched over, he stumbles back into the room, and I advance, making sure the door swings shut behind me.

I follow up with an uppercut that sends him flying back and into a sofa chair. I haven't used my knife yet because I need to make sure he's a Forsaken. The curtains in the room are all drawn, blocking out the sun, but there are probably still some humans hiding in this hotel. When my opponent rolls to his feet and snarls before charging me, I know he's a Forsaken.

Game on.

When the Forsaken closes in, I swing with one arm and slice with the other. My fist slams into his jaw, and my blade cuts across his chest. He staggers back, looking down at the black blood already saturating his shirt.

"You're dead," he growls before coming at me again with zero finesse and even less tactical skill. He's all swinging arms as he tries to ram me. At the last moment, I drop low, taking out his legs. He goes sailing over my head and into the wall face-first. His head and shoulders disappear into the plaster, and I bark out a laugh.

"Rumors of the combat skills of Thorne's soldiers have been grossly overblown."

With a litany of curses, the Forsaken rips himself out of the wall, causing another shower of plaster dust. His black hair is gray with the particles and it now looks like I'm facing off against someone who was dipped in flour. He swipes a hand across his face, which only smears the plaster.

I don't wait for him to rush me again. Instead, I jolt forward and grab the creature by the shoulders, then slam him into the opposite wall. I deliver another blow to the head and follow it up with a jab to the gut.

He hunches over, and I grab his arm. I ram my knife through his wrist, pinning it to the wall behind him.

He lets out a wail, but I crack his temple, finally knocking him out. The last thing I need are his screams bringing even more Forsaken.

Reaching down, I grab the blade at my ankle and secure his other arm to one of the wall's studs. When this dude wakes, we're going to have a talk.

There's a crash farther into the room, and I freeze. We're not alone.

A whimper follows the noise. I glance at the unconscious Forsaken hanging from the wall by the blades in his wrists, satisfied that I have at least a couple of minutes before he comes to.

Taking careful steps, I stalk across the room toward the closed door. Must be the bathroom. Listening carefully, I pick up more than one set of breaths on the other side of the door.

I reach over my shoulder and grab the crossbow slung across my back, loading it quickly. The automatic pistols holstered under my arms might be more useful against whatever is in the bathroom, but they're loud.

I kick in the door and a female screams, throwing her body over someone else.

"Please don't hurt us," she sobs.

I lower the crossbow. It's two humans. A man and a woman. And from the looks of it, the Forsaken has fed on both of them.

Of the two of them, only the woman is conscious. I return the crossbow to my back and put my hands up in front of me.

"I'm not going to hurt you. I'm not like that creature."

Tear tracks run through dried blood spatters on her face. She's clad in nightwear and shaking violently. She cradles a man's head and shoulders in her lap. He's an unnatural shade of white, but he's still breathing. There's a piece of fabric tied around his neck that's half-saturated with blood.

"Can you help us?" she asks.

I nod, even though I know there's only so much I can do.

"Stay here," I order, and the woman flinches. I do my

best to soften my voice. "I'm going to go take care of—" I can't say *Forsaken*, she won't know what that means. "Of the person that hurt you. Don't come out. I'll be back."

Grabbing a washcloth, I shut the door behind me and prowl toward my prey. I left him alive for questioning, but now that I have humans to help, I need to make this quick.

I slap the Forsaken across the face. "Yo, ugly dude, wakey wakey."

He rouses quicker than I expected and tries to surge to his feet, but I slam a hand against his throat and hold him captive against the wall. He spits Enochian words at me I don't understand. Most likely cursing me to the depths of hell.

"Where's Thorne?"

More Enochian. With my free hand I punch him in the ribs, hearing them crack.

"Let's try that again. Where's Thorne? And how about a human language this time?"

The Forsaken tries to spit in my face, but I lean out of the way. Black blood and saliva dribbles from his mouth.

"Why would I tell you anything, you disgusting half-breed."

Using my free hand, I jam the washcloth I snagged into his mouth to muffle his screams. This next part is going to be really unpleasant.

"Maybe this will change your mind."

I jam my thumb and index finger into his eye socket, hardening my features to keep from grimacing at the repulsive task.

The Forsaken bucks and pulls against the blades holding his arms in place. He screams into his gag as I root around his orbital cavity. When I have a hold on the gelatinous organ, I yank my arm back. The eyeball pops out with the optic nerve still attached.

"Well, look at that," I say conversationally. "It didn't pop." I tilt my head at the Forsaken and stare into his remaining eye. "And still attached, which means you could still save it. So tell me, are you ready to talk?"

The Forsaken isn't ready to talk until I pull the other eye out. In under ten minutes I've squeezed out of him the location of the Forsaken in the hotel and that Thorne and Seraphim are holed up in the Royal Suite on the fifth floor.

This Forsaken isn't high enough on the food chain to know all their plans, but he did know Thorne returned with the second orb over an hour ago and that they don't plan to bring the barrier down until nightfall, when the Forsaken can participate in an attack. The sun sets early this time of year, but it still gives me a cushion of several hours, which is the first break since this whole mess began.

My hands are sticky with black blood and vitreous humor. I rub them on the bedding. The dead Forsaken is slumped on the ground somewhere behind me. I hastily wipe both blades off on the blankets, then return them to their sheaths.

Rubbing my jaw, I head for the bathroom to deal with the humans huddled inside. I open the door slowly so as not to frighten the woman. The man is still passed out, which is going to be a problem.

Bending over, I snatch a couple of crumpled towels. I rip them into strips that can be used to bind both their wounds. The woman watches me with wide eyes.

I hand her the pieces. "Use the towels to bind both your wounds as best you can."

She nods and gets to work.

Leaving the bathroom, I search the room, turning up drinks and snacks still in the mini-bar. Spotting a duffle bag, I empty it and shove the food and drinks in there. Next, I strip the bed and knot together the sheets, thin comforter, and a few extra blankets. Shoving open the curtains, I pop the window open. Three stories up would be a relatively easy drop for a Nephilim, but deadly to a human.

There's a groan from the other room as the man wakes.

Good.

When I return to the bathroom, the man is sitting up with his head in his hands. The woman rubs his back. He has a new towel bandage around his neck, upper arm, and thigh.

"You have to leave. Daytime is the safest time to travel. Don't go out in the streets at night, do you understand?"

The woman nods. The man lifts his head, his gaze only half-focused. Frustration floods me. I don't have time for this.

"Come on. You've got to go."

With help, the man pushes to his feet. His steps aren't stable. He leans heavily on the woman to move forward. I'm going to have to lower both of them down. No way are they going to be able to get to the street on their own.

I grab the makeshift rope I made out of bedding and head toward the couple. "I'm going to secure this around you both and lower you to the ground."

The woman gasps, bringing a hand up to cover her mouth as she stares in horror over my shoulder at the dead Forsaken.

I feel a twinge of guilt. I should have covered it. It's a grisly sight, and these two have been through enough.

I clear my throat. "Sorry, I should have—"

"No." She stops me with a shake of her head. Her eyes fill with flint and fire. "He was a monster. He deserved it, and worse."

I nod back at her. She's a fighter. Good.

There's nothing left to say as I secure a sheet around the couple.

"You can't lower us both down," the man argues when I have them both positioned by the window. "We weigh too much."

"I'm strong. I won't drop you."

His Adam's apple bobs as he considers me.

"Listen, your only other option is to stay in this room and hide. Which might be safer, but if I were in your position, I'd want to get as far away from this hotel as possible. Either way, you need to make up your mind right now."

"Who are you?"

"It's not important. I need you to trust that I can get you out of here safely. If you can't do that, I'm leaving."

The woman touches his shoulder. "Think of what he did to that monster. He can do this."

The man finally relents. Once they crawl out the window, it takes less than a minute for me to lower them to the street. When their feet touch the ground, they only glance up at me once before scrambling away from the hotel as quickly as they can. I don't wait to make sure they make it out of sight. I have somewhere else I need to be.

# 42

## ASH

*I*'m not settled until the chopper's landing skids touch down in Brockwell Park. We got word on the flight down from the highlands that Thorne has both of the orbs, so I keep expecting Fallen to drop out of the sky at any moment. There's a parachute strapped to my back, but, considering the last time I had to bail out of a plane, it's hardly a comfort.

The rotor blades whir above our heads as we pile out of the fuselage. Greyson's leg is splinted, so Killian helps him disembark. Nova, Ciara, and I follow.

We had to skirt central London. It took an extra half hour, and even though it's only mid-day, I don't like how low the sun is positioned in the sky. Once it disappears, we'll be at a severe disadvantage.

A makeshift military base has been set up in the flat park. As we head toward the Humvees and green tents set up a couple hundred yards away, the chopper that brought us here takes off again.

Something is definitely going down. There's tension in

the air as we join the angel-borns rushing back and forth between tents like busy worker ants.

I hear a familiar voice in the crowd call Greyson's name, and turn to see Sterling jogging toward us. With disheveled hair, blood-spattered clothing, and a bruise high on his cheekbone, he looks as rough as the rest of us. He clasps hands with his twin and they quickly embrace.

"You look terrible," Sterling says when they pull apart.

"You're not winning any beauty contests right now, either," Greyson returns.

"At least all my joints are still functioning."

"Yeah, well, you should see the other guy." Greyson's lighthearted demeanor disappears in an instant. "I shot him in the chest, and he just flew away. I don't know what can stop him."

Sterling's grim expression matches his brother's. "Yeah, we have a true fight on our hands." He skims his gaze over the rest of us, a brittle smile plastered across his face. "Good to see you guys all in one piece. Our group is down to two. Steel's out there, looking for Emberly—or rather, Seraphim."

A rusty blade pierces my gut at the reminder of what happened to Emberly and the trap Seraphim set for us that I skipped right into.

"Come on, Sable will want to see you. We might have located their headquarters. The Elders are planning now."

Sterling turns on his heel and heads toward one of the tents. He tosses the flap out of the way and motions all of us inside what's obviously the main hub of operations.

It looks like we walked into a high-tech command center rather than a tent. There are computers everywhere. I'll bet

Sterling straight-up started to drool the first time he laid eyes on them.

Sable and Deacon are on the other side of the tent with three of the Elders. To get to them, we have to navigate through unfamiliar techie equipment. The Elders must have pulled in the Keepers.

There are schematics of buildings and zones of London on large monitors throughout the space, dotted with icons that likely indicate groups of angel-born.

I always knew that at our core, Nephilim are a well-oiled and highly organized military group, but seeing it first-hand is still eye-opening.

Killian and Ciara stop us before we reach Sable, to say they're going to check in with their squad. Nova tilts her head at our group to let her parents know she's sticking with us. Killian tells Nova to stay alert, and Ciara hands her daughter an extra dagger to sheath at her ankle. Each member of the family lifts an arm and places a hand on the shoulder of the person to their right, creating a circle. Leaning forward, they touch foreheads, then break apart. Pride for their daughter shines from Killian and Ciara's eyes before they head in the opposite direction.

We're still several paces from the group of Elders and leaders when Sable's voice rises. "We can't just blow up the hotel. We don't know that there aren't humans inside. Not to mention two of our own are in there."

Malachi, the cherub Elder, crosses his arms over his chest and shoots Sable a hard look. "If we don't shut down their operation, a catastrophic number of humans will die when the barrier comes down. This plan could mitigate millions of future casualties. Steel entered that building of his own accord. We will do what we can to get a message to him to get out."

No one notices us, and that's for the best. This conversation is heated.

"And what about Emberly? Do you just consider her collateral damage?"

No one speaks for a moment.

"What about her?" Malachi asks. His voice dips with false composure. "Your own intel told us it's not Emberly anymore, it's Seraphim." He pauses just long enough for an inky sort of foreboding to settle in my chest. "With everything going on, we can't afford to make her a priority beyond neutralizing her. She's to be considered a high-value, high-threat target as dangerous as Thorne—maybe more so—and to be taken out without hesitation."

No. I slap a hand over my mouth to muffle my gasp. Greyson grabs my other hand and squeezes.

Sable's eyes flare and she takes a step toward Malachi. Deacon, a silent statue behind her, reaches forward and grabs her bicep, staying her movements. Going up against an Elder is not a good idea. Besides being a politically dangerous move, our kind gains power with age; the Elders of each line are literally the most powerful Nephilim on Earth—or they were until Emberly showed up.

There's another tense moment of silence. I glance around at the adults, expecting one of the other Elders to object, but they don't. Zara's and Draven's silence speaks volumes. They support Malachi. There's no one else to speak up for Emberly, Steel, and the humans besides Sable and Deacon.

"I wasn't even aware angel-born had access to surface-to-surface missiles." There's a hint of accusation in Sable's voice, and by the way Malachi's eyes narrow, he heard it.

"We're working with the human military."

What? In the history of our people, we've never aligned ourselves with the humans. I glance around the small group and it's obvious I'm not the only one shook by that announcement. Only the Elders don't react.

Sable swallows her shock and tries to reason with Malachi. "This plan is folly and riddled with holes. To destroy the hotel, you'll end up leveling the whole block, if not more. There are humans hiding all over London that will be killed. And what will it really accomplish? The orbs aren't likely to be destroyed by a human weapon, and we're not even sure Thorne or *Seraphim* are even in The Savoy."

Malachi sighs and crosses his arms over his chest. His body language broadcasts loud and clear that he's done with this conversation. "Our best guess—again, from your intel— is that they are."

"But it's a guess. Steel saw Silver at the hotel. That's literally all we do know. The orbs could be somewhere else entirely."

Silver? I twist to my right, where Sterling and Greyson stand. Except for Sterling's slightly narrowed eyes and a hardening of Greyson's jawline, neither one of them reacts to the mention of their sister.

"Enough." Malachi's voice doesn't raise, but I feel the authority he wields as he straightens. "This isn't your decision. I shouldn't have to remind you that during crises, the Elders assume command of the body of Nephilim."

"What about sending a contingent of troops in? It's a mistake to—"

"No. The mistake was made when you allowed a group

of youths to run around the UK with those orbs. If you had done the right thing and told the Council they were missing from the vault, we wouldn't be in this mess. So, that is quite enough. I asked for your input, and now I have it. That is all I require from you."

Malachi isn't pulling punches.

I hold my breath, waiting to see what Sable does next. I'm proud of her for not backing down, but there's only so much she can do against the authority of the Council. But there are several Elders missing from this conversation. Would Sorcha and the others agree with Malachi's proposed course of action?

"Give me three hours." Sable's voice is even, not betraying a hint of anger or fear. "I'll go to The Savoy and do recon myself. Give me a chance to see if Thorne and the orbs are there, and make sure Steel gets out safely."

Malachi's mouth puckers. He shifts his gaze to Zara and Draven. The dominion Elder steps forward, her sharp reverse bob swinging with her movements. Her keen gray gaze rakes over Sable.

I find all the Elders intimidating, but Zara is somehow even more so than the rest. As the Elder of my angel-line, I probably should feel a kinship toward her, but the vibes she throws off are chilly, which is unusual for a dominion.

"You have less than two hours," she says. "Sunset is at 4PM. The missiles will launch then unless we have definitive proof that the orbs, Thorne, and Seraphim are not in that hotel. The Forsaken will emerge at nightfall. If we don't already have the upper hand, this very well may be a fight we can't win."

Sable nods in agreement. She turns to leave, but Malachi's next words stay her steps.

"Sable. Once we have this situation under control, we *will* revisit your repeated lapses in judgment over the last week."

Sable's face doesn't change as she swivels her head to glance at Malachi. She nods again, then strides toward us.

Deacon clenches his fists and jaw as he glares at the cherub Elder, who has already dismissed everyone to speak with Zara and Draven. Even in the midst of a group of angel-born, Deacon scans for trouble as he follows Sable, making it clear he has her back.

Sable's game face is on when she reaches us. "Come on," she says. "We've got work to do."

# 43

## STEEL

*I* wipe at the layer of blood and sweat coating my brow. Taking out the Forsaken guarding the stairwell would have been easy if I hadn't had to worry about stealth. Buckets of blood in the stairwell is an instant tip-off of foul play, whereas missing guards is just a mystery. If any one of the four Forsaken I snuck up on had so much as raised their voice before I could silence them, I'd be in a world of trouble right now.

After snapping each of their necks, I hauled their bodies to a hotel room to finish them off. It was a gruesome and time-consuming job that I'm glad to be finished with.

I crack the stairwell door and peer into the fifth-floor hallway. The Royal Suite takes up the entire right side of this floor and has multiple entry points. When it's clear there's no one there, I slide through the doorway, making sure the heavy metal fire door clicks silently shut behind me.

The first door I reach is small and unassuming. Definitely not the main entrance of the suite, which is the double door I spot farther down the hall. This one looks more like a butler's entry, which is exactly what I need.

I don't hear anything from behind the door, so I start to work on the lock immediately. Using one of my blades, it takes less than thirty seconds to pop the lock. I slide into the suite and start searching for clues. After checking one bathroom and bedroom, I enter the main lounging space. I don't get two steps before a roar sounds from the other end of the suite.

"That's enough poking and prodding. Get out!"

My blood starts to boil. Thorne.

A door slams and feet pound against the carpeted floor as he heads in my direction. It takes a second to force myself to move. What I really want to do is smash Thorne's face in. Instead, I squeeze myself into a closet right before he enters the adjoining room.

He mumbles about the incompetence of his healer, then flops onto a couch or sofa chair. I can't tell which because I can't see through doors.

"You're bleeding all over the upholstery."

My blood chills to ice. It's Emberly's voice, but not her words.

"So? You never cared where I bled before. Or if I bled, for that matter."

"I happen to like this suite. Maybe I'll make it one of my residences. And when you talk like that, it makes you sound like a sullen child. Only weaklings put Band-Aids on cuts and have their booboos kissed. I've raised you to be many things, but weak isn't one of them."

Hearing her voice shreds me, not because it sounds like Emberly, but because it doesn't.

Thorne's laughter drips with bitterness. "You're calling

what little involvement you had in my surviving through adolescence 'raising me'? That's generous."

There's a loud sigh. "When will you stop whining about things—" Seraphim cuts herself off. When she speaks again, her voice shakes with rage. "I told you to get rid of that thing."

"Does it make you nervous?" Even though I can't see Thorne, I know he's smirking. I can hear it in his voice.

"It doesn't make me nervous. It makes me furious."

"To know that even you have a weakness? You don't need that bauble to remind you of that. Good thing I can dreamscape or you'd still be comatose right now. I never did get a thank-you."

Seraphim roars, then something large smashes against a wall. Maybe a piece of furniture?

"I thought you didn't want this suite damaged," Thorne taunts.

"If I see that bracelet anywhere near me again, you won't have to worry about one of your enemies shooting you in the chest, because I'll do it for them."

Bracelet. It has to be the one Emberly spoke of. Why else would it enrage Seraphim?

I have to take shallow breaths through my nose to keep myself under control. That bracelet is all I need to bring Emberly back. I get it, slap it on her wrist, and make sure it doesn't come off until we figure out a way to force Seraphim out of her.

Seraphim stomps away and a few seconds later, a door slams at the opposite end of the suite. I'm stuck in this stupid closet until Thorne leaves too.

There's a pain-filled grunt. It's obvious Thorne can't stand without difficulty.

Shot in the chest. I wonder who did that? I hope it was someone I know.

Thorne's breathing is heavy as he walks to a different part of the room. He might be a powerful angel-born, but he's not indestructible.

Glasses clink together and liquid pours. He's close enough to the closet I'm crammed in that I can hear him gulp down the liquid in two swigs and then slam the glass back down on its tray.

Thorne curses under his breath, and if it was anyone besides him, I might feel bad for the poor bastard. I didn't expect Thorne and Seraphim to have a regular mother-son relationship, but even I'm taken aback by the obvious iciness between the two.

Seraphim strikes me as one of those mothers who would eat their young. Small pity she didn't. I have to wonder if it would take much pressure to shatter whatever messed-up bond holds them together.

Thorne pours himself another drink and downs it as quickly as the last, then leaves the suite altogether, slamming the door behind him. I only wait five seconds before emerging from my hiding spot.

I rush to the living room and scan every surface, looking for that bracelet.

There it is, tossed onto a coffee table. Snatching it up, I turn it over in my hands. It's just a strip of gold with the single embedded white stone. Exactly like Emberly described.

Tension sheds from my shoulders.

I have the bracelet. It's going to be all right. Now I only have to figure out how to get this thing around Seraphim's wrist without getting blasted by angel-fire.

I shove the spirit gem jewelry into an easily accessible pocket.

"Well, well. What do we have here?"

Emberly leans against a wall on the other side of the room. If hearing her voice turned my blood to ice, seeing her stops my heart.

This isn't Emberly at all. The way the girl in front of me holds her body, the expression on her face, and even her clothes scream *Seraphim*.

A sardonic smirk lifts the corners of her mouth. She taps a finger against her lips as if she's considering the situation.

"I would ask if one of my subjects brought me a plaything, but I'm pretty sure you brought yourself." A husky laugh rattles in her chest. "How foolish."

I'm not scared of Seraphim, there's too much hate in my heart for her to feel fear, but I am incredibly wary. As a seraph Fallen, she was undeniably powerful. With her powers combined with Emberly's, she's probably as close to unstoppable now as any being can get.

I lift my hands in front of me, hoping to bring her attention away from where the jewelry bulges at my side. There's no way she saw me pocket the bracelet. If she had, she wouldn't be so calm.

Seraphim pushes off the wall and sashays toward me, her hips jutting suggestively with each footstep. I hold still, waiting to see what she'll do next.

When she's only a foot away, she lifts a hand and trails a finger down my neck and over my chest.

This creature may look like Emberly, but it isn't her. Her touch makes my skin crawl. I can't help flinching under the caress.

Knowing how uncomfortable she's making me, she smiles and runs her tongue along her upper teeth.

I school my features with difficulty and remind myself that keeping her close will help me get the bracelet on her wrist. I just need to swallow my revulsion.

"Such a pretty shell," she sighs. "And Legion was one of my favorites. I was so looking forward to our time together."

I lock myself down and force a bit of awe into my voice, stretching my acting skills. "You look just like her."

I move a hand toward her face. Faster than I can track, Seraphim catches my wrist, stopping me from brushing the strands of hair behind her ear. Her eyes narrow in suspicion, and I hide my internal grimace. My acting skills need some work.

Digging deep, I pull forth as many memories of Emberly as I can. The first time I saw her, surrounded by Fallen and holding her ground like a warrior. Laughing with my brothers in the Seraph Academy cafeteria. The way she ducks her head when she's nervous. How crazy sexy it is when she chews on her full bottom lip, and how I can't keep myself from touching it when she does.

I look into her midnight blue eyes and force myself to look past Seraphim and see Emberly.

Her pupils expand. With her fingers still wrapped around my wrist, I slowly place my other hand to her shoulder and trail a hand down her arm. Entangling our fingers, I bring our entwined palms to rest over my heart. All without breaking our gaze.

"Hmm," she makes a purring sound deep in her throat. "Perhaps there's still some fun to be had?"

Releasing her hand, I lean in at the same time as I reach

for the bracelet in my pocket. I'm a hair's breadth away from her lips and the jewelry, when suddenly I'm airborne.

I slam into the wall and then go straight through it. I bounce off the bed in the next room, then roll to the floor.

Crawling to my feet, I shake my head. Drywall dust and bits of plaster rain off me.

There's a chuckle, then Seraphim ducks through the hole in the wall she created when she threw me through it. She gingerly walks over, staying away from the mess to keep her white clothes clean.

"Oh darling, that was good, but what sort of idiot do you think I am? Also, I like my bedmates relatively clean." She pulls her upper lip back from her teeth to show her disdain. "You're covered in more than one species' blood and frankly, that's just gross."

Seduction plan is a non-starter, time to move to something more aggressive.

Jolting to my feet, I rush her. She swings an arm to bat me away, but I anticipate the move and dip under the blow, ramming into her thighs and sending us both sailing back through the hole and into the other room.

Straddling her waist, I reach for my pocket, but she punches me in the chin, causing me to see stars before I can get the bracelet. She shoves me off her and into the buffet table.

Glass shatters and wood splinters. Before I can regain my footing she's there, fisting the front of my shirt and lifting me off the ground.

"That was very stupid." There's a spark of red in her eyes.

I aim a punch for her face, hoping to stun her, but she leans out of the way and my fist only meets air.

She growls, then slams me against the wall again.

I bring an arm up and swing down against her forearm, breaking her hold on me at the same time I reach for the knife sheathed at my waist.

I swing wildly, not wanting to actually cut her. Twisting, she evades the blow. She hits me in the gut with a front kick that has me reeling backward until my back knocks into another wall.

I need to create an opening to grab the bracelet and slap it on her wrist, but she's too good a fighter. She blocks every move I make with ease.

A roundhouse kick to my temple sends me to the ground.

With a flick of her wrist, twin balls of fire appear in each palm.

I may be part angel, but angel-fire will burn me as easily as it will a Fallen or Forsaken.

"That's quite enough," she says.

"But we were just getting started."

With angel-fire blazing in each palm, she doesn't expect me to charge, so that's what I do.

Pushing to my feet, I slip the bracelet from my pocket and reach for her. Time seems to stretch in the next fractions of a second. Seraphim twists her hand, shooting angel-fire at me. She expects me to duck out of the way, but I keep coming until her palm rams into my shoulder, sending angel-fire up and over my shoulder and down my arm.

The agony is instant and intense, but I close myself off to it and slap the cuff with the white gemstone over her wrist.

The angel-fire extinguishes immediately. Seraphim's eyes widen and her mouth drops open right before she passes out. I catch her body before it hits the ground, gritting my teeth against the pain radiating from my charred shoulder and arm. Worth it.

I lay Emberly on the ground and do a quick check to make sure I didn't injure her. She looks unscathed.

"Emberly, love, I need you to wake up."

I'll give her thirty seconds to regain consciousness, or I'm throwing her over my shoulder and carrying her out of here, caveman-style.

I tap her cheek. Nothing.

I crouch to pick her up when the suite door flies open. Thorne strides through the door, scanning the wrecked room before settling his gaze on me and then Emberly. "What have you done?"

An expletive forms on my tongue. Time for round two.

# 44
## STEEL

*I* rise, stepping in front of Emberly's sleeping form to create an obstacle between her and Thorne. He stands several feet away, fists clenched and nostrils flared. There's a red splotch on his chest where his bullet wound still leaks blood.

Good, he's weakened. I'm going to need every advantage possible to get us out of here.

"Normally I wouldn't thank a dude for giving my girl jewelry, but in this case, I don't mind."

Thorne's gaze snaps to the ground behind me, then back up. Fury hardens his features and he rushes me. I'm expecting it. It's what I hoped he would do.

When he slams into me, I twist and shove, throwing him past me and straight into the wall of windows. Thorne goes crashing through the glass, then disappears.

Giving Emberly a quick glance to make sure she's still out, I sprint to the windows, hoping to see Thorne's body splattered against the sidewalk below like a busted blood bag.

No such luck. He's gone. He probably phased before he hit the ground.

I cast another glance in Emberly's direction and shove a hand through my hair, knowing I have only moments to decide my next move.

My love for Emberly far outweighs my hate for Thorne, but will we be able to make it out of here with him still around?

I let loose a curse, then phase into the spirit realm.

Thorne circles the dusty rose spirit sky once before veering straight toward the hotel. Shifting into an eagle, I jump out the window; my only thought is to keep him away from Emberly.

He takes the bait and follows me up into the air.

From several hundred feet above The Savoy, I can see the Fallen stationed all around the city and in a perimeter around the hotel.

The momentary distraction costs me. Thorne is right on my tail.

I loop at just the right moment and a ball of silver fire shoots past me.

Diving, I tuck my wings tight to cut through the air. The ground zooms up to meet me, and I spread my wings to slow my descent. I'm not looking to break my neck on the landing. My shoulder screams at me, and my wing almost collapses.

I shift into a lion as soon as my talons scrape the ground, rolling once before regaining my footing, and spin in time to see Thorne land.

We run at each other. I go up on my hind legs, and we clash.

He punches my ribs, and I snap at him with my jaws.

Extra muscle and stronger bones protect me in this form, so I don't even flinch from his jabs.

I swipe across his chest with a clawed paw, ripping through shirt and flesh.

He shoves me off of him and spins. The metal tips of his wings slice into my face under my eye, and I back away.

When he comes at me again, he goes straight for my injured shoulder, getting a cheap shot in on my burnt flesh.

Snarling, I shove him to the ground. He's ready for that move though and uses his strength to throw me over his head. I smash into a bench, cracking it in half.

With a shake, I lumber to my feet just in time to dodge a volley of Thorne's electric angel-fire.

I growl in frustration that Thorne can keep me at a distance with his angel-fire alone. I can't take him down if he keeps lobbing those fireballs at me.

In a blink, I shift back into a man.

Pulling both automatic pistols from their holsters, I return fire with bullets. He dives out of the way of the spray. I rush him, guns still spitting fire. Only a few bullets find their mark in Thorne's flesh, but that wasn't the point. I just need to get close enough to engage him in hand-to-hand combat.

When my magazines are empty, I drop the pistols and hammer my fist at his face. He dodges, but my knuckles still graze his cheek. Thorne comes back at me with a punch aimed at my burnt shoulder, but I twist before he can land the blow.

Snatching my knife, I turn and arc it toward Thorne's side. He knocks my wrist before I can bury the blade between his ribs, shattering some of the bones and forcing me to drop the weapon.

Gritting my teeth, I transform back into a lion, ignoring the pain when I put weight on my now-injured wrist.

Thorne flexes his wings, a sure tell that he's going to slash out with them again.

Letting loose a roar, I spring at his back while he's mid-spin. Digging my claws into his shoulder, I clamp my jaws around the base of one of his wings and shake my head while my powerful paws shred his back.

I bite down even harder, crunching the wing bone beneath my teeth.

Thorne shouts in fury and pain, but the noise only spurs me on.

With one final shake and downward swipe of my claw, one of Thorne's wings rips free from his back.

I spit out the severed appendage. The metal tips clang as they hit the ground.

Thorne drops to his hands and knees in front of me. Blood streams from multiple deep claw marks along his shoulder and ribs. He reaches back and touches the foot-long stump that used to be his wing.

I shift back into my original form. I want to finish him off as myself.

Taking two steps, I punch him in the face. One, two, three times before he slumps and falls to the ground.

I'm panting heavily. My own blood and spittle drips from my mouth. Swiping an arm across my face, I wipe it away.

I look around for my knife to sever his head, but don't see it. Grabbing Thorne's unresponsive body under the arms, I heft him up and drag him over to the river's edge. I make sure to snap his neck before I throw him in, so he won't have time to heal and wake before drowning. His body hits the Thames with a splash, then he sinks. Bubbles break the surface, and I hear someone shout my name.

Turning, I gaze up at the hotel behind me. Emberly stands where Thorne's body smashed through the window. I shift into an eagle and fly up to her.

# 45

## EMBERLY

*J* almost can't believe what just happened. I came to, alone in a room that looked like it had gone up against a tornado and lost. When I rushed to the broken window and didn't see anything below, I phased just in time to watch Steel throw Thorne's motionless body into the sparkling spectrum waters of the Thames. I screamed Steel's name, and when his eyes connected with mine he transformed into an eagle, his wings pumping to reach me.

I step back to let Steel glide into the room, still struggling to catch up. I don't know what's more jarring, the shock of being back in control of my body or watching Thorne die.

Steel transforms into himself before his talons even skim the ground. He's in front of me in a flash, wrapping me in his embrace. The feel of his strong arms snaps some sense back into me, and I wind my arms around him.

A sob builds in my throat and bursts free. He rubs a hand up and down my back to soothe me. I get control of myself, instinctually knowing now's not the time. I pull back from him and a quick wince flits across his face. He has a cut high on one cheekbone and he's a gore-covered mess, but by far the worst injury is his burnt shoulder and bicep. Skin is missing from patches, and everywhere else, the flesh is bubbled and bleeding.

"Did Thorne hit you with angel-fire?" I gasp.

I ghost my hand over the wound, not wanting to hurt him. When he doesn't answer, I lift my face to search his gaze.

Seeing the truth, I bring a hand to my mouth in horror.

"I did this." It isn't a question.

"No." Steel shakes his head. "Seraphim. Not you." His eyebrows drop low and he slouches so we're at eye level. "That creature, that monster, is not and will never be you."

I nod. He's made his point. He doesn't need to know it still hurts my heart to know his pain was caused by my hand. It doesn't matter that I wasn't in control.

"Thorne . . ." I have to swallow the sudden lump that clogs my throat. "Is he . . . gone?" I can't bring myself to say "dead."

"Yeah, he's gone." Steel searches my face to gauge my reaction, and I don't hide the hint of sadness over Thorne's demise. It comes from the part of me that held on to the hope that he'd come around someday. The part that saw his potential buried under a lifetime of abuse.

I place a hand on Steel's cheek.

"You brought me back," I whisper.

"I said I would."

A smile curves my lips. "Is that your way of saying 'I told you so'?"

He covers my hand with his own. "No. That's my way of saying I love you."

My breath catches in my throat. Those three words are powerful and carry meaning, and although I've no doubt the depth of Steel's feelings for me anymore, those are words we haven't openly declared to each other—and I have absolutely no fears saying them back to him.

"Steel, I—" I gasp when an errant thought pushes to the forefront of my mind at the exact wrong moment. "Shira. Did you find her?"

Steel slow blinks as he changes gears, then shakes his head.

"Shira, right. No, but I think I know where they're holding her. I ran into a very talkative Forsaken earlier." Steel's grin has a wicked edge that makes me want to know more . . . but also not. "We've got to get out of this room anyway. This place is crawling with Forsaken. The likelihood of one of them having seen my brawl with Thorne is pretty high."

"It's probably too much to hope that they'll disperse when they find out Thorne is out of the picture, right?"

"They'll still follow Seraphim."

That gives me pause. "I'm Seraphim."

"Emberly, we'll figure out a way to get her out of you. As long as that bracelet is on, she's not coming back."

"No, I mean they don't know that I'm *not* Seraphim." I jog over to a curtain flapping in the breeze and yank the tieback off of it. I toss it to Steel. "Give me your crossbow and wrap that around your wrists. We're going to find Shira and then walk right out of this place."

"Brilliant." He shucks the crossbow off his shoulder, then hands it to me. "Let's check the suite for the orbs first. I'll be happy if we can walk out of here with our lives and Shira, bonus if we find the orbs."

We spend an extra few minutes checking for the orbs but can't find them. If we get Shira and me out of the hotel, the orbs' powers will be somewhat nullified without angel line blood to activate them, so we decide it's not worth the risk to keep looking.

We phase back into the mortal world before leaving the suite. With a loaded crossbow pointed at him, Steel goes in front of me with the fake binding on his wrists. We run across the first group of Forsaken the moment we step into the hallway. I yell at them to mind their own business and they scurry right along.

Once they leave, Steel and I exchange a look. This is going to be so much easier than fighting our way out.

"Stairs or elevator?" I ask.

"Stairs. Let's not push our luck. I already cleared them anyway."

I raise my eyebrows. "You were busy while I was out."

A brittle laugh rattles in his chest. "You don't know the half of it. We can swap stories when we're out of this mess."

"Deal."

The stairwell is free of Forsaken, just like Steel promised. We make it down to the ground floor. Steel turns to me right before pushing open the door. "Shira's being held in a small banquet room called the Sorcerer Room."

I grimace. "That sounds ominous."

"Let's hope not."

Steel shoulders the door open and fake stumbles into the hallway, pretending like I just shoved him. Two Forsaken look up from their conversation, and I pretend to ignore them. As Seraphim, a couple of Forsaken would be beneath my notice.

"Keep moving," I bark at Steel, who is limping along in

front of me. I wonder if we're overselling it, but the Forsaken don't utter a word as we pass.

We turn the corner, and the hallway widens. There are doors on the right with plaques announcing each of the rooms' names. We pass the Iolanthe Room and the Mikado Room, then see the sign for the Sorcerers Room. We pull open the door and slip inside, shutting it behind us.

Shira is tied to a chair in the middle of the all-red room. She lifts her head, revealing that she looks even worse than the last time I saw her. Steel and I both rush to help her out of her bindings.

"Are you the good Emberly or the evil one?" she asks as I tug at the rope around her chest.

"I'm me," I assure her. "We're getting out of here."

We have Shira almost free when voices ring outside the door. Steel and I exchange a worried glance.

"Play along," I whisper to Shira as we throw some loose ropes around her to make it look like she's still bound to the chair.

"Hit me," Steel says as the voices get louder.

"No," I whisper-hiss at him.

"Emberly," he growls, "just do it."

"I'm not going to—" The doorknob turns and I swing toward Steel. I mouth "sorry," then backhand him. My hand connects with his cheek right as the door pops open. Steel reacts as if I put everything I had into the strike, when really I hardly touched him, and rams into the wall before sliding to the ground.

"Your half-breed life means nothing to me, so you had better watch what you say," I say without emotion.

I turn toward the intruder, my game face on. I almost let it slip when I see who it is.

Silver stands in the doorway with four Forsaken behind her. Her gaze tracks from me to Shira and then lands on Steel and holds. Her nostrils flare.

"I didn't know we had extra company," she says.

"Why would I apprise you of something that doesn't concern you? You have your orders and I expect you to stick to them."

Her gaze snaps to mine, not hurt by my words, but a bit startled. Shoot, did I play that wrong? I didn't think Seraphim would be soft toward anyone, but maybe Silver is the exception.

"Leave us," I order. "I don't want to be disturbed while I'm with these two." Well, I'm committed now.

Silver tilts her head, but after a beat she nods. "We'll wait out here until you're finished. I have updates for you."

That won't do. I need the corridor clear to escape. My gaze flicks to the windows. On second thought, it's better to go out that way instead, but I still want to know about this update.

I straighten my spine. "Tell me now."

"I can wait until you're finished," she says. Her eyes shift back toward Steel, who lays in a crumpled heap in the corner, faking unconsciousness.

"I won't ask twice," I warn.

Silver puckers her mouth before offering up the information. "The orbs are positioned on the roof like you asked, and the charges have been set. Everything is in place."

So that's where the orbs are. Getting up to the roof to nab them and back out of the hotel is too chancy, but maybe when we reunite with the other angel-born, we can come up with a way to retrieve them. I don't know what charges she's talking about but asking for an explanation will definitely give away our ruse.

"Good. Now get out," I snap.

Silver's eyebrows pinch, but she starts to back away. She's about to close the door when her gaze drops to my wrist and holds.

Both of us freeze. She knows.

She barks a word I don't understand, then flies at me.

The Forsaken in the hallway rush into the small room behind her. Steel pops up to intercept them, and Shira shakes off her fake bindings and goes to help.

Silver's on me the next instant. A blow to the stomach sends me reeling into the wall. She pulls daggers from sheaths at her hips and comes at me.

I have no weapons to defend myself with, so I have to duck and twist out of her reach to keep from being sliced.

"She's weak on her left side," Steel shouts as he snaps the neck of one of the Forsaken.

Silver snarls and shoots a glare at Steel. I take advantage of the distraction by kicking one of the blades from her hands. She comes at me with a renewed sense of purpose. The room is so small, there isn't much space to maneuver. I miscalculate a block and the blade cuts my forearm.

The Forsaken battling Steel and Shira get distracted by the smell of my blood, and Shira is able to take another one down. At least the injury is good for something.

Listening to Steel's advice, I land a punch to Silver's left ribs. She hunches, and I grab her wrist, twisting the blade out of her hand in a move that would make Deacon proud.

Losing her blade doesn't stop Silver's attacks. She comes at me with fists and feet, and the dagger I took from her is almost a hindrance. I don't really want to hurt Silver—she's Steel's sister.

I crack the butt of the weapon against Silver's jaw. She stumbles back and rubs the point of impact.

"You don't have to do this," I huff. "We can all leave together."

Her upper lip pulls back into a feral snarl. "Don't you get it by now? I don't have to do this, but I sure want to."

She darts at me faster than I expect. Her fingers wrap around my wrist, finding the bracelet keeping Seraphim at bay, and I panic.

She yanks, and I plunge the blade between her ribs. It sinks to the hilt.

Both our eyes go wide as we realize what I've done. Her mouth opens, but her body crumples to the ground before she even gets a word out.

I stare in shock at Silver's lifeless body, the handle of her own dagger sticking out of her chest. A pool of blood starts to form beneath her.

I just killed Steel's sister.

A spark of gold catches my eye. The bracelet she pulled from my wrist is clutched in her hand. I go to grab it, but I can't move.

No. No no no. This can't be happening. I haven't passed out. I should still be in control.

I scream at my body to move, but it doesn't obey my commands. Instead, my head tilts up and my eyes scan the room. Shira is slumped in a corner, and Steel battles the remaining two Forsaken.

My mouth opens and a foreign word emerges. It's guttural and the syllables feel sticky in my throat. The Forsakens' heads snap in my direction. Another unwanted word slides over my tongue, and they drop to the ground on their bellies.

I have no idea what's happening, and neither does Steel when his eyes find mine. I try to scream at him to run, but instead my lips curve into a smile.

Recognition flares in Steel's gaze, but it's too late.

Seraphim lifts my arm and shoots a stream of angel-fire right at Steel that propels him into the air and slams him against the wall.

I claw at the confines of my own mind, desperate to find a way to break Seraphim's hold on me, but it's no use. When I wink out a moment later, I don't even know if Steel is dead or alive.

# 46

## ASH

*W*hy does it have to get dark so early here? It's only a touch after three in the afternoon, yet the shadows have lengthened enough that some Forsaken have ventured out of their hiding spots. We've already had two run ins, but we're only a handful of blocks away from The Savoy.

Sable waves us into an alcove off the street. Deacon, Sterling, Nova, and I follow and then fan out around her. I look over my shoulder and see Sable check her watch. Concern furrows her brow.

"We'll make it," Deacon says.

She doesn't look as sure as she pulls a slim phone from a pocket on her tactical vest to check in with Greyson, who was forced to stay behind at the base because of his injured leg. To say he was unhappy with that decision would be to put it mildly, but he's become an invaluable link to base and the goings-on of the Elders.

Sable asks Greyson a few questions, then hangs up.

"No changes," she announces. "The strike is still on for sunset. We have less than an hour."

"It could be worse," Nova says. "At least they didn't push it up."

I nod grimly in agreement.

"Come on, guys. Let's keep moving." Sterling has been unusually stoic and highly motivated since we struck out. With each block we gain, his mood sours a bit more.

The rest of us check with Sable before moving on. She nods and gestures toward the street, and we're off again. We gain ground in a leapfrog pattern, making sure we have eyes in front of us, behind us, and on the surrounding buildings. We were shot at by Forsaken taking shelter in the high rises that line the London streets a few blocks back, so we're particularly cautious about what might be hiding just out of sight.

There's an explosion somewhere in the city. The ground shakes and the boom is loud enough to rattle the glass windows around us. Plumes of smoke rise in the not-so-far distance.

We freeze when another bang rings out and then detonations start going off like popcorn, each one louder and closer than the last.

"Take cover!" Sable yells, and everyone scrambles to comply.

Nova and I sprint for the entrance of a nearby theater. We dive through the doors right as the world explodes behind us. The building vibrates, and the windows shatter.

Nova and I huddle with our arms over our heads. The blasts continue for another thirty seconds at least before petering out. When they do, the air in the theater is thick with particles and sediment. I cough into my arm. It's super hard to breathe.

Nova looks up at me, a thin layer of dust coating her hair and shoulders. She ticks her chin toward the doors, and I nod. We have to figure out what happened.

With careful steps, we emerge from the theater into a cloud of dust so dense I have to keep my hand on Nova's back to keep from losing her. I'm forced to pull my shirt up over my mouth to filter the air so I can breathe. Car alarms and what sounds like stone crumbling is all I hear.

Slowly the air starts to clear, and we're able to see several feet in front of us. Then a half block.

There's not a window in site still intact. Chunks of concrete litter the ground.

"Ash, look," Nova says, pointing to the right.

I gasp. There's no more street. Instead, a demolished building blocks the way.

"There's someone down there trying to climb the rubble," I say.

Nova and I exchange a glance, then take off. We can tell it's Sterling when we get closer. By the time we reach him, he's already ten feet up.

"Sterling," Nova calls. "Get down. You can't climb that, it's too unstable. We'll find a way around."

Sterling looks over his shoulder. There's a cut at his temple dripping blood, and he's as filthy as the both of us.

"There's no way around. They blew buildings to create a blockade around the hotel. Scaling this mess is the only way to get there."

Oh gosh. This is bad.

Footsteps rush from behind us, and Nova and I immediately twist to defend ourselves, but it's only Sable and

Deacon. They look okay, mostly, but Deacon holds his left arm.

"Are you guys okay?" Deacon asks.

We nod.

"Sterling, get down from there," Sable calls.

"We've got to keep going," he yells back without even bothering to turn.

"What about the spirit realm?" I ask Sable. "You and Deacon could fly us over the blockade."

"That's not going to work. I phased a minute ago to check it out, and this area of the city is crawling with Fallen. We'd never make it."

"Well, what are we going to do?" I ask.

I glance up at Sterling, who's still climbing his way higher. Maybe that's our only option?

A shot rings out and Sterling loses his footing. Another shot pings and I see a chunk of debris explode right near his head.

"Sterling, get low," I yell. "They're shooting at you."

Sterling finally listens and slides back down to the ground as more shots ring out. Bullets pepper the ground near our feet, so we dive under a slab of debris that used to be an exterior wall. We have to crouch or hunch to fit in the space.

"We're so screwed," Nova says as shots continue from multiple directions. "Total sitting ducks."

"Everyone stay covered but see if you can tell where the shooters are."

I drop to my belly and scooch forward in an army crawl. It takes a minute, but I finally spot a Forsaken peeking out a window with a rifle in her hands. She takes aim in our direction and I shuffle back. Before she can get off another shot, someone appears and shoves the barrel skyward. Taking a fist full of the Forsaken's shirt, they yank her forward, tossing her from the window. The Forsaken shrieks as she plummets to the ground. Her screams are abruptly cut off when she splats on the pavement.

There's a break in the gunfire, as if the other Forsaken shooters can't believe what just happened.

Then all hell breaks loose.

People start appearing and disappearing in the streets and the buildings around us. Bullets spray everywhere. More Forsaken fall from buildings. The ones that don't die on impact are finished off by the mysterious newcomers.

"Who are they?" Sterling calls over the chaos as the five of us remain hunkered down.

I look to Sable and Deacon, whose attention is glued to the action unfolding around us.

"It's got to be some sort of top-secret Nephilim special ops team, right?" At least that's my best guess. Regular angel-born aren't taught to fight by bouncing back and forth between the mortal and spirit realms, but maybe we should be. What's going on all around us is a cross between a choreographed dance and organized anarchy.

The gunfire ends, and the sudden quiet causes my ears to ring.

"Those aren't any Nephilim I've seen before," Deacon says.

"Me either," Sable confirms.

Feet pound in front of our hiding spot as someone drops from the sky. A man squats down, peering under the slab of stone where we're crouching.

"We cleared the area. You can come on out," he says, his words tinted with a faint accent I can't quite place. He straightens and backs away a couple of steps to give us room to crawl out.

"Whoa," Nova says as dozens of unfamiliar angel-born phase back into the mortal world behind the stranger.

Our whole group tenses. Out of the corner of my eye, I see Nova and Deacon slowly unsheathe weapons.

I take a second look at the stranger who addressed us, waiting for what will come next, and notice he's old. Not old in a decrepit way, but in the weathered way that only a few of our Elders have. His deeply tanned skin is marred with lines and forehead wrinkles. The hair on his head is dark brown, but there's a touch of salt in the scruff of his facial hair.

"Who are you?" Sable asks.

He starts to answer when a young angel-born with dark curls and black wings steps forward. "We shouldn't be wasting our time with these ones while my father's murderer is still out there," he says. His green eyes broadcast his clear dislike of us.

"Aero," the older man snaps. "Silence, or I'll send you back to Eden."

With a scowl, the young angel-born retreats a step. The older man, the obvious leader of the group, takes a moment to scan the rest of his people. The unfamiliar angel-born exchange glances and shift their weight, a clear indication of their unease, but no one else speaks up.

After an elongated pause, the leader nods, convinced there won't be another outburst, and diverts his attention back to us. "Shira and Emberly are my kin. We've come to help."

Kin? I look more closely at the speaker and notice his eye color is the same dark blue shade as Emberly's.

"Are you Nikias?" Sterling asks as he steps forward.

"I am."

"Shira told me about you."

Nikias arches one of his eyebrows. "Did she now?"

"She's in trouble," Sterling goes on. "We're running out of time."

Sable moves forward and extends her hand to Nikias, who shakes it without hesitation. "I'm Sable. We'll accept any and all help, but we have a lot to catch you up on."

# 47

## STEEL

*W*hen I come to, the first thing I notice is the acrid taste of the air. The second thing is that I can't move. I'm sitting with my back pressed up against a metal rod. My hands are secured around it and behind me by thick rope. The third thing is that I hurt everywhere.

I glance down at my chest, surprised there isn't a hole there from Seraphim's angel-fire, but what's left isn't pretty. My shirt is a glorified rag, and my chest is a blackened and bloody mess. The lightest breeze scrapes against me like blades.

It doesn't matter. I'll heal.

"I could have easily killed you already, but considering all the trouble you've caused me, I'll get more satisfaction from having you witness my victory. Who knows? I may keep you around as a plaything for my subjects when the world is under my rule."

I look up and watch Emberly—Emberly's body—stride toward me. We're on a flat roof. The Thames is on one side, and what's left of London stretches out in the other direction. I snap my gaze to her wrist, and it verifies what I already know: the bracelet is gone.

Emberly is gone.

Seraphim squats in front of me and holds up her arm so I have a better view of her naked wrist. "If you're looking for that ugly piece of jewelry, I'm happy to report it's gone for good this time. Not that it matters. I have Emberly sealed in such a tight corner of her own subconscious that not even a spirit gemstone could pull her to the surface this time." She stands and stretches, then looks down at me with a smile. "I learn from my mistakes."

She's lying. She has to be.

The plan is the same as it was when I entered the hotel. Subdue Seraphim and lock her away until we figure out how to yank her out of Emberly.

"What now?" I ask the monster that wears my girl's face.

"Now, the fun begins."

Seraphim gestures to the side, where Shira is horizontal and strung up facedown several feet in the air. Her body sags in the middle. Her head hangs forward, her hair obscuring her face. She dangles over what looks like a large bowl or shallow trough, and in the base both orbs sit—one blue, one silver.

This is bad.

"Funny things happen when these two orbs are around each other," Seraphim says conversationally. "Their power fights against each other, keeping them both in check. One pushes you into the spirit realm, and the other holds you into the mortal world. Yin and yang. Right and wrong. Good and evil. Very on-brand with the Creator's vision of the world, wouldn't you say?"

I jerk my chin, flipping a chunk of hair out of my eyes. "I don't presume to know the mind of the Creator, but considering He created you, I'd say He's down with letting evil exist."

"Ah, the self-righteous doctrine of the Nephilim. You half-breeds like to believe you're superior, but somewhere along the way you've forgotten you're all legacies of the Fallen. A poor substitute for the real thing."

"Does that include your own son?"

By now she must know he's gone. I hope that bringing him up will throw her off, but Seraphim simply smiles back at me, amused.

"Especially Thorne. Being bested by a lesser being," she tilts her head my way, "proves he wasn't fit to rule and is no true son of mine."

Man, that's cold. With a mother like Seraphim, no wonder Thorne was so messed up.

"I am somewhat disappointed about Silver, though. I had bigger plans for her. It's a shame, really."

I narrow my eyes. Silver and Emberly fought in the Sorcerer Room. The fact that Seraphim is back tells me that Silver won, so I don't know what she's going on about.

"Did Silver finally come to her senses and turn on you?" I scan the roof, looking for another captive, but I only see Shira and Seraphim.

"Oh, but you don't know?" Seraphim's slow smile causes unease to slither in my gut. I shift uncomfortably. "Your Emberly put a blade right in your sister's heart. Just finishing the job you started, I suppose."

The blood drains from my face.

I didn't see it happen, but one minute I was fighting two Forsaken, and the next I was blasted in the chest by angel-fire. Could it be true? Could Emberly have killed Silver?

"So much raw potential." Seraphim sighs, but her sadness doesn't ring true. "She would've been a real asset. If the other half-breeds fall in line like she did, I'm sure I could find a place for them in my new kingdom."

I clamp my mouth shut and school my features. I don't have the luxury of processing Silver's death right now, especially when I know Seraphim watches me. Silver attacked Emberly, and if Emberly did kill her, it was in self-defense. I shove my feelings down to be dug up later. I have a job to do, and I can't let anything get in the way.

Lifting my chin, I stare directly into Seraphim's eyes. She pouts when it's clear that's the only reaction she'll get from me.

"It's almost time," she says as she casts her gaze westward.

The sun's belly touches the rooftops of the downtown buildings that still stand. She plans to bring down the barrier between the worlds at sunset. How many minutes until the sun disappears altogether? Ten, twenty? There's not much time left.

Shira groans, coming awake slowly. Seraphim's smile sharpens and she saunters over to Shira, another toy for her to play with.

My stomach turns. Whatever it takes, I have to get that monster out of Emberly.

I test my bindings. My hands are numb because the ropes are wrapped so tightly around my wrists, and my injured shoulder screams as I pull. The rod at my back holds. I rub my hands back and forth, hoping to find a jagged edge, but there's nothing on the cylinder rough enough to fray the rope. With Seraphim's back turned, I snarl in frustration.

"What the heck?" Shira says. She tries to fling her hair out of her face, but all it does is swing back and forth along with her body. "What kind of weird—" She freezes.

Her breathing picks up when she spots the orbs beneath her. It's a few beats and then she starts thrashing in earnest. The twin poles she's suspended between groan.

Seraphim picks a blade up from the ground—she has a collection of them laid out on the ground like a surgeon would display their scalpels—and levels it under Shira's chin.

"Seraphim," I yell. "Don't!"

As if my words will do anything to stop her. Still, I can't just sit here and watch her slice into Shira.

Shira stills to keep her throat from the blade.

I continue to yank at my bindings in a fruitless attempt to free myself.

Seraphim looks back at me. "Don't what?" she asks with false innocence. "Don't do this?" With a flick of a wrist, she slices into Shira's neck.

# 48

## ASH

*I* try to keep my eyes open, but the struggle is real.

"Hang on," Deacon yells in my ear right before he banks left.

Hang on? Hang on to what? I'm strapped to him with a makeshift harness—my back to his chest—as we fly low over the river. There's nothing for me to grab but air.

I pry my eyes open and am almost blinded. The bright glow from the water in the spirit realm helps camouflage the six of us as we head toward the hotel. I can hardly see Sable and Nova or Nikias and Sterling, even though they can't be more than fifteen feet on either side of us.

Sounds of the battle raging between Nikias' soldiers and the Fallen can be heard behind and above us. Nikias and Sable both agreed that a whole contingent of angel-born warriors wouldn't be able to make it past the perimeter blockade the Fallen created around The Savoy, but they would make one spectacular distraction. They staged an attack on our enemies, giving our small group a chance to slip past their defenses.

We're almost to the strip of land that runs next to our target location and haven't been attacked, so I guess that means the plan worked.

A streak of gray slams into Nikias and Sterling, and they crash into the water. A giant Fallen swoops back into the sky and shouts a command.

"Almost there," Deacon shouts over the noise. The strain in his voice is unmistakable.

I crane my neck to search for Nikias and Sterling in the water behind us, but all I can see is the blinding glow from the water.

Deacon wraps his arms around me as he prepares to land. Tilting us so we're no longer horizontal, he flares his wings.

My body lashes forward with the sudden slowdown in momentum, but the strap around my chest and the band of Deacon's arms hold steady.

We're about to land on a patch of grass when we're struck from behind with a bone-jarring hit that propels us forward and into the ground. I take the brunt of Deacon's considerable weight as we're crushed to the earth.

I have enough sense to squeeze a hand under my body and release the latch on the strap that connects us, and not a moment too soon because something lifts Deacon back into the air.

I look up and watch Deacon smash into the side of a building. A gray-skinned Fallen stomps after him, but Deacon recovers quickly, popping to his feet and folding his wings close until they melt into his body.

Thank goodness most angel-born with wings can make

them appear and disappear at will. The extra appendages can actually get in the way during hand-to-hand combat.

The clang of metal striking metal sounds to my left. I jump to my feet and run to help Nova and Sable, who battle a pair of Fallen.

Pulling the retractable spear out of the sheath along my leg, I push the button for it to unfold. It snaps into place quickly, and I launch it at the back of the Fallen bearing down on Nova.

My spear strikes the Fallen through the neck. He immediately drops his sword and grabs at the spearhead protruding from his throat. That hit won't kill a Fallen, but it's definitely going to slow him down.

Nova takes advantage of the distraction and jumps into the air. With a downward swing, she buries a hand axe in the monster's skull. He tips over like a slow-falling tree.

Nova yanks her weapon from his head when I reach them. I bend down to retrieve my spear when Nova plunges a dagger into the Fallen's eye socket. It comes free with a wet suctioning sound. She sheaths both weapons.

"What?" she says when she catches me staring. "Haven't you heard of double-tapping?"

"Better safe than sorry?"

"Exactly." Nova jerks her chin and says "Sable," then takes off.

With spear in hand, I follow. It takes all three of us to fell the next Fallen, and we're a sweaty, bloody mess when Sable finally delivers the death blow.

With my hands on my knees, I gulp in air and scan the area. Nikias and Sterling are still nowhere to be seen. Deacon's gone as well. Nikias' angel-line warriors battle

Fallen in the distance. I can't see them, but I can hear the battle and death cries.

"Where are the angels?" I ask, forcing my body to straighten. "I get that they won't appear in the mortal world, but they should be here in the spirit realm, fighting beside us." Our small angel-born army won't last much longer against this many Fallen.

Sable shakes her head. "I don't know, but the hotel is on the other end of this park."

"What about the guys?" I ask.

"They know the objective. They'll be heading for the same spot. Let's go."

We've barely run half the length of the park before a female Fallen drops in our path. I can see our target over her shoulder. We're so close.

Nova pulls curved daggers and rushes the Fallen, with Sable close on her heels. I skirt the fight, planning to sweep her feet out underneath her.

I'm in position when a cloud of sparks appears above the Fallen's head, then a black panther drops on her back. The cat latches its jaw around the curve of the Fallen's neck and bites. Black blood spurts from the wounds. With a shake of its head, the panther rips a chunk of flesh from the Fallen and then drops to the ground.

Nova doesn't miss a beat and scissors her blades across the Fallen's neck, severing her head from her body in one powerful motion. The head tumbles to the ground and the body follows soon after.

The panther bounces around Nova like a kitten. "I found you!"

"Tinkle. I missed you," Nova says as she drops to her knees. Tinkle bumps up against her and starts to purr.

"Camiel?" Sable asks when Tinkle rolls on his back for belly rubs.

"On his way. I'm faster."

There's a ringing, and Sable reaches into her pocket and pulls out a phone. "Greyson?"

The frown on Sable's mouth deepens as she listens to whatever Greyson says on the other line.

I shift my weight back and forth and check the sky. We have to have at least twenty minutes until sunset.

Someone calls Sable's name, and I look over to see Deacon jogging toward us. Like the rest of us, he's a bit beat up, but alive.

"Are you sure?" Sable asks Greyson over the phone just as Deacon rejoins us. She nods once and says, "You did everything you could. I've got to go."

She hangs up and shoves the phone back in one of her pockets. "We have five minutes to clear the area. They're launching early."

# 49
## STEEL

"No!" I roar as Shira's blood dribbles down into the trough beneath her. Seraphim didn't cut deep, but a steady stream of blood drops into the bowl and trickles toward the orbs.

Shira renews her flailing, which only seems to amuse Seraphim.

"I'd save my energy if I were you," she tells Shira. "I'm not quite ready to bleed you dry. But if you'd like to speed the process, be my guest. The more you fight, the faster your heart will pump and the more blood you'll lose."

The first drops of Shira's blood gather at the center of the bowl and a blue fire engulfs both orbs.

"What's happening?" Shira demands, her voice streaked with panic.

"They're just warming up. Trust me, the real fun won't start until you pass out from blood loss. Punching a few holes in the barrier will be nothing compared to what will happen when the orbs are submerged in a vat of your extra-special angel-line blood."

Seraphim runs her finger through one of the red streams, then brings it to her mouth. She seals her lips around her fingertip, closing her eyes as if savoring the taste. She shivers, and when she lifts her lids, her eyes glow red.

"Yum. Extra special *and* extra tasty." Seraphim pats Shira on the head, who bucks and starts yelling at her in a foreign language I don't understand.

"Why are you doing this?" I yell to get Seraphim's attention off of Shira. I don't need to know the actual answer. I already know Seraphim's insane, not to mention inherently evil. That's enough of an explanation for me.

"You're kidding, right?" she asks with a brow quirked in annoyance.

"Did you not get hugged enough as a baby angel, so you're angry at dear ole dad?" I ask.

"Oh, the answer is much simpler than that." She cocks her head and her creepy serial-killer smile returns. "I can, and so I will."

With a twist and a flick of her wrist, she carves a long cut in Shira's arm. Shira screams. Blood travels from the cut on her forearm down to her elbow and then drops into the bowl. Blue light starts to pulsate from the orbs.

Frowning, Seraphim scans the skyline. I follow her gaze, but besides a wrecked city, don't see anything.

"They're early," she mumbles, more annoyed than alarmed.

Turning back to Shira, she pulls a blade across her neck, starting a red waterfall.

Shira gurgles, choking on her own blood.

For half a second, I'm stunned. Absolutely frozen.

Shira's blood falls onto the orbs, and the blue light

blooms, creating what looks like a sci-fi force field that engulfs Shira.

I go ballistic, thrashing at my bindings without thought of harming myself, only of saving the bleeding girl in front of me. I hurl insults at Seraphim that would make Sterling blush. The metal pole behind me starts to groan and bend.

"Calm down," Seraphim says. "I didn't cut that deep. It will take several minutes for her to die."

The light surrounding the orbs grows, swallowing Seraphim. For a moment I can only see the outline of her body through the blue glow, and then it washes over me as well. When it does, there's a strange sensation in my body, like when I shift into one of my other forms. The feeling passes an instant after it begins. From within the force field, the sky isn't blue anymore—or even pink like the spirit realm. Instead, it's tinted purple.

I flex my muscles, renewing my efforts to break free. Power I usually only have access to when I phase into the spirit realm infuses my body. I don't think about how it's possible or even what it means. I just gather my angelic energy and force myself to shift.

# 50

## ASH

Sable's wings appear in a flash of raven feathers. "You guys clear the area," she orders, her gaze focused on the hotel a block away. "I'm headed up to the roof."

"I'm going with you," Deacon says and brings forth his wings as well. "It's not over yet. Girls," he says to Nova and me, "get as far away from here as possible."

Nova looks ready to argue when six Fallen drop in front of us. Shoot. We don't have time for this. Emberly, Steel, and Shira don't have time for this.

We move into defensive positions, but before the Fallen can attack, streaks of gold and silver shoot over our heads and land behind the Fallen with a thud, shaking the ground beneath our feet.

The Fallen twist to face the new threat, a line of armor-plated angels. Camiel is in the lead.

"Told you he was on his way," Tinkle quips.

Camiel pulls a long sword from its sheath at his hip. With a slight jerk of his chin, the angels on either side of him rush the Fallen.

The battle between the two clans of heavenly beings is vicious. The Fallen fight with their weapons as well as fists, claws, and sometimes even teeth. The angels battle with blades and fire, and clearly have the upper hand. It isn't long before black blood soaks the battle ground at their feet.

Once their opponents are dispatched, all but two of the angels take to the air. The noise of war sounds across the city. Camiel's angels have finally entered the fight.

"We're running out of time," Sable tells Camiel. "The Elders are going to bomb that hotel because they think Seraphim and Thorne are held up inside with the orbs."

"Where have you been," Nova demands. "Your daughter is in there."

Oh snap.

I steal glances at the two intimidating angels at Camiel's side, but their expressions are as cold as stone. They either already know about Emberly or have extremely good poker faces.

Camiel's brows pull together in annoyance, but he still answers. "Held up. Fallen started wars all over the world. We didn't realize they were distracting us from London until the Celestial found us. How long until the air strike?"

"Any minute now," Sable says.

I glance up and notice a blue glow from the roof of The Savoy. It's expanding like a bubble and rapidly engulfing the hotel.

"Look," I yell, getting Camiel and Sable's attention.

"It's started," Camiel says. He jerks his attention back to Sable. "I'll stop those missiles. You get to that roof and stop the ritual."

He crouches and with a flap of his wings, shoots into the

air and phases into the mortal world, immediately disappearing from view.

Deacon, Sable, and the two angels take off. They fly in the direction of the hotel roof, leaving Nova and me on the ground.

"You've got to be kidding me," Nova shouts. "Argh."

I hear my name and spin.

Sterling and Nikias sprint toward us. I point toward the hotel, and Nikias takes flight immediately. Sterling reaches us a moment later, dripping wet.

Tinkle disappears in a shower of sparkles, only to reappear as a dragon.

"Hop on," he tells us.

Oh no, not more flying.

Sucking it up, I climb onto his back behind Nova. Sterling scrambles up as well, soaking my back when he shimmies in close.

"We're on," Nova shouts, and with one powerful downstroke of Tinkle's leathery wings, we're airborne and headed straight for the roof.

# 51
## STEEL

*M*y paws pad against the rooftop. My claws dig in, searching for purchase on the smooth surface.

Seraphim hasn't even noticed that I've broken free. Her attention is on something outside the expanding blue dome, and all the better for it. I'm running into this fight with a severe handicap. I have to incapacitate Seraphim without killing her. I won't risk serious injury to Emberly in order to defeat the monster who hijacked her body.

I jump, aiming for Seraphim's chest. Twin bolts of silver light shoot through the blue dome and hit Seraphim in the chest before I can reach her.

I land, my claws carving deep gouges into the roof as I skid to a halt, then change directions.

Two angels have a hold of Seraphim. Terror explodes in my chest. They're going to kill her.

A massive roar rolls from my chest and explodes out of my mouth as I rush the trio.

Seraphim's hands light with angel-fire. Veins of electricity run up and down her arms, and she blasts the angels off of her. Smoke rises from them when their bodies hit the ground, but they don't stay down for long.

There's a commotion behind me, but I can't afford to look. I'm closer to Seraphim now, so when I jump, this time I reach her before the angels, making sure my claws don't dig into her flesh as I knock her over.

Seraphim gets her legs between us before we even get to the ground. As soon as her back touches the roof, she kicks me off and over her as if I'm a kitten rather than an eight-hundred-pound animal.

I soar through the air and over the side of the roof. I fall two stories before I shift into an eagle and fly back up. Just as I reach the ledge, four Fallen land on the roof and surround Seraphim. I scan the skies and notice Fallen and angels battling all around us.

That's when it hits me: Seraphim really did it. She brought down the barrier and merged the mortal world and spirit realm.

My talons skim the roof, and I shift back into a man. The angels Seraphim blasted face off against the Fallen and Seraphim. There's a split second when I'm frozen with indecision on which side to take. When the angels rush Seraphim with their weapons drawn, instinct decides for me: Protect Emberly at all costs, no matter what.

# 52

## ASH

$\mathcal{W}$e reach the rooftop, and it's pandemonium. A battle rages on one side between Fallen and angels. There's a lion in the mix that must be Steel.

"Sterling, no!" Nova shouts as Sterling vaults off Tinkle.

He lands on the roof in a crouch, then runs to the opposite side where someone hangs facedown, suspended between two poles. Sable and Deacon are already there, working to free them. Nikias holds his hands against their neck.

Tinkle touches down on the roof, and Nova and I slide off his back. The Celestial changes back into a flying squirrel almost immediately, trailing us as we rush in the same direction as Sterling.

My heart jumps into my throat when I realize the person Sable and Deacon just freed is Shira. Her body flops lifelessly as Nikias and Sterling catch her and then carry her away from the giant bowl of blood beneath her.

So much blood. There can't be much left in her body.

Nikias and Sterling lay Shira on the ground. Her once

tan skin is chalky. Nikias' hands are coated in her blood. There's a cut on her neck still leaking, but the flow isn't much.

Something streaks over our heads. I glance over my shoulder to see two Fallen land on the roof. Sable, Deacon, and Nova rush to cut them off. Tinkle zips behind them, leaving a line of sparks through the air.

I stay with Nikias and Sterling to help with Shira. Sterling shucks off his tactical vest, then pulls his shirt over his head. Bunching the material up, he shoves it over Shira's wound and holds it in place.

"Easy, son," Nikias says. "You need to put pressure on the wound, but not too much or you'll choke her."

Sterling nods and lets up on the pressure. "Is she going to be all right?"

Nikias' gaze moves toward the bowl of Shira's blood, then back to his unresponsive family member. His face is almost as white as hers as he shakes his head. "She won't be unless I can get her to a healer, fast. We brought one with us from Eden, but she's on the north side of the city."

Sterling and I both look in that direction. Fallen and angels battle in the sky and on rooftops. The sun has almost set, and we can hear the shrieks of the Forsaken as they crawl from whatever holes they hid in during the day.

"You won't be able to make it there without someone watching your back," Sterling says, voicing the sentiment we're both thinking.

Nikias casts a glance at the chaos around us. Nova, Sable, and Deacon have taken down one of the Fallen, but battle another. The other side of the roof is even crazier with angels and Fallen attacking one another.

Through the Fallen and angel bodies, I catch a quick

glimpse of Steel and Emberly, but it's impossible to say who's winning.

Closer to us, Nova drives a sword through the heart of the second Fallen just as Deacon decapitates it with an axe. They look about, ready to rush into the other fight when Sterling yells Sable's name and then waves them over.

They're all breathing hard when they join us.

"How is she?" Sable asks.

Deacon and Nova keep their eyes on the sky, wary of the next attack.

Nikias quickly explains how he has a healer that might be able to save Shira's life, but he needs to get her to the north side of the city. It's obvious what needs to be done. The angel-born with wings have to help Nikias get Shira out of here, but Sable hesitates.

"We'll stay to help," Sterling says. Nova and I nod our agreement.

"I just—I can't—" Sable says.

"You have to go," I tell Sable. "She's going to die if you don't."

"We've got this," Nova says. "We'll fight as a unit and protect each other. Besides, we have Tinkle." She tips her head toward the squirrel at her shoulder.

Sable takes a deep breath. After checking the sky another time, she nods.

Nikias rips a piece of his own shirt and ties a tourniquet around Shira's throat, doing the best he can to stanch the flow of blood while still letting her breathe.

Sterling throws his shirt and vest back on; the former is soaked with Shira's blood.

Nikias stands with Shira in his arms, ready to take flight, when the sky explodes.

# 53

## STEEL

*I*t's no use, the angels won't listen to me. Every time I get close enough to tell them to stop, one of them swats me away. I'm glad no one's tried to smite me with their angel-fire, but I'm getting nowhere fast.

I drop to the ground to dodge a Fallen's meaty arm as he swings for my head. I'm about to pop back to my feet when something detonates in the sky above our heads, throwing me back down and everyone else off their feet.

Windows shatter in the building beneath us, as well as all over London. The origin of the explosion was somewhere in the atmosphere above us. As the red and orange of the blast begins to fade, the white cloud left behind stands out against the darkening purple sky.

Pushing to my feet, I scan the surroundings. The sky has been cleared of Fallen and angel battles. At the other end of the roof, three angel-borns jump from the ledge, their wings pumping as they flea. One of them cradles a body.

Sharp relief blooms in my chest when I realize Shira is no longer hanging and bleeding over the orbs. Looking back to the receding forms, I recognize Deacon and Sable. I squint at the third figure carrying Shira. Is that Nikias? It definitely looks like him. I don't know how the angel-line Neph joined this fight, but I'm glad for it.

I start to search for Seraphim when I catch Nova, Ash, and Sterling standing back to back as several Fallen approach. My brother and friends don't have wings; they won't be able to flee.

I'm torn about what to do when someone lands with a thump and shouts Seraphim's name. I catch a flash of black wings as the angel-born rushes past me.

Aero.

The fool is going to get himself killed. I only half-care, but he's running toward Seraphim with murderous intent and my instinct to protect Emberly pushes everything else aside.

With a burst of speed, I sprint after Aero, tackling him well before he reaches Seraphim. Flaring his wings, Aero tries to fling me off him. We tussle on the ground until I flip him on his stomach. With my knee in his back, I hold him down with a hand on his neck and his arm wrenched up behind him.

Aero spits obscenities as he squirms beneath me. His clothes are torn and bloody. It's clear he's been through an ordeal, but he still has a dose of fight left in him.

"Stay down," I order. "You're out of your league here."

"She killed my father! She's going to pay." Aero's body vibrates with rage. I'd feel more sympathy for the dude if his father hadn't tried to kill Emberly. For that fact alone, I don't care one lick that Stavros is gone.

I growl in frustration. I don't have time for this. The struggling angel-born beneath me is a liability.

Releasing my hold on Aero's neck, I lift my arm to cold cock him when a body smashes into me. I'm knocked off Aero and pinned to the ground by a large angel. He quickly shoves to his feet and rushes back into the battle between Seraphim and her Fallen.

I spring up in time to see Aero take to the air and shoot toward Seraphim. I'm about to morph into an eagle and give chase when Seraphim spots the black-winged Neph. With a flick of her wrist, she flings a bolt of angel-fire that sends Aero crashing back to the rooftop.

I sprint toward the downed angel-born as he stumbles to his feet, holding his burnt shoulder. A Fallen reaches him before I do, picks him up by the throat, and punches through his chest. When he pulls his hand back, he takes bits of Aero's flesh and bone with him, leaving a clear hole in his chest cavity. The Fallen tosses Aero to the side without a second thought. His lifeless body flops and lands next to the corpse of a felled angel.

I feel a twinge of pity for the headstrong angel-born, but then a Fallen attacks. I'm forced to defend myself or succumb to the same fate as Aero—and I don't plan to follow his lead.

# 54
## ASH

*F*allen drop from the sky on every side. Nova, Sterling, and I pull our weapons, and Tinkle transforms into a gorilla. Not as good as a dragon, but considering his fickle nature, I'm not complaining.

The three of us do our best to remain back to back in a tight circle as we fight, with Tinkle creating general havoc for the Fallen, but with all the slashing and jabbing and kicking, we eventually get separated.

Sterling and I have just managed to take down a Fallen together when the door to the hotel slams open.

A Forsaken with a tactical crossbow at the ready bursts onto the roof. She takes aim at Nova, and a scream rips from my throat.

A white stream of angel-fire hits the Forsaken in the back, shoving her forward, but it's too late. She already loosed her shot.

The bolt sails straight toward Nova's head, but before it can connect, a flash of gray juts out in front of her, blocking the path of the projectile.

Nova, and the gorilla that just jumped in front of her, crash into the low railing behind them.

The Fallen who took the shot is down, but already getting back to her feet. With a battle cry, I chuck my spear at her head. The weapon cuts through the air and lodges in her skull. I don't know if it penetrated far enough to kill, but it will at least put her down so someone can finish her off.

I sprint to Nova and Tinkle's side.

Tinkle lays on the ground with the arrow sticking out of his chest. Nova is crouched over him. The Celestial's breathing is labored and there's a wet rattling sound with each inhale and exhale.

My brain tells me something I refuse to believe. There's no way Tinkle can be dying. By his own admission, Celestials are all-powerful. How could he be felled by a single arrow?

Nova runs her hands over Tinkle without touching him, clearly not knowing what to do.

"Where's Camiel?" Nova cries. "He'll know what to do."

I look skyward, where the cloud from the explosion is still dissipating. Angel or not, I don't know how Camiel could have survived a blast like that.

Tinkle's gorilla face scrunches in a very humanlike grimace of pain. He lifts his hand, maybe to pull out the arrow, but it falls heavy back at his side.

"I would like for you to see me as me . . . before I die."

"No, don't say that." Tears stream down Nova's face and splash against Tinkle's large chest. "You're a Celestial. You can't die."

"I'm afraid I may have exaggerated my omnipotence a

tad." He coughs, and a silver stream of liquid starts to leak from his mouth.

Sterling appears and hands me my weapon. "I finished off the Fallen you speared," he says, then looks down at Nova and Tinkle. "Is he going to be okay?"

I shake my head, my vision blurred with my own tears. "I don't know. I don't think so."

A faint glow appears around Tinkle's body, followed by a flash of light. From one blink to the next Tinkle goes from a giant gorilla to something else entirely. His tiny body is small enough for Nova to pick up and hold in her hands.

He's a little silver being, humanoid in form, with large black eyes, and a pair of wings that remind me of a dragonfly. He's not much bigger now than he was as a squirrel, which probably explains why he preferred that form so much. There's no arrow lodged in his chest anymore, but it doesn't seem to matter. The damage has already been done.

"Don't be sad," he says with a soft smile as he stares at Nova. "It is my great honor to die for someone I love."

Sterling and I both drop to our knees to get closer to the tiny Celestial. My heart bleeds for him.

Nova is practically sobbing. I've never seen her this undone.

"Tell Emberly I like her all right." His words are only a faint whisper at this point.

"Tinkle, no. No no no," Nova says as he lies limply in her hands.

"Okay, tell her I love her too." He tries to chuckle, but the sound is all wrong. He takes one final breath, then goes still.

Tinkle's body dissolves into sparks that slide through Nova's fingers like wisps of smoke before blinking out of existence.

I hold my breath as if the act will freeze time, in complete and utter disbelief at what just happened.

A light shines from behind us, and I crane my neck to see Thorne standing above us.

A bolt of terror shoots up my spine. Thorne's face is lit by the white angel-fire running up and down his arms, but his expression is unreadable. His clothes are wet and torn, and only one wing arches behind him. A bloody stump protrudes where the other one should be.

His eyes look past Sterling and me, to Nova.

"You did this," she screams. She tries to launch herself at Thorne, but Sterling tackles her to the ground.

I stand with my weapon in hand and at the ready. I know Thorne will easily defeat me, but Tinkle isn't the only one willing to die defending his loved ones.

With one more glance at Nova, Thorne turns and takes off in the other direction, yelling his mother's name.

# 55

## THORNE

"Seraphim!" My mother's name shreds my throat as I scream it.

Her electric angel-fire, now amplified by Emberly's power, burns a hole straight through the angel's chest in front of her. She only lifts her red-tinted gaze to me after she's finished him off. The rooftop is littered with Fallen and angel bodies, and a feral sort of pleasure lights her face.

I've lived in a world of carnage my entire life, but for the first time, I'm sickened by it.

Bending over, Seraphim swipes her hand over the defeated angel's forehead. The tips of her fingers come away coated in gold blood. She sticks two in her mouth and licks them clean as she saunters toward me.

"So, you survived," she says.

*With no help from you.*

A pair of humans fished me out of the river after the realms collided. Humans saved me when my subjects, and my own mother, didn't even bother looking for my body.

"You're maimed." Her lips peel back in disgust as she takes in my missing wing.

"You need to stop this." I point toward the horizon.

In the distance, a horde of angels heads our way. Despite how powerful she may be, there's no way she can win. All that will come about from fighting now is more bloodshed on every side.

She glances over her shoulder at the swarm and shrugs. "Let them come. The Forsaken are no longer held captive by the sun, and I can defeat whatever enemies my Fallen can't take down."

"Mother, we were wrong to start this. The spirit realm should have been enough. It's time to end this."

She narrows her eyes and the red in her irises flares with anger. "So, it's come to this, has it. You're betraying me and what you've worked your whole life to achieve? And for what?"

"Near-death experiences tend to give new perspective."

My moral compass might be skewed, but I know enough to know that this is wrong. I've always known on some level —I just didn't want to see it. Believing that the strong have a right to rule over the weak was a simple way to live, but shades of gray have slowly leaked into my soul since the day Emberly walked into it.

I don't know who I am anymore, or what I stand for. But for right now, I know this madness needs to end.

"You're not worthy to rule. You never have been," she spits.

"Enough."

"It will never be enough," she screams.

"So be it."

Before she has a chance to react, I lift my palms and

throw every ounce of strength I have left into a powerful ball of electrified angel-fire. It hits her right in the chest, and her eyes go wide.

It may be Emberly's face she wears, but the look of rage that shines from her eyes is all Seraphim.

I force myself to continue pouring energy into the stream of angel-fire pounding my mother. Her head snaps back. Her screams of wrath and agony rip into me, but I don't stop.

"Thorne, no!" Steel bellows.

I ignore the annoying Nephilim but can't help imagining the horror he must feel as he watches his love burn to ash. I hate the guy, so I don't care.

As I blast Seraphim, I watch Emberly's alabaster skin char and start to flake away.

Steel rushes for her, but his friends hold him back. He fights against all three of them, but he'll be too late.

# 56

## EMBERLY

*S*eraphim's scream of rage pierces the abyss. Fissures appear, and pinpricks of light filter through the darkness. For the first time since I was sealed in the prison of my own mind, I can feel my body. But I'm on fire and burning to embers, so I almost wish I couldn't.

*No. This body is mine,* Seraphim shrieks. *You can't have it.*

The words are meant for me, and rattle around my mind like nails driven through my skull.

I try to open my eyes, but when I do, Seraphim slams my lids closed. I don't fight her on that because the world is bathed in blue and white angel-fire far too bright to see through.

My muscles lock as I'm scorched from the inside out, but through the agony I can feel something else—Seraphim's fury, but also her fear.

We're both trapped in a body created for one soul, and I know that after this battle, only one of us will remain.

Oh gosh. It hurts. It hurts so bad, but the unrelenting onslaught of angel-fire does something to loosen

Seraphim's control. It's not enough to vanquish her from my body, but it gives me the chance I didn't have before.

The chance to fight back.

I stoke my power, moving it throughout my body, letting the angel-fire blasting me from without charge the fire from within. Still, Seraphim's hold remains strong.

*I am the first seraph. You're not powerful enough to beat me.*

I ignore Seraphim as she continues to lash me with words. This isn't a traditional fight. I can't use my fists or even my powers to beat back the evil that clings to me. This is a battle of wills, and I know that my desire to protect the people and relationships I've forged this last year is stronger than Seraphim's obsession with power and revenge. My motivations are pure and untainted, where hers are polluted with darkness—and darkness can never stand up to light.

I fill my thoughts with as much light as I can. Inch by inch, moment by moment, her grip on me lessens. With every piece of her that becomes unrooted inside my body, she fights that much harder to regain her hold. It's not enough. It will never be enough. Because this body is *mine*, and evil can't have it.

# 57

## THORNE

*E*mberly's back arches as I continue to pummel her with pure angel-fire. A gray substance leaks from her pores and peels away from her skin, forming the thrashing shadow figure of my mother hovering several inches above her body. Tentacles of darkness cling to Emberly, but determination is etched on her face as she continues to expel Seraphim from her system.

My arms shake with fatigue even as my mind wars with myself over the choice I made, telling me it's not too late. But that's a lie. I stepped over a line that can't be uncrossed, and my world will never be the same because of it.

A cry bursts from Emberly's throat as the last remnants of Seraphim are purged from her system. What's left of my mother hangs in the air for a moment before exploding in a burst of ash and fire.

A single tear trickles down my face.

It's done, and all that's left of me is a shell. My legs give out, and I crash to the ground.

# 58

## EMBERLY

*I* hurt everywhere, so I don't think I'm dead.

I blink my eyes open. I'm on my back, staring at a dark purple sky. White and red pinpricks of light shine through a cloud of hazy smog.

"Emberly!"

I turn my head and watch Steel sprint toward me. He drops to his knees a few feet away and slides into me. He doesn't waste any time crushing me against his chest.

"I thought he killed you. I thought you were gone."

"Thought who killed me?" I croak. My throat feels burnt and raw.

Steel pulls back and cups my face in his hands. He scans my features, then does a quick check down my body.

"Thorne," he finally says. "He burned Seraphim out of you with angel-fire. But I thought—" Emotion clogs his throat and he has to swallow before going on. "I thought he was killing you."

"Umm . . ." I blink back at Steel. I don't know how to feel

—glad that Seraphim is gone or shock that it was Thorne that freed me. "That's unexpected."

"Ah, guys. I hate to break up the love fest, but . . ."

I look to the side and Sterling, Nova, and Ash are there. Sterling points to the left, where Thorne struggles to his feet. He stumbles once and then limps closer. Everyone tenses.

"The orbs need to be removed from the blood," Thorne says. "It's not too late. The veil doesn't drop all at once. It will expand out from this point of origin, but if we remove the orbs from the blood—their power source—the spread will stop."

Behind my friends, I notice a large, oval bowl. It's filled almost to the brim with red liquid.

My stomach roils in disgust, but I will it to chill the heck out. Now's not the time to lose my last meal.

"Who's blood is that?" I ask.

"Shira's," Steel says.

I push to my feet and then turn in a circle. There's carnage everywhere. Fallen and angels, but I don't see Shira anywhere.

"Where is she?"

Ash lays a hand on my arm. "She's been taken to get help."

I don't understand how she could have possibly survived so much blood loss.

"And the orbs are in there?"

Ash nods.

I look at Thorne. "And to stop the mortal and spectrum worlds from merging, we need to get them out?"

Thorne nods.

"Then what are we waiting for?" Nova asks.

With a grunt, she goes to kick the bowl, but before her foot connects with the rim, she's thrown back. In an instant, Thorne's by her side, trying to help her back to her feet.

"Don't touch me," she snaps at him, and he backs away, looking confused over his own actions.

"The orbs are protecting themselves." Thorne looks at me. "We need to overpower them."

"How?"

Thorne closes his eyes, and with obvious effort, produces a ball of white angel-fire in his palm. "With this," he says, then looks at me. "But I can't do it alone. I'm too tapped."

I lift my hands and call forth my power, producing sparks at my fingertips. I'm not at a hundred percent, but I'm also not completely drained.

"How do we know you're telling the truth?" I ask.

Thorne lifts his upper lip and snarls, "Do you really have much of a choice right now?"

He has a point, and I hate that. My only comfort is that there's no way we can make things worse than they already are.

With lips pressed into a hard line, I nod.

Thorne and I slide into position across from each other. I make my friends, including Steel, promise to stay a safe distance away before I form a ball of angel-fire in my hands.

"We hit them at the same time," Thorne says.

"Why are you doing this?" I know every moment is precious, but I have to know. What happened to make Thorne change his course so drastically?

His gaze lifts from the blood drenched-orbs and connects with mine. "I wish I knew."

I open my mouth to question him, but Thorne starts

counting down from three. When he reaches one, we both release our power, sending streams of angel-fire at the orbs. Our energy hits an invisible dome around the orbs and bounces back at us. Thorne and I slide back several feet across the roof's smooth surface.

Steel yells my name, but I shake my head to keep him away.

As we continue to hammer the dome with angel-fire, my body weakens. I grit my teeth and reach even further into my reserves. Sweat beads on my forehead and my arms shake. I release a warrior's cry as I push even more of my power, more of myself, into breaking through whatever field of protection the orbs have created.

Our combined angel-fire grows even more intense, sliding over the invisible shield and revealing the outline of the dome. The brightness makes my eyes water; the heat recoils back at me in waves.

I can only just make out Thorne on the other side of the blood bowl. The effort this costs him shows on his face and in his shaking limbs.

We're both spent and expelling power we don't have to spare. We're not going to last much longer.

*Keep going. Keep going. Keep going.* I chant to myself as I push my body past its limits.

Something shifts. There's a crack in the dome and some of my angel-fire leaks through. Seconds tick by that feel like hours. More cracks appear.

"It's working," I shout.

Thorne nods without taking his gaze from the bowl.

A spiderweb of cracks splinter over the dome. It holds for two more breaths before shattering completely, throwing the orbs' energy and our own back at Thorne and me. I don't have time to brace myself, and it hits me with the force of a tsunami, blowing me across the roof.

I hit the ground and hardly feel a thing. My body shuts down, function by function. The last thing I see before my eyes close are the gold and silver wings of an army of angels as they descend from the sky above.

# 59

## EMBERLY

*W*hen I wake, I know immediately that Steel is pressed up behind me. His hand rests on my hip and soft breaths puff against the back of my neck. I'm starting to really appreciate the art of spooning.

I lift my hand and start to trace invisible patterns on his bare forearm. When his arm twitches and he nuzzles his face into my hair, I know he's come awake.

"How long have I been asleep?" I ask, my voice scratchy from lack of use.

Steel presses a kiss to my neck that makes me shiver, then sits up. I roll onto my back to stare up at him. His hair is smooshed flat on one side, and he blinks lazily as he begins to fully wake.

"Almost three days."

"Dang." I sit up as well, scooching so my back rests against the headboard. "I knew I needed a nap, but that's extreme."

"Last I heard, Thorne was still out too. Whatever juice

you both had to dig up to break through the force field around the orbs really took it out of you guys."

No doubt.

I glance around the room, wondering at its familiarity. "Are we in Eden?"

The furnishings are similar to the bedroom we slept in at Nikias' home.

Steel scrubs a hand over his head, ruffling the flattened strands as he stares at me. "Yeah. You passed out in London. When we transported you outside of the merge zone, you were still in the spirit realm. This was the safest place I could think to take you until you woke up."

"Is it really safe though, after what happened with Stavros? There have to be angel-born in Eden that hate me."

"Nikias made sure everyone knows it was Seraphim and not you who took out Stavros. Aero would be my biggest concern, but he tried to go after Seraphim in London and was killed."

My heart drops with the news about Aero. I didn't know him well, but the senseless loss of life is still sad.

"Nikias has launched a full investigation to suss out any of Stavros' potential co-conspirators." Steel takes my hand. "And I don't plan on leaving your side anytime soon."

The world is a different place than it was last week. I want to know what we're all facing. I take a deep breath and then ask Steel for the details of what happened after I passed out.

"It worked," Steel says. "You and Thorne cracked through whatever protective shield the orbs cast around themselves, and we were able to pull them from their power source."

The power source being a vat of Shira's blood.

"All of London, and a decent chunk of the surrounding suburbs, were lost. They're calling it 'The Merge Zone' because within that area, the spirit and mortal worlds collided, creating a new dimension. The Fallen roam free, and the Forsaken can walk in the daylight there."

"How is that possible?"

Steel shrugs. "Who knows? But I'm sure it makes the idea of combining the orbs again even more attractive."

I huff. "I guess that's a problem for another day."

"Yeah."

"What's going to happen to Thorne?" I ask.

Steel shakes his head. "That's above my pay grade, but I'd imagine nothing good."

I chew on my lip, torn. "He saved me, and we wouldn't have been able to get through the barrier around the orbs without him. That should count for something."

"He did a lot of harm before that. A significant number of lives were lost in this war. Human, angels, and angel-born alike. I'm not sure his decisions at the end will cancel all that out. The consequences of Thorne's actions, even if the true mastermind was Seraphim, are far-reaching."

I nod in understanding, glad that I wasn't entirely wrong about Thorne. But Steel's right, he did a lot of bad things. Even a lifetime of good can't erase that.

Steel inches up the mattress so he's closer to me.

"I'm so glad you're all right," he says, sincerity wiping his face clear of all hardness. His gaze bounces over my face, not settling in any one spot for long.

"I'm just glad everyone else is all right."

Steel's gaze connects with my own and he goes silent. He takes a deep breath, and I start to worry.

"Steel. What's happened?"

~

I cry into Steel's shoulder when he tells me about Tinkle's death and that Camiel is missing but presumed dead after intercepting a missile that would have blown us to bits. "The Angel of War would be very hard to kill," Steel says as he rubs my back. I hiccup from crying so much. "His own kind searches for him. There's a chance he may just be badly hurt and not recuperated enough to find help. If anyone is too stubborn to die, it's Camiel."

I nod into his shoulder, afraid to really hope.

There's something we haven't discussed yet. I loosen my arms from around Steel's neck and pull back. "Steel, your sister. I'm so sorry."

He winces. I hold my breath as I wait for him to say something. I wouldn't blame him if he hates me, but I desperately hope he doesn't.

"They found Silver's body in the Sorcerer Room." He rubs his bloodshot eyes, evidence the last few days weren't as restful for him as they were for me. "Seraphim didn't even bother to have her covered."

I force the next words out of my mouth, frightened that they'll change things between us. "I didn't mean to kill her. Everything happened so fast. She kept coming at me. I couldn't get her to stop. I'm still not even sure how—"

"Emberly," Steel presses three fingers against my lips, only removing them after I quiet. "I don't blame you for Silver's death. It may have technically been you who ended her, but she chose the wrong path again and again. It was always going to lead to the same place—her death. I'm heartbroken and still coming to terms with the fact that it was me who put her on that path, but she had the opportunity to start over and didn't take it."

There's nothing to say, so I reach forward and wrap my arms around Steel, offering him what comfort I can. He buries his head in my hair and hugs me back. His body is strung tight as a bowstring, but after a few minutes, he starts to relax. When he pulls back, his face is a bit lighter, though still weary.

"Thank you," he says, then intertwines his fingers with my own.

I lean back against the headboard, my chest heavy with loss. "What happens now?"

"There's a lot to do." Steel squeezes my hand. "You and Nikias have been granted spots on the Council as the seraph- and angel-line representatives."

I scrunch my nose. "I'm an Elder?"

Steel smiles at my reaction. Dipping his head he says, "Your Supreme Highness."

I roll my eyes.

"The humans know more about us and the reality of their world than they ever have before. Malachi and the other Elders have been in contact with a select number of human governments, especially in the UK and America, where the attacks occurred."

"That's surprising. I was expecting a major cover-up."

"Yeah, but that's not all. Angels and Nephilim are working together in London to evacuate humans."

"Working together?"

That's almost too much to believe. Camiel himself said that he didn't think that would ever happen.

"Nikias was appointed special liaison between our two

species, and we seem to have struck an accord with the angels, at least while the world works to restore order."

"That's a big step for both sides."

He nods in agreement.

"The humans are building a wall around the merge zone. Apparently, they're having a problem with people trying to sneak in."

"That's suicide," I say, then pucker my mouth. Talk about walking right into a lion's den. "What a mess."

"Yeah, it's certainly that."

I furrow my brow, already overwhelmed. "Do we have to go back right away? Could we take a few days to just . . . be?"

Steel leans forward, placing a chaste kiss on my lips. "Of course," he says when he sits back.

The door swings open, and Sterling barges into the room. Seeing me sitting up in bed, he turns his head and yells, "She's awake!"

Feet pound on the stairs down the hall and then Greyson bounds into the room, followed by Ash. Ash skirts Sterling as she runs to the bed.

"You're finally awake," she squeals as she nudges Steel out of the way. With a chuckle, he stands and leans up against the wall next to the headboard.

"How do you feel?" Ash asks, her concerned gaze bouncing over my face.

"Like myself."

She lets out a relieved breath of air. "Thank goodness."

Sable and Deacon walk into the room hand in hand. I catch Sable's gaze, then lift my eyebrows in question. A touch of pink colors her cheekbones, but she just smiles back at me.

When I look around at my friends, some of the heaviness lifts from my chest. But someone is missing.

"Where's Nova?"

Ash and Sterling exchange a look.

"She's at the Elders' compound," Sterling says.

"Oh." Maybe her parents wanted her there?

"I don't think she was up for seeing all the Celestials here in Eden," Ash explains. "Tinkle's death was hard on her."

Oh gosh, that didn't even occur to me, but it makes perfect sense. I loved Tinkle. He'll always have a special place in my heart, but there's no denying Nova had a unique bond with him. Considering he also died to save her, she must be a wreck right now—at least on the inside. Knowing Nova, she's probably broadcasting to the world that she's totally fine.

A fresh wave of sadness threatens to drown me. For Tinkle and for Nova.

"Were you there when it happened?"

Ash nods. "He wanted you to know that he loved you."

Fresh tears gather in my eyes. "I wish I could have done something to help. It feels like this is all my fault."

Sable steps forward, letting Deacon's hand slip from her grasp as she does. "Oh no, honey. Don't think that. What happened to you was not your fault. No one blames you, and we're all here for you."

A wan smile is the only thanks I can offer.

"And I know what it feels like to wish you could have done more," Greyson says. "I was benched because of a broken leg." There's a tightness around his mouth and eyes. "It didn't feel good."

Deacon claps Greyson on the shoulder and tells him, "Every extra minute you gave us helped."

"Thanks, man."

"The angel-born in Eden had a memorial service a few days ago for the warriors they lost. We thought that once you woke up, we could plan our own for Tinkle and . . ." Ash bites her lip before awkwardly finishing the sentence, "anyone else we might want to honor."

She means Camiel, but I'm not ready to mourn him before I know he's truly gone.

"I'd like to honor Tinkle." I wipe away the tears that didn't fall from my eyes, then offer her a smile. "I think that's a great idea."

"Word is my cousin is finally awake."

Sable and Greyson step to the side to reveal Shira standing in the doorway. Her face is a smattering of fading bruises, and there's a bandage over her throat.

Guilt rolls over me fast and hard. I may not have technically put her through this ordeal, but if it wasn't for me, it wouldn't have happened.

"What are you doing out of bed?" Sterling rushes to her side. "You're supposed to be resting."

He tries to take her hand like she's an invalid and walk her back out the door. Shira swats at him and slides farther into the room.

I glance at Ash, who's smothering a smile behind her hand.

Sterling acting as nursemaid—I never thought I'd see the day.

Sable clears her throat. "I think I hear Nikias calling for lunch. Let's go check it out."

"I didn't hear anything," Sterling says, but Greyson is

already grabbing him by the back of the shirt and hauling him out of the room.

Ash turns to me after Sable and Deacon leave. "See you downstairs in a bit?"

"For sure. I need to stretch my legs." I wiggle my toes underneath the blanket.

I assume Steel is going to follow her out, but he walks across the room and settles into a chair instead. Cocking my head, I give him a funny look.

"I know it's going to be annoying, but you need to give me a little time. I was serious before. I'm not quite ready to let you out of my sight."

"What about when I go to the bathroom?"

"I'm okay waiting behind the door as long as I can still hear you."

I grimace. "Ew, Steel."

He grins.

I shake my head, but I don't mind if he stays. We're going to have to renegotiate the bathroom privacy though.

I settle my attention on Shira, who stands awkwardly in the middle of the room, looking like she's not sure if she's going to bolt or not.

"Shira," I start, "I'm so very sorry for—"

She holds up a hand, halting my words. "I know that wasn't you. I only wish I'd listened the first time you tried to tell me."

"Still . . ." I take in her injuries again. Her clothes hide her arms and legs, but I think she limped when she walked in the room. "If it wasn't for me, this never would have happened. You almost died."

"True, but if it wasn't for you, the angel-born from our line would still be hiding away in this town. There's a big world out there that we've been scared to be a part of, but having seen some of it for myself, I think it's past time we broke out of this bubble. I'd go through all this again if it meant true freedom for my people. And I couldn't be prouder that we added another powerful warrior to our family."

I open my mouth to argue, then close it again. After taking a deep breath to rein in a bit of my emotions, I try again. "Thank you for saying that."

Shira lifts her chin in recognition and then tips her head toward the doorway. "I can hear the boys raiding the pantry. I'd better get down there before they tear the place apart."

My smile is watery. I can't seem to keep my waterworks at bay today.

She turns to leave but pauses at the door. "You coming?"

"Absolutely. There's nowhere else I'd rather be."

# 60

## EMBERLY

*T*he warm Mediterranean breeze ruffles the leaves on the trees around us and circulates a fresh burst of citrus-tinted air. My face is tilted toward the sun, my eyelids lowered, as Steel plays with the ends of my hair while I rest my head on his lap. The remains of our lunch rest on the other side of the plaid blanket beneath us.

It's been three days since I woke up. In that time, I've done my best to keep everything going on outside of Eden's bubble out of my mind. Here, alone with Steel after a midday picnic, I can almost pretend he's a regular boy, I'm a regular girl, and we have regular problems. I know we can't stay like this forever, but it's still nice to pretend.

"Do you know what the others are up to today?" I ask.

"Nikias offered to give a tutorial on phase-fighting. Ash and Deacon seemed particularly interested," Steel replies. "They were thoroughly impressed when the angel-line warriors swooped in to save them."

"I heard it was pretty remarkable to see them pop in and

out of worlds. I'm honestly surprised the Academies don't already teach combat that way."

Steel shrugs, jostling my head. "I think Sable might start campaigning to get it added to the fight training, but Nephilim are pretty set in their ways."

I can't argue with that. I'm sure some of the Elders' heads are about to explode with all the changes. Humans knowing about the spirit world, working with angels, a whole new merged dimension in the lower part of the United Kingdom.

I blink open my eyes and squint against the brightness. Steel's head is ringed in a halo of light. I can only just make out his features.

"A fighting tutorial sounds like something you'd be down for."

Glancing down at me, Steel brushes a wisp of hair off my forehead.

"I have better places to be," he says with a smile.

I blush. Seeing the reddening of my cheeks, Steel leans over and kisses the tip of my nose.

"I'll bet Sterling didn't join the others," I say. "He's probably still hovering over Shira. I heard her yell at him to stop trying to hand-feed her earlier."

Steel shakes his head. "Dude's coming in a little hot. He's going to smother her."

"Sterling is irresistible. He'll wear her down eventually."

Steel chuckles. "Or maybe he's finally met his match."

I laugh along with him. "Oh, I hope so. That would be a good show for the rest of us."

We fall silent and my mind starts to wander. I close my eyes against the sun's rays.

"Have you heard anything from Nova?" I ask. When Steel doesn't answer, I crack an eyelid.

"Last I heard she was trying to get on one of the teams to return the orbs," he finally says.

Seeing my frown, Steel tries to reassure me. "Nova has always liked to process things on her own. I'm sure she'll be back soon."

I nod, but I'm not so sure. Steel knows Nova better than I do, but I have this gut feeling she's on a path that diverges from ours, at least for now. I hope I'm wrong.

I take in a deep breath of honeysuckle- and lemon-scented air. "So, where do we go from here? We can't stay in Eden forever."

Steel pauses before answering. "Well, with your new Council duties, finishing your training, and the wedding plans, you're about to be a very busy little angel-born."

"Yeah, that's a lot and—wait. Wedding plans?" I sit up so fast Steel jerks out of the way to keep from getting head-butted. "What wedding?"

Lifting my hand, Steel slides something on my finger. "Ours."

I look down and almost choke.

"What. Is. That?"

Steel grins. "You know what that is."

A filigree rose gold band with a milky, pear-shaped gem circled by small diamonds sits on my left ring finger.

Steel just put a ring on it.

I stare at Steel, wide-eyed. "Steel, we can't get married. I'm only seventeen. You're nineteen. We're too young."

Steel plays with my hand, running his fingertips over my knuckles. "Angel-born are very long-lived. Age doesn't mean much to us."

"By that reasoning, we're practically babies!"

He looks up at me through his fringe of dark lashes. His teal eyes shine bright. "Do you really care about doing things the way the world tells us we should?"

"Well, um . . . maybe?"

Bringing a hand to my face, Steel brushes wisps of hair behind my ear. He cups my face and runs a thumb back and forth over my cheekbone.

"The truth is, I don't mind waiting as long as you'd like. We're soul-bonded by choice. I love you, Emberly, and I know you love me. That won't ever change. I simply want to make my intentions toward you clear, to you and to the whole world. As long as I'm by your side, the timeline is completely up to you. I'll wait an eternity as long as I know you're mine."

I take a deep breath, puffing out my cheeks before releasing it slowly. Am I really going to do this?

The answer is yes, yes I am.

"I love you."

Turning my hand over, I lace our fingers.

"Yes, I'll marry you."

A smile spreads over Steel's face, crinkling his eyes. He pulls me toward him and kisses me. Just like every time we come together, I can't seem to get enough.

Who knows how long it is before I have the sense to pull away. When I do, Steel's lips are swollen and red and there's a flush on his face. I smile, pleased to know I'm not the only one in this relationship who comes undone by kisses.

"Just so we're clear," I say. "I'm not even ready to *think* about having children for another hundred years, at least. Maybe more. Probably more."

Steel rubs his brow. "I'm on board with that. You know

my family is known for being prolific in the baby-making department."

I put my head in my hands. "Oh my gosh, twins. I may never be ready for that."

Chuckling, Steel tugs my hands from my face and kisses my forehead.

"Wait, you didn't get down on one knee. You have to do it again or the proposal doesn't count."

"We're sitting down. And that's a human tradition," he laughs at me.

"And this isn't?" I hold up my hand, wiggling my ring-clad finger.

"A little blending of traditions never hurt anyone. But in this case, it's more than just an engagement ring." Taking my hand, he brings my fingers to his mouth and kisses the tips. "The stone in the middle is cut from the spirit gem that kept Seraphim suppressed. I had someone find the bracelet you took off at the Elder's compound. This ring is a symbol of my love *and* a form of protection."

I cock my head, touched he put so much thought into it. It's also a little weird.

"You know Thorne gave me that bracelet?"

"I do."

I scrunch my nose. "And you don't have a problem with me wearing something that came from him?"

Steel takes a deep breath, sobering.

"I'm never going to like Thorne. But I think in his own weird and warped way, he tried to protect you. If he hadn't given you that bracelet, I would have lost you back at Whitehold. Seraphim would have possessed you immediately, you never would have destroyed Legion, and we wouldn't be here today." Steel runs his fingers over the top of the white gemstone. "I don't think you'll ever have to worry about being possessed again, but this gem will make you less of an obvious target for Fallen. Tinkle's not around anymore to shade your aura."

"So you got me a practical, tactical engagement ring?"

*How romantic.* I must have a sour look on my face because Steel starts to laugh.

"I could have given you the biggest diamond on the planet, but this gem is rare and precious, just like our love."

Oh, well that's better.

I go in for another kiss but freeze when we hear voices. I glance up to see Nikias and an unfamiliar snowy-winged angel walking toward us.

Steel and I share a look, then get to our feet. There's nothing between Nikias and the newcomer's body language that says we should be alarmed, but an angel in Eden that isn't Camiel is cause for concern.

The pair reaches us at an unhurried gait. The angel's gold-plated armor is almost blinding in the mid-day sun. His midnight skin sparkles as if he was brushed with gold dust.

"Emberly, Steel," Nikias starts, "this is Ramiel."

Ramiel tips his head in greeting and then regards me with uptilted gold eyes that are almost too large for his face. His jaw is square, and his straight nose widens slightly at the end. He's certainly an impressive being, but it's his presence more than his appearance that has me worried.

"What's happened?" I ask.

"Ramiel asked to speak with you." I narrow my eyes in suspicion, and Nikias adds, "He was close with your father."

"Have you found him yet?"

I haven't mourned Camiel because I refuse to believe

he's gone. What Steel said about him is right: If anyone could have survived the blast, it would be Camiel.

"I believe Ramiel has something to give you." Nikias nods to a small wood box Ramiel holds between his hands. It's about the size of a music box.

"I'll leave you to visit," Nikias says.

Rather than walking out the citrus grove the way he entered, Nikias flaps his wings and takes flight, taking the more direct route.

Steel reaches forward and encloses my hand in his own, offering me silent comfort.

"What's this all about?" I ask.

"I came to give you this." Ramiel holds out the box for me. I take it reluctantly. "It was Camiel's, and I believe he'd want you to have it."

I don't like the direction this conversation is going. My spine stiffens involuntarily, as if my body is already preparing for something my mind hasn't acknowledged.

"We still haven't found him," Ramiel says. "It doesn't mean we won't, but I won't lie and tell you I hold out much hope."

I look him over more closely, noticing how his armor resembles Camiel's.

"Are you supposed to be his replacement? The new Angel of War? I didn't expect angels to give up on their own so quickly." It's impossible to hide the bitter note in my voice. Truth is, I didn't even try.

Ramiel quirks his head, but his expression doesn't change. "Camiel said you were direct. I can see he wasn't wrong."

"He told you about me?"

I didn't think Camiel told anyone about me.

He nods. "He did. But to answer your question, no, I'm not replacing Camiel. I'm only a stand-in for the time being. I have my own duties to attend to."

I glance down at the box in my hand, then back at Ramiel.

"What's in here?"

"Camiel's most treasured possessions. He wouldn't have showed them to anyone else, and I expect if he returns he will want them back, but in the meantime, I felt that as his daughter, it was best you kept them safe."

I blink rapidly as tears fill my eyes. I have to clear my throat before speaking. "Thanks. I'll keep this safe."

Ramiel tips his head, then bows. The gesture makes me uncomfortable. No one should be bowing to me.

"I have to leave, but it was an honor meeting you, Emberly. I have no doubt our paths will cross again."

I don't know why they would, but I nod at Ramiel anyway, and he takes that as a cue to depart. With one mighty downswing of his white wings, he's airborne. I don't watch him leave because my gaze is fastened on the box in my hands. My mind whirls with possibilities of what it holds. What would a seraph angel consider his most treasured possessions?

"Hey," Steel says. "You don't have to look right now. You can give it some time."

"No, I want to know," I say with a shake of my head.

I crack the lid, and the breeze catches a piece of paper inside, tossing it in the air. With a gasp, I drop the box and make a grab for it.

I snatch the paper between my fingers right before it floats away, realizing only when it's in my grasp that it's a photograph.

I blink down at the image. At first, I think it's a picture of me with a wig, but that's not me at all. The photo is of a small family. I recognize Camiel. He's dressed like any of the angel-line Nephilim in Eden. His gold wings arch behind him as he grins down at the woman beside him that he has his arm around, and the small, bald baby cradled in her arms.

"That's my mother," I whisper. This is the first photo I've seen of her. Nikias probably has a photograph or portrait of her somewhere, but when I was in Eden before, I was too overwhelmed and preoccupied to ask to see one.

Steel steps in close and peers at the photograph from over my shoulder.

"And that angry little one must be you. I'm sorry to say, but you weren't the cutest baby."

"Steel!" He's not wrong. In the picture, my face is red and scrunched, but I lightly elbow him in the ribs. "I was crying."

He kisses me on the neck, as if that will soften the blow.

"You look so much like your mother."

I trace her face with my fingertip. Her head is no bigger than the size of a quarter in the photo, but I can still tell we have the same dark blue eyes, the same slope to our nose, and the same full lips.

"She was beautiful," he says.

I smile. "Yeah, she was."

"What's this?" Steel asks.

Bending over, he picks up the box I dropped as well as a small square of yellow fabric that fell out.

"I don't—" Wait. I think I know what that is. "When I was found as an infant, I was wrapped in a yellow blanket. I think that might be a piece of it."

I reach for the piece of fabric, and Steel hands it to me. I rub it between my fingers, the texture instantly familiar. The tears that were only threatening before, spill out and run down my face.

Camiel kept a piece of my baby blanket all these years.

"Hey, come here." Steel gently turns me and folds me in his arms. The front of his shirt soaks up my tears as he rubs a hand up and down my back. "I'm not saying that I agree with Camiel's decision to let you be raised in the mortal world by humans, but it's obvious how precious you are to him."

I appreciate Steel referring to Camiel as if he's still here, rather than already gone like everyone else. But what if . . .

I lift my face to Steel. A wave of vulnerability makes my limbs weak. I know my pain is reflected in my gaze, but I don't try to hide it from him. He's my person. I won't hide parts of myself from him anymore.

"What if he's gone? Then I'm back to not having family anymore."

"Oh, Em." Steel lifts a hand and wipes the wetness from my cheeks. "Haven't you realized you'll never be without family ever again? Ash and Nova would do anything for you. Greyson and Sterling already consider you a sister. Blaze and Aurora would trade me in for you in a heartbeat if they could." A laugh escapes me because that might be right. "Sable loves you like a daughter, and Deacon is so unbelievably proud of you. He's told any angel-born in Eden who will listen that he was your first trainer. And you also have Nikias and Shira now. I know they already consider you family and don't ever intend to let you go."

My heart goes from empty to bursting in the course of a few sentences. Steel's right. These people who I love so much, whether blood related or not, are my family. It doesn't take away the pain of losing Tinkle and possibly Camiel or erase the years I grew up without knowing what it was like to be loved, but the things I've gone through make me cherish the people I do have all the more.

"And you have me." Steel gazes at me with unfiltered adoration. "And as far as I'm concerned, it's my job to make sure you never feel alone again."

"How did I get so lucky?"

"How did *we* get so lucky?"

I tuck the photograph and piece of fabric back into the box, gently closing the top. There's a fullness in my heart that wasn't there a few minutes ago.

"Should we go tell the others the news?" Steel asks.

I nod. "Ash is going to flip out, but she'll make the most beautiful maid of honor."

Steel grimaces. "Well, actually, they all kinda know it's coming."

"You mean to tell me Sterling was able to keep it a secret? My mind is blown."

"Everyone knows it's coming *except* Sterling."

I laugh. "Wise choice."

We share a kiss and then clean up our picnic. With the blanket bundled up under his arm, Steel holds out his hand for me, and I take it. We leave the orchard the way we'll face the world from now on: hand in hand.

∾

# ANGELIC CLASSIFICATION
## IN ORDER OF SPHERE

**Angelic Spheres** – The nine classes of angels are divided equally into one of three spheres. Each sphere has related roles and responsibilities and it's believed—but not proven—that the most powerful angels are from the first sphere with decreasing power down to the third.

**Seraphim** – Literally translated as, "burning ones," seraphim are the highest angelic class and considered the most powerful. Part of the first sphere of angels, these supernatural beings are said to have six wings and protect the throne of their Creator. There are no known Nephilim from the seraphim line, because not a single seraph angel rebelled and therefore there are no seraph Fallen.

*Known Descendants – Emberly & Thorne*

**Cherubim** – Part of the first sphere of angels, cherubim are the highest angelic class that rebelled. The Nephilim of this line can typically shift into one of three different forms in the spirit realm: a lion, an eagle, or a bovine. It's very rare for a Nephilim to be able to shift into two or all three of these forms.

*Known Descendants – Steel, Greyson, Sterling, Aurora, Blaze, Eloise, Laurent, Silver, & Malachi (Cherub Elder)*

**Thrones** – The thrones are part of the first sphere and are said to be natural protectors. Nephilim of this line can manipulate and build wards to protect the academies and compounds from supernatural enemies by pulling on energy contained in underground springs.

*Known Descendants – Deacon & Draven (Throne Elder)*

**Dominions** – Part of the second sphere of angels, Dominions regulate the duties of the lower angels as well as govern the laws of the universe. Dominions are considered to be divinely beautiful with feathered wings of various colors. The Nephilim of this line value friendship, family, and loyalty and tend to be the peacemakers of the angel-born world.

*Known Descendants – Ash & Zara (Dominion Elder)*

**Virtues** – These angels are known for their signs and miracles. Part of the second sphere, they ensure everything is acting the way it should, from gravity keeping the planets in orbit, to the grass growing. Nephilim of this line can control natural elements in the mortal world, but their abilities are more powerful in the spirit realm.

*Known Descendant – Sorcha (Virtue Elder)*

**Powers** – Part of the second sphere, these angels are considered the warriors of the angel hierarchy. As such, they are always on the frontlines of battle. They are known to be single-minded and focused on their cause. Nephilim of this line are skilled in combat and have a knack for military strategy. They are able to manifest wings in the spirit realm.

*Known Descendants – Nova, Killian, Ciara, & Lyra (Power Elder)*

**Rulers** – As part of the third sphere, these angels guide and protect territories and groups of people. They preside over the classes of angels and carry out orders given to them by the upper spheres. They are said to be inspirational to angels and humankind. Nephilim of this line tend to manage and govern different bodies of angel-born. Their natural talents veer toward shepherding and their powers manifest as defensive rather than offensive.

*Known Descendants – Sable & Arien (Ruler Elder)*

**Archangels** – These angels are common in mortal lore. Part of the third sphere, they appear more frequently in the mortal world than other classes of angels—with the exception of the angel class. Tasked with the protection of humanity, they sometimes appear as mortals in order to influence politics, military matters, and commerce in their assigned region. Nephilim of this line are skilled chameleons. They have the easiest time blending in with humans and many of them work as Keepers.

*Known Descendant – Riven (Archangel Elder)*

**Angels** – Perceived as the lowest order of celestial beings, angels—sometimes called "plain angels" or "guardian angels"—belong to the third sphere. Their primary duties are as messengers and personal guards. Nephilim of this line were believed to have been murdered over two millennia ago, yet it was recently discovered that they'd survived the massacre and were thriving in a hidden community, Eden. The powers of the angel-born of this line are still being discovered, but they greatly exceed what was previously recorded.

*Known Descendants – Emberly, Shira, Aero, Stavros, Nikias (Angel Elder)*

# NOTE FROM THE AUTHOR

While this story is fictional, the emotional struggles these characters face are very realistic. The self harm that Thorne inflicts on himself is not healthy and should not be glamorized, condoned, or promoted. Mental illness is real, dark, dangerous, and lonely, but **you are not alone.**

If you are thinking about harming yourself, or are concerned that someone you know may be in danger of hurting himself or herself, call the **National Suicide Prevention Lifeline at 1-800-273-TALK (1-800-273-8255).** It is available 24 hours a day, 7 days a week and is staffed by certified crisis response professionals.

# GLOSSARY

**Angel** – A winged supernatural being who protects both mortal and spirit realms from Fallen and Forsaken.

**Angel-born** – The common name for Nephilim. An elite race of supernatural warriors born of human females and male Fallen, and their descendants. They have varying powers and abilities based on their Fallen ancestor's angel class. They are stronger, faster, and their senses more enhanced than humans.

**Barghest** – A serpentine, dog-like creature most commonly known as a hellhound. Barghest have elongated muzzles and their bodies are covered in scales. Several rows of spikes protrude along their spines and a tuff of needle-like hair crowns their heads. They exist only in the spirit realm and are known to be highly aggressive, only trainable through the use of Enochian commands.

**Celestial** – A fabled supernatural being that acts as a protector for angel-born. Nephilim tell their children fairy tales about these creatures, but their existence has never been confirmed.

**Council of Elders** – Comprised of the oldest Nephilim in each of the seven existing angelic lines: cherub, throne, dominion, virtue, power, ruler, and archangel. They are the closest thing to a ruling body the Nephilim have, yet—unless there is a global threat—their normal duties are to act as judges to help settle disputes between angel-born.

**Elder's Compound** – A highly protected stronghold where the Elders of each Nephilim line are based, which consists of several buildings including lodging for over three hundred occupants, training centers, a vault for cherished Nephilim artifacts, and two pyramids. The compound is located in an area of Egypt called Farafra that's known for its hot springs.

**Fallen** – Angels who rebelled and were banished to Earth as punishment. They retained their strength, immortality, and wings, but lost their class specific angelic powers. They are unable to access the mortal world.

**Forsaken** – Fallen who have merged with a Nephilim—or willing human—and taken on the form of their host's body. They are able to travel between each realm unencumbered. Their appearance is hideous in the spirit realm, reflecting their true nature. Forsaken thirst for blood—although it's not their primary source of sustenance—and are unable to withstand the sunlight in either realm.

**Keeper** – Nephilim tasked with monitoring and collecting information about the human race.

**Mortal World/Realm** – The dimension on Earth where humans reside.

**Nephilim** – The proper name for angel-born.

**Phasing** – When a Nephilim, Forsaken, or angel travels from the mortal world to the spirit realm or back again.

**Seraph Academy** – One of nine secret academies around the world devoted to the education and training of Nephilim children. Nephilim youth attend the academies from age eight until twenty, at which time they are considered fully trained. Seraph Academy is located in the Colorado Mountains near the town of Glenwood Springs.

**Spectrum World** – What Emberly calls the spirit realm.

**Spirit Gem** – Small gems or stones of different colors that originate from the spirit realm and have various uses and properties. Some examples include concealing powers, amplifying natural abilities, creating shields, controlling objects or people, or forcing people into or out of the spirit realm. It is believed that there are yet undiscovered varieties of gems still hidden in the spirit realm. The orbs in the Council of Elders vault are both large spirit gems. Until recently, the Nephilim were not aware of their existence.

**Spirit Realm** – The plane of existence that can only be accessed by supernatural beings. The spectrum of colors differ in this realm and sound can be seen as ripples through the air. Angels spend the majority of their time in the spirit realm warring with Fallen for control of territories. Nephilim's angelic powers activate in this realm.

**The Great Revolt** – When the Nephilim rose up against the Forsaken and Fallen who had enslaved and used them as vessels for Fallen.

**The White Kingdom** – Also known as "Whitehold" this fortress is located in the Laurentian Mountains of Quebec, Canada. This stronghold was the primary training ground for Fallen and Forsaken and ruled by Thorne and the seraph angel, Seraphim. It remained a secret from the Nephilim for hundreds of years, but since its discovery it has been abandoned.

# PLEASE WRITE A REVIEW

amazon                                    goodreads

Reviews are the lifeblood of authors and your opinion will help others decide to read my books. If you want to see more from me, please leave a review.

Will you please write a review?
**http://review.UnleashingFire.com**

Thank you for your help!

*~ Julie*

# ACKNOWLEDGMENTS

I can't believe my sophomore series is wrapped. I'm not gonna lie, I'm not ready to leave these characters behind! *whispers* So maybe I won't. Stay tuned! *wink wink nod nod*

It would be impossible for me to acknowledge every person who helped me turn the *Fallen Legacies* series into a reality, but I'm going to give it a go! *cracks knuckles and neck*

I owe a giant squishy "thank you" to my amazing virtual assistant, Kelly Stepp. I have been so incredibly fortunate to have some really talented people in my corner, and Kelly is one of them. On top of being a Rockstar social media marketer, she's so kind and knows exactly when I need a cute puppy gif or meme to pull me out of the writing pit of despair. *whispers* All authors are needy, and if they tell you otherwise, they're lying. Every author should have a "Kelly" in their corner...but if someone tries to take her from me, I'm gonna get stabby!

Speaking of people in my corner, I need to dump some "thank you confetti," on Heidi, Sarah, Erin, and LeAnn. They keep my Facebook fan group chugging along so I can disappear into my writing cave from time to time. Without them I wouldn't be able to balance my social media marketing and writing. Also, they are some of the coolest people I know. I'm pretty sure a lot of my readers prefer them to me...and I'm not sad about it!

A shout out goes to my father-in-law, Bernie, who reads every book I write! I'm so blessed to have in-laws who are so supportive of my dreams.

I've said this before and I'll say it again, I would not be able to do what I do if it weren't for my hubby, Lucas. He's the other half of my publishing machine, and the other half of my heart.

Everyone in my Fallen Legacies Launch Group deserves a million, "thank-yous." They are my people and are always there to help spread the word about a new release, root out rogue and stubborn typos, and cheer me on. Without their support and love of my make-believe worlds, I'd surely run out of writing steam. #PleaseNeverLeaveMe

My friend, Carrie, is a saint! She reads all my rough drafts before they go through a lick of editing! It takes a special type of friend to provide honest and helpful feedback while still staying positive enough to keep me motivated. I treasure her and how much she's taught me about how to be a true friend.

And last (but not least), a special "thank you" goes to Red Bull for providing my writing fuel and giving me wings. If you're ever looking for an author sponsor, #CallMe. I will work for free Red Bull!

# GET UPDATES FROM JULIE
## JOIN MY NEWSLETTER

Please consider joining my exclusive email newsletter. You'll be notified as new books are available, get exclusive bonus scenes, previews, ridiculous videos, and you'll be eligible for special giveaways. Occasionally, you will see puppies. 🐶

Sign up for snarky funsies:
**JulieHallAuthor.com/newsletter**

I respect your privacy. No spam.
Unsubscribe anytime. 💜

# JOIN THE FAN CLUB
## ON FACEBOOK

If you love my books, get involved and get exclusive sneak peeks before anyone else. Sometimes I even give out free puppies (#jokingnotjoking).

You'll get to know other passionate readers like you, and you'll get to know me better too! It'll be fun!

Join the Fan Club on Facebook:
**facebook.com/groups/juliehall**

See you in there!

~ Julie

# ABOUT THE AUTHOR
## JULIE HALL

My name is Julie Hall and I'm a *USA Today* bestselling, multiple award-winning author. I read and write YA paranormal / fantasy novels, love doodle dogs and drink Red Bull, but not necessarily in that order.

My daughter says my super power is sleeping all day and writing all night . . . and well, she wouldn't be wrong.

I believe novels are best enjoyed in community. As such, I want to hear from you! Please connect with me as I regularly give out sneak peeks, deleted scenes, prizes, and other freebies to my friends and newsletter subscribers.

**Visit my website:**
JulieHallAuthor.com

**Get my other books:**
amazon.com/author/julieghall

**Join the Fan Club:**
facebook.com/groups/juliehall

**Get exclusive updates by email:**
JulieHallAuthor.com/newsletter

**Connect with me on:**

- facebook.com/JulieHallAuthor
- bookbub.com/authors/julie-hall-7c80af95-5dda-449a-8130-3e219d5b00ee
- goodreads.com/JulieHallAuthor
- instagram.com/Julie.Hall.Author
- youtube.com/JulieHallAuthor

# BOOKS BY JULIE HALL

**Stealing Embers (Fallen Legacies Book 1)**

www.StealingEmbers.com

**Forging Darkness (Fallen Legacies Book 2)**

www.ForgingDarkness.com

**Unleashing Fire (Fallen Legacies Book 3)**

www.UnleashingFire.com

## LIFE AFTER SERIES

**Huntress (Life After Book 1)**

www.HuntressBook.com

**Warfare (Life After Book 2)**

www.WarfareBook.com

**Dominion (Life After Book 3)**

www.DominionBook.com

**Logan (A Life After Companion Story)**

www.LoganBook.com

**Life After - The Complete Series (Books 1-4)**

www.LifeAfterSet.com

# AUDIOBOOKS BY JULIE HALL

**My books are also available on Audible!**

http://Audio.JulieHallAuthor.com

Made in the USA
Monee, IL
06 August 2021